SHIELD AND COVETED SPLENDOR

ENERGY OF MAGIC
BOOK SIX

J.E. NEAL

For my mom —
For teaching me to believe in my own magic

CONTENTS

CHAPTER 1

NAVIGATIONS

RAINER LAWSON

"So, he asked Fionna to come with him to Sydney and she agreed?" Even though this was the third time she'd restated this question, Emily still sounded thoroughly irritated.

"According to Garrett, she called him as soon as Dan left to go get his stuff this morning," Rainer confirmed. "On top of everything else, Logan and I are supposed to keep him from freaking once he realizes what he's committed himself to." Rainer wondered how exactly they were supposed to fulfill Garrett's orders.

"If he gets her there and then freaks and breaks her heart, you won't have to worry about it. I'll kill him myself," Emily spat.

Rainer grinned at her vehemence.

Logan pulled his lips away from Adeline's. "Em, we're just as shocked as you are." They'd been getting a jump start on their honeymoon in the back of the Hummer.

"Do you think you could leave her clothes on until we get to the hotel?" Rainer harassed.

Adeline blushed and giggled, and Logan rolled his eyes. "I can't help it if my wife can't keep her hands off me."

Adeline looked like she wanted to melt into the floorboard.

Rainer and Emily had endured Logan referring to Adeline as his wife and vice versa forced into conversation at every available opportunity all morning long.

With a tight clench of his jaw, Rainer tried to remember that they were excited and that he was happy for them. He told himself that once they spent a few days wrapped up in each other, they wouldn't feel the need to announce their new marital status every few moments.

Emily shot him a grin that let him know she was thinking the very same thing.

He pulled into the Iodex parking deck. After they unloaded the luggage, Rainer casted the car and then led Emily to the private tarmac. Governor Haydenshire was there waiting on them with their tickets.

"That depends on who the other ticket is for, Daniel," the governor sounded wary as he talked on his cell phone. After a period of silence, Governor Haydenshire looked genuinely pleased. "Sure, I'll take care of it. I'm the one forcing you to take a vacation. If you'll assure me that she moves more than your obsession with Wretchkinsides, I'll arrange a ticket for Ms. Styler right now." His grin spread broadly across his face.

Whatever Vindico was telling him, he was elated to hear. After a minute, concern etched the governor's face.

"All right, I believe you, but you listen to me, son. Don't take her to the other side of the world, decide this is more than you want to deal with, and break her heart. Do you understand me? If you make a commitment to her, we will all help you keep her safe. You deserve to live outside of that tomb. This time let me help you." The governor gave a silent nod. "Just please, for me, don't screw this up, Dan." He ended the call and moved to the gathering of pilots, coolant officers, and flight attendants of his own jet.

"I'm going to add another passenger, Glenda."

"Sure, Crown Governor." She was eager to help.

An hour later, Emily and Fionna were tucked up on one of the plush bench seats that ran along one side of the Crown Governor's jet. They were whispering heatedly and giggling. They would both occasionally glow red in their embarrassment over whatever they were discussing.

Vindico looked annoyed as he sat in his seat and flipped through a magazine that was on the plane.

Logan and Adeline were in the small bedroom off the passenger area with the door closed. They'd both insisted that they were going in there to talk. No one had believed that for a moment, but they'd kept their thoughts to themselves to save Adeline embarrassment.

Rainer fully planned to harass Logan about his out-and-out lie, later on.

Dan kept glancing Rainer's way, but he also seemed unable to keep his gaze off Fionna for any real length of time. He very obviously wanted Emily to leave Fionna alone so that he could have her attention all for himself.

Rainer figured that was a good sign so he didn't comment. He kept a close watch over Emily though and tried to hear any part of her conversation. The whispers were too soft and too rapid for him to pick up on much.

With what appeared to be a haggard, steadying breath, Dan stood and moved to Rainer. "Could I ask you something?"

"Sure." Rainer shrugged and followed Vindico's eyes back to the ladies.

"Up here." He gestured to another seating area at the front of the plane, just behind the cockpit.

There were seven pilots and cooling officers flying the jet, which would put them in Sydney in a little over ten hours.

Rainer followed Vindico to the bench seat at the front of the plane. Whatever he wanted to know, it was making him extremely uncomfortable.

"Are you okay?" Rainer quizzed. If his boss had suddenly decided that he shouldn't have invited Fionna along on their trip, Rainer was going to shove him out of the plane over the ocean. The thought settled firmly in his mind as he awaited the response.

Dan looked surprised by the question. "Yeah, I'm great, actually." He appeared shocked by the truthfulness of his reply.

"Good." Rainer was still waiting for the impending question. He began to wonder just what had happened between Fionna and his boss. It appeared to have been much more than sex.

"Uh,"—Vindico drew another deep breath—"I was just wondering if you'd help me with something, I guess." He still looked pained.

"Sure. What?"

"It's…been a while since I was at the academy." Rainer knitted his brow. This question was starting off oddly. "And, you know, I've never really…" he continued to try to formulate his question, "dated any Gifted women," he finally managed.

Rainer nodded but still wasn't certain what his boss needed to know.

"I remember Will and Garrett teaching a few guys how to cast a woman," he managed to get out in a husky whisper. "I didn't really need to know that at the time, but I do need to know now. It's important, and I was wondering…" he hemmed again.

Rainer took pity on him. "If I could teach you how?"

Air released from his lungs as he gave a quick nod. "And, also, if you could never mention this conversation to anyone, I'll owe you. As your boss, that seems like it puts you in a pretty good position."

Rainer chuckled. "I'll teach you, and I won't tell anyone. You don't owe me anything if you just won't break her heart."

"Why does everyone think I'm going to do that?" Vindico sounded highly offended.

Rainer studied him incredulously. He didn't really want to give voice to that answer.

"Okay, fine. I've been an ass, but I'd…uh,"—he turned to make certain Fionna wasn't paying him attention—"I'd like to make this a really great week for her."

"Okay," Rainer agreed. He was certain there was more Dan wasn't saying, but he wasn't going to push. He didn't want to do anything to ruin this for either of them.

They moved to the set of seats that faced the front of the plane. The backs of the chairs would block what they were doing from the girls' prying eyes. They'd suddenly become very interested in what was being discussed.

Vindico smiled his appreciation as he took the seat beside Rainer.

He tried to think of the best way to explain how to cast someone without being crude. "Uh, you…you know, you and Fionna…last night."

Vindico laughed at him outright. "Slept together? Yeah."

"Right." Rainer willed away the blood pooling in his cheeks. "Okay, so you know when you do something so you, uh…have her energy…in your hands," he finally forced. There wasn't really a delicate way to explain this. He went so far as to mimic fingering someone.

"Yeah." Dan didn't seem to have any issue with anything Rainer explained. He watched Rainer's every move.

"It's easiest after you've done that."

"Okay." He was growing impatient quickly.

"Anyway," Rainer refocused, "if you use some of her erotic energy to summon with, and then you add your own soothing and calming energies, you just sort of move the cast up her from her…" He couldn't think of a word for vulva that he would be willing to use in front of his boss, especially since the woman with the body part he was referring to was seated not ten feet away from them. He gestured to his own crotch, and Vindico nodded his understanding.

"Lock onto her at her opening. Move the cast up until you feel where she opens way up. That's where you seal her off, but keep pumping your own soothing energies into her for several seconds after it's sealed. That will keep it from making her uncomfortable."

Dan looked concerned. "If they do it themselves, it makes them uncomfortable?"

"Yeah, a little. Em still does it herself occasionally," he whispered, "but she usually asks me to because the way I do it just sort of… makes her want more. She gets a pretty heavy dose of my energy when I close her," he managed to force this information out of his mouth.

"I didn't know that."

"And you know about the twenty-four hour thing?" Rainer felt the very odd role-reversal taking place.

"That's how long it lasts, right?"

Rainer nodded. He almost laughed out loud as he thought that

Vindico should have been at the academy a few weeks ago for amative energies week.

Suddenly the girls' voices picked up in their excitement.

"I almost died. I mean, wow! He's huge," Fionna gushed. Emily was laughing hysterically. "Seriously, I almost want you to see it just so you'll believe me!"

"I'll take your word for it," Emily assured her as they erupted in another round of hysterical laughter.

"Please tell me they're not talking about what I think they're talking about." Dan looked thoroughly embarrassed as he made his plea.

Rainer grimaced and nodded. His mind rejected the information he was being force-fed.

A little while later, Logan and Adeline emerged. They were still gazing adoringly at one another as they took one of the small benches and began cuddling.

Dan finally requested that Fionna come sit with him, which she agreed to happily.

Emily fell into Rainer's lap. "What were you and Dan talking about?"

Rainer shook his head at her. He brushed a kiss on her cheek. "Not how vertically gifted my boss is like you and Fionna were," he chastised.

Emily's face turned the color of her hair. "I didn't *want* to know that. She just kept talking about it!"

Rainer cracked up.

Fionna and Vindico remained locked in deep conversation for the rest of the flight. Occasionally, Rainer would hear one of them laugh, and several times they stopped talking in order to indulge in passionate kissing, but they definitely seemed thoroughly engrossed in one another.

When the plane finally landed at Kingsford Smith, they thanked the pilots and coolant officers as they grabbed the luggage.

Emily's entire being lit up as she took in the warm air and sunshine of the Australian coastal city. Adeline appeared to have enjoyed the flight and the ten hours of Logan's undivided attention, but when they landed her nerves returned in full force.

"Hey." Logan kissed the side of her head as they made their way off the plane. "It's our honeymoon. You aren't allowed to be nervous until we go to the palace."

A hesitant smile formed on her face. "But my father is somewhere in this city," her voice shook.

"Okay, but if he happens to be in the honeymoon suite of the Kingsford Wellborn, I'm still gonna make him leave."

Dan and Rainer rolled their eyes. They exchanged some money, then located the City Circle train and all made their way to the Kingsford Wellborn Hotel and Day Spa.

"It's Tuesday morning here, right?" Emily quizzed.

"Yeah." Rainer grimaced. They'd effectively lost an entire day in their ten-hour flight, and it was somewhat disconcerting. They walked from the train station to the Kingsford Wellborn.

Adeline was suddenly nervous about staying in such a swanky hotel. Logan tried to reassure her while he gave the hotel clerk his name.

"Ah, yes, our honeymoon couple." The clerk smiled kindly, and Logan beamed. "Right this way, Mr. Haydenshire. We have your suite ready." The man gestured to the elevators.

"We'll see you later," Logan offered with a slight wave. Emily and Fionna were still whispering to one another, but now their conversation appeared to be about the hotel.

The vast entryway, which was several stories high, contained an extravagant bar area situated off of the restaurant. One side had entrances for the world-renowned Kingsford Wellborn Day Spa.

As he watched Fionna and Emily gaze longingly at the spa, Rainer assumed the ladies would be spending a day there at some point. Dan noticed as well. He and Rainer shared a chuckle. Rainer had never seen his boss so eager to please anyone.

"A spa day!" Emily exclaimed.

Fionna was nodding. "Okay, but I don't want Adeline to feel left out, so whenever she wants to go."

"We'll have to get her out of bed with my brother first."

"Good luck with that," Rainer teased.

Vindico stepped up as another clerk greeted them.

"Dan Vindico," he drawled confidently. "And I'm not certain what room Crown Governor Haydenshire booked for me, but let's go ahead and upgrade that." He winked at Fionna.

Rainer thought the move was a little showy, but Fionna looked thrilled.

"Actually, Mr. Vindico," the man smiled kindly, "aren't you here with a Mr. Lawson and a Ms. Haydenshire?" He studied the screen on the computer in front of him.

"That's us." Rainer stepped up. The man gave Rainer another smile as he nodded. "I was just going to see if you'd be interested in two of our premiere ground-level suites. They're each three-room complexes with extended king beds, and they share a private pool. Only the four of you would have access to that particular pool."

"Whatever you want," Vindico assured Fionna.

Rainer started to roll his eyes. His boss appeared to have forgotten that he and Emily even existed and would also need to agree to the arrangement.

"The rooms don't join. You would only share the courtyard and pool in between. It offers a great deal of privacy, ma'am." The clerk seemed to have determined that Vindico was captaining the ship and Fionna was all that mattered. Rainer sighed.

"That sounds like fun if Rainer and Emily want to." Fionna gently reminded Dan of their presence.

"Sure," Emily replied, after she and Rainer had a silent conversation with their eyes and very slight nods. It was the kind of conversation a couple that had been together for a lifetime could easily have.

With that, they were each given the keycards to the suites. Another attendant rolled a luggage cart to them, loaded up all of the bags, and gestured for the four of them to follow him.

The ladies decided to meet at the pool in a little while as Dan and Rainer unlocked the doors to their rooms. Vindico grabbed Fionna's hand and tugged her away from Emily.

This thoroughly delighted her as the girls laughed at him outright, and though he was smiling, Rainer got the distinct impression he wanted to be alone with her. He was growing weary of Emily and Fionna's almost magnetic attraction to one another.

Rainer smirked. *Emily knows her vastly better than you do, man. You're gonna have to step up your game if you want her to choose you over Em when we're together.*

CHAPTER 2

LEARNED CONVERSATIONS

After he guided Emily through the door ahead of him, Rainer began studying the space. It was a rather nice three-room suite. The room they'd stepped into was a modern living room, with several low-slung love seats and chairs decorated in sleek black and white.

The photos on the walls lacked color as well but were charming shots of surfboards and surfers from many decades before. There was a large television and a small desk in a corner.

Off the living room was a kitchenette complete with a wet bar. He led Emily farther inside the suite toward their bedroom.

A posh, king-sized bed dominated the space. One wall held a cutout with glass shelving and several large shell displays. You could see from the bedroom into the living room. Opposite the bed was a dresser with a large mirror.

There were sliding-glass doors off both the living room and bedroom, which looked out on the swimming pool in the courtyard outside their room and then to the beach beyond.

The pool area was bedecked with several wicker lounge chairs and couches. The deep indentation of the concrete building along with the abundant landscaping did indeed mean that the pool area could only be seen by the people occupying the two suites.

Emily began unpacking as Rainer lifted suitcases onto the bed for her. He pulled his cell phone from his pocket.

"I think I'll just call Logan and see what they're up to," he teased.

"You should. They've been driving me crazy since the wedding." She shook her head. A deep yawn overtook Rainer. Something about the long plane ride and the loss of an entire day made him tired.

"So, now will you tell me what Dan wanted to know?" Emily turned the full power of her eyes on him as she wound her arms around his neck.

She arched her back and gave him an exquisite view of her stunning cleavage. Rainer gave her the growl she was after. He waggled his eyebrows and grabbed her backside.

"Are you trying to seduce me into betraying a confidence, Miss Haydenshire?" A broad, delicious grin spread across her beautiful face as she nodded. "I'll tell you, but don't say anything to Fionna."

"Okay," she agreed, but then redacted. "I mean, as long as he's not cheating on her or anything like that, because I'd have to tell her that."

Rainer shook his head and kissed Emily's forehead. "No, baby. It seems like he might've fallen for her just like Garrett predicted. He just wanted to know how to cast her."

"Oh, that's such a good sign! You told him how to do it so it doesn't do that thing where it hurts for a minute, right?"

"Yeah, of course."

"Good, because Fionna's on cloud nine, so I really hope he doesn't screw this up."

"I told him I would only teach him if he wouldn't break her heart." He tried not to think that his saying that would definitely buy him several points in Emily's book.

"Aww," she swooned, "you're the best."

Rainer squeezed her tightly before yawning again. "I don't know why I'm so tired." He rubbed his eyes.

"You always get tired when we fly," she reminded him. He smiled. She knew him better than he knew himself.

Just as Rainer was enjoying that thought, Emily's phone chirped. She pulled it from her purse and studied the screen confusedly. Her brow knitted.

"What's wrong?" Rainer quizzed.

"It's Adeline. She says Logan's freaking out about the beach. She wants to know if you'll talk to him."

"What's wrong with the beach?" Rainer flung open the sliding-glass doors from the bedroom and stepped out toward the ocean. From his vantage point, it appeared to be like any other beach. It had much larger swells than they had at home, and the ocean was definitely bluer. It was beautiful, but Rainer couldn't fathom what would be wrong with that.

He stepped back into the room. Emily was flipping through a binder on the bedside table with information about the hotel, Manly Beach, and Sydney. Her mouth fell open as she turned the page and then bit her lip in an effort not to laugh.

"What?" Rainer moved beside her.

"Manly Beach was voted one of the world's top ten topless beaches," the copy of the award in the binder announced proudly.

A broad grin spread across Emily's face as she rushed to the living room and threw open the sliding-glass doors to take in the beach. The view from their bedroom was on an angle, and the one from the living room offered her a more direct view of the ocean.

No wonder Logan's freaking out. He has every right to, Rainer thought furiously as Emily spun around and rushed back inside. Her face held a mix of stunned disbelief, delight, and piqued intrigue.

They stared at one another for a long, drawn minute as defiance set in her eyes, and a war began in his head. He heard the phrases he knew he should never utter pulsing through his mind as she stated, "We're about to fight about this, aren't we?"

Powerless to stop himself, he spat, "We are if you're under some great misapprehension that you're going out there topless."

Fury flashed in her eyes. He watched her tuck her hair over her right ear purposefully. He knew what was coming. She crossed her arms over her chest and narrowed her eyes.

He needed to stop. He needed to calm down. Ordering Emily Haydenshire not to do something was the quickest way to get her to do the very thing you did not want her to do. He'd been with her since they were toddlers. He knew this, but he just couldn't force himself to think rationally.

The possessive, chauvinistic part of his brain won out above all reason and all ability for him to stop talking. He fired back. "Those are mine! You are mine, and no one else gets to see them, ever!"

"Oh really," she spat in acrid defiance. "I'm not your personal property! And I will do whatever I want to do, whenever I want to do it!"

He continued on stupidly. "You will under no circumstances go out there without a top on."

"Watch me," were her parting words as she stomped out of their suite and slammed the door behind her.

Revulsion washed over Rainer as he thought of other people seeing what he considered to be his and his alone. It threatened to push him right over the edge. He ground his teeth and clenched his fists as he began to pace.

A minute later, a knock sounded harshly on their door.

Well, look who came to her senses. Rainer stalked to the door and threw it open. To his shock, his furious glare landed on Logan not Emily.

"What do you want?" Rainer stomped back into the suite.

"Hey, I'm not the one you're mad at. I happen to agree with you if you and Em are fighting about what Adeline and I are fighting about, anyway."

"She is not going out there topless," Rainer insisted to Logan, though some small part of his rational mind, still vying to be heard, tried to tell Rainer that Logan had no control over his little sister.

"You don't have to tell me that." Logan followed Rainer into the suite and shut the door.

He was now not only furious with Emily for wanting to go out topless, but he was also worried about where she'd gone and why she hadn't returned.

"Why does Adeline want to go out there topless? I mean…ugh!" Logan fumed.

Rainer shut his eyes, nodded, and then began to accept his defeat.

"You know we can't stop them. I don't know what to do."

Logan fumed. "Those are…I mean…she's not…and no one else should ever…" He seemed to realize that he hadn't formed a complete sentence. He shook his head in disgust.

With a slight chuckle despite his own annoyance, Rainer completed the thoughts for his best friend. "Those are yours. She's not going out there like that, and no one else should see them ever."

Logan laughed and lost his angry, frustrated expression momentarily. "Yes," he huffed. His fury returned quickly. "And I sure as hell don't want you and Vindico seeing her like that, and I don't want to see Fionna or my little sister like that." He scowled at the thought.

Another minute passed, and Rainer and Logan settled into their acrimony.

Dan looked highly agitated as he moved across the courtyard between his suite and Rainer's. He gave a quick knock on the glass door before sliding it open.

"Can I come in?" he asked, though it was far more of a command than a request.

"Why not?" Rainer quipped. He didn't particularly care that it was a rather disrespectful retort to give his boss.

Dan didn't seem offended. To Rainer's shock, a wry grin spread across his face as he took in Rainer and Logan's scowls.

"All right, can I make another deal with you, Lawson?"

Rainer sighed and tried to regain the ability to speak to his boss with respect. "I guess."

"I'll just go ahead and tell you two…" Vindico began, but then halted abruptly. He went back to the door and slid it closed before starting again. "Fionna is…well…" he hemmed, but then shook his head and started again. "I really want to get to know Fionna better. As stunned as I am to say this, I really want to make this work for as long as I can. Being with me is complicated and obviously dangerous." A slight shudder worked through his body.

Logan and Rainer shared a quick, confused expression as they nodded.

"So, I have to work this carefully. If you'll help me out, since I'm not quite as experienced with Gifted women, especially Receivers, as I am with other women, I'd really appreciate it. I figure you've been with a Receiver since birth, so you're probably the guy to talk to." He offered props to Rainer, who couldn't help but grin. "So, if you'll help me, then I can help you out with a little advice."

"Advice about what?" Logan asked.

Vindico chuckled and took a seat on one of the couches in the living room. Rainer and Logan followed suit.

"Seeing as your wife and your fiancée,"—he gestured first to Logan and then moved his gaze to Rainer—"are both in my suite, one of them in tears, and seeing as how they interrupted what was looking to be a really great afternoon, how about we start with advice about the reason you're fighting."

He looked highly annoyed about the fact that his and Fionna's time had been interrupted.

"Sorry," Rainer apologized.

"S'okay," Vindico sighed but couldn't quite hide his irritation.

"Of course Emily's crying." Logan rolled his eyes.

Dan nodded but then furrowed his brow. "Why did you assume it was Emily?" His tone shifted. He sounded the way he did when he interrogated a criminal.

"Emily cries all the time."

Rainer decided to go on and help Dan with the first lesson he could teach him about being with a Receiver.

"No, she doesn't." Rainer threw a glare at Logan. "Receivers are able to feel people's emotions in the energy all around them all the time. You know that, but have you ever really thought about what that must feel like for them? There's a reason Receivers don't like big crowds. If you watch Fionna and Emily at their challenges, they both relax when the aegis is set. It blocks out all of those emotions for them. They can't concentrate when they're bombarded, and if someone they care about is upset or angry, they feel that more than anything else, especially when you've been together as long as Em and I have."

He sincerely hoped teaching Vindico about Fionna wasn't going to somehow backfire and make him run. To Rainer's relief, he seemed extremely intrigued.

"So, that's why Fionna looked like she was going to cry when Emily showed up in tears."

Rainer nodded. "Fionna and Emily are really close."

"Yeah, I noticed." He didn't look quite as annoyed by the information as he had earlier. "Is that how she is with all Receivers or only Emily?"

"It's really just the two of them. Receivers are usually close and enjoy hanging out together because they get how the world feels to each other. But Emily and Fionna are on the same team, and even though Fionna is a far more powerful Receiver, they really get each other. Fionna's kind of crazy powerful, but Emily is very strong in her Predilect as well. The ring makes her even stronger than she is without it. They understand what the other goes through."

"Go on," Vindico urged.

"So like you said, Emily is crying. She's crying because she's mad at me, but she's also crying because I'm mad at her. She can feel all of my anger because we're so close physically."

As Rainer explained the way Auxiliary Predilects worked, guilt washed over him and took up ruthless residence in his gut. While trying not to focus on the guilt, he drew a deep breath. "So, Fionna and Emily have stayed together. They see each other all the time. They hang out even when they aren't at practice. They share makeup, food, drinks, everything. When Emily's upset, Fionna feels that more strongly than she would if she saw someone crying she'd never met before, but that would upset her as well if she could pick up on their energy."

"That's why Rainer lets Emily get away with murder," Logan scoffed.

Vindico's brow knitted, and Rainer knew he wanted to ask something.

"I'm really glad to help. I didn't say anything earlier because I didn't want to freak you out, but you've been with her one night and I've never seen you look so happy. I know it's complicated, but if I can help you make this work, I want to."

Vindico gave him a genuine smile. "Thanks, I really appreciate that." He was still considering. "Okay," he drew a deep breath. He looked rather uncomfortable. "Are you all right talking about your sister sleeping with him?" He gestured to Rainer as he posed the question to Logan. "I know that I personally don't care to hear about any of my sisters' sex lives."

Logan shrugged. "I want to hear whatever the advice is about my wife and the topless beach, and like you said, he's been with her since birth. Half the time I can hear the two of them going at it in their room, so I'm kind of used to the idea by now."

Rainer's eyes goggled. Heat pooled in his cheeks.

After joining in Logan's laughter, Dan went on with his question. "You said Fionna and Emily are very close and feel each other's emotions strongly, but that's because they've spent so much time together and they're friends. After last night, shouldn't Fionna feel me stronger than she feels Emily?"

Impressed with the question, Rainer reminded himself that he'd just promised he'd help him so he shot straight with him.

"Yes and no," Rainer hemmed. He watched his boss become impatient as he awaited the rest of the answer. "Some of it depends on how safe you made her feel when you were together."

Deep concern etched his chiseled features.

"Receivers are so open, and feel things so deeply, they develop their own kind of internal emotional shield as children." Rainer drew a deep breath and tried to decide the best way to explain this. "Like you said, Em and I have been together forever, so she always feels safe with me. She's never really held much back when we're together like that. There was once when she felt like I'd really let her down, and when we made up I could tell she was guarded." Rainer recalled their make-up sex after he'd been to The Tantra.

"So, if Fionna was afraid she was going to share her powerful emotional energy bond with you and then you were going to bolt and never call again, or hurt her in any way at all, she was probably guarded when you were together. She can take everything she feels from you without allowing you to feel everything from her.

"I guess, to answer your question, Fionna feels safe with Emily because she knows Emily isn't going to hurt her. She trusts Em.

Receivers need to feel that emotional safety. They need an emotional shield, either their own internal one or an Ioses Shield."

He debated momentarily, but then he continued. "Or she may have laid it all out for you when you were together, and now she's terrified you're going to hurt her, so she's clinging to Emily. She's going back to a place she feels safe."

Rainer suddenly missed Emily, and he wished he hadn't been such a jerk. Regret swirled in the pit of his stomach.

Shock was the predominant expression on Vindico's face. It seemed to permeate his entire being.

As his dejection built, Rainer decided to go ahead with the rest of what he considered necessary information if you were going to be in a successful relationship with a Receiver.

"There's a reason Ioses Predilects and Auxiliary Predilects tend to do so well together. There's a reason the legends exist. She needs you to protect her and make her feel safe, and you need her to navigate the world. She'll make you feel and use your heart, not just your head. Being inside one of our shields is the only way a Receiver is ever truly calm. We're the only ones who can block out the emotions from everyone around them. Sometimes they need to be in a completely safe place just to process all of the emotion they have to feel on any given day. But in return, they can take on all of the terror that can be trapped inside a shield that we aren't able to get rid of because it's locked in our barrier. She'll make you a better person if you'll let her."

Dan nodded. "So, the reason she acts like she'd rather spend time with Emily than with me is because she doesn't feel safe with me?" His voice sounded distant and pained.

Rainer tried to soften the blow. "It's not quite that harsh," he redacted. "It's just that she knows Emily better than you, and it's probably going to take her a little while to really trust you the way she trusts Emily or Garrett."

"She feels safer with Garrett than she does with me?" Devastation drowned Dan's tone.

Logan looked concerned over his reaction as he forced a chuckle. "She is, like, one of maybe five women in the greater DC area who hasn't ever slept with my brother, and she and Garrett have been really good friends for a long time. He takes good care of her, and she does the same for him." Logan's explanation did elicit a small smile from Vindico. "Honestly, I'm not sure Garrett would've gotten through Cal's death without her. You're going to have to prove yourself to her the same way Garrett has. He's never let her down. You just said you wanted to make this work, so do it. Prove to her that you're not going to walk away this time. You kind of have a reputation that isn't helping your cause." Logan pointed out the cold hard facts.

"Yeah." Vindico looked truly disturbed as he glanced back across the pool to his suite. With a slight headshake, he seemed to pull himself from his reverie. "Okay, so you'll tell me if you think of something else I need to know."

Rainer considered for a minute. He wasn't certain his boss would let his guard down again so he decided to tell him everything he knew. "Receivers are so incredibly powerful, but their power is in emotion so they get discounted all the time. That wears on them. Emotions are so compelling they scare people. I mean, think about it. Emotion rules the world. For a lot of people it's easier to write Receivers off than to accept what they're telling you."

Concern creased Vindico's brow as he nodded. "Anything else?"

"They're usually fairly sentimental because they can feel the emotional energy that went into a gift or an event. It doesn't have to be a big expensive thing, just something they can feel your effort in."

This seemed to please Dan. "Okay, anything they universally hate that I should avoid?"

Rainer considered. "Nothing's universal, but anything that diminishes their reads tends to frustrate and frighten them."

"Explain that."

"Storms or clutter for instance. Anything chaotic makes it harder for them to read through and they navigate the entire world through emotions. When something affects their ability to read the world around them, it would be like if all of a sudden you couldn't cast a shield. They lose a little of their power and their ability to navigate the world. Think about how terrifying that would be. But when things are kind of settled or clean or whatever, it lets them process emotional energy easier so they're confident in what they're feeling."

After drawing a deep breath, Dan nodded. "Okay, anything they universally love?"

"Water," Logan and Rainer answered at the same moment. They pointed out the doors. The ladies had emerged from Fionna and Dan's suite and were sitting by the pool with their feet dangling in the water.

Rainer nodded. "Emily loves the beach over anything else. It centers Receivers. To some degree, it will even wash away the residue of the emotional energy they get overwhelmed with. That's why they're out in the pool now. Em's trying to wash off the way our argument made her feel."

"I really appreciate all of this. Seriously, thank you," Vindico offered humbly.

"No problem."

Dan smirked for a minute before he began. "The thing about this being a topless beach, just stop. This isn't as big a deal as you're making it, and you're driving them crazy." He gestured out the window to the girls.

Emily's eyes were red and puffy. Rainer's guilt increased, and Logan rolled his eyes.

"Not every guy on the beach is as interested in seeing theirs as you are," Vindico assured them.

Rainer huffed. He found that very hard to believe.

"Oh, so you want to see Adeline and Fionna like that, then?" He effectively trapped Rainer.

"No," he vowed.

Dan laughed. "I'd hold my judgment on seeing Fionna. Believe me, it's a sight to behold."

Rainer was lost in a sea of guilt, regret, and gall that Emily was going to parade around topless on a beach, and there was nothing he could do to stop her.

"Trust me, Lawson. Emily doesn't do to everyone what she does to you. To me, she'll always just be Will and Garrett's annoying kid sister, and eventually one of my best officer's wives, but nothing more."

Rainer sighed. "Thanks, but I just don't get why she wants to do this so badly. You may not be looking at her, but other guys will."

Logan nodded his agreement.

"There are several reasons they want to do it."

Spite-filled indignation had Rainer throwing his arms out and deciding he'd love to hear this.

Vindico seemed lost between chewing Rainer out for his disrespect and genuinely trying to help him. He glanced back toward Fionna. Determination pulsed in his shield. It was so potent in that moment that Rainer and Logan could both feel it.

"She wants to do this because she's twenty years old, and this is new and exciting and just a little bit bad in her mind. She wants to rebel, and not to throw your own words back in your face, but you need to listen to your own advice because it's good."

Rainer furrowed his brow as Vindico continued.

"She feels safe with you, and if you'll get over yourself and go out there with her, you can let her rebel a little and keep her safe. That's what she really wants. She wants her Shield." Then a goading grin formed on his chiseled features.

"I'm willing to bet thus far, you've rather enjoyed Miss Haydenshire's rebellious side. As I recall, the story is that she dared you to kiss her. Then there was the sex, and the belly shot, and I overheard our new Crown lamenting a decent-sized tat of your crest on her hip. Throwing all of that in her father's face was fine, but this isn't, because now you feel like you have to share her in her rebellious state instead of being the one on the receiving end of it."

Rainer couldn't argue any of those points which only irritated him further. "I just don't want her to do this."

Logan was still nodding. "And Adeline's never done any of that stuff Emily's done. Why does she want to go out there and let everyone see that?"

"You just answered your own question, didn't you?" This seemed to thoroughly confuse Logan. "She's never done anything rebellious, and now she has your ring on her finger and it seems like maybe you've finally convinced her that she's worth something. She feels safe and content, and not to sound like an asshole, but I really think they both want you two to see them like that.

"Like I said, it feels just a little bit bad to them. Women need to know they drive you wild. Being desired is a hell of an aphrodisiac, but whether you're happy about it or not, here's the deal, guys—this is a losing battle. You need to stop trying to fight it and go along with it. You might even enjoy it if you give it a chance. Take it from me, ten years your senior and with vastly more experience with women. You won't stop them, and if you keep acting like this, you're just going to push them harder. You might just push them farther than even they want to go."

The harsh reality of Dan's warning mixed into the volatile cocktail of guilt and irritation already swirling in Rainer's stomach.

"Yeah," he finally had to agree. "I know, and I'm sorry Em interrupted you two."

"No, it's fine. I really appreciate everything you told me. It was worth it. I want to figure out how to make this work."

"Do you really think it's dangerous for you to date Fionna?" Logan broached. "Do you really think he'd try something like that again even though she's Gifted and incredibly powerful?"

Vindico narrowed his eyes. His jaw gave a fierce clench as he glared hatefully. "I'm not sure, Haydenshire, but I'm sure as hell not gonna take any chances."

"Yeah, okay, I know," Logan tried to cover his gaffe. "You know all of Elite will help you keep her safe."

With a quick nod and glance at his watch, Vindico sighed. "I can't figure out what the hell time it is, but I'm starving." He stared out at the girls once again and then offered, "You wanna go get whatever meal it is, and then I think Fionna wants to go shopping. That would keep them off the beach for a while."

Rainer and Logan were appreciative of the fact that even though they couldn't stop Adeline or Emily from sunbathing topless, it was still an appealing idea to delay it.

CHAPTER 3

PRAYERS AND CONFESSIONS

DAN VINDICO

Dan was stunned and reeling from the fact that Fionna felt safer with Garrett Haydenshire than she did with him. Garrett may've been one of Dan's closest friends, but he was still an asshole when it came to women.

Dan's dogged determination took over a second later as he gazed at her sitting sweetly on the side of the pool beside Emily. She was trying to make her friend feel better about the fight with her fiancée.

He would make her trust him. He would make her feel safe and secure with him if it was the last thing he did. He had one week to convince her to date him in secret. He had just a few short days to convince her that he was worth all of the shit that would come with that.

If you can just somehow make her fall for me, I swear I'll catch her. It was the first breath of a prayer he'd prayed since he'd escaped Moscow. Oddly, some part of him actually believed it was heard and just might be answered as well. Maybe the legends were wrong. Maybe it was Receivers who saved Shields. He tied more negotiations to this prayer than he should. *I can do this if you could just help me keep her safe, please.*

His standard speech that he'd rattled off the night before, standing in her living room, seared through his mind, and he felt sick.

How could he have stood there and lied to her and then carried her upstairs and been with her? He had a great deal to make up for. The realization of that coupled with everything he'd just learned about Receivers made him nauseous and dizzy.

The fact that Fionna might have been holding some of herself back when she'd been with him was more than he could fathom.

How could there somehow be more of that heavenly feeling? How could her body contain more light? It didn't seem possible. He couldn't believe that anything could have felt as amazing as being with her and penetrating the heart of her did. The fact that there could be more that she'd kept from him made his determination all the more focused.

Suddenly, nothing mattered more to him than peeling back the layers of Fionna Styler, learning her inside and out, until he'd experienced all of her. After quickly pushing away his ponderings about whether or not that would mean she would experience all of him, he moved to her.

Dan squatted down beside her as she grinned up at him. She squinted in the noonday sun that had her body glowing with warmth and tender care.

He brushed an errant hair, blown by the breeze coming off the ocean, behind her ear and moved slightly so he blocked the sun from her face. "We were thinking you all might be hungry. I'm pretty sure they have some groveling to do. So, how about after that, we all go to lunch, and then I do seem to recall promising to take you shopping, Miss Styler."

Emily shot Rainer a look that said he was going to have to do some big talking before she would let him off the hook, and Rainer looked up to the task. Fionna seemed pleased he was going to apologize.

"Normally I would never turn down an opportunity to shop," she informed him. After sharing his adoring grin with her, Dan nodded. He was thankful for every piece of information he could glean about her. "But we were thinking maybe we could get some lunch and then go swimming." She gestured to the pool.

"I actually ordered lunch before you got mad and came to find Emily," Logan admitted to Adeline.

"She wouldn't have gotten mad if you hadn't acted like a prick," Emily sniped, and Dan choked back laughter.

"Thanks, Em. How would you like to go swimming now?" Logan glared at his little sister.

"Logan." Rainer shook his head and narrowed his eyes.

"Ah, siblings." Dan tried to smooth over the comment. He was growing irritated with Lawson and Haydenshire's childish antics and arguments. He had one week, and he planned to use each and every moment of it to win Fionna Styler.

Fionna patted Emily's hand sweetly. Dan watched her soothing Receiver's cast work through Emily's pale skin. Jealousy seized his soul.

"Would you please come back to our suite and eat with me? I will try to apologize for being concerned about your safety and your modesty." Logan just couldn't let it go.

Emily rolled her eyes as Adeline stood. She gave Logan a frustrated sigh. "I will come back and eat with you, and then I will tell you why that was not at all an apology. Then I will hang out with you, because I love you even though right now you are being what Emily just called you." Everyone laughed as the tension eased.

A few minutes later, Dan followed Fionna back into their suite. He closed the glass doors that led to the pool.

"What's your favorite kind of food?" He was one hell of a detective. He could attempt to learn about her and figure out where to take her for lunch all at the same time.

By the end of the week, he wanted to know everything about her. If he could just tap into a few of her dreams and fantasies, if he could somehow get her to share herself with him, maybe he could figure out how to be with her without getting her hurt.

She considered for a few seconds. "To cook or to eat?"

In all of the many years he'd interrogated criminals and witnesses alike, Dan knew a thing or two about interpreting people's responses. Answering a question with a genuine question meant that she was not only thoughtful but that there was a great deal to be found out about her.

"Either," he allowed. Dan found himself unable to take his eyes off of her. She seemed genuinely pleased he wanted to know more about her.

She shrugged. "I don't know. I love to cook, and I kind of go through phases. I just recently ended my Italian cooking phase when I gained eight pounds." She laughed at her own admittance.

He shook his head. "You are stunningly gorgeous, baby doll." He was doing this. He was going all in. "What would I have to say to get you to get back into Italian cooking?"

A delicate blush crept up from her chest. The color rose in her cheeks a moment before they glowed enticingly. The effect simultaneously drove him wild and told him that not only did she not think she was attractive, but also that she wasn't complimented that often. He found that hard to believe as he continued to study her. She seemed to force herself to continue.

"As for eating, I kind of like to try new things and then see if I can figure out what's in them. If I like them, I'll try to recreate them sometimes with my own twist." Her eyes lit with an enchanting sparkle as she talked about this practice, and a broad grin spread across her face.

Dan planted a kiss on top of her head. He had three sisters. He knew there was more.

"Okay, so no absolute, favorite dish or that thing you go out and get when it's the time of month that makes you want to eat whatever it is that you eat?" He chuckled at his own rambling question.

Fionna laughed at him outright. "How'd you get so smart, Chief Vindico?"

His jeans constricted as she called him by his title.

"Three sisters." He held up three fingers. "But you didn't answer my question." She seemed hesitant to answer. "Come on, it can't be that bad." He needed her to relax and let him in, even just a little at a time.

"Okay, I'll tell you, but then you have to tell me something about you," she negotiated.

Dan held up his hands in mock defeat. "Deal."

After wrinkling her nose adorably, she drew a deep breath. "I don't do this every, *every* month, but occasionally I really want a deep dish, meat lover's pizza with extra onion, and some Ben and Jerry's Karamel Sutra ice cream, and maybe an entire bag of chocolate-covered macadamia nuts that my grandmother sends me."

She covered her face with her hands and looked like she was afraid he was going to suddenly become disgusted with her and demand that she leave.

Dan forced out a chuckle, but he was concerned over her reaction. He seated himself beside her on the couch.

"See? That wasn't so bad, and the great thing about that is, other than the macadamia nuts which it sounds like your grandmother has the market on, those are things I can pick up for you and bring over if you're in the mood for them."

He was playing his hand extremely carefully. He wanted her to know he had no intention of going anywhere, even if she was cranky, irritable, bloated, and all of the other things he was well aware could come with being female.

Stunned disbelief broadcast from her features. "Really?" Her brow knitted. "You would do that?"

Dan began mentally lambasting himself, but he decided to jump in with both feet. "Apparently, my reputation is worse than I even knew, and this is sort of all new for me. Me asking you to come here with me is unlike anything I've ever done, but if you'll give me a chance, if you'll help me learn how to do this right, I would really like to be in a serious relationship with you. There's kind of a bunch of shit that would require, but can I just have this one week to try to prove myself to you? Please?" Terror filled his heart yet again as he awaited her answer.

"Tell me what all of your tattoos mean."

His brow furrowed until he understood she was testing him. His reply held the answer to his plea. If he blew her off and made up some bullshit about his ink, she would know, and that would tell her he hadn't meant what he'd just said about being in a relationship with her.

She knew his tattoos meant something deeply personal to him. They weren't just random pieces of artwork he'd gotten drunk one night and had someone do. Each of them held a piece of his soul.

He swallowed hard and pulled off his T-shirt. "Uh, the one on my back is for Amelia, but you probably knew that." He pointed to the large Celtic cross and vines of flowers over his right shoulder blade. Amelia's initials and birth and death dates were intertwined in the roping on the cross and in the flowered vines.

Fionna looked devastated as she placed her hand tenderly on his back near the tattoo. "I really am so sorry for your loss."

He knew she truly was. She didn't want him to hurt. Her strength and honesty helped him to go on. He drew another breath.

"Uh, this one,"—he pointed to his left bicep—"is the Kanji sign for warrior." He pointed to the symbol inside the circle of Latin words.

She nodded and kept her hand on his back. He felt it. The hypnotic, intoxicating peace washed over him. Her energy permeated the skin of his back. She was giving him strength and peace. Her acceptance soothed his soul like nothing ever had.

He panted. It was incredible. He wanted to strip her down and lay her out. He could think of little else but plunging her depths. He wanted to feel more, but he forced himself to go on.

"Uh," he breathed and tried to remember where he'd left off.

"These are Latin." He circled his finger around the words that encased the symbol of the warrior. She studied them intently like nothing had ever meant more to her.

"What do they mean?"

"Uh, these,"—he pointed to the words over the symbol—"mean relentless pursuit. And these,"—he moved his hand to the bottom of the ring of words—"mean vanquish defeat." He studied her and tried to gauge what she was thinking.

"I hope that's not about another woman." She grinned at him. That heavenly smile lit the darkest places in his battered soul. The way she seemed to accept every piece of him was astonishing.

"Relentless pursuit might just be about you, baby doll." Her smile stretched the width of her face. He glanced down at the tattoo on his chest and hesitated for a moment.

"You don't have to tell me anymore," Fionna offered. "I think I know what that one means." She could feel his terror and his sorrow. She could feel it all.

He understood in that moment that he could keep nothing from her, but with sudden realization, he also knew that he didn't want to.

"No, I want to tell you." He was going to do this. He was going to let her in. "Uh, that snake is a Cascavel cobra. It's one of the most vicious snakes in the world, and it was the name one of Wretchkinsides's top guys went by. He, uh..." He choked but then forced himself to continue. "He had a penchant for casting snakes and using them. He was the one who kidnapped Amelia, and he's the guy I killed several weeks ago when we tried to rescue Samantha Peterson. He did some heinous things to the women he kidnapped for Wretchkinsides. Hence the spear through the snake."

He forced the words from his lips. The harrowing grief fought its way back into his heart and into his soul, but she felt it as well.

She flooded him with warmth and the dizzying energy that made him feel the hope that vanquished the fear. She made him believe, for the first time in a long time, that life might really be worth living.

She smiled up at him and swallowed down fear of her own. "Okay," she nodded. "I want to do this. I want to be in a relationship with you, but just me, okay? No strippers. No one else. I still don't know what all this entails. You keep saying there's other stuff, but you aren't ready to tell me yet. So, let's just have an amazing week together," she stated knowingly.

She'd just made his entire world fall into perfect accord. Dan nodded. "Of course. I don't do the more than one woman thing. I told you last night I broke it off with Bridgette when I signed the papers to get her out of jail on her prostitution charge. I asked if she wanted me to get her a job at another club to make sure she's safe, but she refused. Other than that, I'm out." While forcing out his mind's badgering reminders that he wasn't good enough, he decided he would find a way to make himself good enough for her.

Dan pulled her to him and paused for a split second. He gazed at her lips, hungry to feel her again as he leaned and devoured her mouth.

She slid her hands down his bare chest and let her thumbs drag over his nipples. He groaned from the sensation.

His own reactions continued to shock him. His reactions to her weren't calculated. She made him say, do, and feel things he never thought possible.

He didn't make noises like that, noises that let women know he was turned on and wanting them. He made women make sounds like that.

He would never have revealed even that much of himself to anyone, but somehow she was able to cut through all of the layers of pain and volatility, all of the fear and revenge, all of his pure bullshit, and find him underneath it. To his utter shock, she seemed to like what she discovered.

A low, delicious moan stuttered from her as Dan edged the knit shirt she was wearing up and slipped his hands to her waist. Suddenly he felt seventeen again, like he had no self-control whatsoever. He pushed her shirt up higher until he reached her bra.

With a quick move, he lifted the tight shirt over her cleavage and pulled down the cup over her right breast. Her nipples throbbed. They pulsed for his starving mouth. He moved his lips to her as a desperate moan sang from her soul.

Her head fell back. She pushed what she wanted tended to in his face.

His body ached for her in desperate craving need. He wanted the delicious drug that made everything between them perfect and beautiful, and that gave him peace. It was a sensation he couldn't recall ever feeling before.

"Tell me, baby doll," he commanded as he huffed hot breath over her nipple. He caught the rhythms of her energy again as he began to understand more about being with her. "Tell me what you want me to do."

He let his thumb circle her nipple. He watched it pucker raw and beg for his attention. "I know what you need. I'm going to give it to you, but I want to hear you say it. Tell me." Her energy arced rapidly, and he reveled in his education.

"Please, please," she whimpered. Her head shook as her body began to writhe in his arms.

"It hurts, doesn't it?" He gently touched the deep-brown tip as her body flinched and tensed in her need. "And I know how to make it feel better. Just tell me."

"Suck me," finally spilled from her lips, and a deep growl seared from his chest.

He lowered his head and lapped his tongue over the swollen, puckered mound. Dan worked quickly. He pulled her breast deep into his mouth and sucked fervently. He had it. He could feel it wash over him again. It wasn't as strong here as when he took her, but it was slightly stronger than when he kissed her.

He pulled and sucked until she was quaking and moaning from the sensation. The very essence of her moved through his mouth. Unable to stop himself, not even taking a moment to consider that some women didn't like it quite so intense, he somehow knew that she would. He let his teeth slide tenderly along the swollen curve, and then nipped the most sensitive part of her breasts.

She went wild. Her eyes flashed in heated desire as she pitched and writhed.

He reached back, desperate for more, and popped the clasp of her bra with one hand. Her breasts spilled forward as he groaned in need.

Dan moved his head to her left breast and began to lave that one as well. He bathed her nipple with his tongue and lifted their heavy weight in his hands. He squeezed and groped her. He tended to the fevered swollen mounds of flesh as she cried out for him. She trembled for him. It drove him wild, but a moment later she backed away.

"Dan." She tried to catch her breath.

"I wasn't finished. Come here to me," he demanded. Her breath came in quick gasping pants as she nodded.

"Oh god, I know…but…" She swallowed down her own need and desire. "Aren't we supposed to go out to lunch with Emily and Rainer?" She didn't appear to want to leave any more than he did. All thoughts of food had been replaced with a voracious hunger for everything that resided deep inside of her.

While biting back the string of curse words that threatened to spew from his mouth, Dan drew a deep breath. He forced himself to think with the head above his belt line.

"I've never been on a real vacation, other than my parents dragging me to the Outer Banks every freaking summer growing up, but I will say, the next time we go on a trip, I think I would prefer to travel without Lawson and Ms. Haydenshire if it's all the same to you."

Fionna chuckled and shook her head at him. After giving her a wry grin, he joined in her laughter as she rehooked her bra.

"I'm not certain if I'm more astonished that you've never been on a vacation or that you're already planning our next one."

With a quick glance at his watch, Dan smiled and winked at her.

"Actually, I'd say Rainer has at least five more minutes of groveling before Emily gives him back his all-access pass."

Fionna's adorable laughter delighted him. "And how exactly do you figure that?"

"Since I believe I heard that he actually said the words, 'those are mine, you are mine, and no one else will see them ever,' then yeah, that's at least another five minutes."

Dan shuddered over Rainer's horrible choice of verbiage. Fionna nodded as they both cracked up at the rather chauvinistic declaration.

"He's really so sweet to her though. He's just very protective. You should have seen him when she was getting her tattoo. He was a disaster. It was kind of adorable. He really, really loves her. You know?" She lost all sense of teasing in her realization.

Dan studied her for a long moment before nodding his understanding. "Yeah, I do know, and I would have to say the ridiculously overprotective thing tends to come with the Predilect." He watched her eyes close and hoped she caught on to what he was insinuating.

"Is that a warning, Chief Vindico?" She turned her inquisitive eyes back on him.

"Yeah." He paused. He was taken aback again by her tender beauty and the way she understood him as he concluded, "It definitely is."

With a broad grin, she drew a deep breath. What he'd said had made her happy. He could feel it suddenly. The energy he'd drawn from her breasts still resided inside of him.

"Good," she breathed, "because I think I could really get used to that."

Dan brushed a kiss across her forehead. He inhaled the sweet scent of her hair. The vanilla and coconut musk filled his lungs and then his soul.

"Good…because Lawson and I have a lot in common." He gave her a cocky grin, but she didn't return the smile. She studied him more intently.

"Dan," she eased. He didn't reply verbally. He simply raised his eyebrows. "I know this is kind of moving really fast, and I guess I sort of knew you in school, and I graduated with Kara and everything, but…" She seemed to try to weave her feelings into a tapestry of words. "What I'm trying to say is that I understand that you aren't ready to talk about any of it yet, but I already knew you weren't able to save Governor Peterson's daughter when you killed that guy." She gestured to the snake on his chest. She hemmed again as pain etched her expression and her voice. "Everything leaves its mark, and if you ever want to talk about it, I'm here."

She offered without expectation that he would delve into the hellish abyss that was Cascavel. It was a patient offer, one that would remain standing until he was ready to accept it.

Dan swallowed down the raw emotion that had come on him suddenly. He tried to navigate his way back to the incredible woman standing before him. The long, confusing paths seemed too much to walk alone anymore. "I may take you up on that."

He couldn't do it, not yet, but with stunning realization, he understood. Until that endless moment with Fionna, he'd never even been willing to consider talking about it with anyone.

She seemed perfectly fine with his reply. She gave him a smile that he swore could light the entire world and then handed him his shirt.

With a wry grin, he chuckled. Very few women ever asked him to put his shirt back on. He considered everything she'd just said.

"You graduated with Kara?"

Fionna nodded and checked her makeup in one of the mirrors that hung on the living room wall.

"That's good. That way you missed most of Lindley's insanity when she was at Venton." He tried to piece together his life in relation to hers.

Fionna giggled and seemed to recall Dan's youngest sister. "I might have missed most of it, but I was there the day she came to class with no clothes on. It was my senior year. It was the day the Angels were coming to see me challenge, actually."

Dan shuddered. He shook his head. The tales of his sister's antics were known far and wide, and the embarrassment she'd brought his family infuriated him.

Fionna grabbed her purse and put on some lip gloss. She grinned at him as she considered. "I always sort of thought of Lindley as being misunderstood."

"People who are insane can be difficult to understand."

Fionna chuckled. He could sit and listen to her laugh for hours. The thought frightened him momentarily. *Don't screw this up, Dan.* Governor Haydenshire's words lit in his mind, and his determination to do this right reaffirmed itself.

Fionna bit her lip as she stared at Dan. She wanted to ask something.

"Go ahead." She shook her head. "Come on, although, I will say that if it's about my sister, it's probably true."

He took Fionna's hands and pulled her to him. He wanted to feel her body next to his. She buried her head in his chest and let him cradle her tenderly.

She seemed unable to keep herself from his care. The motion soothed his weary soul.

"Did she really offer to give Chancellor Wilshire a blow job every day if he wouldn't make her go to her classes her senior year?" The question seemed to have spilled from her beautiful lips without her permission, but he wanted her to ask anything she wanted to know.

"Yes." Dan cringed as he recalled that phone call.

"Wow," Fionna gasped.

"Yeah."

A distraction came in the form of Rainer and Emily knocking on their door.

Dan linked his hand with Fionna's. Walking in the bright sunshine with her beside him was heaven. He wanted to live in the light and the warmth of her. No one on the streets of Sydney paid them any attention at all. It was blissful perfection.

They didn't have to walk far until they'd stumbled upon a sandwich shop just a few blocks from the hotel.

Dan was pleased Fionna held his hand the entire walk and talked to him more than she talked to Emily. But once they were seated, she and Emily sat beside one another and leapt back into an animated conversation.

The frustration must have been evident on his face because Rainer chuckled. "It's gonna take more than one day," he whispered so quietly that the women didn't seem to notice he'd spoken.

As they perused the menu, Dan slid his right hand under the table and squeezed Fionna's thigh. She gave him that grin again, the one that was somehow sexy as hell and sweet as heaven all formed on one set of luscious lips.

They discussed options of things to try, and after they'd ordered, everyone joined in a conversation about the things they liked.

After their food arrived, Dan watched Rainer feed Emily bites of the rice salad that went with his soup and sandwich. Dan also took in Fionna's reaction to what he considered over-the-top doting, but Fionna smiled and plunged her own fork into the beet salad she'd ordered and seemed to love.

As the waiter returned to provide them with ice cream menus and to collect their lunch plates, Fionna's eyes goggled. Dan turned all of his attention to her, but she leaned toward Emily, placed her hand in front of her mouth, and whispered in Emily's ear for several long seconds.

Emily grimaced and then bit her bottom lip in concentration. Her eyes lit, and she leaned back in to whisper a quick response in Fionna's ear.

Fionna nodded and then Emily leaned back in, but this time Fionna shook her head. Emily considered again. Then with a nod she continued the conversation.

Fionna looked relieved as she nodded and hugged Emily. Whatever Emily's solution to Fionna's problem was, she deeply appreciated it.

Rainer had watched the entire exchange along with Dan's reactions. He took Emily's hand and smiled at her.

"Come on. You two are driving him crazy." He gestured to Dan.

"Oh, sorry." Fionna grimaced, and Dan glared at Rainer. He didn't appreciate being called out. "Just girl stuff." Fionna was uncomfortable suddenly.

"It's fine," Dan assured her, but he was more intrigued with the fact that in one quick grab of Emily's hand, Rainer had her. Emily's attention was all his. She gazed at him, and Rainer returned the gesture. They could have been the only two people in the restaurant, or in the entire world, for that matter.

After picking up the ice cream menu, he leaned closer to Fionna. "They have a caramel chocolate, and I could help you with the sutra positioning when I get you back to the room," he flirted shamelessly. With a wry grin, she shook her head and giggled.

"That sounds good, but we should try something we can only get here." Her breath danced heatedly on the skin of his neck. His stomach clenched in hopeful anticipation.

Dan leaned and kissed her cheek. He was unable to help himself. The motion seemed to delight Fionna, and hope sprang once more in his heart.

"Let's split one," she urged.

Dan was well aware that this was a tactic of women to keep themselves from eating more calories than they thought they should. He decided to allow it for now. He didn't want to call Fionna out on it.

"Sure, whatever you want," he agreed as he recalled Rainer's comment that Fionna and Emily had shared food and drink and therefore energy.

The waiter returned for their orders.

Rainer smiled. "Yeah, she'll have vanilla with extra cherries, and I'll just have a scoop of chocolate chip." He hadn't even had to ask Emily what she'd wanted.

"Uh," Fionna looked uncomfortable as she studied the menu and Dan. "Do you want to try the hokey pokey?" she quizzed hopefully.

Dan nodded. "Sure."

The waiter applauded Fionna's choice by telling her that it was a delicacy from New Zealand, but his eyes remained just a moment too long on Fionna's chest once she'd handed him the menu.

Dan ground his teeth and shot the waiter a vexing glare. He got the message and scooted away to retrieve their ice cream.

As it turned out, Fionna's choice was excellent, vanilla ice cream with candied honeycomb pieces in it.

Dan enjoyed the ice cream almost as much as he enjoyed watching Fionna devour it.

When she'd had enough of it that he could taste her energy in his bites, he was done for. He wanted her all to himself and took to feeding her the ice cream just so he could taste the spoon after she'd had it in her mouth.

Fionna seemed delighted with the gesture, and Rainer nodded his approval.

CHAPTER 4
EAGER

The ladies still wanted to try out the private heated pool, but Rainer had pled a nap, so they'd agreed to swim in a couple of hours.

As they returned to their suite, Dan asked, "Do you want to go out and see the city, or go down to the beach, or just hang out?" He was perfectly willing to do anything at all as long as he got to spend every moment with her. "I promised to take you shopping. We could do that." He'd never had the desire to spoil a woman so thoroughly.

Fionna considered, and then that intoxicating grin spread across her face once again. "You just want to see me topless," she teased.

He gave her a cocky grin and chuckled, "Always."

She glanced out to the pool and ocean beyond.

"I don't know," she hemmed. "The time difference is kind of crazy. I'm a little tired too."

Dan kicked off his shoes and pulled off his shirt. He tried not to be delighted at the way her eyes traced his chiseled pecs and abs whenever he did that. He moved to the largest couch in the sitting room of their suite, reclined against the arm, and gestured for her to join him. "Come here to me."

She slid off the sandals she was wearing and glided to him. She

41

sighed contentedly as she let him cradle her on his chest. He considered for a moment and then went on with his question.

"I've heard Garrett and Emily call you Fi. Can I call you that?"

She smiled against him. As she relaxed, he could pick up on more and more of her energy. It rolled in placid waves.

"Of course. Everyone calls me that." She cuddled her face deeper into his chest, and he kissed the top of her head.

"What did you ask Emily at the restaurant?" he quizzed and then clenched his jaw. He shouldn't have asked. He wished he could take it back. Her cheeks flushed against his chest. "You don't have to tell me," he feebly backtracked.

"No, it's okay. I guess I didn't really think about the fact that we're spending the week together and sort of agreed to kind of, maybe start a serious relationship, but we really don't know much about each other."

Suddenly worried that she was regretting her decision, Dan edged. He didn't care for the *kind of*, and *maybe* portion of her declaration.

"I would really like to know everything about you, but I'd be willing to take a crash course if you're offering one."

"She grinned. "I'm just scared eventually I'm going to tell you something you don't like." Her energy seized as if her body was warning her off.

"I don't think that's going to happen, so give me a try?"

She raised her head. Blood pooled quickly in her cheeks. "You promise not to think I'm, like, a sex addict or anything?"

He laughed out loud which only made her blush more pronounced. "Because that would be such a huge turnoff."

She rolled her eyes. "I kind of do some things differently. I don't usually sleep in anything. I believe it's healthier not to. I think your skin and your soul need to breathe when you sleep. My body needs a chance for all of the emotional energy I've had to absorb all day to dissipate." Her body tensed and braced for rejection that certainly wasn't coming. Dan willed her to understand that.

"And since me coming with you was kind of last minute, I forgot to pack the couple of nightgowns I bought and used when we were in Brazil. I remembered stuff I wanted to wear for you before, but I guess I sort of forgot the after part." The admission seemed to have cost her quite a bit. She tucked her head back into his chest and hid from him.

Dan nodded. He cradled her tighter. He wanted her to know he was already crazy about her. If what she was trying to tell him was that she was different from the duplicated drones he'd been banging without thought or care for the last decade, he needed her to understand that nothing in the world sounded better than that.

"Okay, I have several questions." She raised her head hesitantly. "What did Emily have to do with all of that?"

"Oh." Fionna seemed relieved with that particular question. "I told her I forgot pajamas because she already knows I don't wear anything to bed. At first, she said that you'd already offered to take me shopping, but I can't actually let you buy me stuff like that." She sounded as if the very idea was preposterous. "And then she said she thought she'd brought a nightshirt I could borrow, because she normally wears Rainer's shirts to bed."

Dan tried to decide what to ask first. "I'm just gonna ask everything I'm thinking, and you answer whatever you want."

"Okay." Fionna giggled, probably at the desperation in his voice.

"First, why can't I buy you stuff like that? Second, when I said a serious relationship, I meant that. If you normally sleep naked which, other than the fact that I assume some other guy has had the pleasure of you doing that with him, is a huge turn-on,"—he made her blush again—"why can't you sleep that way with me? You did last night, and it was incredible." He sincerely hoped she'd found it just as exhilarating as he had. "And if you were uncomfortable sleeping here with me like that, why don't you just borrow one of my shirts?"

With another deep breath, she appeared to force herself to go ahead and complete her confession.

"I was kind of trying not to show you how scattered I can be right off the bat. You know, maybe save that for after the second time we sleep together or something." She shrugged. "If I borrowed Emily's gown, then I wouldn't have had to admit to you that I forgot mine. And as long as we're taking Fionna 101, no, I haven't ever slept like that with another guy." She sighed after her confession.

Dan waited. He knew there was more. She seemed to want to fill the silence, so she went on, "I, uh, I've never let a guy stay over with me before you, and I'm not into that whole walk of shame thing, so I always invite them to my house and then make them leave."

Everything she said brought about another round of questions Dan desperately wanted answered.

"I don't think you forgetting something you don't normally use when I gave you approximately an hour to pack for a week-long trip to the other side of the world makes you appear scattered. I think I forgot my shaving cream, and I've had a week to pack." The relief on her face made him continue. "And I've never stayed over with anyone either. I hope me asking didn't put you in an uncomfortable position, but honestly, sleeping with you like that drove me wild. I wanted to hold you, and protect you, and keep you warm. I wanted to keep you safe. I don't want you to do anything that makes you uncomfortable, but I would be honored to hold you all night, every night we're here. Naked in my arms sounds like absolute perfection to me." Dan needed to tell her the truth.

She looked overwrought. Her energy picked up. He could feel it as she lay against him.

"I was really happy you asked to stay," she admitted hesitantly. "If you'd left, I would've cried for a long, long time."

Her raw, tender confession touched Dan in the places he'd thought were dead and gone, the places she'd filled and soothed the night before. He held her tightly, not certain what to say.

"I don't ever want you to cry, sweetheart, and..." He hesitated. His mind was at war with his heart and his soul. *She'll make you feel, not just think. She'll make you a better person if you'll let her.* Rainer's words pierced through Dan's reluctance. "Fi, I'd like to stay over or for you to stay at my house whenever you want."

He was dumbfounded by the ease with which it rolled off of his tongue. That was the only way a relationship between the two of them would work, he reminded himself.

"Okay, you have to stop," she whispered, and Dan's entire body seized. He'd gone too far. He'd pushed further than she was ready. He started to backpedal, but she continued, "I feel like I'm in this fantastic dream, and I'm about to wake up and you're not going to have said everything I've wanted you to say, and then I really am gonna cry."

Utter relief flooded through him as he held her close. He exhaled the bitter regret that had worked through him so quickly, and he allowed himself to breathe once again. Since she was providing him with information with relative ease, he kept up his questions.

"So, back to why I can't buy you things like that…"

She scoffed and rolled her eyes. "You brought me here. I didn't pay for my plane ticket or any part of this really nice suite. You wouldn't even let me pay for my lunch. I can't let you take me shopping and buy me clothes for a week."

He studied her incredulously. "Baby doll, I asked you…no," he corrected, "I *begged* you to come here with me. I meant what I said. I will take you out and buy you anything you want. You didn't have to pack anything at all. I'm just thrilled you're here."

"Thank you, but you don't need to spend money on me. I'm happy I'm here too."

As he thought over her response, he took a guess. "This wouldn't have anything to do with the fact that you make ten times what I do, would it?" She was the highest paid Receiver in Summation. He knew she was well paid for her work.

She grimaced. His assumption was correct, and some moron had given her hell over that before him. Anger roiled in his chest.

"Guys get all weird about that," she conceded.

Dan shook his head. "I don't know who you've been with before me, but you're an amazing athlete, and as I'm certain you are aware, the Angels make the city and the Realm quite a bit of money. You should be paid well for what you do. It doesn't bother me in the least, but when I asked you to be in a serious relationship, I meant I want you to be my girlfriend, and that means when we go out, I pay.

"If I coerce you into flying around the globe with me, then I get to buy whatever you need when we get there. And, as I am the guy who has to give legal approval to the Angels' contracts, I know what you make. Just trust me, I make a good living being top of the food chain at Iodex, and for the past ten years or so, I've eaten ninety percent of my meals in the Senate cafeteria. My house is paid for. My bike is paid for. So, other than occasionally buying a bottle of Scotch, a few beers, and gas, I don't spend much money. Let me spend some on you. Nothing would make me happier."

She still seemed uncomfortable with the concept, but she shrugged her agreement.

"Actually, the first thing we have to buy you is a helmet," he informed her with another wry grin. *I could put her in a full helmet and feel her hold on tight while I take her for rides on my bike. No one would have a clue who was with me. This could work.*

"Oh really," she drawled.

"Really."

"You know, my car has two seats, and I don't have to mess up my hair to ride in it," she informed him with a great deal of sass.

"Helmet hair is sexy, baby doll. Trust me." He made her laugh, but his brain continued its negotiations. *I can never ever be seen in her car with her.*

Eventually, Fionna was yawning more than talking, and she fell asleep once again curled up on Dan's chest. He debated momentarily and then eased her shirt up only enough for her stomach to be against his, so he could place his hands on the small of her back.

He closed his eyes and focused on her energy as she slept.

He wondered if all Gifted women felt so incredible if you got that close to them. Dan decided they didn't. They couldn't. It was only her.

As he began to understand the rhythms her body made, she once again hypnotized him. She was happy, peaceful, and content in his arms.

He'd never felt anything so fulfilling as he held her in his protective embrace and watched her sleep.

CHAPTER 5
THE CHICKEN QUEEN

an and Fionna joined Rainer and Emily in the pool outside their suite. Emily was seated on the side with her legs dangling in the water. Rainer was standing in the pool between her legs, smiling up at her.

Dan entered the pool via the steps and offered his hand up to Fionna.

"Do you know how to swim?" he quizzed as she let him guide her in. She almost laughed in his face, but she bit her lips together and nodded instead.

Emily giggled. "Fi's an amazing swimmer. She taught the kids at the orphanage while we were there. She's like a mermaid."

"Wow." Dan smiled at Fionna. He let his voice take on an appropriately impressed tone. "You'll have to tell me about Brazil."

"It was amazing," Fionna gushed and then turned to Emily. "I got a letter from Aida."

"What did it say?"

Whoever Aida was, she clearly meant a great deal to both women.

"It made me cry so hard. She kept saying how much she missed us and wanting to know when we were coming back. I sobbed for an hour before I could even write her back."

Emily nodded her understanding.

Rainer moved placidly through the water until he was right beside Dan. "Really sweet little girl at the orphanage they both fell head over heels for," he explained. "Aida's a Receiver too. Ask Fi about it later. She'd like that."

"Okay, let's chicken fight," Emily urged a few minutes later. Rainer shook his head at her.

Fionna looked excited by the idea as she moved close enough to Dan to lean her head on his chest. "You want to?"

"I'm good with anything that gets my head between your legs, baby doll."

She waggled her eyebrows as that adorable giggle echoed in the hollow recesses of his soul. After giving him a naughty wink that made him ache, Fionna spun away from him.

"Okay," she chanted, "whichever couple wins gets to use the pool tonight all alone."

Dan smirked. He rather liked his odds in this scenario.

Rainer looked embarrassed, but Emily was intrigued.

"Deal," she agreed.

"We will never ever discuss this at work," Rainer negotiated.

"Agreed." Dan nodded his acceptance of the deal with a chuckle.

With that, he dipped under the water and came up rather smoothly with Fionna seated on his shoulders.

Rainer attempted the same move, but Emily was distracted. As she tried to position herself on his shoulders, Dan continued to flirt shamelessly.

"So tonight, after we win," he informed her, "I'm gonna do the same basic thing only I'm gonna turn you around."

Fionna's abdomen clenched in anticipation as she leaned down and murmured, "I can't wait."

Rainer edged toward Dan and Fionna with Emily on his shoulders. Fionna and Emily were both laughing and attempting to trash talk, which Rainer and Dan found hysterical.

Emily reached for Fionna, but Dan backed her away. Fionna laughed and stuck her tongue out at Emily.

Eventually Fionna caught Emily's hands, and the fight was on.

Rainer and Emily had clearly played before and had a decent move where Rainer would back up quickly while Emily grasped Fionna's hands in an effort to pull her off of Dan's shoulders.

"Wait 'til he moves back again," Dan instructed. She kept her arms locked tightly with Emily's.

Rainer stepped back quickly, but this time Dan leaned toward Rainer as he retreated, and Fionna leaned upwards. She placed her crotch on the back of Dan's head and pushed at the same moment. Emily's back hit the water.

Fionna cheered as Dan lowered her back into the water and then caught her in his arms. He kissed her heatedly.

"Ever skinny-dipped, Chief Vindico?" Fionna teased when he pulled his mouth away. Dan grimaced. He didn't really want to tell her the truth.

"Never with anyone as gorgeous as you," he offered one of his signature phrases hopefully.

With a dramatic eye roll, she didn't in any way give him the customary response. Fionna laughed in his face. "Wow," she drawled sarcastically, "use that line much?"

Dan let his head drop in defeat. He found it odd how much he liked the fact that she wasn't going to take his crap.

She turned away from Dan again and teased Emily.

"Don't feel bad. I was actually the chicken-fighting queen of the middle school I went to, all three years." She effectively cracked Emily and Rainer up.

"Well, I bow to Her Majesty the Chicken Queen," Emily joked as Dan reveled in Fionna's laughter once again.

"Hey, I saw in that binder in the rooms,"—Fionna changed course quickly, taking no time to revel in their victory—"that the room-service people will pack you a picnic to take to the beach. Let's do that for dinner." She turned back to make certain it was all right with Dan as she eased back to him. She seemed to want his arms around her as much as he wanted to hold her.

He enveloped her body in his own. "That sounds perfect, sweetheart."

Emily swooned over the gesture.

Dan did think it sounded like a great idea. Seeing Fionna topless in the sunset made his entire body ache, and if they stayed at the hotel, he could get her back in bed, or in the pool, even faster.

Rainer looked morose.

Dan mouthed the words, "Losing battle."

Rainer pretended not to see him.

"That would be fun." Emily rolled her eyes when she took in Rainer's expression.

"We could wear tops," Fionna offered. She clearly didn't want to cause another round of arguing.

"No," Emily huffed. "I could finally have a tan without lines." She shot another irritated glare at Rainer.

Dan had already conjured up several fantasies of Fionna on the beach, in his arms, topless against him. He threw Rainer a look that said for him to get over it or else.

With a defeated huff, Rainer rolled his eyes. "Whatever you want to do is fine," he lied, and everyone knew it.

"He will eventually get over this," Emily assured them.

"I'm not really thinking so." Fionna looked truly concerned over Rainer's reaction.

"He will," Dan joined in, "right about the time she whips her top off. Trust me."

The ladies laughed as Rainer blushed yet again.

"Okay, well, I think we'll just let you two work that out, and we'll go order the picnic," Fionna eased. "And really, Rainer, if it makes you uncomfortable, I'll wear a top. It's fine."

Certain he'd like to throttle Rainer Lawson right about then, Dan narrowed his eyes.

"It's fine. I'll be fine." His face turned crimson in his embarrassment. Fionna pulled Emily close to her face.

"If he freaks, just text me and I'll wear a top. He's really hurting. I can feel it. I know you can too. Don't be so hard on him. He loves you so much." There seemed to be absolutely no doubt. She could apparently read Rainer with ease. "It's kind of sweet." Fionna continued playing peacemaker.

"It's kind of over-the-top," Emily argued.

Before Fionna could offer to wear a top to the topless beach yet again, Dan grabbed her hand.

"Come on. We'll get enough food for everyone." He led Fionna out of the pool.

CHAPTER 6

TO FIGHT YOUR OWN SHIELD

RAINER LAWSON

After he handed Emily her towel, Rainer left her standing beside the pool and went back in the suite. He was still pouting.

"Rainer, please," Emily begged as she followed him inside.

"Fine, whatever you want." He moved away from her again and closed the bedroom door behind him. The door opened immediately, and Emily marched in.

"Look," she demanded. "I'll wear my top out there and leave it on, and then when you see that it's really no big deal, I'll let you take it off. You can do your obsessive watching over me thing that you do until you stop freaking out about it."

"Whatever, but I'll be perfectly honest with you. Letting you take your top off out there"—he threw his thumb angrily in the direction of the beach—"will be one of the hardest things I've ever done, and you know all of the things I've done."

He willed his temper to remain in check. It was a mighty task. She looked deflated, and he felt guilty again. He couldn't redact his statement. It was the absolute truth. Angry tears pierced her eyes, and her chin quivered.

"You know, you don't seem to mind my lack of modesty when I'm pulling my clothes off for you or when I'm splayed out on the hood of your Porsche," she vaulted furiously.

With his eyes goggling, Rainer felt like she'd slapped him. "That's different, and you know it!" he shouted. This brought on sobs.

"Stop yelling at me! I didn't do anything wrong!"

A tidal wave of guilt threatened to engulf Rainer.

After forcibly willing down his anger, he breathed. "So that doesn't bother you? Believe me, guys are going to be looking at you. Obviously they're going to look. You're gorgeous, and,"—he paused but then decided to go on—"you've got a hell of a rack. Men are going to drool." The statement alone made him queasy.

"That's what I keep trying to tell you. It's really not that big of a deal. There are lots of women of all shapes and sizes out there. No one is gawking at them."

Rainer decided to change tactics. "And that doesn't bother you either? That I'll be seeing all of the women out there?" This bit of information did bother her, and Rainer was hopeful.

"No," she forced, "because you're a gentleman, and you'll be looking at mine. They kind of all look the same anyway."

"And where was all of this tolerance when I had to go to The Tantra?" Rainer spat.

"No one out there will be shaking theirs in your face," Emily came right back. "And I've learned a thing or two since then. I grew up. I completely overreacted about that. I told you that."

He suddenly realized that this wasn't going to go away. She was right. He couldn't have it both ways. He couldn't have the girl who paraded around for him in a corset and heels or the one who told him to take her hard and fast on the hood of his Porsche and expect her to be a prude on a topless beach.

The more he protested, the more determined she was going to become. He knew this, and it was the straw that broke the proverbial camel's back.

"All right, baby. If you really want to do this, we will, but I'm not kidding you. I'm going to freak if I see another guy ogling you. That's more than I can take. I'm your Shield."

"Okay," she agreed, and then gave him his favorite mischievous smile. She laid her head on his shoulder.

"I'll even let you put suntan lotion on them," she teased and elicited a slight chuckle, which was the most Rainer could come up with at the moment.

CHAPTER 7

HUNGRY PAST
DAN VINDICO

Dan was finishing the order for a picnic for four when he temporarily forgot how to speak.

Fionna paraded out of the bathroom wearing nothing but a white, tie-side, barely there bikini bottom.

"Uh, sir?" the woman on the other end of the phone asked concernedly.

"Oh, uh, sorry. Yeah. I'll pick it up in a little while." He stared as Fionna opened one of the bags she'd packed. She removed a plastic bottle that appeared to have a homemade label on it while she shot him looks that threatened to make him spontaneously combust.

She sauntered toward him. Her eyes darkened with every step she advanced. Dan tried to remember how to hang the phone back in its cradle. Watching her full, ample breasts sway as she walked was all he was capable of doing.

After giving her a very appreciative, hungry grin, Dan let a low whistle slide between his teeth. He thoroughly delighted her.

"I need some help," she informed him in a sexy coo.

"Do you, baby doll?" He grabbed her backside and pulled her into him as she nodded. "And what can I do for you?"

She shivered slightly. His trousers strained as his heart picked up pace. He reveled in the feeling of it all. She held up the bottle expectantly.

"Could you rub this all over me?" she challenged with a sultry smile.

"I think I can handle that." He removed the bottle from her hands.

"I thought you probably could."

He took her hand and guided her to the couch. While he let his voice take on a sexy edge, he seated her.

"Lie down for me, baby," he commanded. With a sexy grin, she reclined on the couch. He studied the bottle momentarily. *Hawaiian Princess Sun Rub From Iona Farms*

With a slight shrug, he lathered his hands and began with her neck. The scent of coconut, honey, and hibiscus perfumed the air. He rubbed the lotion into her soft, tender skin.

He let his fingers knead her muscles. He worked out the stress and strain he wasn't even aware she was carrying until he'd begun the massage.

She moaned as he loosened the knots. The sound made his own muscles clench and tighten in anticipation. As she'd lain out on her stomach, denying him what he really wanted to put lotion on, he slid his hands down her back and thoroughly enjoyed the way it dipped in a perfect arc just before it swelled to her gorgeous ass. Her eyes were closed, and she laid her head on her folded arms.

"You and Amelia never went on a vacation anywhere?" she quizzed suddenly.

He forced himself from his abstraction and tried to focus on what she was saying rather than on her luscious body.

"Uh." He shook his head and tried desperately to focus. "No," he answered. "She went with me a few times to the Outer Banks, but Will and Garrett and all of my friends were at Virginia Beach, so I was always irritated with my parents while we were there.

"We got engaged before I graduated, and she wanted to buy a house near our folks. So, that's what we did." Dan was shocked yet again at how he could discuss any part of Amelia with her and somehow it seemed bearable. She wasn't jealous. She didn't want him to forget his former life. She wanted to know more about it.

"Is that still where you live?" she whispered hesitantly.

"No." Dan shuddered from the thought. He tried to modulate his voice. His tone was making her nervous. He could feel that as he lathered her skin with the lotion. "Uh, no." He commanded himself to draw full breaths and try to explain everything to her gently. "I sold it a few months after she was killed. I bought a place in a Non-Gifted neighborhood that's closer to work. Maybe you could come over after we get back. I probably need to clean first though."

Fionna flipped onto her back, and Dan's thoughts instantly went back to her phenomenal body.

"You don't seem like a slob." She studied him.

Dan recalled Rainer saying that Receivers hate clutter because it affected their reads, so he rushed to reassure her. "I'm not a slob. I'm just never home. I send all of my laundry out, and I think the most I've ever cooked in my kitchen is coffee and maybe some toast. I should probably at least change the sheets and make it look like someone actually lives there before I let you see it." Dan wanted her to know if he somehow convinced her to be with him back in DC, he would do everything right by her.

He rubbed lotion over her shoulders, then skipped her breasts entirely and moved to her svelte stomach. She poked her bottom lip out in a delicious pout. The move made him chuckle.

"Don't worry, honey. I'm saving the best for last."

He stifled a groan as her nipples began to pull taut and darken. She wanted his attention, but he continued to make her wait. He wanted the anticipation to build.

After working his way down her stomach, he pressed until he'd slipped his hands under the bottom of the swimsuit. Her breath caught as she let her eyes open slightly.

"I don't think I'll get much sun under there," she teased.

"Oh, okay." Dan wasn't playing her game. With a wry smile, he noted her pout as he moved to her thighs. "Spread your legs for me, baby doll."

Her breath stuttered deliciously. She let her legs fall to the sides, and he re-lathered his hands. He massaged up her legs and worked until he was rubbing the most sensitive parts of her inner thighs. He slid them higher and let his thumbs rub between the top of her thighs and her lips.

She panted. With a knowing smirk, he slipped his thumbs under the crotch of her swimsuit as a quick raspy moan escaped her mouth.

He traced her lips. "Is that good, honey, or did you need some more?" She writhed under his touch.

With a quick hungry moan, she pulled the slight, beaded strings holding the swimsuit to her body.

He growled as he watched her reveal those lush folds, already swollen and hungry for his length. Dan dragged two fingers on either side of her slit after he pulled the swimsuit away from her. He watched her lips throb and glisten for him.

With tender care, he eased her apart. He wanted to see the pulsing, pink flesh as she writhed and bucked. She needed to be tamed.

A low, fervent moan escaped him as her body began to roll.

"I need you, honey. I don't think I've ever wanted anything as much as I want you right now, and I know you want it too. I can see how wet and needy you are. Let me have you. Let me make it feel better. Let me show you how good I can make it feel when I take you from behind. Let me own you."

She trembled with a wild look in her eyes.

Dan paused. His natural reaction would've been to grab a condom at that moment before he warmed her up and had his way with her.

Suddenly, he found the very idea appalling. Anything that would block the indescribable sensation of her surrounding him, of her energy permeating him, of releasing himself inside of what had to be a portion of heaven, horrified him.

With a determined clench of his jaw, Dan watched her beautiful body writhe in hunger, and he forced himself to remember everything Rainer had taught him that morning.

She was astounding. He hated the feeling that there was even more about being with her that he was so inexperienced with.

A loud moan cried from deep within her. Dan managed to remember that he needed to have her erotic energy in his hands. He slipped two fingers inside of her as she cried out for him. The sound drove him wild.

He could feel it, the sweet essence of her. It wound around him, binding, restoring, soothing, and mending his fractured soul. He pushed deeper as she bucked in ardent need.

"There's my good girl. This is what you really needed my help with, isn't it?" He curved his fingers and coaxed the spot that made her body pulse and tense as she pulled him deeper. She began grinding and thrusting as she tried to fuck herself with his fingers.

"It's all right, sweetheart. I'm gonna take good care of you." His voice was low and reverent in his deep desire. A few more of his signature moves formed in his mind as he gazed at her body trembling for him.

With his left hand, he pushed down gently on her mound as he stroked with his right hand deep inside of her.

"Oh yes," she gasped, and he smiled. He was fairly certain that was one she hadn't felt before.

Suddenly, the astounding feeling of her washed through him again. She was exquisite. Her energy and her body rolled in craving need. He couldn't get enough.

"You're still swollen so nice and tight. Seems like you might need a few rounds tonight."

Her breath hitched in her outcries. She wanted more. He could feel it, as he was able to concentrate on her energy. "Are you up for that, baby doll? You up for me now, and then when I get you back in that pool? You gonna be a good girl for me and take it twice?"

"Please, please" she begged in need acute to the point of pain. Her lips clenched. The liquid form of her energy slipped around his fingers. Not certain how much longer he was going to last, with her begging and her body pulsing and fevered, Dan leaned so he was closer to her face.

"I'm gonna cast you. Then I'm gonna fill up that sweet wet hole. Make you take it hard until I explode inside of you. I'm gonna fill you full of me and make everything better."

She halted abruptly. Her body shuddered as she forced herself to stop feeling what he was doing to her.

"No, wait!" she panicked.

Dan halted instantly. He pulled his hands away. She looked terrified, and it cut him to the core.

"What's wrong, sweetheart?" He was shocked yet again that the sudden halt of his progress didn't bother him in any way. Deep concern filled his shield.

She was scared. He had enough of her in his hands to feel her panic. She swallowed hard and shook her head. She was concentrating on something. She scooted away from him.

"Fi, baby come on. Tell me what's going on. We won't do anything you don't want to do." Vile revulsion washed over him. He would never force her to do something she wasn't comfortable with.

"I set the cast yesterday just before the party, but I can't figure out the time thing. Was that twenty-four hours ago?" her voice trembled, and tears formed in her eyes.

"It's okay." Dan wrapped his arms around her, but she was hesitant. Something had made her wary of him, and his heart ached. Nausea set in his gut.

"Baby." He held her tight and refused to let his hands move anywhere that wasn't her back. He rubbed soothingly. "It's okay. If it's still set, then I'll feel that once I'm in there, and if it isn't, then I'll seal you off. If you want to stop, we will. I'll do whatever you want."

"Have you ever done that before?" Her face held a mixture of terror and grief.

Dan hesitated as he brushed her cheek with his thumb. "Truthfully, no," he admitted, "but I'm pretty sure I can. I did get some good instructions."

She nodded hesitantly

"Tell me what's going on. What happened? Did I do or say something you didn't like?"

She drew a deep, steadying breath, and he felt it again—the awe-inspiring sensation moved through him. She was drawing from him in heavy doses. He panted as she pulled in his protective care.

She drew strength from him as well. He closed his eyes and gently pushed everything he had to her. He let her take as much as she needed in endless supply. He wanted her to drain him dry. It was heavenly.

"I don't usually let guys cast me." She still sounded frightened.

"Okay." Dan waited patiently. He knew there was more.

"My job depends on me not getting pregnant."

He continued holding her to his chest, rubbing her back and letting her draw from him as she needed his energy. He was desperate to do more to soothe her. He added calming waves to his secondary bands so she could pull both. She relaxed against him, but the fear remained.

Dan's stomach knotted as he worried about the reason she didn't let other men cast her. While holding her tenderly, he didn't even have to concentrate to let his shield encapsulate her.

If she needed to feel safe, that's exactly what he would do for her. He'd never shielded a woman. Amelia couldn't have felt anything if he had, but when he held Fionna in his rhythms, he was filled with peace, and warmth, and an emotion he couldn't quite name.

"Wow," she whispered in awe as his fierce shield surrounded her. His adoration was in the very air she breathed.

"Tell me, honey. I know there's more. I've got you. You're safe." He kept the full force of his double-banded shield locked tight around them. "I'm right here."

"When I was a lot younger…" she choked. His gut clenched. "I was with this guy, and he said he could cast me, so I let him." She spat the regret from her mouth, and fury began to sear through Dan. "He was horrible at it, and he hurt me really badly." Dan let his eyes close. His overly-muscled arms tensed of their own accord. "But then he just went ahead with everything. It was awful, and I hurt for days. I was completely freaked out for weeks because I thought he probably didn't do it right and that I might be pregnant." Her body shuddered from the haunting memory.

While he fought the desperate desire that permeated every fiber of his being to hunt the guy down and shatter every bone in his body, Dan tried to remain calm.

"Did you tell him to stop?" Bile rose violently in his throat as he awaited her answer.

"Kind of," she hemmed. "Yeah," she finally admitted. "I kept thinking it would get better, and I didn't want to make him mad."

She said nothing to keep Dan from wanting desperately to fix it so that whoever the prick was, he would never have sex again.

"I'm sorry." She looked devastated, which effectively shook Dan from his infuriated preoccupation.

"Baby, why on earth are you sorry? You did nothing wrong. The asshole who did that to you did everything wrong, and if I ever convince you to tell me his name, I'll make absolutely certain he is well-informed of what I think of what he did, but you have nothing to apologize for."

This elicited a small smile. "No, he was just a stupid kid. I was apologizing for shutting this down. I really didn't mean to." She seemed confused by everything that had happened.

Dan was still in shock. She'd just hesitantly admitted that she'd been forced, and now she was the one apologizing. What the hell? Why was the world so fucked-up and why were women always, always the ones who were the most abused?

"Look at me." He pulled away from her but widened his shield so she still felt safe as he took her hands and stared into her eyes. "Sweetheart…" He squeezed her hands gently and willed calm into her as he decided to lay it all on the line. "Last night,"—he drew a deep breath as shame began to creep in—"last night was about sex."

She nodded and cast her gaze to the ground.

"But it's about so much more than that now, and I told you I'm no good at this. It's been over ten years since I was any good at this, and then *I* was just a stupid kid." He gently touched her chin and guided her gaze back to his. "I only wanted to be the one to set the cast because I want to take care of you. Not because I'm some macho prick who has something to prove. If it makes you uncomfortable, then I'll back off and let you take care of it until you're ready to give me a shot.

"I understand why you're hesitant. I need you to know that I would never, ever hurt you, and that I sure as hell wouldn't try to keep going if I ever thought you were hurting in any way for any reason. If you say stop or wait or indicate in any way that I'm not making you happy, then we stop. That's what happens and that is always what should happen." He was still sickened by her story. "And that includes because something scared you, even if it's a memory that didn't have anything to do with me."

"I know." She never dropped his gaze as she moved back toward him. She wanted to be held. He let go of her hands and wrapped his arms around her. He cradled her into his chest. The motion soothed her. He could feel it, and he reveled in his education of her.

Dan brushed a tender kiss across her forehead and allowed himself a moment to let his eyes trace down her body, still naked and in his arms.

Her cell phone chirped, and she seemed momentarily confused as to whether or not she should check it. Dan released her, and he dropped his shield. The last of the impassioned lust they'd created still pulsed in the air. She moved to her bag and picked up her cell.

"It's Emily. She says they're heading out and..." She scrolled down and then giggled. It was one of the sweetest sounds in the world. That and the way she moaned and panted his name when he brought her to climax. "She wants you to tackle Rainer if at any point he attempts to throw a towel over her on the beach."

Dan laughed. "I can probably handle that, but Lawson's quick."

She replied and then gave Dan a sorrowful look.

"I really am sorry." She gestured back to the couch.

Dan shook his head as he moved to her. He lifted her chin in his hand.

"You have nothing to be sorry about." He was still devastated that she thought he would be upset with her for needing to stop him from taking part in their physical relationship so that he could learn more about the emotional one they were delving into. "Let's go to the beach, and then later if you're up to it, we'll see what I can do to rectify this." He mimicked her gesture toward the couch. A sweet smile spread across her beautiful face. It faded quickly though, as she studied him.

"Dan," she whispered.

"What, sweetheart?" He drew her back to him. He needed to feel her safe in his arms.

"Why don't you go ahead and set the cast?" she choked but then forced herself to continue. "And then we can go out with Rainer and Emily. If you're sure that doing that won't make it worse for you."

Dan weighed all of his options. He needed her to trust him. That was the only way this would ever work. It was more than that though. He *wanted* her to trust him. He wanted her to trust him with everything.

"Are you sure?" He studied her as she nodded. She held his eyes with her own.

He prayed he still had enough of her energy in and around him to do this, and he nodded. "Go sit back down and relax for me."

She drew a deep breath and moved back to the couch. He needed to prove himself to her. He joined her and held her tenderly in his arms. His heart ached from her story and from the way she looked so small and timid in his long, overmuscled arms.

"First of all," he soothed, "setting the cast doesn't make a guy any more horny than he was several minutes ago." That elicited a small grin. He drew a deep breath and kissed her head. "You tell me if anything I do doesn't feel the way it's supposed to, okay?"

She gave a slight nod. He summoned and used the very last of her erotic energy that still danced in the air around him.

"Relax for me, baby. I've got you." Suddenly, he knew what to do. He understood what had to happen. He was a decent healer from all of the times he'd healed his officers in the field. He moved slowly and added in his own soothing and calming energies in heavy doses as he tenderly placed his hand on her mound. Dan concentrated. He let the combined energies move up her, and with delicate precision, he tenderly sealed her off and filled her with calming, soothing waves. When he was certain she was closed completely, he pulled his hand away.

"Okay?" He kept her tucked in the safety of his embrace. She looked astonished.

"Wow!"

Dan chuckled as relief filled him.

"That was,"—she shook her head—"wow." Her eyes flashed in shock as he allowed himself to laugh outright.

To prove his point about the guy being a total shitbag, Dan winked at her. "Are you ready to go to the beach?" He handed her the swimsuit she'd been wearing.

"You're kind of amazing."

She'd just made his entire year, but Dan shook his head. "I've been called worse, trust me."

She pulled on the entire swimsuit, top included, and asked if he'd help her tie it in back.

"I'll be much better at untying this," he teased her as he tied the bikini top tight.

They picked up the picnic and headed out to the crisp, blue waters and bright, white sands of Manly Beach.

CHAPTER 8

DEEP IN THE SEA

The ladies both left their tops on as they found a set of umbrella-covered beach chairs and ate their picnic. The numerous kinds of sandwiches and gourmet chips were all delicious.

Logan and Adeline joined them a little while later.

Fionna gave Logan a sorrowful gaze as he settled near her. "I feel really bad that we're all on your honeymoon with you."

Logan grinned. "I feel really bad that you're all on my honeymoon with me too."

Everyone laughed.

"Logan," Adeline whispered in what Dan assumed was supposed to sound scolding if you were Adeline Haydenshire. This only made Logan laugh harder.

"Look who decided to come up for air." Rainer chided his best friend.

"Hey, even I have to recuperate occasionally." He sounded rather macho and elicited eye rolls from Rainer and Dan as he continued to laugh.

A moment later, Rainer was gasping as Emily pulled off her top.

"It's like a Band-Aid," she sassed. Everyone cracked up, and Dan immediately turned his gaze to Fionna.

"Geez, Em, I'm trying to eat." Logan was scooping up the remnants of his sister's dinner and helping himself.

"Can it, Logan," Rainer demanded.

Fionna and Dan choked back laughter.

Dan appreciated the fact that though Rainer didn't want her out there topless, he wasn't going to allow her brother to harass her either.

Fionna reached back to untie her own top, but Dan had bound her in it tightly.

"Uh, little help please, Chief Vindico." She giggled.

Dan shot her a cocky smirk as she turned around, and he untied her. He planned on releasing her in all the different ways he knew how as soon as he got her back to their room. He stifled a groan as the bikini top pulled away from her ample cleavage.

Adeline couldn't seem to muster the courage to remove the top of her suit.

Fionna grasped Emily's hand. "Let's go swim."

Emily followed her toward the water. Rainer looked sick as he swept his eyes over the beach making certain no one stared at Emily for any length of time.

"Losing battle," Dan quipped again. Rainer rolled his eyes, but Dan was watching Fionna. She dove into the ocean and rolled onto her back. A mermaid indeed, she appeared to have been born in the sea. He'd never seen anyone move with such grace and allure in the ocean's tides. It was as if she commanded the energy of the water.

With a defeated sigh, Rainer kept his eyes locked on Emily as she played in the incoming tide.

"So, how's it going?" He gestured his head to Fionna, though he was intent not to look at her breasts. That was a feat Dan was rather impressed by. He couldn't seem to look anywhere else.

He watched them sway seductively with her body as she lounged and frolicked in the water. Occasionally, she would catch a wave and body surf. Dan had never before been jealous of the ocean.

"Good, really good." He was excited by the truthfulness of his statement.

"Good," Rainer mimicked as he gave Dan a genuine smile.

Fionna's cell phone rang in her bag. After a brief pause, he turned back to Rainer. "And thanks for the instruction this morning. That was…" He tried to think of how to compliment Rainer for his lesson.

"Helpful?"

Dan smiled. "Very."

"Glad to be of service." Rainer was still watching over Emily obsessively. Adeline stood and moved to the girls in the water. The top of her swimsuit was still firmly covering her chest.

"How'd you get her to do that?" Rainer demanded of Logan.

"I didn't. So, I'm going to go with lack of self-esteem and daddy issues. I can't believe I'm saying this, but now I kind of wish she'd take it off."

Fionna's cell phone began ringin again, and Dan turned to glance at her bag.

"Should I?" He already knew the answer as he watched Logan and Rainer shake their heads.

"Not unless you're trying to piss her off," Logan warned.

"Right." Dan turned his attention back to the fantasy he was watching play out with Fionna topless in the waves as the surf washed over her gorgeous body.

At that moment, Emily sauntered over to Adeline as the waves rolled away before churning back to kiss the shore. She quickly popped the clasp of Adeline's swimsuit and pulled it away from her. Adeline gasped her shock but then began laughing.

"Geez," Logan spat. "Emily!" he bellowed, but the ladies were too far away to hear him. "Would you please do something about her?" he demanded of Rainer.

"Why, because you're too stiff to walk after that?" Rainer came right back, and Dan cracked up.

With an eye roll, Logan huffed, "It would've been way hotter if it hadn't been my sister." Rainer joined in Dan's laughter.

A few minutes later, the ladies made their way back to the chairs where the men were seated as the sun dipped low on the horizon.

Fionna was shooting Dan looks that threatened to make *him* unable to walk. After she'd toweled off, he took her hand and pulled her onto the chair with him while he fought with everything in him not to grope her luscious tits.

"Your phone rang a couple of times," he informed her just as he started to wrap his arms around her.

"Oh." She looked surprised as she stood to retrieve her bag. The phone started again before she reached it.

With a knowing grin and a distinct eye roll, she pulled the phone from her bag. "Hey, Daddy." She situated herself back in Dan's lap.

"Maylea, where are you?" Dan could hear her father's concerned greeting through the phone. It was rather early for her father to be awake back in the States, and Dan wondered how Fionna had gotten her nickname. He continued to listen. Fionna's jaw clenched against his chest.

"I had a last-minute invite to go on a trip." Several seconds of silence passed. "I came to Sydney with Emily and Adeline," she offered hopefully.

Logan, Rainer, and Dan all stifled laughter. Fionna rolled her eyes and smirked.

"You do know Adeline. She just married Logan Haydenshire." Logan beamed as Adeline chuckled at his exuberance. "Yes, Logan's here," she stated hesitantly. "Uh, youngest besides the twins," she informed her father as everyone laughed.

"No, you're thinking of Levi. No, that's Connor. Garrett's not here," she eased and then rolled her eyes again. "I'm certain Logan would keep me just as safe as Garrett does."

"Safer," Logan vowed, but Dan clenched his jaw. Fionna didn't need Logan or Garrett to keep her safe.

"Uh, yeah, Rainer's here with Emily. Yeah." Fionna tensed and was quiet for another moment. "Dan Vindico," she informed her father hesitantly. Although Dan couldn't quite make out all of Fionna's father's words, his tone raised several decibels.

"Daddy, be nice!" Fionna commanded.

Dan let his head fall in defeat as Rainer and Logan gave him sorrowful glances. "No, he won't," she responded to what Dan was certain was a reminder that he would break her heart. "I mean...I really hope he won't." Fionna swallowed down a sudden onslaught of threatening tears.

No, I won't. The vow pulsed in Dan's shield. He let the fear wash over him and then settled into the idea as he listened to Fionna defend him to her father.

He began to feel the peace that being beside her always brought him. He was going to prove everyone wrong. He would figure out a way to be with her and how to keep her safe. He wasn't going to break her heart, not when she was the woman who had located his own after all of these years he'd been certain it was dead and gone.

"Daddy, go bake muffins, and let me talk to Mama," Fionna demanded angrily.

She turned back to Dan and mouthed an apology. Dan shook his head and pulled her back to his chest. She could talk as long as she needed. He just wanted her to stay right there with him.

"Maylea, my sweet girl," Dan heard her mother gush as she came to the phone. Fionna's entire face lit to the sound of her mother's voice. "So, you're in Sydney?" Her mother sounded thrilled for her. Fionna was now leaning against him completely, and Dan could easily hear the conversation. He tried to determine Fionna's mother's accent. It sounded Spanish.

"Yes, ma'am," Fionna agreed.

"When will you be back?" her mother asked, though Dan noted that it didn't sound like an inquisition, just a genuine curiosity.

"Well, uh, Saturday there, but it will really be Sunday here, because it's Tuesday night here now. It's confusing." Fionna shook her head.

"And this boy your padre is yelling about and kneading bread dough that we will eventually use to re-brick the house—is he cute, Maylea?" Her mother laughed heartily. Fionna joined in.

She shot Dan a vexing grin. She knew when she was reclined on his chest he could hear both sides of the conversation. She giggled.

"Not really," she teased, as Dan feigned heartbreak. She laughed at him outright. "I'm just kidding. He's a dreamboat," Fionna sassed as Logan and Rainer immediately began harassing Dan.

"Aww, Chief Dreamboat," Logan goaded.

"Just because we're on vacation doesn't mean I can't fire you, Haydenshire," Dan informed him as everyone continued to laugh.

"Remember love may be hiding in the unlikeliest of places. We may not know when we will stumble upon it, but we know when we've found it because we can't live without it," Fionna's mother reminded her. Dan listened intently.

"I know." Fionna sighed. "I don't think we're quite to all that yet, okay?"

"Really, because even though you are my Maylea, you don't often fly across several oceans to spend a week with a dreamboat at the drop of a hat. And you sound like someone might've just proven that the clouds are made of fairy floss, like you used to tell your Papa when you were a little kekei." Fionna's blush grew more pronounced.

"Okay, I have to go. I'll call you when I get home. I love you, and tell Daddy I love him and that I'll be fine." With that, Fionna ended the call.

Not certain what to say, Dan settled for holding her close and allowing his mind to ponder everything Fionna's mother had just pointed out and her use of both Spanish and Hawaiian words.

While refusing to meet Dan's gaze, Fionna turned all of her attention back to Emily.

Her mother made her uncomfortable, and she immediately turned back to Emily. The harsh sting of rejection pierced through him.

"Adeline, Emily and I were thinking that maybe we could do a spa day since the spa here is supposed to be phenomenal. Would you like to come?"

"That sounds expensive," Adeline lamented. Emily and Logan both rolled their eyes.

"It's our honeymoon, and Dad's paid for everything so far. Go have a good time. It's fine," Logan urged.

"Do you want to go tomorrow, or before we go to the Premier's castle Thursday, or we could go Friday?" Emily pushed.

Fionna grinned. "Let's go tomorrow or Friday, because once we get all gorgeous, the boys have to take us out."

Dan chuckled and brushed Fionna's chestnut tresses behind her shoulders. He began dragging his fingers through the soft, thick locks, gently separating where the ocean had tangled it.

"I think you're already beautiful, but I'll take you anywhere you want to go while we're here." Dan continued playing calmly with her hair and hoped she wouldn't note the caveat to his promise just yet.

Her energy eased and relaxed as she lay against him. His hands in her hair seemed to calm her rhythms where they'd been ragged and irregular when she'd been on the phone with her parents.

Fionna smiled and finally allowed Dan to catch her eye. She must've been frightened that what her mother had informed her of on the phone would scare him off. Dan tried to think of some way to reassure her.

"Whatever day you decide to go, we could hang out and find somewhere nice to eat for dinner," Rainer suggested.

"Why is it that women think that once you go and get all buffed and waxed and painted, we want to take you out? What we want is to keep you inside all to ourselves," Dan flirted shamelessly.

Logan and Rainer laughed, but he didn't care. The utter delight that lit in Fionna's eyes and the broad grin that spread across her face were more than worth it.

"We're going to a spa, honey. Not in for a car detailing," she harassed him. Dan joined in her laughter. He kissed the top of her head and decided to revel in the fact that she was now using pet names for him and was comfortable enough to chastise him.

"Why don't you all go on tomorrow? We might need to do something with your dad on Friday," Logan said.

"Please stop calling him that. He doesn't even know I exist," Adeline scoffed.

With a sigh, Logan nodded. "Okay, well, whatever we find out at the palace, it might need to be dealt with later in the week, so why don't you go to the spa here tomorrow?"

"It'll be fun," Emily promised. "Here, why don't we go back in, and I'll call and make the appointments?"

"Okay," Adeline finally agreed. "I'll come help you." She stood and pulled her top back on. Emily promised to text Fionna with the appointment times.

CHAPTER 9
MY SOLEMN VOW

As soon as Emily left, Fionna's energy spun in nervous, jagged twists once again.

Dan wrapped his arms over her. "Are you okay?"

"Yeah." She stared out at the endless Pacific Ocean. The sun was giving off its last vestiges of light, and the number of beach dwellers dwindled as the tide continued its slow churns. Night crept over them and bathed them in its soothing darkness.

"Do you want to go in, sweetheart?" Dan tucked Fionna's head under his chin.

"Do you mind if we stay out a little longer?"

He noted that it sounded like a desperate plea. Her eyes never left the rhythmic waters. He wondered if she wanted to get back in the ocean. Was more water required to wash away what she was feeling?

"I don't mind at all, as long as I get to hold you right here." He ran his hands up and down her arms as he cradled her to him. A slight shiver worked through her body. "Are you cold, baby doll?"

"Just a little. I'm okay."

Dan grabbed one of the large beach towels she'd thrown in her bag. He wrapped it around her and then leaned back in the chair.

He pushed radiant heat out of his pores until she relaxed completely. She gave him a sweet smile, the one that made contentment flow through his veins and lit his world. It was the one he found himself hoping he could call his own at some point in the near future.

"I love the beach." She tucked herself into his protective embrace. "It's my favorite place in the entire world."

"I'd never seen the Pacific before now. I've really only been to the Outer Banks and to Virginia Beach. I went with Will and Garrett a few times when we were kids." He shut down the memories quickly. He didn't want to think about Amelia being at the Haydenshires' beach house so many years before.

"I hope my mom didn't freak you out," she finally confessed what was plaguing her soul.

"I'm fine. I wish your dad didn't already hate me."

"He'll be fine. He's kind of got that overprotective thing going on as well, only…he's kind of an ass about it usually."

Dan nodded his understanding. "I know what kind of reputation I have. Your dad has every right to hate me, but I promise you, as difficult and complicated as this might be, I want to do this right. I don't know where it may be heading, and I can't even promise that I won't freak out at some point, but I'd like to prove myself to you. I really want to be in a relationship with you, and that's not something I ever thought I would say again. I just have to figure out if that's possible. I have to keep you safe." Dan pricked the surface of the conversation he'd wanted to wait until the end of the week to have with her.

Fionna nodded, and Dan saw tears begin to trickle down her cheeks. They reflected the moonlight on the water.

"Baby." He panicked and turned her so she could bury her face in his neck. He began wiping away her tears as her breath stuttered. "Please don't cry." Her tears broke his newly resuscitated heart.

She lifted her head and stared him straight in the eye. Her jaw clenched in determination.

"Please don't break my heart, just please," she pled with those huge sienna eyes that seemed to reach down into his soul with every tender gaze. Dan felt like he'd been sucker punched. He clung to her. "I'm trusting you."

"I have no intention of doing anything of the sort. Please just give me a chance to show you."

She nodded and buried her head in him again as he surrounded her with his body. They sat there quietly taking in the serenity of the calm evening air and the relentless crash of the waves as they broke on the shoreline.

As she calmed and he kissed away the last of her tears, he decided to see if he could learn more about her.

"Can I ask you something?" She nodded, and he continued to push calming energy through his chest and into hers. "Why do your parents call you Maylea?" She grinned just from hearing the name. "It sounds Hawaiian."

"Yeah, it is." She sounded impressed he'd known that. With a slightly abashed sigh, she hemmed, "My dad's been calling me that since I was a toddler. In Hawaiian, it means wildflower. He thinks I'm wild." She rolled her eyes.

"When I was little, he said he would tell me not to do something and then I would immediately do it, and they would send me to my room and I'd go happily and play. So, then they tried putting me in a chair at the kitchen table, and I would sit and sing. So, then they sat me in the corner, and I pretended to draw pictures on the walls with my finger. My mom started calling me wildflower, because she used to say that I'll bloom wherever you plant me." She sounded thoroughly embarrassed about the reasoning behind her name.

Dan chuckled and brushed a kiss into her hair. "It sounds like you were just a sweet, happy little girl."

"Yeah, my grandmother says they finally gave up on punishing me until I was older." She wrinkled her nose. Dan laughed again. She was adorable.

"It's under the surfboard tattoo on your ankle, right?"

"You saw that?"

"Uh, yeah, honey, I saw it all, remember?"

She giggled, and his heart timed its beats to hers. The sweet sound of her laughter undid him.

"I remember, believe me. I'm hoping to be reminded again here in a little while," she flirted suggestively, and Dan growled in her ear. "I just didn't know you were paying attention to my ankles."

"I was paying attention to every inch of your beautiful body." His promise made her energy swirl rapidly.

As he let everything he'd felt from her the night before replay slowly in his mind, he longed to have her again. He ached to make her feel him and to satiate the desire pulsing in her energy. He wanted to fill her with his strength and his protection, wanted her to have all of him.

He kept both of their bodies covered in the towel and gave in to his longings. He slipped his hand up her side and spun his index finger over her nipple. It was already puckered from the breeze coming off the water.

"When you took your top off..." he whispered in her ear and kept his hand massaging her right breast. She panted against him. "You made me ache. I wanted to pull you under me, suck you until you screamed for me, and then fill up that sweet, wet hole. Make you take it hard and fast until I filled you full. I couldn't think about anything else but how good you feel when I'm deep inside you."

A low fervent moan echoed from her. He made certain no one was near enough to have heard her or to see either of them. He let his right hand slip off of her breast and glide down her stomach. He began massaging her left breast with his other hand as he dipped his fingers into the bottom of her bikini.

"Please don't stop," she begged as her body writhed against his, and she spread her legs farther. "I can't take it if you stop again. I need it," she pled for the relief she knew he would provide.

He throbbed hard and eager against her back as another moan spilled from her lips.

"You need it, baby doll?" he growled as she shuddered against him. "I've got everything you need, and I'm not going to stop until you just can't take it anymore."

Her entire body quaked and pitched over his.

He pushed his hand into her bathing suit and cupped her mound. He edged her lips apart with his fingers but didn't enter her as she began to beg in heated whimpers of desperation.

"I feel it, baby. I feel how wet and hot you are. Such a good girl for me. You want it, don't you? You need me to make it feel better."

She shuddered against him. "Please, please." Her words were desperate and aching. Her lips clenched against his fingers. He teased them until she began to beg in earnest.

"I want you to lie right here and let me touch you until you come in my hand. Then I'm going to take you back to the room and lay you out, and I'm going to make love to you, Fionna. This isn't just sex anymore, baby. You're mine."

She gasped for breath, and her body begged for more.

"Relax for me. Let me make it all better." He slipped two fingers deep inside of her and let the physical form of her energy wash over him in a heated tidal wave of ecstasy. "It feels good when I touch you right here, doesn't it?" He wanted to hear her tell him as he curved his fingers and moved over her most sensitive spots.

"It feels amazing. Please don't stop," she gasped in a heated pant. Her breath hitched as she tried to quiet her moans.

"When I get you back in the room, I want to see you clench and drip for me, and then I'm gonna lick you right here." He added to the intensity of his strokes inside her and slid his thumb through the liquid heat before he teased her clit tenderly.

His name fell heavily from her lips. The sound drove him wild as desire and need coursed heavily through his blood. "That's right. That's my good girl. Tell me who owns this sweet pussy." Her rhythms arced high from his possessiveness and his praise. She was perfection.

She trembled and swelled, and her energy began to spike in hard, jagged arcs. She was almost there. Being outside held her back, but he was going to give her what he'd promised her.

Deciding to test what he was fairly certain was one of her kinks, he growled, "I'm gonna suck those sweet lips and drink you. I want to taste that honey you make for me. So fucking perfect. Like candy made just for me." He had her.

Her body released her energy. It flooded around his hand and permeated his body. It traveled up his arm and filled his shield. He reveled in the ecstasy of her uncoiling and opening all around him.

She turned and clung to him. She hid her face in him as he

wrapped his arms around her. Dan kept her covered as she trembled. Her body tensed and writhed from the powerful orgasm he'd just given her.

"I've got you, sweetheart. I'm right here." He caressed her face and allowed her to hide from the world inside of his embrace. "I would never have let anyone else see that. That's only for me." He wouldn't let her down, not now, not ever.

Dan closed his eyes and tried to steady his breath. His entire body was hot-wired and thrumming for her. Insatiable desire pulsed in his shield. It craved her rhythms.

He'd always prided himself on his longevity, able to provide multiple releases for his partners. His double bands used to make him able to achieve two himself if his partner was up for it, but she was just too much, too perfect, and he hadn't done that in a decade.

As soon as he plunged her depths, he was set to detonate. He panted as he let her body relax after her release.

Get it together, Vindico. She deserves the best of you.

She stilled and clung tightly to him. She seemed fearful of what they'd just done and where they'd done it.

"I'm gonna take you inside, baby. Are you ready?"

She gave a heavy nod. Her eyes were dark. Her lips were swollen. Her body longed for more. She wasn't satisfied and neither was he.

With one quick move, he pulled the T-shirt he'd worn out to the beach over her head and threw the top of her bikini in her beach bag.

She stood to allow him to get up, but her legs trembled slightly. With a smirk, Dan leaned and scooped her into his arms with ease.

"I'm going to take care of you, baby doll. Give you everything I know that beautiful body needs, and I'm gonna hold you all night. I'm never going to let you go. I plan to make you unable to walk every night for as long as you'll let me."

He glided toward their suite. He kept her cradled to him as he slipped the keycard through the lock on the door. He dropped her bag on the floor as she leaned up.

"Don't you want to use the pool?" Her voice was still raspy from her pent-up need and her release.

Dan shook his head as he pulled back the down coverings and

smooth bamboo sheets on their bed. He laid her down tenderly. He cradled her between the pillows at the top of the bed and the gathered sheets and comforters that he'd pushed toward the end.

"This isn't about sex anymore, honey, I told you. And right now, I'm gonna lay you in this bed, and I'm going to make every inch of you belong to me."

CHAPTER 10
ANGELS AND DEMONS

"I'll be back in a little while. I won't stay so late tonight." He said the words, hoping to appease her, but not really meaning them. He was sick to death of fighting with her about it and everything else.

"Dan, come on. You haven't been home in forever. We never talk anymore. We just fight. Please just stay with me tonight, please." The pleading pain in her eyes irked him.

"Amelia, baby, come on. Not this again. I need to work. I almost have this guy."

"That's all you ever do...work. I'm tired of being here all alone. It's scary here so late at night."

"You'll be fine. I'll be back in a little while." He lied again.

"I'm asking you please don't leave me tonight. I really am scared." He pulled her close and kissed her forehead.

"I'll be back as soon as I finish the documents for this guy, Pendergrath. I think I found his safe house."

He opened the door, and she huffed audibly. Angry tears pricked her eyes. Her arms crossed over her chest.

"Why are we even getting married if you're never going to be here?" she spat.

"Just stop. I'll be back later. I love you."

"Right," she fumed.

Can't imagine why I don't want to be home when all she does is bitch. He rolled his eyes and slammed the door.

Dan awoke gasping for breath and covered in sweat as he jerked upright in bed. He held his head in his hands and let it fall between his knees.

The same damn dream. He tried to remember how to breathe as he dragged his hands over his face. He wiped away sweat and terror from his brow. Salt scraped over his skin as he tried desperately to remove the remnants of his nightmare from his face.

Someone moved. His head jerked to the side wildly. Why was there someone in his room?

Fionna… He gazed at her longingly. His own personal angel sent to pull him from the depths of hell. He didn't deserve the reprieve. People he loved got hurt. People he loved got killed.

Please don't break my heart. I'm trusting you. Her words branded themselves into his brain. They mocked his shield. He shook himself from his hellish abyss.

After swallowing back an onslaught of terror, he reached and touched her skin. He could feel it—the soothing, tender balm that came only from her. She soothed him even in her sleep.

She moved, and her eyes blinked open hesitantly.

"Dan?" She sat up beside him.

"Hey, baby. I'm sorry. I didn't mean to wake you up," he choked. "I, uh…I think I'm gonna go run on the beach. I'll be back in a little while."

She studied him without reply. With her intoxicating, languid motions, she took both of his hands in her own and casted him. She covered him in the safe, soothing energy that made him feel whole and alive. His breaths came easier. The harrowing fear abated instantly.

"I think you've been running from nightmares for a really long time, sweetheart. So, if you want to run, then I'm going with you. If you want to talk, then I'll listen. If you just want to lie here and let me make you feel better, I can do that too. But I don't think running away is really getting you anywhere."

With a slight nod, he refused to think anymore. All he wanted was to feel her. He lay down again and let her soothe him back to sleep.

Sunlight poured into the room a few hours later, and Dan awoke again. He sensed the absence.

"Fionna?" His eyes methodically searched the room. Where was she? *Please, don't let her have left me.* Panic shot through him like ice through his veins.

"I'm sorry." She rushed back in the room from the sitting area carrying a tray of food and mugs of steaming coffee.

"I was making coffee, and I ordered some breakfast. I was heating it up. I thought I'd finally gotten you back to sleep." She smiled at him adoringly as she glided toward the bed. She set the tray on the table beside him.

Dan forced a smile. He felt like a weak child.

"I'm fine," he lied. "I just wondered where you'd gone."

She didn't look like she believed him at all.

She'd pulled on the white dress shirt he'd flown to Sydney in, but she was wearing nothing else. As Dan's body began to steady, he regained the ability to take in the abject sex appeal that stood before him. His ego rejoiced. His shirt on her gorgeous curves was like a flag on a conquered fortress.

"Thank you," he managed as she handed him his coffee.

"I wasn't sure how you liked it, so I just brought the cream and sugar and everything with me." She looked like it was some kind of failing on her part that she didn't know how he liked his coffee.

"Honey, this is perfect. You really didn't have to do all of this. I'm fine."

She smiled at him and leaned to brush a tender kiss along his jaw.

"I know, but we're on vacation. I thought it might be nice to have coffee in bed. Maybe we could talk. I didn't do this because I thought something was wrong."

Dan decided to just go with it. Every time he spoke he said something wrong.

"I do normally run every morning." He shuddered as he recalled what had happened a few hours before when he'd awoken from the harrowing nightmare, the one that had haunted his dreams for ten long years.

With another one of those intoxicating smiles, Fionna nodded. "Yeah well, I mean, obviously I can tell you work out." She slid her hand along his bulging bicep.

His ego relaxed, and he chuckled.

"We run and work out hard at practice all the time, so I usually give myself Tuesday and Thursday off unless dancing and singing around my kitchen barefoot while I cook or extreme shopping count as working out." She blushed and let him know that she was giving up more of herself. She was letting him peel back another layer. He just had to keep his head in the game.

Dan brushed her hair behind her shoulders. He was delighted she felt like talking. "I'd really like to see that sometime."

"Trust me, you don't." She laughed and shook her head. It was the most beautiful sound in the world. Suddenly she slid her bottom lip through her teeth and seemed to draw on deep resolve.

"You know, if you want a great workout while we're here, we could go surfing."

"You surf?" He was extremely impressed as he watched her nod.

She crossed her legs in front of her and took a bite of a breakfast roll with bacon, egg, and avocado. Her eyes closed in delight.

He noticed the tattoo on her ankle and then gently cradled her face in his powerful right hand. He guided her eyes back to his. She smiled from the tender caress.

"What do your tattoos mean?" The one on her ankle was an intricate surfboard with scrolling waves surrounding it. There were pictures in the waves that Dan hadn't really studied yet.

Under the board itself was her childhood nickname. It clearly meant a great deal to her. She tensed uncomfortably, but she never dropped her gaze from his.

"Please tell me. I want to know. I don't even know your middle name, and I want to know everything about you. Please." He was unable to make himself stop begging.

"Okay." She nodded but seemed momentarily unable to go on.

Dan's mouth moved of its own accord. "Uh, my middle name is Arthur. You know, after my dad, and I don't ever really sleep all that well. The night I stayed at your house is the longest I've slept without waking up in…about ten years, I guess," he choked as the realization hit him hard. "I usually wake up really early, run at least five or six miles, then go to the office and hit the gym there. I lift every day even though I probably shouldn't. Sometimes I work out before I go home as well."

"So you'll be able to sleep." Fionna immediately figured out his secret and his shame. He nodded.

She remained quiet and held his hands in her own. He allowed the words he seemed unable to halt to continue to pour from his mouth.

"After Amelia died, I was really fucked up." He swallowed hard. He wasn't certain why he was telling her all of this, but his confession felt like she was pulling him up from a riptide. It felt as if he might be able to surface from the choking waters as she supplied oxygen to his drowning lungs.

"I got two DUIs that my dad and Governor Haydenshire covered up for me if I agreed to stop drinking, so I started using."

She nodded and began supplying him more of the energy he was quickly becoming addicted to. It was so much better than any of the drugs he'd consumed. It felt like he was inhaling life not death.

"I failed one of the Senate drug tests, and Crown Governor Lawson stepped in. He made the test disappear, and then he sent Rainer to stay at the Haydenshires for several weeks while he and my dad cleaned me up. He moved me into his house. I talked to him after he told me about Maggie dying and leaving him with a four-year-old. He knew what I was going through. Like I said, I was a walking disaster. He was the only person who got through to me. He really was a great man.

"He also promoted me over several guys who'd been in Iodex a lot longer than I had. He made me the youngest Chief in the history of Iodex, but he told my dad and Governor Haydenshire and the whole board, who thought he was nuts, that I could do it. He knew I needed the responsibility, that it would drive me, and it would be a way to end Wretchkinsides."

She blinked back tears as she continued to send her heavenly rhythms through his own. "I'm so sorry," she choked as tears poured down her face. Dan shook his head and wiped them away.

"I didn't mean to make you cry."

"No, it's okay. I just hate you went through all of that." She supplied her soothing life source to him in ample doses.

Whatever he'd said, she suddenly decided to answer his questions.

"I actually have two middle names." She took in his reactions with careful study. He nodded, eager to hear more. "I added the second when I was fifteen and could legally change my name, but my parents were fine with it."

Dan was now extremely curious.

"What are they?" he begged again.

She offered him another hint of the smile that soothed his soul.

"Originally I was Fionna Kalani Styler, but now I'm Fionna Kalani Halia Styler." Her energy turned nervous suddenly.

"What do they mean?" He began to suspect that there was a large portion of Fionna's life he'd completely missed.

"Kalani means from heaven or heavenly." She wrinkled her nose as her cheeks colored.

"Well then, I'd say that's perfect. I might start calling you Kalani." Dan only added to her embarrassment, but he'd meant every word. He wanted to know why she'd added the second name. "What does Halia mean?"

She drew a deep breath and let her eyes close for an extended blink. "Uh…Halia means in remembrance of those who have gone before us, and that even if they aren't here, they're still with us. They'll always be a part of us." Her chin trembled as she choked out the meaning.

Dan pulled her close. He reclined back on the pillows and held her tightly to his chest. Her tears beaded and flowed over his skin.

"What happened, baby? Who went before you that wasn't supposed to?" He was unable to believe what she was saying. She sat back up and scrubbed her hands over her face. Dan followed her, now extremely concerned.

"Can I tell you something that you can't tell Rainer or Logan?

Emily doesn't even know. Garrett knows about my mom but not all of this."

He grasped her hands and returned the energy he'd just drawn from her. He supplied her with strength where she'd supplied him with peace.

Supremely honored by her request, Dan nodded. "Of course. You can tell me anything. I would never tell anyone."

"Okay, just let me say all of this, please, even if I cry."

He nodded. If she just needed him to listen and not respond, that's precisely what he would do. She closed her eyes and drew from him deeply. He felt the energy leave him, but it didn't weaken him in any way.

"The woman you heard me on the phone with last night isn't my mom." Her voice snagged on her emotion. "I mean, she is my mom, but she's my stepmom," Fionna fumbled over her words. "My mom was Hawaiian, and she's who named me Maylea. It's called an *inoa welo*, a name someone gives you based on a personal trait. It's... important in Hawaiian culture. More important than your legal name."

Dan nodded but didn't want to interrupt. "My mom and dad used to own a bakery on Kauai. My grandparents have a huge farm there. That's where I grew up. My mom was a Scholera Predilect, and she taught kids to swim and surf. She was an amazing surfer. I grew up swimming and surfing and paddle boarding almost every day, while Dad ran the bakery." She looked like that particular part of her childhood meant a great deal to her.

"When I was thirteen, my mom and dad and I hiked up to Hanakapiai Beach on Sunday afternoon for a picnic, just like we always did," she choked again, but then swallowed down her terror and continued. "There are really strong tides there. You have to be a really strong swimmer to even get in the water. We'd just started eating when we heard screaming. This tiny little boy had walked away from his grandmother and had gotten swept up in the tide." The tears poured from her eyes now.

Unable to sit there and watch her cry, Dan cradled her to him. He kissed her forehead and held her tenderly. His heart fractured, and the scars she'd mended began to ache. She didn't have to go on. He understood.

"Anyway," she forced, "I'm sure you know what happened. My mom went in, but the tide was too strong. They both drowned." She shuddered and began sobbing.

"Baby, I'm so sorry." Dan could no longer keep from speaking. She seemed to understand.

"So, that's what the tattoo on my ankle is for, but there's more I need to tell you." Dan immediately went back to listening. "Anyway, I refused to go back to the beach. I refused to surf. I refused to do anything. My dad and I weren't that close, and I was so mad at him because my grandmother tried to tell him not to take us to the beach that day. I wouldn't leave Tutu's house—that's my grandmother.

"Anyway, he was so worried about me that he moved us to Texas, close to where he'd grown up. He's originally from Mexico. A couple of months later, he met Gretta. That's who I was talking to last night. Gretta used to sit for hours and talk with me about my mom. She kept her pictures out in our house. She taught me to make Hawaiian foods and took me to see my grandparents in Kauai.

"When I was old enough, she made my dad let me go back every summer to live on the farm. She encouraged me to keep surfing and taking hula. She talked my dad into letting me change my middle name. She taught me that just because someone isn't here with us anymore it doesn't mean that you don't still love them or that they aren't still very much a part of everything that you are." Her tears returned. After wiping them away, she sat up so she could look into his eyes.

"I guess that's what I'm trying to tell you." She kept her tear-filled gaze locked on his. "I know you still love Amelia, and I'm fine with that. I don't think I could ever be in a serious relationship with someone who stopped loving a person just because they aren't here anymore. She's a huge part of who you are, and she always will be. So, please know that I understand how much you still love her. I know you miss her. You should miss her. You're supposed to. I don't believe it has to be an either-or proposition. You don't have to give up your love for her because of me or anyone else."

Fionna bit her lip momentarily but then concluded her confession. "I think, if you'll just try, there's enough room in your heart to love Amelia and to love me if you wanted to." She made her offer without expectation that he would, but he already did. He knew instantly. She knew as well.

"You are so fucking amazing," Dan gushed as tears poured down his face. They fell onto the sheets below them and met hers as they cried together.

Fionna laid her head on his shoulder. The motion set firmly in his heart.

"I do, okay. I really do, and I swore I never would again. I'm scared as hell. I'm terrified, baby. I just don't think I can say it yet. Please know, even if I can't tell you, I do feel it. I have to figure out how to keep you safe."

She nodded against him. "It's fine. You don't ever have to tell me, as long as I can feel it too. You have a lot of stuff going on in there, but last night when we were together, I could feel it."

Dan gave in to the emotion he'd been waging war against since she'd begun her story, the weight of what he'd carried with him since he'd dropped the rose on that casket. He began to sob the tears he'd refused for a decade. He let her soothe him and cling to him.

When he finally regained the ability to do anything but cry, she kissed his cheek and smiled his smile.

"And my Angels tattoo means that I was twenty-one and just made the team, and my best friend became the captain, and we went out, got drunk, and got Angels tramp stamps, and I really regret that." She seemed to revel in his laughter as he nodded his understanding.

"What about my favorite?" He rubbed his eyes. They were clouded from his tears. Then, with a genuine smile, he slid his hand from her mound to her hipbone along the tattoo of flowers.

"Yeah, I figured you noticed that one right off." She laughed.

"There's a reason it's my favorite." He was impressed with how he was able to joke after such an emotional night.

She grinned broadly. "Those are violet hibiscus flowers and pink plumeria. We have them all over our farm in Kauai. Purple hibiscus means that life is very delicate and that we should appreciate each day we have because none of them are guaranteed, and plumeria means new beginnings." Her tears and her lengthy confession seemed to have left her tired.

Dan was overwhelmed as he gazed at her. He cradled her face tenderly in his hand and brushed her hair behind her shoulders.

"You are the most beautiful thing I have ever set eyes on, and no, that's not a line or something I've ever said to any other woman, ever. The most amazing thing is that you're even more beautiful inside than you are on the outside, and I know I'll never deserve you."

"That's not true."

He shook his head. He knew it was. "I will do my damnedest to be everything you need me to be. Just know that I'm still not really the way I'm supposed to be, but I'm trying."

"No one is the way we're supposed to be. Life is a journey, don't you think?"

"Maybe," he allowed hopefully. She gave him that smile once again, the one he decided then and there to claim, and then a mischievous look sparkled in her eye.

"Okay, enough tears. Let's do something fun, and then if you'll let me, I'm going to teach you to surf."

"I thought you were going to the spa." He didn't want her to miss out on fun with her friends because he'd come unglued.

"I am, but our appointments aren't 'til eleven. It's barely seven."

"I'm sorry I woke you up last night."

"Dan, stop. Remember that thing we both feel but we're not talking about yet? That means if you can't sleep, I can't sleep either."

He didn't want to argue with her, so he just leaned and kissed her cheek.

"Okay, Miss Fionna Kalani Halia Styler," he quoted just to hear her giggle again.

"It gets really long if you have to write it down." She continued her infectious laughter.

"Whatever you want to do, I'm game. You just show me the way."

Her entire body seemed to glow with her ethereal light, and he was mesmerized.

"I get to ask you five rapid-fire questions, and you have to answer without thinking about it. Just say whatever pops into your head first."

"And then I get a turn," Dan negotiated.

She agreed after a moment of consideration. "Ready?"

"Ready." He chuckled at her exuberance.

"Favorite thing to eat?"

"Steak rare and potatoes with cheese and those little green onion things on them."

"Scallions," she provided for him. He laughed and nodded his agreement.

"Okay," she considered. "If you had a day where you could do anything you wanted, what would you do?" she quizzed and then added, "If you say work, I will pinch you and not in a fun way."

Dan laughed. "Can I see the fun way first?"

She rolled her eyes and shook her head at him.

"Up until a few days ago, my answer would most definitely have been work, but now," he considered, "I'd spend it with you just trying to make you smile."

"That's so sweet."

He gazed at her adoringly.

Her smile turned naughty as she goaded, "Favorite sexual position?"

He smirked and fired back, "Doggy-style," instantaneously.

"Figured," Fionna sassed as he winked at her.

"Favorite lingerie?"

"For me or you?" he teased her just to keep her laughing.

"Me," she huffed.

"Hmm…"

"No thinking, just whatever pops into your head."

"Something dirty, black lace, crotchless, that doesn't cover much, with black stiletto heels." He watched to see just what she thought of that.

To his delight, a broad grin spread across her entire face. She was thrilled.

"Okay, favorite kind of Scotch, and will you teach me to drink it?"

"That's two questions, sweetheart," he harassed.

"You can punish me for breaking the rules later," she came right back.

"Is that a promise?" He thoroughly enjoyed watching the blush that was rising from her neck to color her cheeks. "Single malt Talisker 18, but it's kind of expensive, so you don't need to buy me any and yes."

Fionna looked very pleased with all of his answers.

"My turn." He wasn't letting her get away with not letting him play.

After a begrudging eye roll, she nodded. "All right, your turn."

"The first four are the same."

"I was afraid of that," she admitted. "Uh, my favorite thing to eat would probably be sushi or poke really. It's a Hawaiian thing. Poke nachos actually. A day to do anything I wanted…?"

"Uh, no thinking."

Her mouth twisted in consideration. "I would wake up in your arms, and you would bring me coffee in bed, and then spend the whole day with me shopping for shoes and lingerie, which are my two most favorite things to buy. See? You got extra information," she sassed as he listened intently. "Then we would go back to my house and cook a delicious dinner, and then you would do deliciously dirty things to me all night long."

"Done." His vow made her blush even more pronounced, but she very conveniently stopped talking. "Uh, Miss Styler, there were two more questions."

"I know." She giggled. "I don't know. I like them all. I can't choose just one."

Dan laughed outright at her excuse. "I'll take your top three then." He rubbed her thigh. He was unable to keep his hands off of her.

"Ugh." She looked thoroughly embarrassed. "I don't know all of their names," was her next excuse.

He raised an eyebrow and gave her a cocky grin. "You could show me or vividly describe them." He tried not to enjoy how cute she was when she was embarrassed.

"Fine, I like the one you said, only when I'm kind of lying on my stomach." Dan smirked. "And last night was really hot, and the first time at my house. I don't know. I just like being with you like that. It's kind of incredible," she finally admitted in a fretful huff.

While feeling like a king, Dan winked at her as elation filled his soul. "Well,"—he kissed her overly pink cheek—"we could try out a bunch of different ones and you just tell me what you like. Let's hear about this lingerie?"

"That's really personal." She laughed at her own joke. *I could sit and listen to her talk and laugh for the rest of my life.* The truth welled from his soul. He kept his game face on.

"Baby doll, I've seen it all, and believe me, your body drives me wild. You said lingerie was one of your favorite things to buy, so I assume you must enjoy wearing it. So, what's your preference if I should take it upon myself to buy you something just for the purpose of tearing it off of you?" He flirted as she wiggled beside him in delight. She considered for a moment.

"I really love the whole thigh-high stockings with the seams up the back, and a garter belt, with a thong and a really sexy matching corset or bra. Oh, and high heels, preferably Blahniks or Louboutins. And I also love waist-cinchers that are lacy and beautiful. But really I love it all. I love how sexy I feel when my bra and panties match. I try really hard to always match them."

She used her hands to describe the pieces. She was thrilled by the thought of wearing it.

"And no one has ever bought me lingerie before, so that would be amazing." She seemed unable to stop talking. "I guess I would have done really well in the forties when women wore stuff like that."

"Oh, I'd say you'd be pretty damn hot in them right now, and I would thoroughly enjoy seeing you in it all and then taking it all off of you, sweetheart." His cock strained and the real estate in his boxers became nonexistent.

Fionna looked delighted with his assessment, but then goaded, "Okay, you have one more question, and then we're going to surf. We're missing the best swells."

"You understand I've never even held a surfboard." Dan was mildly uncomfortable trying things he'd never done before in front of her. Deep desire to impress her tensed in his shield.

"I'll teach you. It'll be fun. I promise."

If it made her that happy, he'd attempt to walk the Pacific. After quickly deciding to let her off the hook, Dan pulled her to his body, then he wrapped her up in his arms.

"When's your birthday, Fionna?" he asked as his final question.

She smiled against him. "April 26th."

He memorized that information with a nod, then began wondering if she would mind delaying his surfing lesson for just a little while.

He needed to feel her again. He needed to permeate her completely. He needed to share himself with the woman who'd saved him.

CHAPTER II

ALL YOUR SECRETS I WILL KEEP

Dan used his chin to ease Fionna's face to the side. He slid his stubble along the thin skin as he granted himself access to her neck. He began to kiss and huff hot breath as he moved upwards toward her ear.

After brushing a tender kiss on her earlobe, he slid it gently between his teeth and began to suck. Her echoed, hungry moan made him grin.

"There's something I'd really like to do before my surfing lesson, baby doll." His tone was rough from his emotion and his desire.

He let his hands glide over her thighs. He grasped her hips as his need throbbed against her abdomen. With quick work, he loosened the few buttons of the shirt she'd clasped.

She began to pant and let her head fall back. She wanted more. He kissed along her collarbone as he let his hand slip from her waist to her backside. He spun his tongue in the hollow of her throat and grasped handfuls of her luscious ass. He kneaded her with desperate greed.

Her body trembled in his arms. She grasped his biceps in aching desire.

With sudden realization, Dan knew why he wanted to be with her again so suddenly. He needed her to feel it. He needed her to feel the

99

love he couldn't yet express any other way. He knew it was there, and it was all for her.

"I want you to feel it again, baby doll. I want you to feel how much I..." he halted. He was simply unable to say the words, but his mind and his body were drowning in the emotion.

She lifted her head and gazed at him with a fiery storm in the depths of her eyes. Her body rolled in hunger as she nodded heavily.

"I want to feel it. It feels amazing. When your body is pressed against mine, when I can really feel how you feel, when you're deep inside of me, it's incredible," she urged him onward.

A low, thundering groan echoed from deep within Dan's chest as she pulled away from him and stood beside the bed. She had a naughty half grin on her face, and her hair was tangled on her shoulders. Her lips were swollen ripe and flushed. They needed to be kissed. They tempted and begged him as he took her in. The fire in her eyes lit explosively. Her body was obscured slightly in his shirt. Her nipples were already strained and throbbing.

Dan knew if he spread her legs and saw what she was hiding, her pussy would be swollen, the color of a pale rose against her beautiful deep olive complexion, and dripping wet for him.

She looked every part the sweet girl who wanted to play sex kitten for just a little while, and the effect nearly drove him over the edge.

"Come back here to me, baby doll. I wasn't near finished." His commanding thrum made her rhythms arc in excitement. And he continued to revel in his education.

"I was just thinking I might go put on some heels."

He stood beside her, wrapped his arms around her, and crushed her lips to his. He devoured her mouth. She wasn't going anywhere except to his bed and then into the depths of ecstasy at his hands if he had any say at all.

He slid his hand under the shirt once again. He grasped her backside and massaged as he dipped his tongue into her mouth and sucked her bottom lip hungrily.

"You don't need heels, honey. I've got several plans for you, and heels are going to get in my way."

"Oh yes," she panted. Her energy spiked hard, just like it did when he brought her to climax, but she fought it willfully. Her body shuddered with the effort as she pushed it away.

Thus far, she'd clearly been playing with boys who were weak and indecisive. Boys who, Dan was certain, probably talked a big game to get her into bed and then left her unfulfilled.

Idiots who couldn't see that getting a woman like Fionna Styler to take her clothes off was only a very small portion of the game.

The way she moved, the way her body responded, everything about her was sensual. Desire swam in the very aura of her. *No wonder she likes toys*, Dan thought wryly.

He laced his fingers in her hair and grasped it at the nape of her neck. He tugged and watched as her head fell back while a heated moan spilled from her lungs.

He worked his lips down her neck. He sucked the thin skin, swirled his tongue over her, and inhaled her heady scent.

He knew exactly what she wanted though she'd never ask. He knew how to develop her fully and allow her to own the sexuality that brimmed so copiously just under the surface. It was just out of reach if you didn't know how to access it.

She needed a man who knew what he wanted and how to make her every fantasy and desire a reality. Not an insipid fool who asked her what she wanted, how she wanted it, and if his anemic member was too much for her, in an effort to stroke his own ego as he lost it all before she'd even begun.

Visions of nameless, faceless boys, who asked if she'd like to change position, almost made Dan laugh out loud. All of the virgin school boys who couldn't even speak loud enough to say the words she required, who had no clue what they held in their inexperienced hands, who couldn't read a woman like Fionna if she'd inked what she required across her luscious curves, could turn and walk away.

She deserved more. She deserved better, and that's precisely what he was going to give her.

She was a woman, and Fionna Styler had sensuality, tenderness, desire, and femininity coursing through her veins and spilling from her pores. She needed someone who knew how to touch her and where to kiss and lick her, where to suck, and bite, and pull, and strike, if she was in the mood, to allow her the passion she craved but was terrified to ask for.

He continued to kiss and suck her neck as he took her hand. He slipped it in his boxers and wrapped it around his length as desperate moans quaked from her body.

"Feel what you do to me. Feel me throb in your hands. That's all you."

She spiked again. She grew frantic as he continued to lave her neck. She squeezed his length and caressed him. She ran her hands up and down his shaft and head. It drove him wild.

She'd bared her soul to him. She'd shared her spirit and her energy. She was letting him in deeper with each conversation, and that was so much more than taking her clothes off.

His body ached. His cells reverberated with the need to feel her, to permeate her, to suck and mark her, to make her all his own.

"Do it," she begged in a heated whisper. He grasped her breasts and dragged his teeth over the delicate skin where her neck and shoulder joined. "Just do it. I need it, please," she begged as her firm grip, the tenacious shield she kept on her own erotic desires, began to slip away.

Dan's heart pounded. He could feel her desperation and her tentative shame.

"You want to be marked, baby doll? You want people to know you've been with me?" He knew precisely what she longed for. "Good. I want everyone to know who you belong to."

A moan in the tenor of a scream echoed loudly from her and answered his question.

Fully confident of the fact that he could heal her when he was finished if she wasn't quite ready to show off what she'd begged for, Dan slid the shirt back and sucked the very top of her breast until he'd marked her.

"That's my good girl. You're all mine," he growled and then moved back to her neck as he sank his teeth in and sucked hungrily. He marked his territory thoroughly.

He let his fingers trace along the center of her backside and then to the pulsing wet center of her. She went wild. She grasped and clawed his massive arms, unable to remain still. "That's it, baby. Claw me. Fuck me up," he urged.

"Oh my god," she whimpered.

He left her aching in desperation as he pulled his shirt off of her. He reveled in all of her luscious curves. He picked her up, laid her back in their bed, and crawled over her.

While bathing her body with his tongue, he sucked her nipples that were swollen and drawn so tight she was desperate for relief.

He moved down her body. She arched her back. Her hands grasped the sheets below her. She needed to hold on to something as he leaned her over slightly and kissed from her right breast down her side.

He halted at the indentation where her side began to swell into the gorgeous curve of her ass, just above her hipbone, and he sucked again. He'd never heard her moan so loudly as she begged for more.

After he'd left his bite there, he rolled her to her side and dragged his teeth over the top of her backside. She writhed and unending moans quaked from her.

He sucked her here as well until she was wearing his mark. Then he eased her to her back and moved to her swollen, fevered lips and spread her legs. He continued to lick and suck. He used his tongue to give her the force and friction she begged for. Then he gently tugged her right lip with his teeth, and then soothed the exquisite pain he'd left.

He growled as she clenched and spilled herself into his mouth. He drank the liquid form of her energy. He sucked every last drop like a parched man offered life's water on his deathbed.

She writhed and bucked. She couldn't contain the ecstasy. Her legs spread farther as her hips gave needy, desperate thrusts. She was ready. She needed to be tamed.

Dan let one hand trace from her breasts to her lips as he stacked several of the pillows beside her. When he finished, he grabbed her hand and sat her up.

The wild, impetuous look in her eyes had him aching to bury himself inside her and make her take him until she was screaming his name and begging him for another release.

"Lean over, baby doll. Shake that sexy ass for me before I fill you full."

Her body pitched. Her eyes flashed. She gasped for breath, unable to believe he knew precisely what she longed to hear.

"Now," he demanded, and she nearly came again from his orders. "Be a good girl, and do what I say."

"Yes," spilled from her mouth as she positioned herself over the pillows and followed his orders. He growled fervently as he grasped her hips.

The reason she liked his favorite position, only lying down, was fairly rudimentary for those who knew what they were doing. It allowed her to feel everything he had in all the right places, but he was about to teach her a thing or two about what she thought she liked before she'd been in bed with him.

She threw her head to the side and shot him a look that dared him to take her hard as she shook it for him. Her back dipped low, and she propped up on her elbows. It was one of the most erotic things he'd ever seen. His blood seared with need.

"Take it, honey. Take it like my good girl," he commanded as he grasped her hips and jerked her back over him. He pierced her as she screamed her approval. She lost all sense of what he was certain she would consider appropriate behavior, and it drove him wild.

He'd tried to prepare himself for the feeling, but it overwhelmed him every time he had the extraordinary pleasure. Their energy combining, her energy filling and restoring him, wasn't something he'd ever become accustomed to. He could never prepare for something so extraordinary.

He kept his thrusts deep and unrelenting. He watched himself as he pounded her depths.

"That's it, baby. That's what you needed. It feels better now, doesn't it?"

She cried out his name and pushed herself back against him, nearly ending him, but he refused the release that throbbed in his groin. She clawed the sheets under her.

"Harder," she begged.

He grasped her backside fiercely and lost any sense of restraint. "Take it," he growled and hammered into her hard and fast.

A split second later she tensed and shuddered as the orgasm crashed through her. He eased his thrusts and let her waves wash over him until she was ready for more.

"I know you need more, baby doll, my greedy, greedy girl. Tell me."

"More, please, please" she begged when she could catch her breath.

"Such a good girl. Begs for my cock." He thrust hard again and buried himself inside of the liquid perfection of her. He leaned and traced one finger from the very top of her spine, all the way down the center of her back, over the throbbing nerve endings centered in her backside, until he reached the place he was forming around his length.

She went wild. He knew she would, and she came again. He allowed her climax to fully develop before he started again.

He wasn't going to last much longer. She was too much, too perfect, too tight, wet, and fevered. He wanted to explode inside the heart of her.

Her muscles clenched tightly around him, only furthering his imminent release. He forced it away by sheer strength of will. He wasn't leaving her before he was thoroughly spent and he was forced to return from their otherworldly ecstasy.

His vision split. He dragged his hand from her backside to her breasts. He grasped them firmly and pulled himself deeper as he kneaded the fevered mounds. He pounded into her. She was made for him alone. He continued his hungry claims.

Just as he lost the ability to fight his own release, he caressed her nipples between his thumbs and forefingers.

As her entire body tensed, he gave a twisting squeeze. She threw her head back and convulsed. Her body rose up to his head, and she lost it all as he exploded inside of her. He forced his energy and his release in deep.

When he'd regained the ability to breathe, Dan withdrew and fell to the bed. He immediately took her and held her in the safety of his embrace. He knew what was likely to follow all of that.

As she began to recall everything she'd begged for, he would adamantly refuse to allow shame to cast a shadow on her finally owning what she wanted.

"You are absolutely amazing. That was the most incredible thing I've ever felt, and no, I've never said that to anyone else either," he informed her in complete honesty.

Her last climax was still quaking through her, but she was trying to will it away.

"Uh, wow." She clung to him and buried her face in his chest.

Dan cupped his hand and pulled light from the only lamp lit in the room. He tried to give her a little time and space to assure her that he'd thoroughly enjoyed everything she'd begged for.

He turned to his side and kept her pressed to him. He shielded her from the rest of the world with his body. After pulling the sheets back over them, he covered her up and held her close.

"Are you okay, baby?" He tenderly ran his hands over her body and brushed her hair behind her. He tried to discreetly heal the marks he'd left in case she didn't want to think about them or have to ask.

"That was incredible," she admitted as she let him hold her and protect her deepest desires from the inflicting world.

"That's what happens when we're together. You are just absolute perfection. I don't know how I got so lucky," Dan assured her as he worked.

In a few hours, she was going to a spa with Emily and Adeline. Dan was certain that they, at nine and ten years her junior, didn't know enough about themselves or their own sexuality to even begin to understand her needs and hidden desires.

"You just keep blowing my mind." She finally allowed herself to really speak and open her eyes as he chuckled. He continued working on the deep purple mark he'd left on her backside.

"Uh, could you?" Her face glowed crimson as she turned to her side to see the already healed marks he'd left there. She furrowed her brow. Her release had hidden his casting and healing her. She hadn't felt it. He was already a part of her energy.

"I'll always take care of you, baby. Anything you want, I'll do, and I would never allow anyone else to have any part of that." He held her eyes with his own and never dropped her terrified gaze.

Tears sprung to her eyes as he finished his work on her backside and then slid his hand up to embrace her fully.

"Okay, where have you been all my life?" She tried hard not to cry.

With a soft chuckle, he kissed her forehead and kept her in the serenity of his embrace.

"Being an idiot, but I'm here now. I'm not going anywhere."

With that, he surrounded her body with his. His shield set over her, soothing her, and making certain she felt safe and secure.

His entire body made a vow to her that he would protect her vulnerability with his very life.

CHAPTER 12

TALES OVER BURGERS AND BEER

RAINER LAWSON

Emily picked up her cell phone as she pulled a bite of the toast they'd ordered off of her plate. She grinned broadly as she read the text.

"Who's that from?" Rainer smiled at her delighted grin.

"It's Fionna. It says she's taking Dan surfing, that they'll meet us at the spa at eleven, and then it says 'wow just wow.'" A fit of giggles overtook her.

Rainer laughed. "I take it they had a nice night then."

As she finally regained her calm, Emily beamed. "Do you think this could really work? Do you think he'll really fall in love with her? Maybe they'll get married!"

Rainer decided to hope against hope that what Emily was saying might actually happen. He wanted that for Dan as much as she wanted it for Fionna.

"I wouldn't use the word married, or wedding, or marriage within earshot of him right now, but he's falling for her, trust me."

"Where are you taking us tonight after we're all glamorous?" Emily kissed his cheek and wrapped her arms around his chest from behind him. Her hands caressed his pecs.

Rainer spun and wrapped his arms around her. He settled them on the top of her backside.

"Wherever you want to go as long as you meet me back in this bed after dinner."

She giggled and then kissed his jawline. "I'll think about it."

"Logan and I will find something. A nice restaurant or a club or something."

She shook her head. "Not a club. Somewhere quiet and romantic."

"Okay, do you want to go with the four of them or do you want me to find somewhere just for us?" He wanted to get everything right. He had a lot to make up for. He still felt bad about their fight and the way he'd acted about the topless beach. After he'd gotten over himself, he'd thoroughly enjoyed the display. And she'd been right. No one really seemed to care.

"I think we're supposed to all go out together, but Fionna needs to see if Dan has a romantic side. They still don't really know each other very well."

Rainer nodded. "Quiet and romantic. I got it."

A little while later, he walked Emily to the spa door. He wasn't comfortable with her walking alone down the corridors of the Kingsford Wellborn in nothing but the robe the spa had sent to the room when they'd made the reservations. She carried a duffle bag with her selected outfit for their night on the town.

Dan was dropping Fionna off and giving her a rather heated goodbye kiss when Rainer and Emily approached.

Emily cleared her throat, and after several seconds more, Dan finally pulled back though Fionna looked mutinous.

Logan and Adeline appeared off the elevator, and after making sure the ladies were situated, Logan spun to Dan and Rainer.

"I really want a burger and a beer," he begged.

They meandered out of the hotel and into the streets of Sydney.

"So, Adeline said the words candlelit like three hundred and ninety-seven times when I asked what kind of place she wanted to go tonight," Logan joked.

Dan and Rainer agreed to look for a place appropriate for taking the ladies when they emerged from the spa. Vindico pointed to a burger joint that advertised a vast beer selection. They took a booth in the back corner.

"How was surfing?" Rainer quizzed as he took the menu from the waiter.

"Fionna had fun. She's amazing. Even the guys we rented the boards from were impressed."

"Where'd she learn to surf?" It wasn't a common skill for your average Virginian.

Vindico shrugged. "No idea."

Rainer wondered momentarily if he was lying, but it didn't appear so.

"How goes the sex fest?" Rainer harrassed Logan.

Vindico chuckled as he flipped through the menu.

"It's great when she's not freaking out about meeting her father or about going to a spa." Logan turned his attention to the waiter as he approached.

They all ordered burgers and beer and settled into the Australian pub.

"I thought you drank Scotch," Logan quizzed Dan suddenly.

He gave him a mocking grin. "Not in the middle of the day at a burger joint as that would make me an alcoholic with extremely poor taste."

Rainer and Logan laughed. Rainer couldn't recall a time he'd seen his boss joke with such ease or seem so relaxed.

"Do you have a plan for tomorrow night, Haydenshire, or are we just going to show up and hope for the best?"

"I'm really worried actually. Ad is coming unglued, and you saw how she was at the hotel. Now we're going to this guy's castle. I'm certain her mother's apartment would fit in their servants' broom closet. I'm terrified she's going to see the palace and make a run for it."

"What are you going to do if he recognizes her?" Rainer finally asked the question he'd been dying to know since they'd first begun planning the trip. "She doesn't look anything like Candy. She must look like him."

Dan nodded. "I couldn't find any photos of the Premier's sons when they were in their twenties, but there are two of them she favors."

Logan considered. "If he doesn't freak, I think that would be perfect. We can get the whole pretense over with right away."

Dan and Rainer considered that as the waiter returned with their plates and beers.

"Why was she nervous about the spa?" Rainer picked up his burger but then returned it to his plate. It was too hot to bite into.

"Man, do you remember the couple of weeks during our sophomore year when I had to go pick her up in the mornings and bring her over so she could shower because Candy failed to pay their water bill?" Logan reminded Rainer rather indignantly.

Dan shook his head. He looked disturbed by the story. "We should have stepped in earlier."

"Dad finally paid the bill. He waited a week, hoping that Adeline would finally give in and come live with us, but she wouldn't. Adeline didn't grow up getting her nails done all the time like Em did."

Rainer nodded and then followed Vindico's lead. He summoned and cooled his burger before diving in.

"What else do girls do at spas anyway? It can't take six hours to get your nails done."

Dan chuckled and took the last sip of his beer. He raised the empty glass to the waiter. "They didn't tell you what they're having done today?" They both shook their heads. "You'll enjoy this, trust me."

After finishing his own beer, Rainer nodded to the waiter as well.

Logan knitted his brow. "What do you mean I'll enjoy it? Isn't *she* supposed to enjoy it?"

After considering for a moment, Dan smiled. "They will. Well, they'll enjoy some of it, but trust me, they're there for us."

Logan looked incredulous. "She's not there for me. I mean, I don't care if she wants to go as long as she's not naked and letting some guy rub oil all over her." In true Logan Haydenshire format, he made everyone laugh. "I always think she's beautiful. She's my wife. I thought she was beautiful the week she went without a shower, when she was too embarrassed to tell me that they didn't have any water."

With a wry grin, Vindico raised his glass to Logan this time. "That, my friend, is true love. But just trust me, she'll be stunning when she leaves there tonight, and she'll want you to tell her and to show her."

Rainer picked up on something else he'd said, but he waited to ask since the waiter had returned to see if they needed anything else. "What do you mean they'll enjoy some of it?" He studied Dan closely.

"I grew up with three younger sisters, not to mention dating a long litany of women after Amelia died. They put themselves through a tremendous amount of pain because the world is designed to make them think they have to. It's ridiculous, but they're there because they want us to admire what they have done."

This brought Logan and Rainer up short.

"What kind of pain?" Rainer demanded.

Logan shook his head. "I don't want her to be in pain."

"Why do they go if it hurts?" Rainer still didn't fully believe what their boss was telling them.

After taking a quick bite of his burger, Dan supplied, "They go through a lot of shit trying to be what the world tells them they should be, which changes constantly by the way. What the spa is selling is a few minutes of confidence for them. And that, gentlemen, is sexy as hell. She wants you to show her just exactly how gorgeous you think she is."

"But I already think that and do that," Logan stammered uncomfortably.

"Ah,"—Vindico drew another sip of beer—"but this will be a whole new Summation challenge, because after all they have done, and taking a day to allow themselves to really relax, they'll actually believe it."

Rainer considered as he continued to eat. He couldn't come up with anything anyone could do to Emily to make her more beautiful.

I thought she was the most beautiful thing I'd ever laid eyes on when she was in a hospital bed bandaged head to toe. He shuddered from the memory.

There was certainly no reason for her to be in any pain on his account. He wondered what Emily might be doing just then. He was eager to pick her up for their dinner.

"Okay, enough about spas. I want to know what you said to the Russian board. You promised," Logan urged Dan.

Shame broadcast from his chiseled face. Rainer wondered if that meant he'd learned the lesson Governor Haydenshire had been trying to teach him. "You don't really want to know."

"I overheard some of the retelling. I just want you to fill in the rest."

"Which part did you hear?"

"What you told the Crown he could do on his way to hell."

He cringed. "Your dad should have fired me."

"But he didn't, and you won't do anything like that again, blah, blah, blah. What did you say?"

"He's like a dog with a bone," Rainer explained "You might as well tell him. He won't let it go."

"Does this good cop, bad cop routine work on the governor?" It seemed Dan wasn't going to be played.

"It worked better when we were kids," Rainer admitted.

"And it works better on Mom," Logan explained as the whole table laughed.

With a defeated sigh, he seemed to consider this part of his punishment. He gave a begrudging nod and wiped his mouth on his napkin.

"This story will not be brought up or retold to Fionna under any circumstances," he threatened.

Logan looked offended. "Yeah, because we're pricks like that."

He seemed to agree that Rainer and Logan were pretty good guys as he tossed his napkin onto his empty plate.

"I might've said something about them buying fur coats for their... mistresses," Vindico edited, but Rainer knew instantly.

"You didn't call them mistresses."

"Damn, I taught you to read people too well."

Rainer laughed but kept his eyes trained on Vindico. He hadn't answered the accusation.

"I called Pendergrath several less-than-complimentary names, and you heard the pathetic group of useless cowards part. I told them to enjoy their payoff." He looked furious as he recalled the event.

Logan and Rainer shared a quick glance.

"What'd you call their mistresses?" Logan edged. "We'll never say anything."

"Cum bunnies," he admitted in a regret-filled whisper.

Rainer choked on the beer he'd just swallowed.

"Damn," Logan gasped. His mouth fell open as Dan shut his eyes and nodded his head.

"Okay, how'd you get to Paris?" Logan asked when he regained the ability to talk.

"That's a much better story." He seemed relieved he'd concluded the other line of questioning. After he retold the harrowing story of escaping to a convent, climbing border gates, and two harrowing hitchhiking stints, they paid their bill and left the burger joint.

CHAPTER 13

BUFFED, WAXED, AND BEAUTIFUL

At ten 'til six, Rainer paced outside the spa. He checked his watch and sighed. He missed Emily. He'd liked being with her constantly the past two days, and he was still worried about Dan's declaration that something she was having done in there was going to be painful.

Logan exited the elevator after having showered and changed into slacks and a button-down shirt. He moved quickly toward Rainer. "They're not out yet?" He peered through the fogged glass doors, though no one could see in the spa.

Rainer shook his head. "It's not quite six."

Vindico stalked down the corridor. He pulled his shirtsleeves out of his jacket. Rainer wondered if he should have worn a jacket. He felt underdressed.

"You eager to see her or something, Lawson?" Dan quipped.

"Always." Rainer assumed his anxiety must be evident on his features.

"Yeah, well, you're in for a treat." He gestured his head toward the door, and Rainer saw Emily coming through it. She looked absolutely stunning.

"Wow!" He smiled as she walked excitedly toward him.

"Fionna and Adeline are finishing getting dressed," she informed

Dan and Logan, who also told her how lovely she looked which made her glow.

Rainer quickly pulled her away from her brother and his boss. He moved them farther down the corridor.

"You look amazing." Her skin was glowing radiantly. Her hair was fixed in tousled waves down her back and over her shoulders. Her lips were full and ripe, and Rainer fought the urge to devour them right there. There were other things that were a little different, but Rainer couldn't quite figure out what they were. Dan had been right. She looked more confident.

"I knew you'd be waiting on me, so I hurried. I missed you." She bit her lip. He stifled a groan as thoughts of him biting her lip swept through his mind.

"What all did you have done?" He tried to distract himself from his lust-filled thoughts. She giggled, but then stopped abruptly as Adeline and Fionna made their way out.

Dan and Logan's eyes goggled appropriately.

"Wow, you look great," Logan gaped.

Vindico gave Fionna a much cooler smile and a, "Stunning, absolutely stunning."

Dan Vindico

Dan wasn't playing anymore. He had her. He just had to keep her safe. She no longer sought Emily with regularity. She moved right into his arms, right where she belonged.

Their travel companions needed to go. He wanted to spoil her rotten. He needed to show her what they could be as soon as he ended Wretchkinsides.

He needed to lavish her with attention and make her understand if she would stick with him while he ended the Interfeci, as soon as his work was complete, he'd tell the world she was his.

"I missed you," he half whispered and half growled in her ear. The sexy grin that was on her beautiful face had his groin on high alert.

"I missed you too."

"Did you enjoy your day?"

"Not as much as I plan to enjoy my night, but I had a few things done I'm hoping you'll really like."

"Baby, I'm loving everything I'm seeing right here. You look phenomenal. The most beautiful thing I've ever laid eyes on."

Her energy trilled in delight as she beamed at him. "Does that mean I should just leave this dress on all night?"

"Uh, hell no. Don't worry. I'll get you out of it."

The luscious fire he loved began to churn in her eyes. She moved closer. She wanted him. With a timid hunger that swam in her rhythms, she laid her head on his massive shoulder, and he wrapped her up in his arms.

"We don't have to go out tonight, baby doll. Let me take you back to our room. I'll order you anything you want and spend the night consuming you." She grinned against him.

"We have to go with them. Emily and Adeline talked about it all day. They're really excited."

Dan knew he wouldn't be able to talk her out of going if she thought she might hurt Emily's feelings, but he was intrigued that she wanted to stay in with him. He sighed and decided to go along. Arguing with her was not an option.

"Whatever you want," he soothed. She brushed her lips along his jawline as she raised her head.

"We can spend a long time together when we get back." She lost a little of the hunger and slipped back into the version of herself she let others see. "I did have fun." She cracked up suddenly. Dan was thrilled to hear her laughter.

"I have to tell you this. Emily casted me while I was getting waxed. I think the spa employees think we're insane because we were holding hands while they were ripping wax off of our va-jay-jays." She giggled hysterically as Dan shook his head. She was adorable.

"I look forward to seeing that, Miss Styler." He knew she waxed. He'd known from the moment he'd unzipped that leather skirt in her bedroom, but the soft, sweet, lush feeling of the day of the appointment wasn't something he'd gotten to enjoy with her yet. His trousers strained as he pictured her waxed bare and on full display for him. She blushed slightly as she grinned at him.

"But don't say anything. Emily's going to surprise Rainer tonight. She's never had it done before."

Dan cracked up as he took her arm, and they followed several yards behind Rainer and Emily out of the hotel.

"First of all, that's not something that I would generally bring up at dinner, and second, Lawson may have a heart attack. She should at least warn him."

To his delight, Fionna was still laughing. Dan's heart picked up pace.

"Yeah, well, Adeline did the same thing, so…." She choked back hysterical laughter as they both tried to envision Logan's reaction.

Dan could feel the warm, healing balm permeate his body as he stared at her smile.

He certainly couldn't wine and dine her at all once they were home, so he decided to make the entire evening magical for her. The opulent restaurant, a few drinks, dinner, dancing if she wanted, and then he would take her to bed and give her every single thing her body craved.

CHAPTER 14

A NIGHT OUT

RAINER LAWSON

As they entered the swanky restaurant, all of the ladies grinned. "Wow!" Emily gasped as she took in the rich colors of the darkened restaurant, with baroque architecture, soft leather couches, and inlaid booths. The tables were candlelit and the sconces on the wall offered just enough light to read the menus and see what you were consuming, but not much else.

Each table offered a different seating arrangement, and Dan had reserved the one that situated each couple at specially designed love seats for two along each side of the table.

A vast bar, with more alcohol than Rainer had ever seen in one location, sat in the center of the restaurant, although no one appeared to be indulging more than they should. The drinks were made to go with dinner. They were high-end brands with high-end price tags.

"This is so nice." Adeline's tone held a mix of admiration and concern.

Fionna nodded her agreement as the maître' d escorted them to the table tucked away in a back corner and concealed with antique Victorian screens.

Rainer seated Emily and then situated himself in the high-backed love seat beside her.

"This is so romantic." Emily seemed impressed. She tucked herself closer beside him.

"I'm glad you like it, baby. You look amazing." Rainer squeezed her exposed thigh in the short, black skirt she was wearing.

Their waiter made his appearance as soon as they were seated. He introduced himself and asked for their drink and appetizer orders.

"Oh, are you going to get Scotch?" Fionna quizzed Dan. Her entire face lit.

With a slight chuckle, he nodded. "I thought I might."

"You promised you'd teach me to drink it."

"Tonight?" He didn't seem to think that was a good idea.

Fionna nodded hopefully.

Rainer and Logan had each tried Scotch once when they'd snuck some out of the Haydenshires' liquor cabinet.

"It burns all the way down." Logan tried to help Dan who looked appreciative of his warning.

"Please." Fionna gave him a look Rainer knew he wouldn't be able to deny.

With a sigh, he nodded. "All right, let's get her a Glenmorangie Nectar D'or, and let's add a little more than a splash of water," he ordered the waiter, who chuckled and nodded his understanding. "I'll take a single malt Talisker, the oldest you have. Don't screw with mine. And waters for both of us."

Rainer ordered Emily's wine selection and the recommended Australian beer. Logan followed suit, and the waiter switched the vast bar menus with dinner menus and left to prepare their drinks.

As Rainer pulled the large menu toward them, they began to discuss what they might like to eat. While using the menu as a screen of his own, he laved her with a kiss and told her how beautiful she was. Emily's eyes darkened slightly as she moved back in for another kiss.

After they selected what they wanted to eat, Rainer kept the menu in place. He saw no reason to remove it. The waiter hadn't yet returned with their wine.

"Did you have fun today?"

"Yes, it was amazing. I've never had so many women touching me while I was naked, or such weird things put on me, but my skin feels so good."

She held her forearm up, and he slid his hand down it. She did indeed feel like silk.

"What weird stuff did they put on you?"

She giggled. "Hot oils and coconut husks and sea salt…oh, and sea shells, and hot rocks."

He bristled. "Hot rocks?"

"Yeah, it felt amazing. It's supposed to help you relax, and I fell asleep while they were doing it." Clearly it hadn't hurt her if she'd fallen asleep, so with a slight shrug, Rainer set their menu down. He ordered both of their meals when the waiter returned.

The ladies elaborated more on their day at the spa as their drinks arrived. They all shared quick, giggling grins occasionally. This made Logan and Rainer extremely curious, but Dan just kept up a steady smirk.

Everyone quieted and watched Fionna take her first sip of Scotch.

"If you don't like it, you don't have to drink it. I'll get you whatever you want," Dan assured her. Fionna seemed excited to try it. "Sip slowly, hold it in your mouth, breathe over it, and then swallow," he instructed.

Fionna brought the glass to her lips, and Dan tensed. His shield gave a slight vibration. She took a slow sip and shuddered forcibly. Her face twisted in a confused pucker. Dan took the glass from her hands.

"It takes a little getting used to." He handed her the water he'd ordered. Fionna began to cough, and he stifled a chuckle.

"Wow." She drew another long sip of water.

"Told you," Logan teased.

Fionna joined in the laughter at her own expense. "I'm going to not try that again for a while," she admitted abashedly. Dan leaned and kissed the side of her head. Rainer had never seen him so attentive with anyone.

"When I said I'd teach you, I was thinking at home just the two of us." He'd clearly been trying to save her any embarrassment. Fionna looked quite touched by the planned gesture.

Their meals arrived, and everyone agreed the food was delicious. Dan ordered Fionna a glass of Pinot, after asking her about her favorite wines.

After a few more drinks, everyone began to mellow and sink into the person they were seated with. As the table was relatively small, and they were all talking to their respective dates, Rainer and Emily only chuckled when they heard Dan compliment Fionna's dress and her reply of, "Wait 'til you see what I plan on wearing to bed, Chief Vindico."

"So, what are you planning on wearing to bed tonight, Miss Haydenshire?" Rainer let his whispered question caress over her neck.

"Nothing," she breathed the word in his face.

Suddenly, eager for their dinner to be over so he could take her up on her offer, Rainer looked around for the waiter to return with the checks. To his chagrin, when the waiter returned, he was carrying the dessert menus.

With a goading grin shot right at Rainer, Dan requested that the waiter leave the menus. He informed him he was certain they all wanted dessert. He knew they'd overheard Fionna's comment, and they'd heard Emily's as well.

Rainer sighed and ordered dessert. Emily decided to just share his, as they'd had a large meal. Adeline made the same request of Logan, who looked thoroughly disappointed since that meant he'd only get half of a dessert. Rainer and Emily laughed at Logan's mournful agreement.

As their desserts arrived, Emily laid her hand discreetly across Rainer's thigh, but the anticipation made his mind spin wildly. Everyone dug in, and in a moment of distraction, she slid her hand higher and gave him a naughty wink.

"Eat, baby," he whispered in her ear. "I'll have my dessert when we get back to the room." Her breath caught as her eyes flashed excitedly. Her energy began to flutter.

She pulled her hand away momentarily as he spoon-fed her the ice cream, covered in berries, that he'd ordered. Eventually the dessert bowls were empty, and the waiter brought the checks.

"Look a little antsy there, Lawson," Vindico harrassed as he stood and helped Fionna with her wrap. Rainer laughed, certain that was true.

"But you're not looking forward to anything at all?" Rainer turned the tables on his boss as the ladies exited ahead of them.

Dan raised his left eyebrow. "Never said that. I just don't like to reveal my cards until I know I have all the aces."

Rainer came right back. "It's not about having all the aces. You just need to know how to play the hand you're dealt well."

"Your dad taught you that." Dan immediately looked reminiscent.

"He did." Rainer nodded. The familiar ache in his chest whenever he missed his father took its customary chokehold. They walked back toward the hotel slowly and took in the Sydney skyline lit from the lights of the Opera House over the bay.

They passed an oddly shaped building a few blocks from the hotel, with a long line of people trying to get in what Rainer assumed was a popular club.

"Oh, that looks fun. Let's go have a few drinks and dance a little before we head back," Emily urged.

As this was not at all what any of the men in the group had in mind, they all stifled their disappointment. Fionna and Adeline agreed that it would be a fun way to spend the evening and that it was still early.

As they made their way to the back of the line, Vindico slapped Rainer on the shoulder.

"See? With women, you need all the aces."

Rainer nodded his defeat. They worked their way through the line until they were standing at the entrance to the multistory complex, with large hanging signs over the door declaring it to be 'The Slip In Night Club: Sydney's hottest night club.'

"Yeah, this is not the hot spot I wanted to be slipping into right about now." Logan made certain only Rainer and Dan heard his quip. They laughed and nodded dejectedly as they studied the club.

The main level was a large dance floor surrounded by booths, with a large bar in the center. The basement was a club with a decidedly darker feel, but the two upper floors were entirely different. One was a beach-themed area, complete with palm trees. Each table was secluded carefully by high-backed booth seating. It was a quiet getaway from the floors below. The top floor was a garden bar where guests could enjoy drinks and dancing on the roof or play pool in the covered areas surrounding the inner garden.

"Where do you want to start?" Fionna eyed Dan sweetly.

"I always prefer to start down and work my way up." There was a naughty glint in his eye as he let his eyes follow a path up her body, starting with her legs and ending with her chest. Fionna smirked over his decidedly dirty remark.

"I know." She waggled her eyebrows.

Dan gave her a low, shuddered moan and led the crowd down to the nightclub in the basement.

CHAPTER 15
TEA WITH THE PRINCE

It rained most of the night and into the morning. Fionna texted Emily and asked if they would go shopping with her and Dan to find something for her to wear to their dinner with the Australian royal family. With the limited time she'd had to pack, she hadn't brought anything but a semiformal dress.

Logan informed everyone that he was spending the day with Adeline alone. He was trying to keep her calm and distracted until the limousine arrived at five to take them to the castle.

"This is going to be fun." Emily was flitting around their suite, getting ready to go shopping. Rainer caught her hand and pulled her to him.

"Have I mentioned how much I really, really like everything you had done at the spa?" He let his fingertips trace over the satin crotch of her panties. She hadn't finished dressing yet.

Emily giggled. "You *have* mentioned that about two dozen times after you freaked out that it might've hurt me," she reminded him of his shock and then concern the evening before.

"Well, I love you and I don't want you to be in any pain. I'm your Shield. But if you're sure it didn't hurt, then I really, really like this."

"I really, really like it too. Fionna was right. The sex afterwards is amazing."

Rainer caught her lips with his own as he allowed their extended lovemaking session from the night before to replay slowly in his mind.

Despite his initial hesitation to go shopping with Dan and Fionna, they did have a good time. Rainer was impressed with Dan's kind, patient demeanor with Fionna, despite being dragged all over Sydney in search of dresses and shoes for the ladies.

At a quarter to five, Rainer pulled on the monogrammed *L* cufflinks that had been his father's and retied his tie as he waited on Emily to emerge from the bathroom.

"Baby, we need to head out. The limo will be here soon," he called after glancing at his watch. Emily emerged a moment later. Rainer's mouth hung open.

"You look phenomenal."

She was wearing the dress she'd originally brought from home, though she'd tried on many others during their shopping excursion. It was a deep purple, silk wrap dress that hugged her curves perfectly. It hung just below her knees, as that had been her father's request. She was wearing one of her grandmother's pearl bracelets that Tad had designed. Her hair was pulled up in an elegant French twist.

"Really?" she fussed.

"You look amazing."

He let his eyes travel the length of her body, until he landed on the strappy high heels fixed at her ankles that completed her perfection.

"Amazing like, hey, there's an okay-looking girl walking down the street, or amazing like, hi, I'm the Crown Governor's daughter, and you might be my best friend's dad?" Her face broadcast her bewildered expression. Rainer tried not to laugh.

"Sweetheart, you look phenomenal, like my beautiful, classy, sweet baby, and her daddy's baby girl, but that's just the perfect amount of naughty once I get her back here and out of that dress."

A broad grin stretched across her features. Her eyes lit at his compliment.

"Do you think Logan managed to keep Adeline calm today?" Emily moved to the mirror over the dresser in the bedroom and rechecked her hair.

"If anyone could, he did. I don't know if you've noticed this, but he does seem to have her number."

Dan Vindico

Dan grimaced as he checked his watch. He didn't want to rush her. He understood the importance women put on an event like this, but he also didn't want to do anything to cast a negative light on Adeline. Making the Premier's driver wait might not be the best way to start off their evening.

"Honey,"—he tapped lightly on the bathroom door—"no rush. I was just checking on you."

She laughed. It was a sound Dan had decided could bring about world peace.

She opened the door slowly. "I swear, I'm not usually this much of a klutz, but I cannot get this strap fastened."

Her warm olive skin glowed in her embarrassment, but Dan was unable to respond as he took her in. She was the most beautiful thing he'd ever laid eyes on. Her hair was pulled up in a loose low bun, with several curled tendrils fixed elegantly around her face.

The dress she'd chosen was a cool aquamarine that dipped low in the front. The shoulders and back were made of delicate lace. The gown fit perfectly around her shapely physique. She was astoundingly beautiful.

She was the absolute picture of elegant grace and poise. She'd applied slightly more makeup than Dan had seen on her thus far. The complete picture overwhelmed him.

"Fionna, you are stunning." The words poured from his mouth.

"Thank you." She seemed embarrassed.

With an adorable wrinkle of her nose, she held up one of the pearl-colored heels she'd selected while they'd shopped. "Could you help me?"

"Of course." Dan took it and her hand. He led her to a chair in the sitting room. He tried not to chuckle as she walked awkwardly on one high heel.

After she was seated, she crossed her legs and offered him her left foot. "I feel like Cinderella." She giggled as he knelt on one knee and slid the shoe onto her dainty foot.

Dan grinned. "I would definitely not qualify as Prince Charming, but I would search the kingdom for you, and I would do just about anything to make you my princess." Her energy spun in elation as he made his vow.

After he buckled the strap at her ankle, he stood and offered her his arm.

"I've been to the Haydenshires' farm dozens of times, and it never occurred to me that Garrett's dad is like royalty. I'm so nervous."

"Governor Haydenshire would be the first person to insist that he isn't anything special. I personally believe the Premier thinks just a little much of himself with the limos and the palaces, but that's the way their Realm is set up." He shrugged. "But, baby doll, you look every part the princess. I can't take my eyes off of you. I cannot believe I'm lucky enough to have you on my arm tonight."

Maybe a dinner date at a castle where I can tell everyone she's mine will make up for the times when I can't. Dan continued to hope against hope.

Logan Haydenshire

"You will be fine. I will not leave your side," Logan vowed for the tenth time in an hour. With every lurch of the elevator, she seemed to fall further apart.

"We are about to just show up at the home of the Premier of the Australian Realm and announce that I am his illegitimate granddaughter and my mother is a prostitute." Adeline blinked back yet another round of tears and hysteria.

"Sweetheart, please," Logan begged as they exited the elevator. "Emily has a good feeling about this," he reminded her. His sister's feelings were almost always right, and Adeline generally put a great deal of trust in Emily.

"You look beautiful," Emily vowed as soon as they made their way to the waiting limo. Logan caught Rainer's concerned glance and shot him a look of abject panic.

Rainer slapped him on the back as he followed Emily into the car and immediately echoed Emily's compliment to Adeline.

She did look stunning. Logan had informed her of this numerous times. She'd curled her hair and pulled just a little of it off of her face, and was wearing an elegant, navy blue gown that showed off the hint of blue in her onyx eyes.

Fionna beamed at Adeline as the driver closed the door to the limo.

"Everything is going to be fine. I can feel it." Fionna squeezed Adeline's hand, and Logan was certain she tried to push her soothing Receiver's energy into Adeline.

Dan couldn't seem to take his eyes off of Fionna, who did look ravishing.

After taking Adeline's hand, Logan concentrated. She let him in, and her ragged energy soothed slightly as he willed calm into her.

CHAPTER 16

THE DAUGHTER OF THE PRINCE

A few minutes later, the limo arrived at a massive stone structure, nothing short of a castle, surrounded by a matching stone and wrought iron gate that enclosed acres upon acres of land. Neither Logan nor anyone in the car had ever seen a dwelling that extravagant much less been invited inside one.

Adeline whimpered and trembled as the limo door was opened.

"I'm right here. We're just having dinner. We don't have to say anything at all if you don't want to. We're just here for Dad," Logan kept up his steady reassurances.

Dan and Rainer both gave him sympathetic looks as they all guided their respective dates up the vast staircase that led to the massive front doors.

A servant of the Premier swung the doors open wide and bowed as they were issued into the great hall. The circular room was awash with marble tile work, gilded busts of the Nguyens' ancestors, and four life-size murals that hung on the walls.

Logan took in the vast, full-length painted portraits of each of the Premier's sons, painted when they were in their early twenties, and he knew that they were had. As he studied the last picture in the lineup—the one of the Premier's youngest son—he stared into the eyes of his wife.

"Oh wow," Emily gasped as she noted the very same thing.

Dan and Rainer shared a concerned glance.

"I'm either going to pass out or throw up." Adeline whimpered.

"Emily," Logan ordered.

Emily nodded and rushed in. She took Adeline's forearm with both of her hands and willed more calm into Adeline than Logan was capable of.

"Here, let me help." Fionna immediately came to Adeline's aid as well. Two more attendants dressed in uniforms, complete with the Nguyen swan crest, appeared.

"Premier Nguyen and his sons would like to extend a formal invitation to the men of the group to join him for a few sporting rounds of clays on the back deck. Lady Nguyen has requested that the ladies meet her in the parlor for tea prior to supper, which will be served in just over two hours, per her request."

"No," Adeline breathed the word. Her voice choked in her terror. Logan's heart ached. He wasn't certain what to do.

Dan stepped in, and Logan was truly astonished at his calming demeanor.

"Fi," he whispered. "He has to go. His father is the American Crown," he instructed Fionna while barely moving his lips. She nodded her understanding.

He moved in front of Adeline. "Adeline, look at me, okay. Deep breaths," he soothed, "just go with Fionna and Emily. Logan isn't going anywhere. He'll be with Rainer and me, but he needs to do this. We can't offend the Premier. You'll be okay. If you want Logan at any time, you can call him or text him, or Fionna can call me, and I will get him to you. I promise I won't let you down." His tone remained steadfast and soothing. The command rang with certainty and calm.

To Logan's shock, Adeline nodded her understanding. She seemed to draw on deep resolve. At that moment, two men entered the vast foyer.

One was the Premier's youngest son, with the very same jet-black hair as Adeline, the same long, willowy frame, and identical eyes. He gaped at what appeared to be his personal assistant. He took one look at Adeline, pale and trembling in the foyer, clinging to Logan and being casted by Fionna and Emily.

He stared into her eyes as his mouth fell open in disbelief. His assistant had a similar reaction.

"Uh, sir, perhaps…I should cancel your appointments for the evening?" the assistant suggested.

"Too right," the Premier's son agreed in a choked whisper. "And for the morrow as well," he said as his tone grew slightly more audible. His assistant nodded while staring bewilderedly at Adeline.

After shaking himself, the man stepped up to Logan.

"Uh, I am Lucas Nguyen." He offered Logan his hand.

With a quick steadying breath, Logan nodded. "I'm Logan Haydenshire. This is my wife, Adeline." He introduced the man to his daughter.

"Holy dooley," Lucas whispered. His breaths were short and ragged just like his daughter's. "Uh, hello, dear. So…nice to meet you."

"Hi," Adeline managed to eke out.

"Uh, sir?" one of the butlers urged Lucas.

After quickly studying the expression on the butler's face, Lucas nodded and then turned back to Logan.

"Has my mother invited them to tea?" Logan nodded. "She should go. My mother is very sensitive," Lucas urged. "But uh,"—he turned back to the butlers—"tell my father and brothers that I've decided to stay in for the evening with our American friends, and that I've detained them in my den for…" He paused, and then added, "…several minutes. Tell them we'll meet them on the deck in time."

"Yes sir," the butler agreed. "Right this way, ladies." He gestured down a massive corridor to the east. Adeline clung firmly to Logan's arm.

"Adeline," Fionna soothed, "come with us. Logan will be back in just a few minutes. I promise. Emily and I will be with you the whole time."

Logan nodded his agreement. "Let me go talk to him, baby." He kissed Adeline's forehead. "I'll be right back. I promise. I won't let you down."

"We'll stay right beside you." Fionna continued to calm Adeline with Emily's help.

"Okay," Adeline agreed in a terrified whisper as she allowed Fionna to forcibly remove her hand from Logan's arm.

"I'll be right back," Logan assured her again as the women led her away. Lucas ran his hands through his hair and stared after Adeline. He swallowed hard and broke out in a visible sweat.

"Uh, I could really use a drink. Would you care to join me?" Lucas begged Logan, Rainer, and Dan, who all nodded their agreement.

They followed Lucas down an opulent marble hallway and up two flights of stairs bedecked with ornate polished fixtures and deep crimson carpeting.

"In here," Lucas gestured as he opened a set of cherry-wood French doors that revealed what appeared to be a lush office, with leather couches situated around the large room.

The walls were covered in heavy, hunter-green silk fabrics. Large portraits of Lucas and his brothers hunting and holding up their kills hung on the walls.

Lucas's assistant followed them into the den and offered everyone drinks.

Lucas shook his head. "I'll get the drinks. Just cancel all of my appointments, and then you're dismissed for the evening, Fred."

"Yes sir," Fred agreed. He turned and gave Logan a speculative nod before he exited.

Lucas moved to a broad, cherry-wood liquor cabinet. As the doors swung open, a rather well-stocked wet bar was revealed. He poured what appeared to be nothing but a shot of gin and drank it in one sip.

"Uh, what can I make you?" He gestured for the three of them to take a seat. He slid bottles around in the wet bar. "I have some American whiskey around here somewhere." His nerves seemed to be getting the better of him.

"It's fine. Why don't we all have a beer, and you and Mr. Haydenshire can talk," Vindico suggested.

Lucas spun. He studied Dan intently for a moment. He was clearly used to being the one who gave the orders. Dan raised his eyebrows. His jaw flexed. He wasn't backing down. Lucas, however, did.

136

"Of course." He pulled three bottled Australian beers from a lower compartment, chilled them with his hand, and handed them out.

Logan drooped slightly under the sheer power of Vindico's hand as he slapped him on the back and urged him on.

"I don't really know where to begin except to just come out with it. She is most definitely your daughter, and she needs your help," Logan stated calmly. He visibly impressed everyone in the room.

Lucas rubbed his temples. He seemed to will calm.

"Uh,"—he drew another deep breath—"I'm so sorry. Tell me her name again."

Fury shot through Logan's veins as he narrowed his eyes. "Adeline," he huffed indignantly.

"He just met her," Rainer whispered.

"I had no idea. You have to believe me. I would never have allowed my child to go on not knowing I was her father."

"We know," Dan agreed as Logan and Rainer nodded.

"How old is she?"

"She's twenty-one." Logan studied Lucas.

"I was seventeen," he murmured then shook his head as the shock washed over his features. He grasped the edge of the substantial desk in the room. "Wait, you said she needs help. Do you need money?" Lucas moved to his desk and withdrew a checkbook from the top drawer.

"No, but that would've been nice twenty years ago."

Lucas looked devastated.

With his eyes goggling again, he sighed and moved to the couch.

"Wait, she's twenty-one? Dear saints, please tell me that woman didn't raise her!"

"If you're referring to Candy, then yes and that's why we're here."

"Who's Candy?" Lucas looked confused again.

"Adeline's mother. The, uh…."

Lucas sighed. "Molly." Logan's brow furrowed and Lucas looked thoughtful. "Uh, American…American…I believe you call them hookers." He landed on the appropriate term.

"She's changed her name several times in the last twenty years or so," Dan commented.

A deep crimson heat spread up Lucas's neck and settled in his cheeks. His blush matched that of his daughter's.

"Not that I know any of you well enough to have this conversation, but seeing as it's my fault you're here, it was my first go. The franger broke. I didn't have a clue what I was doing. She told me not to worry about it when I told her it was my first root. She said she couldn't get pregnant. I was off my face. My brothers arranged it."

Though there was a good bit of Australian slang in the tale, everyone listening got the gist of the story.

"Let's not tell Adeline any of that," Logan commanded.

"Of course not."

"Wait, do you know what a franger is? My God, how could there be so many different forms of English?" he quizzed the air around him as he began to pace.

"We've got it," Vindico assured him.

"I cannot tell you how sorry I am. Of course, I need to go tell her I know." He paused and seemed to gather his thoughts. "Please tell me what I can do."

With that, Logan began the tale of Adeline's upbringing. He started with the story of the way Candy was informed of Adeline's Gifted energies.

"She jerked her shoulder and elbow out of socket because Ad wanted to see a doll in a store when she was four," he spat angrily. Lucas looked physically ill.

Logan moved on to the fact that Candy was high when she gave birth to Adeline, but that Adeline being a Valeduto Predilect had saved her from any permanent harm from the drugs.

"She offered me Ecstasy when I was with her," Lucas recalled.

"I met Ad when we started at the academy. After we started dating, my mom and dad begged her to come and live with us, but she refused until graduation night." Bile rose viciously in his throat as he recalled their graduation from Venton. "Anyway, that's where all the real problems began."

Rainer and Dan seemed to have nothing to add but continued to nod their encouragement.

"I'm so sorry to stop you, mate, but who are they again?" He gestured to Rainer and Dan.

"Oh, sorry," Logan fumbled.

"This is Rainer Lawson, my best friend. He's engaged to my sister," Logan explained as Rainer shook Lucas's hands.

"I'm Dan Vindico, Chief of Iodex in the American Realm. Logan and Rainer are two of my finest officers." He offered Lucas his hand.

"You're the brilliant bastard who told the Russian Crown he could suck your old fella. We heard all about it." Lucas suddenly looked thrilled.

Vindico grimaced. "I was afraid of that."

"Guy's a bloody thief. Every Realm in the world knows."

"It wasn't my finest hour."

"Anyway," Logan redirected.

Lucas immediately turned his attention back to the matter at hand. "Sorry. Please go on."

Logan went over Candy's arrest, and then her blaming the drugs in the apartment on Adeline.

Lucas stood and began pacing again.

"Adeline's never used, but when she was hospitalized..."

"What?" Lucas came back to sit in front of Logan. Terror broadcasted from his features.

"She's all right now," Logan assured him.

"Why was she in the hospital? You don't have a baby, do you?"

"No." Logan's impatience grew rapidly.

"Good on ya. It's one thing to find out you're a father and had no idea. It's another match entirely to find out you're a grandpa as well."

"Could I just finish?"

"It's a lot to take in," Rainer whispered.

A few minutes later, Logan was concluding the harrowing tale.

"So, anyway, I don't really know what you might be willing to do. Our lawyer believes that if you came to the trial and claimed Adeline, informed them that Candy was using when you were with her, and that if you had known of her existence you would have provided for Adeline, it would discredit her entire story.

"If nothing else, by winning the trial, Adeline will be able to continue practicing medicine, which she's extremely talented at and loves. And,"—Logan glanced at Rainer, who nodded for him to go on —"I know you didn't know she even existed, but I love her, sir, more than life itself. She's been through hell, and I just think it might go a long way for her to know that she has at least one parent who actually cares about her."

Lucas studied Logan for a minute.

"Of course. I should have been taking care of her all these years. You and your family have given her more than I'll ever be able to, not that I won't try. I'll do anything in my power to get her out of this trouble, but your father's the Crown Governor. Surely he has more power in America than I ever will."

Vindico stepped in. "That might be true if this trial was being held within the Realm Senate, but this is a Non-Gifted trial. Governor Haydenshire can keep her out of prison, but if she's charged with possession and use of legal or illegal substances, she won't be able to practice medicine."

"If I'd known, I would have brought her here. She would've lived like the princess she is. I feel horrible."

"Do you have other children, Mr. Nguyen?" Vindico quizzed.

"No." Lucas shook his head. "My ex-wife never wanted to have any. It was one of the reasons we split up. Of course, I didn't know about Adeline. Not that she would've changed anything," he corrected quickly.

"Let's maybe not mention that to her either," Logan instructed.

Still reeling from the information that Lucas would've raised Adeline in an Australian castle and that Logan would probably never have met her, he swallowed down heartache. There were too many emotions to sort through.

"May I speak with her?" Lucas broached cautiously. Logan appreciated the fact that Lucas understood that he had no hold over Adeline, and that Logan would set the boundaries for the time being.

"If she wants to, and as long as I'm with her."

Dan gave Logan a nod that said he was deeply impressed.

"When did you marry?"

"Last weekend. This is actually our honeymoon."

"I regret not being there," he commented as the reality of the situation began to settle into his eyes. "You said that you found out about me a week or so ago. Did she use her maiden name?" Lucas asked suddenly.

"No." Logan shook his head. "She didn't want any part of Candy anymore, so she's Adeline Marie Haydenshire." Logan tried to soften the blow.

Lucas shook his head. "The American Realm must be vastly more accepting than the Australian for the Crown Governor's son to have married a woman without a last name."

"Logan's gotten a lot of flack for that over the years," Rainer stepped in. "But he never cared. That's the kind of guy your daughter married."

"Yes, I'd say she did very well for herself all things considered." Lucas offered Logan his hand again.

Logan shook it and smiled. "If she hasn't completely freaked out, I think she would really like to meet you."

"I don't want her to be frightened. I'd really like to know her and do what I can for the both of you. I'd love for you all to stay here at the palace for the rest of your trip if I can persuade you." Lucas looked momentarily like he might drop to his knees and plead.

"Why don't we go get Adeline, and we'll see what she wants to do? She's my top priority."

Lucas was moved by Logan's vow. "I do want you to know that if I'd known all these years, she would've been mine also, and she certainly is now. Everything else can wait."

"I think that would mean a lot to her." Logan gestured to the door.

With another nod, Lucas led the group back down the staircases and through the vast hallways, until they located a small parlor area where the women were having tea with Lady Nguyen.

Lucas nodded to his mother and then turned to Adeline. Logan had already reached her and offered her his hand.

"Adeline, I'd very much like for you and Logan to finish your tea in my den if it would be all right with you," he soothed kindly. Logan gave her a reassuring nod as her eyes sought his.

"Oh, uh, okay. Thank you." Adeline gave a hesitant nod.

"Lucas, dear, I was trying to get to know our guests," his mother informed him, but her expression said that she knew there was a great deal more to the story.

"Yes, Mother, but I'd like to try to get to know my daughter," he shot back instantly.

"I think that's probably a very good idea." His mother gave Adeline a kind smile. "Why don't you drop the gentlemen off on the south deck? Your father thinks he can best the American Head of Iodex at clays." She rolled her eyes as Dan and Fionna chuckled. "The ladies and I will continue to get to know one another, and then we can have a dinner to welcome Adeline to the family."

Adeline looked stunned at the declaration as Logan beamed. With that, Lucas guided Dan and Rainer to one of the back decks and then led Logan and Adeline to his den.

CHAPTER 17
PROTOCOL
RAINER LAWSON

"Clays are skeet, right?" Rainer whispered to Dan.

"I sure as hell hope so."

"I've never shot skeet before."

"It's just like shooting anything else. When it moves, you blast it, and you better make us look good," he demanded through clenched teeth. "I'm still not certain if I should be offended he called me a brilliant bastard."

Rainer shared a chuckle with his boss and then shook the Premier's hand along with two of Lucas's older brothers.

In the end, Rainer shot well. He hit seventeen of the twenty clay targets. Vindico couldn't quite hide his smirk as he shot a perfect score.

The men joined the women, along with Lucas, Logan, and Adeline, in the opulent dining room a little while later.

The Premier had taken to Dan quickly after seeing him shoot. As he gestured for everyone to take a seat, he leaned and kissed his wife's cheek. "Not only is the bastard built like a brick shithouse, but he's a corker of a shot, and we've all heard that he's got a bloody mouth to boot. Tell us the tale, Officer Vindico. Tell us what you told the Russian board. I want to hear it." He held both of his hands up to Dan in exaltation.

Fionna looked extremely curious, and Dan appeared ready to murder as he pulled her chair out for her and then seated himself beside her.

"That's really not a story for mixed company, sir."

Rainer and Logan choked back laughter as Dan continued to dissuade the Premier. Lady Nguyen instructed her husband to have a seat.

"Now, I believe Lucas has something he'd like to share." She opened the floor for her youngest son. Lucas stood. He smiled and moved behind Adeline and Logan. As this was the first time the Premier or his other sons had focused on Adeline, they all held shocked expressions as Lucas began to speak.

"Well," he chuckled, "Adeline, this is my father and two of my older brothers, Arlo and Ethan. This is Ethan's wife, Maribel, and his children, Ollie and Noah." He gestured to his sister-in-law and nephews who smiled kindly. "And this is my daughter, Adeline, and her husband, Logan." He watched as stunned disbelief washed over the features of his father and brothers.

"Obviously, I've missed a great deal of Adeline's life, and I intend to rectify that situation. I'll be leaving for the States to spend the holidays with Logan and Adeline, and to clear up a little matter there. I plan to travel back and forth often."

The Premier stood and moved to Adeline. He welcomed her to the family. He did pull Lucas to the side, and Rainer overheard the word media used several times.

Lucas, however, didn't seem to care what the press or anyone else thought, and told his father that he would be phoning the media himself the following morning.

"Uh, actually, sir," Logan interrupted. "Our lawyer would like to keep the fact that Adeline found her father under wraps until the trial." He took Adeline's hand as she blushed.

"Lawyer?" Premier Nguyen urged his son.

"We'll talk about it after the meal, but certainly, Logan, like I told you both, whatever you want is precisely what we'll do."

"If Mrs. Haydenshire,"—the Premier nodded to Adeline—"has

gotten herself into some sort of trouble, perhaps our legal team should take care of whatever the problem seems to be."

"Adeline hasn't gotten into any trouble. This is all due to the woman who gave birth to her, and our legal team, fine though they may be, cannot practice law in America, Father. I think it best this time for us to let Crown Governor Haydenshire, my daughter, and her husband tell us what they need. That is what we're going to do." Lucas stood firm.

"Your will and estate will have to be changed," the Premier challenged his son.

Adeline shuddered visibly. "No, sir. I really don't want anything except to keep my job," she assured her grandfather.

It was evident to everyone seated at the table that she was using every ounce of determination and fortitude she had to make her plea. "I mean, Logan's always taken such good care of me. He's really all I'll ever need. I just want to work. I love my job so much." She offered Logan a hesitant smile. Logan shook his head as he gazed at her with an expression that said he wasn't certain how he'd gotten so incredibly lucky.

"Yes, well,"—Lucas smiled proudly—"the fact that you've married one of the finest men I've ever had the privilege of meeting is one thing, however, my will and estates will be changed. I will do what should have been done twenty-one years ago, and I will certainly try to make up for what Logan and his parents did on your account. As shocked as I am that I'm standing here looking at you, dear, I cannot tell you how much I would love to be a part of your life."

Tears sheened Adeline's eyes. "Okay, but you don't have to give me any money just because you want to be in my life, and you can think about it. I'll understand if you just want me to go away. Just helping me keep my job is more than I could hope for."

Logan and Lucas shared an extremely concerned glance.

Emily couldn't seem to keep her thoughts from verbalization. "Adeline, stop. That isn't true. He doesn't want you to go away. I can tell. Why don't you ever believe that everyone loves you?"

"I assume this is the way she feels about most things?" Lucas quizzed Logan discreetly. Logan nodded. Pain broadcasted from his features. "Seems I have more to make up for than I ever could have imagined." Determination etched Lucas's face as he turned to the table.

"Let's eat, and I would like to extend a formal invitation for Logan and Adeline and their friends to spend the rest of their stay here in the palace." He turned to his daughter. "I don't have to think about it. I want to get to know you and Logan. I want you to be a part of my life, and I yours. I will make certain that you are cared for in the manner you would've been taken care of if I'd known about you all those years ago."

No one spoke as Lucas took the chair on Adeline's left. Logan was seated on her right.

"I assume your mother will be at the trial," he whispered quietly to Adeline.

"Yes, sir."

"Good. I have quite a few things I'd like to say to her."

Logan couldn't quite hide the broad grin that spread across his face.

Fionna was visibly distressed as she whispered in Dan's ear.

"Prince Nguyen." Dan cleared his throat. "I certainly can't speak for Logan and Adeline, and though Fionna and I truly appreciate your offer, you don't need to house us," he insisted politely. Fionna nodded her adamant agreement.

"Officer Vindico, I will consider it a personal offense if you do not allow me to put you up for the next few nights. I imagine you might be trying to rectify your international image at this point, are you not?" Lucas pointed out with a slight chuckle as Dan grimaced again.

"Perhaps they would be more comfortable in the guest quarters. If Logan and Adeline would feel all right in your apartment, then Officer Vindico and Ms. Styler, along with Mr. Lawson and Ms. Haydenshire, could be accommodated in one of the guesthouses," Lady Nguyen suggested. She was clearly accustomed to playing peacemaker.

Lucas nodded as the servers began bringing out the first course. Adeline was giving Logan terrified glances. Everyone else was still trying to imagine living in a place large enough to have numerous apartments inside of one home.

Premier Nguyen informed everyone that they'd had the chefs prepare Australian delicacies for their grand feast. Fionna, who had moments before looked slightly bewildered at the thought of staying in the Nguyen's guesthouse, smiled.

Dan winked at her as Rainer rubbed Emily's thigh and tried to calm her. Her energy stuttered in nervous pulses from the Premier's insistence that they stay in the palace as well.

"We've prepared the finest in sushi platters for your appetizer this evening," the chef informed them as he stepped out from what must've been the kitchen.

"Thank you, Nigel," the Premier complimented as each person in attendance was given a rectangular-shaped platter that held four small mounds of raw fish in delicate arrangements.

Fionna and Dan shared a smile at the announcement of sushi, but Fionna's face fell when it was revealed. Dan put his arm around her and caressed her shoulder with his thumb. Fionna smiled hesitantly.

"Oh, uh, what kind of sushi is this?" she asked politely. Only those at the table who knew her well picked up on her apprehension.

"So sorry, dear." Lucas stepped up, but he seemed hesitant to direct his attention to anyone but Adeline. "That,"—he pointed to a small mound of translucent, raw white fish stacked on what Rainer thought were some kind of black noodles, "is cuttlefish. It's a local delicacy. It's prepared on Tagliarini pasta. The sauce is made of squid ink." He didn't seem to notice the nervous glances being shared by his guests.

"Those," Lucas went on, "are, of course, spiced prawn on aioli, barramundi sashimi, and those are soused snook." He pointed to the one on the ends of the platters. "Try them. They're my personal favorite."

Fionna nodded, and then shot Vindico looks that said for him to save her now. He glanced around, trying desperately to figure out a way to do just that.

Since there really wasn't any escape, everyone began hesitantly trying the sushi. Adeline forced down a tiny bite of the cuttlefish and squid-ink noodles. She tried very hard not to grimace. Logan attempted to shield her face with his body unsuccessfully. Lucas panicked.

"You don't like it?" he asked, as if this were some kind of failing on his part. "Here, we'll have them make you whatever you'd like."

"No." Adeline shook her head violently. "Please, it's fine, really."

Logan shot Lucas a look that said he needed to back off, which Lucas did.

A few minutes later, the Nguyens were eating happily, and Dan leaned and whispered something in Fionna's ear. Rainer was certain it was a promise that he would take her to get anything she wanted to eat after the meal was over. She beamed at him as color rose in her cheeks.

Emily and Rainer tried some of the sushi. They ate the prawn that everyone but Logan seemed to like. Logan scowled and uttered the words fish-bait under his breath.

Finally, the waitstaff moved back in and removed the sushi platters. The soup course was next, and everyone waited to see what would be revealed as small, covered tureens were situated at everyone's places.

"Uh, this is a Maori boil-up," Lucas informed the guests, though he kept his eyes locked on Adeline. "It's a vegetable soup made with pork and dumplings. It's been a while since I was in the States. I wasn't able to attend your father's ball. I do apologize for that. I believe, when I was last there, I had a vegetable soup made with beef."

Adeline nodded. "Mrs. Haydenshire makes hers with leftover roast." There was a wistfulness in her quiet tone. "It's delicious. She makes it for me when I'm sick."

"Well, I hope you enjoy this as well," Lucas offered hopefully.

With that, everyone lifted the tops of the tureens and picked up their soup spoons.

Emily gave Rainer a relieved smile. The soup was delicious. Everyone relaxed as they settled into the meal and their hosts.

"Uh," Lucas looked extremely uncomfortable. "I would love for you and Logan to stay in my apartment with me. I imagine, with this being your honeymoon, you probably don't want me around too much. I do understand. I'll just be there whenever you'd like to visit," he tried to form his thoughts into appropriate dinner conversation.

Adeline's eyes goggled as her face burned crimson. Fionna and Emily gave her sorrowful expressions. Rainer and Dax shot each other glances that said Logan was going to have trouble fielding this particular conversation.

"Well, that is where the expression comes from, Luke." Arlo laughed and shook his head at his younger brother. Lucas chuckled though Rainer noted a hint of disdain.

Lucas sighed. "My brother's being crass, but there's an expression here." He glanced hesitantly at Adeline, clearly not certain if he should state the expression, but he decided to go on with it. "Uh, off like a bride's nightie." He swallowed a sip of water, before shaking his head and drawing a steadying breath. "I didn't mean to embarrass you. I guess I'm still not certain what to say to you."

"It's okay," Adeline offered in a strangled voice.

"Why don't you tell us about your work at the hospital?" Lucas offered the table to Adeline who looked like she would rather do anything else.

The absolute last thing she wanted was more attention directed her way, but her father, having only known her for a grand total of an hour and a half, had no way of knowing this.

"Well." Adeline reached for Logan's hand, and Rainer knew she was drawing from him in heavy doses. He was supplying her strength readily, though he looked worn himself. "I have six more months of training, but I just passed my oral boards so now I'm allowed to see patients on my own. At the end of my full training, I'll be training another incoming medio student."

"Ad's already been asked to join the top obstetrics medio team at Georgetown, even though she's only been training since our graduation. She's incredibly talented," Logan bragged.

The Premier and his wife smiled and nodded. They looked pleased with Adeline's eagerness for her work.

"Logan is an Elite Iodex Officer under Vindico, here," Lucas informed his father and brothers.

"And you're pleased with his work?" the Premier asked pointedly.

"He's an outstanding officer and a fine man. I trust him with my life and the lives of my men on a regular basis. He saved his brother's life just a few weeks ago. She chose very well." Vindico nodded to Adeline.

Fionna beamed, which seemed to thoroughly delight Dan. Emily smiled at her brother adoringly, only adding to his blush.

"Well, we'll have to see him shoot," the Premier announced excitedly.

"Dear, he's on his honeymoon. Let the lad enjoy himself. I'm certain this has all been rather trying for the both of them." The Lady gestured to Lucas as she rolled her eyes at her husband.

The Premier scoffed and shook his head. "My heavens, Isabel, she's not a dunny door in a storm. The man can take a little time off to enjoy a round of clays."

Dan shuddered. He seemed to be the only American at the table who understood the Premier's remark. Adeline turned to Logan. Her pale skin did nothing to cover the blazing crimson color in her cheeks.

"What does that mean?" she asked in a terrified whisper. Logan shot Lucas a warning glare. Rainer was rather impressed at his determination to shield Adeline from her father's family.

"Forgive them, dear," Lady Nguyen scoffed. "Growing up in a family of all boys made them rather rude despite their years of training. Of course, I'm certain the newly crowned Governor Haydenshire's family must be the same way. I understand that you have a number of brothers, correct, Logan?"

"Yes, ma'am. I have seven brothers living and two sisters. One's due here in a few months."

"Yes, we'd heard your family was going to have another addition. Your mother is doing well, I hope?"

"Yes, ma'am, as well as can be expected. There is some concern over the baby."

"Yes, we heard that as well." The Premier nodded. His tone echoed his concern.

Before another comment could be made, the salad course was served.

"Ah, you've outdone yourself. Barbequed sweet potato, corn, and haloumi salad." The Premier seemed very pleased.

Adeline studied the salad, and Lucas grew more uncomfortable.

"My Lord, Mother. Perhaps when we're serving American guests, we should serve food that is at least recognizable to Americans."

"Oh no. It looks delicious. I just don't know what haloumi is," Adeline explained.

"Oh,"—Lucas nodded—"it's cheese, dear. It's quite good. Try it," he urged hopefully. Adeline took a bite of the salad and gave a genuine smile.

"It's delicious."

After that, Emily and Fionna fielded several questions about Summation and the Angels.

"You should recruit them, Dad. You've got buckley's chance that the Signaliers will be taking any trophies this season," Ethan urged his father. Everyone chuckled as the waitstaff returned with the main course.

"Roo steaks, cottage pie, brussels sprouts, mashed potatoes, and Yorkshire puddings," the chef announced proudly.

"As in kangaroo?" Emily whispered in Rainer's ear.

"Think so, baby." He gave her a concerned smile as she nodded hesitantly.

"Prince Nguyen, what is cottage pie?" Adeline quizzed Lucas quietly.

Lucas smiled. He seemed pleased she'd asked.

"It's a beef and vegetable pie with potatoes on top. If you'd prefer to have that instead of the roo, I'll have them bring you another portion. And please, at least call me Lucas."

"Oh, okay. I'm sorry."

Rainer had become so accustomed to Adeline's quiet demeanor and hesitant disposition it took him a moment to imagine what Lucas must be seeing in her as he studied his daughter.

"You have nothing to apologize for," Lucas assured. Anguish colored his features.

The plates were served, and Rainer and Dan cut into their steaks. They shared a speculative glance as they each took a bite.

Dan was visibly impressed as he cut another bite and nodded for Fionna to try it.

Adeline nodded. "It's very good," she agreed.

"Well, cut her two, Luke. She hardly casts a shadow," Arlo commented as he took another large bite of his steak.

"Yes, well, I wonder where she gets that from?" Lady Nguyen commented. "When Lucas was a teenager, I could hardly find him he was so thin. It didn't seem to matter how much the chefs prepared. He ate and ate and never put on." She gave Adeline a kind smile.

Adeline seemed to find this information interesting. "I always thought I was so thin because I never had much to eat growing up, but Mrs. Haydenshire started making more of my meals when Logan and I started dating, and I still didn't really gain any weight then either."

Everyone nodded, but the look on Lucas's face was a mix of heartbreak and fury as he shook his head and willed calm from the air around him.

Rainer and Emily shared a worried glance. Rainer noted that the Lady was thin and willowy, just like her granddaughter. It was odd for her to be the one complaining about her son's weight.

"What have you all done while you've been here?" the Premier changed the subject.

"You're staying at the Kingsford, yes?" Ethan added.

"Yes, sir," everyone spoke in unison.

"It's lovely," Adeline added. "Our view is amazing."

"We went to the spa there yesterday. Just the ladies, I mean," Fionna added.

Lady Nguyen nodded. "Yes, I enjoy their services myself occasionally."

"And we ate at the Victoria Room," Emily chimed in. "It was such a lovely restaurant. The food was great."

The Nguyens nodded and smiled.

Small talk carried them through dessert. The Premier and his wife very skillfully seemed to plan out the itinerary for the rest of their week. Rainer didn't want to object, but he also wasn't certain they wanted to stay at the castle, or to attend operas, lectures, and teas on a daily basis.

CHAPTER 18

A CHANGE OF VENUE

"Shall I see you all to your quarters?" Lucas took over as their host.

"Really, Lucas, I don't want to put you out. The Kingsford Wellborn is nicer than anywhere I've ever stayed, except maybe the Ritz in Paris, and it was just too nice," Adeline vowed. Logan chuckled at her assessment.

"You've been to Paris?" Lucas was instantly taken with the story. He looked pleased.

Adeline nodded. "Logan took me a few months ago. We went with Rainer and Emily."

"What did you think of the city?"

"It was beautiful, and the food was amazing. I'd had surgery a few weeks before, so I was pleased that I felt up to going. We had such a good time." She beamed at Logan as he draped his arm over her shoulders. "It's crowded though. I don't really care for cigarette smoke and it's everywhere." She seemed to feel the question was a test, and she needed to provide a full answer.

Rainer noted that Adeline relaxed at Logan's touch. Lucas seemed to notice as well.

"Well, I'd really love to hear more about your trip, and spend as much time with you as you have. I do wish you'd stay here, please, Adeline. I'll beg if I must."

After sharing a hesitant glance with Logan, Adeline smiled. "If you're certain you want us to?"

"Nothing would make me happier. I'll just send the drivers to retrieve all of your things."

No one commented, but everyone thought of the things they'd packed that they might not necessarily want other people seeing or touching.

"They're very discreet, of course." Lucas seemed to have understood the group's hesitation.

Dan stepped in. "It isn't far from here. Why don't I take Logan and Rainer back, and we'll pack everything up? You could spend a little time with Adeline."

Fionna looked relieved as Lucas nodded his agreement.

"If that works, I suppose it's all right. My father would like you three gents to play billiards with us tonight in the basement billiards room."

A few minutes later, the group was given a partial tour of the palace. Rainer, Dan, and Logan were given a ride back to the hotel to gather their things.

Rainer was mildly uncomfortable sharing a house with his boss and his newly minted girlfriend, but he wanted to be there for Logan and Adeline.

When they returned, butlers guided Rainer, Emily, Dan, and Fionna out to one of the large guesthouses at the south end of the property.

The guesthouse was decorated extravagantly and was three times the size of the Haydenshires' guesthouse. It offered two vast, well-appointed bedrooms, both with king-size beds, but they shared a bathroom.

Each room had its own toilet and double sink vanity, but they were joined in the middle by a huge, tiled room that contained a Jacuzzi bathtub inside of a shower, complete with bench seating and multiple water heads and jets. The entire area was surrounded by clear glass doors, which would make bathing somewhat uncomfortable if anyone entered the bathroom while it was in use.

Both of the ladies seemed thoroughly worn as they traipsed around the house and were assigned rooms by the rather pushy serving staff.

Dan kept Fionna tucked close to him. She seemed to be drawing from his hand, and he was supplying her with his steady strength.

After they were given the tour, Emily and Fionna asked Rainer and Dan to tell the butlers that they could unpack everything themselves.

Vindico promptly informed the staff that Miss Styler would like a little time alone and not to bother her again. He was polite but left no room for argument.

Rainer wasn't quite as comfortable making the same request, but he muddled his way through.

∽

Dan Vindico

Dan softly closed the door to their assigned bedroom. He could feel Fionna's fatigue and the tension in her rhythms. He moved to her as she began going through her bags.

"Are you okay, sweetheart?" He took her hand and eased the purple satin negligee she'd worn for him the night before from her grasp.

He wrapped his arms around her. He didn't want to go play pool. He didn't want to do anything but hold her against his chest and make certain she felt safe and secure. She buried her face against his chiseled pecs, and his mind became more resolute.

"Yeah, kind of. There was just a lot of emotion at dinner." She tried feebly to explain how the evening had worn her.

"I'm sure. Why don't I tell the brigade of people around here who would probably chew his food for him that they can let the Premier know that I'm not going anywhere tonight? I'm staying right here with my girl."

Fionna's energy began its luscious trill he'd become quite addicted to whenever he referred to her as his girl.

She couldn't seem to resist nuzzling her face against him. She wanted to hide, and he wanted nothing more than to be her Shield.

Dan grinned down at her. He kissed the top of her head. She drew from him, and he moaned.

It didn't seem to matter how many times she helped herself to his ample supplies of energy. Nothing could ever feel so heavenly. With a smirk, he reconsidered. *That doesn't feel quite as good as it does when I pump her full of it.*

With a deep breath that must have contained hard-fought resolve, Fionna pulled away. Dan made no effort to hide his frown.

"No. You have to go. I would be a mess if you didn't. I'd be so worried you'd offended them. Plus, maybe you can figure out what's really going on about Adeline. Lucas and Lady Nguyen felt genuine, but I'm not sure about his brothers or his dad. They felt…odd."

Dan tried to determine what to do. He didn't want to leave, but her plea was fervent. "Odd how?"

Fionna hemmed. She went back to her suitcase and began pulling things haphazardly from it, refolding them, and then rearranging them into neat rows. "I don't know. I shouldn't have said that. I didn't mean to freak you out."

"Honey, you didn't freak me out. Just tell me what you felt."

She grimaced. "Arlo creeped me out. I don't…like him, and the Premier seemed less than happy about Adeline being here." She shrugged and picked up her large toiletry bag. "And poor Adeline, she doesn't know what to do. She wants to make her father happy, but she doesn't want to be here. She's terrified."

Fionna eased to their half of the bathroom they'd be sharing with Rainer and Emily. Dan followed.

"Being a Receiver is just kind of a crazy thing. You can feel what everyone around you is feeling, but you can't really comment or act like you can feel it. People are entitled to their emotions and their own thoughts. I'm sure the Premier is shocked we're here and that he has a granddaughter he didn't even know about."

"I'm sure he is, but I can tell you're uncomfortable being here, baby. We don't have to stay here. I don't ever want you to be anywhere you don't want to be. You're the only thing I'm worried about."

A beautiful grin spread across her features at his words.

"Thank you, but I'll be fine. It'll be fun to be here with Emily. I really do want you to go play. I want to know what they're really thinking. I bet they'll say things in front of you they won't say in front of Lady Nguyen. Then you can come back here and take me to bed."

He captured her lips with his own. In that moment, it was the only thing that made sense to him. The night had depleted them both. She was standing before him with her gown drooping and her makeup worn, and she was still the most beautiful thing he'd ever laid eyes on.

Dan kept his lips soft and lush. He consumed her slowly and allowed his tongue to hesitantly explore her mouth. He cradled her head in his right hand and drew her body closer with his left.

She trembled in his arms. Her breaths came in quick pants of hunger. She pulled away. Her body shuddered. It seemed to argue contentiously with her mind.

Her graceful neck contracted as she swallowed down her need again. The tip of her tongue traced over her kiss-swollen lips. Dan knew she could still taste his rhythms there. He groaned from watching her.

With a knowing grin, she straightened his tie. "You change and go play pool. We'll be right here waiting on you to get back. Maybe we can sleep in tomorrow and just hang out here all alone." She gestured around the large room they'd been assigned and then began arranging some of her many varied beauty products on the counter in the bathroom. Dan understood, and his heart ached. She was trying to order her space to soothe her weary rhythms. *Receivers hate clutter. It affects their reads.* Dan heard Rainer's comment in his mind.

"Are you certain you want me to go?" He reached to touch her hands. The electricity and heat that rose under her skin in a storm of passion that quaked at his touch drove him wild. He was quickly becoming an addict, and he wanted no reprieve. "I'd rather stay here with you and help you unpack." If she needed to arrange and rearrange every single thing in either of their luggage, he would be there to help. Hell, if she wanted him to install shelving and build an entire additional closet, he'd make every effort to do that as well.

"I don't want you to go, but I really think you should." She was trying so hard to be brave it crushed him.

"Fi, baby," he soothed, "let me put you in my shield and hold you. Let me give you some time to process everything you had to feel tonight."

Tears pricked her eyes. "You're amazing," she choked.

"That's you, baby doll."

"I would love to lie in your shield. You have no idea how much it means to me that you know that's what I need, but you have to go. We have to know how they really feel, and you're the best detective in the Realm. Adeline's job depends on this working."

Dan nodded and began pulling off his tie. Lucas had informed everyone that casual dress would be expected for billiards that evening.

After making certain Fionna and Emily were really okay with them leaving, Rainer and Dan made their way back toward the palace.

"Did Fionna ask you not to go?" Rainer asked hesitantly.

"If she'd asked me not to go, I wouldn't be out here," he huffed but then remembered that he owed quite a bit to Rainer on Fionna's account. "She didn't want me to but insisted I go anyway. I wasn't sure what to do." Dan hated that feeling.

Rainer nodded. "Yeah, Em said the same thing. It's hard on them, like I said. If we'd turned down the invite and it offended the Premier, they'd have to not only endure whatever came of that but also feel his offense. But now, they're both in there trying to deal with everything they had to feel at dinner from Adeline and everyone else without a Shield to give them space to process everything."

Dan halted. "Maybe we should go back." He started to turn, but Rainer shook his head.

"You don't want to make her think that you believe she can't process it without you. They're a hell of a lot stronger than us, trust me. Plus, if us turning down this ridiculous game negatively impacted Adeline, that would hurt them way more."

"This entire thing is ridiculous." Dan gestured to the stone entry doors and the castle at large.

"Yeah, and us staying here isn't making anyone happy but Lucas."

They came to another set of cherry-wood French doors that led into the large room which had not one billiard table, but seven along with a vast bar area, leather couches, and huge flat-screen television sets mounted on the walls.

One door was opened just enough for Dan to make out the landscape of the room, but no one noticed them in the hallway. Lucas and his older brothers were talking with the Premier.

Dan halted Rainer from entering, placed his finger to his lips, and edged them out of sight. He *was* the best detective in the Realm, and if his baby wanted him to figure something out, he'd take every available opportunity to do just that.

"How were we to know you'd bang up a whore on your first go? My word, your stuff must be built like a brick shithouse." Arlo laughed. Dan could see Lucas through the small gap the open door allowed him. He rolled his eyes.

"I don't regret anything except the way the poor girl was raised. Did you hear her say she was starved, abused? I can't believe this."

"She'll be apples. Logan seems to have her settled," the Premier scoffed.

"Is he coming to play?" Ethan asked.

"No." Lucas shook his head. He sounded annoyed. "He's honeymooning my daughter, I'd say. He certainly told me where I could go when I suggested he play." He took a sip of a stout drink from the bar.

"Come on, you've been a dad for half a night, and you're already whinging on about her husband." Arlo shook his head.

"He's obviously wild about her and she him," Ethan pointed out as he began to chalk a few cues.

"I've been a dad for twenty-one years. I just didn't know it."

"So, you'll settle her up now and go see her whenever. You'll eat it in the media for a while, but she'll be right," Arlo assured him. "Premier Nguyen's youngest son meets his daughter and her mother, Molly, for the first time." He laughed and took a sip of his own drink.

"All I'm saying is did either of you see the lollies on their head officer's arm? She is abso-bloody-lutely beautiful. I'd be up her like a rat up a drainpipe. In fact, I plan to be."

Fury ignited in Dan's blood. His jaw clenched. His eyes flashed dangerously. Visions of his hands wrapped around Arlo Nguyen's throat filled his head.

Rainer grasped his forearm and shook his head. The frantic gesture was all that kept Dan from busting into the room and beating Arlo into one of those pool tables.

Arlo creeped me out. I don't...like him. That's precisely what Fionna had felt. His lechery had frightened her. Bitter gall and rage fought for dominance in Dan's chiseled body. His shield flared like he'd been hit. Utter hatred filled him readily. It always did.

"Arlo, you're forty years old. Do you ever plan on growing up? I can't imagine why you've never married." Ethan rolled his eyes.

The Premier laughed. "Yes, and I imagine Officer Vindico packs quite a punch. He can shoot a blowfly off a bull's arse and has a bloody temper to boot, so I wouldn't let him hear you talking about Miss Styler like that. I think if he'd asked her at supper, she'd have dragged him to a chapel straight away."

A cocky half grin formed on Dan's face, but Rainer stared up at him in panic. Dan's brow furrowed. He had no idea why Rainer was concerned. He was the one who should be furious.

"Are you really gonna give her part of your estate?" Ethan quizzed Lucas.

"Well, she's my daughter. She looks just like me, and I felt her energy as soon as I laid eyes on her. I didn't even have to be in contact with her. Our patterns are almost identical."

"Well, yeah. Her mum's not Gifted, so she's all you," Ethan explained.

"I feel wretched. An Australian Realm Princess, and she's terrified of everything including me."

"She'll come round, son," the Premier assured.

"Did you see her at dinner? She has to draw from her husband to speak."

"Well, be glad he's there then," Ethan pointed out.

"She'll come on just like Dad said. You have to let her get to know you. Of course, she doesn't trust anyone. She was raised by a bloody wench whore," Arlo huffed.

"Yes, well, I plan to do just that."

With that, Dan knocked on the open door, and he and Rainer entered the grand game room.

CHAPTER 19

THE WRONG MEN TO BILLIARDS

LOGAN HAYDENSHIRE

"Thank you," Logan offered the maid who insisted on unpacking his and Adeline's things. "Could we just have a few minutes?"

"Certainly, sir. Mr. Nguyen alerted the staff. He explained you'd be spending the rest of your honeymoon here, so I'll only come if you call."

Logan nodded. He sincerely wished that Lucas would stop informing the vast staff of their honeymoon status. Adeline wasn't quite as comfortable discussing it as her father seemed to be.

With a quick curtsy that Logan found disturbing, the maid left. She closed the door to the guest suite on her way out.

Logan made it to Adeline in two long strides. He pulled her to his chest and wrapped his long arms around her. "Are you okay?"

She drew from him. It always shocked Logan after all the years they'd been together and all that he'd shared with Adeline that her drawing from him still felt just as incredible as the first time she'd done it.

"It's just so surreal. I keep thinking this is some kind of bizarre dream. I can't seem to figure out if it's a good dream or a bad dream. You're here, so it must be a good dream." She declared all of this while talking into Logan's chest.

A broad grin spread across his face as he kissed the top of her head. "I know it's been a lot, but I think so far it's gone pretty well, all things considered."

Adeline nodded against him. She was suddenly quiet and introspective.

"Hey." Logan pulled away from her just enough to stare deeply into her eyes, the very same as her father's. "What's going on in that beautiful head of yours?"

"I don't know. This isn't normal. People don't live like this." She gestured to the affluent room they'd been given that was surrounded by a palace. "It's just too much, the maids and butlers. Everyone keeps staring at me. Aren't there people that could be helped with all of the money they must spend on all of this? Or…they could invest in medicine and research…or something that's not a castle." She let Logan wrap his arms back around her as she tucked her face deeply in his chest. The world with all of its many problems was just a little too much right then.

"I guess if you'd grown up with all of this, it would seem perfectly normal." Logan tried to keep his tone steady and smooth, the way Rainer always did with Emily.

"I would've still found you," Adeline vowed as tears began to form on her long eyelashes.

"Baby," Logan choked out the word. The thoughts of whether or not they ever would've met if she'd been raised as an Australian Realm princess had terrified her as well.

"I would've." Defiance perforated her words.

After swallowing down the all-consuming emotions that threatened to overwhelm him, Logan drew a steadying breath.

"Listen to me…" He tried to formulate what to say.

But she wasn't finished. "You are the only good thing in my entire life, and I don't deserve you," she declared. Her pain stabbed through him.

"Shh," Logan soothed. "Okay, just listen. I know this is scary, and new, and a lot to take in, but I'm right here with you. That's the only place I will ever be. And I'm not the only good thing in your life. You love your job and everything you've accomplished with your work and in school. That was all you, sweetheart. What I told you all those months ago in your mother's apartment is still true. My life without you isn't worth living, so it's me who doesn't deserve you. But you can have good things, baby. You can have a dad who wants to be part of your life, and you can be the princess I've always known you were, and you can have me, and everything we have back on the other side of the world."

Adeline's jaw clenched against Logan's sternum. "I don't ever want to think about not meeting you." Her exhaustion and terror had finally gotten the better of her.

"I've always wished you hadn't had to grow up the way you did. As much as I despise Candy and the way she treated you, I get what you're saying. I would never say that I was worth what you went through growing up. Never." The very idea made him ill. "But you don't get to be a kid again and try it another way. We get this one shot at life, and I'm just thankful I somehow got lucky enough to get to have this life with you."

She broke down in his arms.

"Logan," she convulsed.

"Shh, baby. It's okay."

"Can you cast me, please?" Her body trembled against his.

"Come here." He took her hand, kicked off his shoes, and threw the silk coverings and the dozens of decorative pillows off of the bed. He leaned back against the pillows he hoped were meant to be slept on, and he pulled her onto his chest.

She had to step up on the stool on the side of the bed just to join him. She was right. This was too much.

It wasn't her, and it certainly wasn't him. In that moment as he wrapped her up in his body and set his shield firmly around the two of them, what he wanted more than anything was to take her home.

He understood her plea was so much more than a need to feel safe. She wanted to be surrounded by something familiar, something that was all him, a place where the two of them could exist all alone without the world intruding and keeping up its relentless assaults.

~

The Premier and Arlo looked startled as Dan and Rainer entered the game room.

"Welcome, gents." Ethan smiled and gestured around the room. "Shall we play English Billiards or American Eight-Ball?"

Dan chuckled and kept steady warning glares directed at Arlo as he shrugged. "I'm no good at either so your choice."

Rainer nodded his agreement.

"Ah, I think we're being bagged, mates." Arlo challenged Vindico's threatening glares.

"No money changing hands here. I don't gamble. This is just a friendly game, right?" Dan narrowed his eyes. "I have a beautiful woman waiting on me in the bed you've so kindly offered us, so I don't plan on staying down here long." His tone spoke volumes that never took on words.

She was his, and he'd not only fight for her, he'd kill over her. As he stared Arlo down, it was apparent to everyone in the room that it would be an extremely poor decision for Arlo to try and use all of his power, all of his money, and his international playboy lifestyle to woo Fionna Styler.

Everyone laughed, though Rainer saw realization settle in Arlo's eyes. It didn't seem to bother him for long. He slapped Vindico on the back with a nod of defeat.

"Don't blame you, mate. Let's just rack 'em up, have a go and a drink. We're all friends here, right, or hell…family." Arlo laughed as Lucas shook his head.

"Let's pour up something impressive," the Premier ordered. "I have a feeling Officer Vindico knows his way around a Scotch bottle."

Dan shrugged. "I've had a few in my day." His slight admission thoroughly delighted the Premier.

Rainer was in awe of how cool Dan was and how he never allowed anyone to see the hand he'd been dealt. His advice from the night before was precisely how he played the game of life. He waited and watched until he knew who held the aces, and then he strategically took them all for himself.

Rainer gave him an admiring smile. He slapped him on the back encouragingly. The gesture spoke volumes as well. There were very few people he allowed close enough to really know him, and over the past six months or so, with all that they'd been through, Rainer had become one of the closest.

Premier Nguyen moved to one of the four liquor cabinets situated on either side of the bar. Numerous taps of Australian beer were on the display along with mugs permanently casted to stay cold.

"How about I pour up glass after glass of, say, this fifty-year-old Dalmore, in exchange for the story of you and the Russian senate, Officer Vindico?" the Premier offered with a goading grin.

Vindico grimaced. "You drive a hard bargain, sir."

Rainer noted that he still hadn't accepted the bargained price for his story.

"I considered opening with a forty-year Macallan, but I want to hear the tale."

"It's really just a narrative of my temper getting the better of me. Like I told Lucas, it certainly wasn't my finest hour." Dan nodded his acceptance of the Scotch the Premier poured and handed to him.

"I know some men rattle off drivel about men losing their temper losing their worth, but I've found in my vast experience that men who are soft and easy are of very little value."

Rainer was handed a glass of the same Scotch.

"That Scotch costs more than you make in three months' time. Drink it slowly and enjoy it," Vindico instructed under his breath.

Rainer hesitated. He didn't want to cough and make a fool of himself.

"That's outstanding." Dan delighted the Premier. He gave a somewhat abbreviated version of what he'd informed the Russian Crown that he could do and what he'd called the governing board at large.

The Premier and his sons roared with laughter as more liquor was passed around. Everyone engaged in a round of eight-ball, and Dan hadn't been lying. He really wasn't very good. After another glass of Scotch, he pointed out somewhat bluntly that he'd never seen the point to the game.

"All right, mate," Ethan goaded him with a grin. "Now let's have the story of what brought on your bailing up the Russian governors. There's got to be more to it than you being mad as a cut snake."

"Not enough Scotch in those cabinets, gentlemen." His tone dared anyone else to ask.

Arlo laughed and shook his head. He shot a smirk at Lucas.

"Hey, Luke, maybe you should go lob in on your house guests. Make sure they got tucked in all right."

Lucas rolled his eyes. "If it's all right with you, I'd rather not think about it," he hemmed momentarily as he set up his next shot. "S'pose I should be thankful he makes her so happy."

Though he'd remained quiet and let Dan, Ethan, and Arlo keep up most of the evening's banter, Rainer stepped up on Logan's behalf. "There's probably a lot you should be thankful for on Logan's account," Rainer stated firmly.

Dan offered him a broad grin and an appreciative nod.

"I know, mate. It's just been such an odd night. You understand, I'm certain. I mean, marrying the Crown Governor's daughter, you must know thinking about my daughter on her honeymoon is a bit odd."

Arlo laughed as he continued his teasing. "I was telling Luke earlier he's been a dad for a few hours and he's already cranky about her and her husband having a naughty. Geez, mate, he married her. What more do you want?"

Everyone chuckled, but Lucas remained concerned.

"I just hope they married for love, and that he didn't take advantage of the fact that she needed a last name," he finally stated his concern out loud.

Fury quaked through Rainer's shield. Anyone who attacked Logan's character infuriated him more than if someone attacked his own. "Trust me, she adores him and he her. They've been together for years. He stuck by her through everything her mother did to her. He took care of her, and he always will."

Dan smoothed over Rainer's visible irritation. "Rainer and Logan have been best friends, quite literally, since birth. Adeline and Logan are one of those couples who are meant to be. They stuck together when the entire Realm tried to pull them apart. I have nothing but the utmost respect for both of them. So, if you're looking for someone wishing to come up with Logan's flaws, you've invited the wrong men to billiards."

"Oh, heavens no," Lucas backtracked. "Like I said, I'm pleased he makes her so happy. It has just been a rather exhausting night, I suppose. I'd retire for the evening and take my worries to my bedroll, but I was trying to let the newlyweds enjoy their evening in."

CHAPTER 20

BETTER EVERY TIME

LOGAN HAYDENSHIRE

Adeline calmed and after a few minutes sat up.

"Would you unzip me?" She pointed to the zipper that ran the length of the back of the dress.

"That *is* one of my favorite things to do." Logan was pleased that her energy had soothed after just a few minutes of being in his shield.

She laughed. The sparkle began to make a slight return to her eyes as he sat up and helped her off of the bed.

"So, you're not getting tired of it? I don't want to become one of those married couples who fight all the time and never has sex."

Though she was mostly teasing, Logan caught the slight concern in her voice. He worked the zipper down her dress.

"That may be the most absurd thing you've ever asked me. I'm still irritated you've worn clothes at all on our honeymoon. Eventually, I plan on taking you somewhere without our friends, and I'm not letting you get dressed for weeks."

She grinned at him. Her energy eased, and her tears dried completely.

Her laugh was one of the sweetest sounds in the world. Logan knew from the first time he'd told a lame joke at the academy lunch table, and she'd cracked up. It was one of his favorite things to hear. He'd never get enough.

"Do you think they think it's rude that you didn't go play pool?" she worried suddenly.

Logan shook his head. He couldn't help staring at her in the slight black bra with lace trim and at her backside in the matching lace panties.

"No, I don't, but I wouldn't really care if they did." He reached and brushed his hand along her exposed backside. He was simply unable not to touch her. She shivered slightly, and he ached for her.

"I want to be with you. This has been a hell of a night. I'm not certain what Lucas was thinking, but I'm not stowing you up in this ridiculous apartment alone after everything you've been through. That's not what marriage means to me. It means if you're going through something then so am I. And if anything at all has scared you, or worried you, or even just pissed you off, then I'm right here to hold you, cast you, and talk to you about it. I'm not down in the basement drinking and playing pool." He hadn't realized until that moment how much the invitation had annoyed him. "I'm your Shield."

"That's because you're the best husband ever." Adeline wrapped her arms around his neck, and he embraced her tenderly.

Exhaustion and worry plagued her rhythms, but he also felt her desire swirling there under the fear. He just had to dissolve the apprehension before he could access the need.

She stared up at him like she was afraid she'd hurt his feelings. "Is it really bad that I want to go home from my own honeymoon?"

Logan shook his head. He kissed her cheek before he pulled off his tie and unbuttoned his shirt. "No, baby. I get it. Believe me."

"I just want to put on one of your sweatshirts, lie on the couch, eat popcorn, and watch *The Godfather* while you hold me."

Logan winked at her. "I didn't pack *The Godfather*, but I get the impression that any of the waitstaff would gladly access it for you if you really want to watch it. How about I put you in one of my T-shirts, cuddle you up in the biggest bed I've ever seen, and hold you all night long."

"That sounds perfect." She slipped off her bra as she climbed up on the step stool to return to the bed. She didn't wait for the T-shirt. Logan certainly wasn't going to argue. He wasn't stupid. If she wanted to be held next to him in nothing but a slight pair of panties, he was only too happy to oblige.

He tried to push away the thoughts of just how quickly he could have her out of the panties. *Hell, I'll just pull them aside,* he thought savagely as he tossed his trousers over the back of a chair and crawled into bed beside her.

She immediately curled up on his chest. The motion made everything in his world perfect.

"Can I have a kiss, Mrs. Haydenshire?" He loved the way her energy leapt when he called her that. She grinned and nodded.

"I really love it when you call me that."

"I really love that it's your name."

Her energy spun in blissful spirals. The feeling overwhelmed him.

"Do you think Lucas is back from playing billiards yet?"

He tried hard to hide his grin as he kissed her forehead. "Why? You planning on getting loud, screaming out my name, banging the headboard against the wall, something like that?"

"Maybe," she finally managed to get out as she giggled at her own joke.

Logan gazed at her adoringly. He could never love anyone more. She stopped laughing as she met his longing gaze.

Just like the very first time he'd ever kissed her, Logan leaned without thinking, without pretense, and brushed his mouth across her lips.

He'd wanted to do it since he'd first set eyes on her at sub-freshman orientation. That night, after he'd thoroughly embarrassed himself at dinner with his family, he'd taken her out on the side porch, and they'd sat on the swing.

She'd been telling him how lovely his family was and how much she'd enjoyed the meal, and he'd kissed her. He couldn't wait any longer. He wanted to taste her and to feel her energy.

He wanted her to stop talking about his family and his mother's cooking. He'd wanted to claim her in some small way all for himself. From that first kiss, he'd known he'd never want anyone else.

Slowly coming back to the present, after a long, drawn-out,

intense kiss, Logan knew she was the sweetest thing to ever fill his mouth.

He let his hands slide down her slender neck. His right hand teased the delicate hollow of her throat and brushed over her right breast. He lifted it, massaged, and felt it swell all for him. He listened to her sweet moans as they filled his mouth.

With a quick study of her, he tried to determine if she was uncomfortable making love in her father's house. He retreated slightly, but she advanced.

A low, rumbling groan thundered from his chest as her eyes darkened from his kiss.

"Let's see here," he whispered as he began kissing down her neck and across her collarbone. "I believe my wife really likes it when I do this." He halted his mouth at her breasts and spun his tongue over her left nipple. It pebbled and throbbed.

He drew her breast into his mouth and sucked fervently as she moaned and panted. Her head fell back. The motion pushed her breast deeper in his mouth and showed her craving need. She trembled as her energy began to swirl in heated arcs all around him.

He moved to her other breast and repeated the process. Her moans were intoxicating.

While letting his hands caress what had just been sucked thoroughly, he moved down her stomach with his mouth.

"Quiet, baby," he soothed. "I don't think your dad wants to hear the sounds you make for me when I do this." He settled between her legs and pulled the thong to the side. He traced his tongue up her slit. The liquid form of her energy flowed readily into his mouth. He began his hungry feast.

"Yes." She quaked and moaned as he dipped his tongue between her folds repeatedly. He kept it up as she began to beg. "Logan, please..." She drove him wild.

"What, baby?" he urged her on as he slipped his fingers inside of her and continued to bathe her clit with his tongue.

"Please, please, I don't want to think anymore. I just want to be with you," she begged. She bucked under his touch and pled for distraction and relief. He was only too happy to meet her every need.

With a fervent growl, Logan moved his mouth back to her breasts as he worked her over with his hands. She writhed and did, in fact, call out his name repeatedly.

"That's it, baby. That's it." He pressed as he brought her nearer. Her body flushed. Her rhythms spiked hard and jagged. "Let it go for me, sweetheart. I'm right here. I want to hear you lose it all for me."

The tension and stress of the night had her fettered and bound. He worked diligently. He curved his fingers and stroked all the right places. He moved his mouth back to her clit and began to suck. She came undone suddenly. It unfurled around him as she cried out and convulsed. Her body writhed under his hands as she clawed at the sheets that probably cost more than he made in a month.

"I'm gonna set the cast, baby, and then I'm gonna make you forget everything but you and me."

Her eyes flashed in desire, and she groaned out her pleas. Logan couldn't quite hide his smirk. If Lucas was home, he surely heard that.

In a quick move, he removed the panties and threw them off the bed. He disposed with his boxers just as quickly. He casted her and then rubbed his cock between her folds.

"You ready for me? I need to be inside you." Her energy arced again, ready for more. She spread her legs farther for him. Her moans streamed from her in unending need.

Logan lowered his hips and slipped deeply into her. Her energy consumed him.

It was so different. It still shocked him. He'd never thought making love with her could be any better, ever. It was a pleasure he'd never deserve, and certainly nothing had ever felt as good as being inside her, but their wedding night had been utter, bliss-filled magic.

Knowing she was his, that she would never be with anyone else, and wearing the ring she'd slid on his finger as he'd made her his wife, was unbelievable ecstasy. Heaven couldn't be any better.

He'd been mistaken that night. It seemed to get better every time he had the pleasure. He began to pump her full of him while lying in her father's castle.

"That feels good, doesn't it, baby?" He thrust against her and moved her body in time with his.

"It's amazing," she gasped as she met his every push. Her body shuddered deliciously, and she clenched. He moaned. The feeling was all-consuming as he added to the intensity of his unrelenting thrusts.

She broke hard around him. She spiraled out of control and let him have all of her. She writhed, unable to do anything but feel the powerful orgasm rock through her in fevered waves.

"I'm not finished with you, baby. I want another one," he demanded, and she called out his name in a passion-filled plea for more. He pumped her full again.

Logan shuddered. Everything in him pulled tight as his release threatened imminent explosion. It gathered fiercely in his groin.

Through sheer determination, he held out until she broke again. His vision clouded. He collapsed on top of her and filled her with everything he was. He wanted her to have it all.

When he regained the ability to breathe, he slipped out of her and pulled her onto his chest.

A few blissful moments later, Adeline leaned and brushed a kiss across his jaw.

"Thank you," she whispered.

Logan laughed and kissed her cheek. "Trust me, the pleasure was all mine."

She tucked closer into his embrace. He pulled the sheets and blankets around her and cradled her tenderly.

"For bringing me here, helping me find my father, and for not going to play pool tonight."

Logan ran his hands up and down her back. He occasionally slipped them to her backside and reveled in her grin against him.

"Again, the pleasure was all mine."

Her energy relaxed into placid waves, and she let him soothe her to sleep.

CHAPTER 21

AN AUSTRALIAN OUTBACK MONSTER

RAINER LAWSON

Rainer and Dan trooped back out to the guesthouse a little after ten.

"So, this is odd." Dan gestured to the house and then to Rainer.

"Yeah, I know. This whole thing is odd. How did we all end up staying here, and I can't believe they thought Logan would play tonight." Rainer was still irritated by Lucas's concerns and Arlo's shock that Logan hadn't played.

They started up the stairs to the front door of the guesthouse. "I'm thinking marriage and lifetime commitment aren't really something they're accustomed to. They certainly don't know anything about being someone's Shield. None of them are Ioses Predilects."

Suddenly, they heard a harrowing shriek coming from the guesthouse.

"Fionna!" Dan threw the door open as he and Rainer summoned.

"Thank goodness!" Fionna gasped. She and Emily were dressed in tiny tank tops and their matching Angel short shorts. They were backed up in the corner of the living room clinging to each other, wide-eyed with terror.

"What's wrong?" Dan had the ladies casted in his shield instantly.

He held that with his left hand and swung his right out. He threw his radar scan around the room in a split second.

"That." Fionna shuddered as Rainer threw his own shield over himself and his boss. Dan turned to the opposite corner of the room.

Rainer dropped his shield and chuckled.

Dan's eyes landed on a rather large spider a moment later. He dropped his shield cast and shot a weak stream of electricity to kill the spider. Then, he turned a teasing grin on Fionna.

"It was huge. Kill it again!" she commanded frantically.

Emily moved and clung to Rainer.

Dan cracked up as he pulled Fionna to him. "I promise it's dead, sweetheart."

"This is one of those boyfriend things you just sort of get used to," Rainer explained.

Dan smirked. "You may have a decade on me in the boyfriend department, Lawson, but this I can do. Three sisters, remember?"

"It was huge," Emily fussed. Rainer grinned at her and nodded.

"And it kept making clicking noises." Fionna shuddered against Dan's chest.

"How long have you two been trapped in the corner?" He was trying very hard not to laugh outright.

"Just a few minutes," Fionna explained hesitantly. Her face glowed in her embarrassment. "We went in the kitchen to make popcorn. When we came back in here, it was just there. It chased us." She scowled and pointed to the remains of the bug with a convulsive shudder.

"It chased you?" Vindico choked back hysterical laughter. After he drew a deep breath and shook his head, he moved away from Fionna slightly. "Let me get rid of it." He grabbed a tissue and then threw away the spider's remains.

"I used to make Garrett come over and kill things for me, but if you want to be my boyfriend then you have to do it," Fionna declared, though her tone was kind. She was still blushing violently.

Dan winked at her. He sank onto one of the large couches in the room and pulled her into his lap. "I'll tell Garrett he can stop moonlighting as an exterminator." He gave her a cocky grin. "You know, if I'm there and you see a bug, I will valiantly step in to save you."

Emily gave Rainer a delighted grin as they watched.

"Aww, my knight in shining armor."

He laughed as he kissed her overly pink cheek. "Yeah, but if I'm not with you, then you have to wait on me to get there."

"Then you aren't allowed to leave," she informed him flirtatiously. "I'm taking you prisoner."

"On that note, maybe we should leave them alone," Rainer teased.

"No." Emily shook her head. "Fi can tie you up later. We were talking until we were so rudely interrupted by that Australian Outback monster." She gestured to the approximate location where the spider had been killed.

"I want to hear about pool," Fionna urged.

Rainer sank down on the sofa opposite Dan and Fionna. Emily curled up beside him.

"Monster, spider, whatever..." he teased Emily over her vernacular.

Fionna came to Emily's aid. "It was huge, and gross, and clicky." She shuddered again. It was very clear from his boss's expression that he found her reaction to be completely adorable.

"Oh, Garrett says to tell you two hi," Fionna remembered suddenly.

"When did you talk to Garrett?" Rainer quizzed.

"Fi's been talking to him since we got here. He was checking on her and on Adeline."

Rainer caught the annoyed grimace that shadowed Dan's face, but he wiped it away before Fionna turned back to gaze at him. "What did they say about Adeline? Tell us everything."

Dan smiled at her and brushed her hair away from her face. "All in all, I'd say Lucas is handling this pretty well. He's envious of Adeline's relationship with Logan, but he'll get over it."

Rainer nodded. The fact that Lucas was jealous of Logan hadn't occurred to him. It seemed obvious when it was pointed out.

"I can't believe Adeline is a princess for real, and she's staying in a palace. I know she's freaking out." Emily's tone was laced with worry.

"Logan's got her. He'll take care of her. He always does," Rainer soothed.

"Yeah, and don't ever tell him I said this, but my big brother is kind of awesome."

"There's a gym here in the guesthouse," Fionna informed Dan with a wry smile.

"Really?" He visibly tried to hide how much the information pleased him.

"Yes, and I'll even work out with you tomorrow, after you tell me all of this business about the Russian Senate or whatever," she bargained.

Rainer's laughed. "That story is clearly worth a fortune, man. You should sell the rights."

Dan forced a chuckle and nodded his agreement. "I told you I'd gotten suspended and that Governor Haydenshire mandated this vacation."

"Yes." Fionna was still grinning at him. "And I intend to thank him profusely the next time I see him. I may get him a gift, but you never told me why you got suspended."

"How about I tell you later, okay?"

Rainer sensed that the matter wasn't open for discussion.

"Okay." Fionna studied him closely.

"So, are we supposed to stay out here all day tomorrow, or can we go out and do stuff?" Emily tried to smooth over the awkward silence.

"I think Lucas wants to show us Sydney's hot spots." Rainer sighed. "He plans on us touring the Opera House and eating there tomorrow night if we want to go."

Emily nodded. "I guess it's good to be friends with a princess."

"I wouldn't call her that if I were you." Rainer shuddered as he considered Adeline's reaction to being called a princess.

"Aww, look, after all these years, I made you sensitive." Emily applauded, and Dan cracked up at Rainer's scowl.

They chatted a little more and took another tour of the house.

Rainer and Dan checked under couches and in the kitchen cabinets to make certain the spider had no friends, per the ladies' request.

Fionna yawned for the third time, and Dan grinned at her. "How about I take you to bed, baby doll?" Fionna waved good night to Emily and Rainer.

"Only after…" She halted and turned back to Vindico from the bottom step. She shot him an extremely naughty smirk. Dan appeared to try to decide how dirty to tease her in front of Rainer and Emily who were already laughing.

"…I check our room thoroughly for spiders?" he joked.

"Yeah, that too."

"I'll be right there." He gestured for Rainer to remain downstairs.

Rainer kissed Emily's forehead and told her he'd be up in a minute. He let his right hand glide over her backside as she climbed the stairs. He enjoyed watching her blush.

"All right, how do you want to work the bathroom thing? I may not mind her lying out topless, but there are a few things I have no intention of letting anyone else see."

Rainer tried not to be offended as he huffed, "Yeah, well, I have a few things I feel the same way about. Just lock both doors if you're in there. We'll do the same, and if you want to shower…" Rainer hemmed over the word together. He knew perfectly well that a great deal of his boss's threats came from the possibility of him and Fionna being interrupted, and the shower was clearly designed to be used by couples. "…at the same time," he finally managed, "then we'll hang out down here."

"And we'll do the same," Vindico agreed.

With an uncomfortable nod, Rainer headed upstairs. Dan checked to make certain the front door was locked and pulled the light from the lamps.

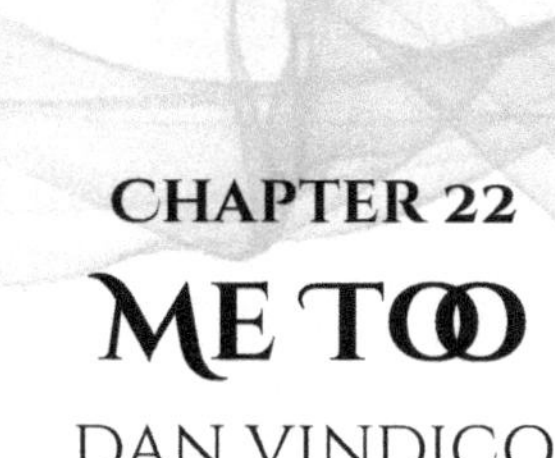

CHAPTER 22

ME TOO

DAN VINDICO

Weary irritability tensed in his shield as Dan turned out the lights and headed slowly up the stairs of the Premier's guesthouse. He began unbuttoning his shirt while thoughts of how they'd all ended up staying there churned in his head. They were jumbled with irritation that Garrett Haydenshire seemed to have a large claim on Fionna, and his annoyance that Rainer and Emily were going to be staying in a room so close by.

He wanted her wild, raw, and loud. He needed her without fear that someone might hear her when he forced those delicious sounds she made only for him from the depths of her soul. He wanted her moans to rattle the heavens and scandalize the saints.

He debated what to tell her about what he'd done and said to the Russian governing board. He knew she was going to ask again. He'd vowed to himself that he was going to let her in and let her know him like he'd never let anyone else, not in the last ten years anyway. He had to. He had to have her trust or when that stupid plane came to carry them back to his own version of hell, she would walk away.

Arlo informing his brothers that he'd be up Fionna like a rat up a drain pipe served to make Dan want to sink his fists into someone or something repeatedly, preferably Arlo, who as far as he was concerned *was* a rat.

Dan knocked on his and Fionna's bedroom door. It felt odd. He awaited a response. He didn't want to just walk in on her, even though they'd grown so intimate and so intoxicatingly close in the last few days. He knew she was feeling a little unsure of herself staying in a strange guesthouse with Rainer and Emily.

Dan drew a deep breath and tried to soothe his own energy. His annoyance with Arlo won out over all of the other aggravations at the moment. He was furious that Arlo had frightened Fionna. And he didn't appreciate his choice of words even if he wasn't aware he was being eavesdropped on. It was one thing to speak admiringly about a woman's looks. It was another thing entirely to make such a crude comment about the woman Dan was falling more in love with each moment he spent in her presence.

The thought paralyzed him. His heart raced. He forced himself to breathe as Fionna called for him to come in. He needed to say it to her eventually if he was going to keep this going and most certainly if he was going to force her to never share their relationship with anyone outside of their families and Iodex.

After deciding that thinking the word was a decent first step, Dan willed repose as he eased the door open.

Fionna was in the bathroom. She was standing in her bra and panties with her hair pulled up in a topknot. She was washing her face.

Dan stared at her with hunger and need pooling in his blood. He allowed himself a long moment. She was absolutely breathtaking. Guilt settled in the pit of his stomach as he acknowledged the fact that he wanted her desperately.

He wanted to drown their long, exhaustive day in the delicious feelings and energy that swirled so copiously within her. He wanted her selfishly and voraciously. He wanted to own her.

She splashed water on her face. A few water droplets made their way down her chest, and Dan fought back a growl as he moved to her. She dried her face and turned to her toiletry bag situated on the counter. She took out another one of those dark brown glass jars and her toothbrush.

Dan didn't want to think anymore. He just wanted her, wanted to taste her, and feel her, and make her feel him. He wanted to pound those sweet lips she'd waxed bare for him, deep and dirty just how she liked it.

He startled her as he entered the bathroom and wrapped his hands around her waist. He kept her back to his chest as he brushed kisses down her neck. He tucked the curves of her luscious ass against his hard-on and watched her eyes flash and darken in the mirror as her torso tensed in anticipation. He reversed course back toward her ear. "Do you feel what you do to me, baby doll? Do you feel how hard you make me?"

With a quick move, he turned her so she was facing him. He braced his hands on the counter and caged her between his body and the bathroom vanity. She gave him a naughty grin as she began to pant.

"I thought I was supposed to be taking *you* prisoner." Her voice was low and throaty as he fed the desire swirling inside of her.

Dan let an aching moan echo from his chest into her mouth as he crushed it to his lips. With a hungry gaze, he gave her a cocky grin when he pulled away. He lifted her backside up onto the sink and wrapped her legs around his waist. He wasn't gentle as he pressed his throbbing erection against her lips, barely covered by the thin cotton G-string she was wearing.

"Another plus of letting me be your boyfriend," he drawled as he unhooked her bra with one hand, "is that if you should need them, I have numerous sets of handcuffs." He pulsed against her as he made his offer.

Dan let the erotic images of her naked and handcuffed to his bed as he drove her wild settle firmly in his mind. Her eyes flashed as she moaned. She was intrigued.

Her rhythms pulsed, but fear flowed through her. He decided to make the offer again later, when he'd made her feel more secure, more settled in their relationship, and when she was ready to give herself and her pleasure over to him fully.

Her heart thundered against his chest as he hoisted his shirt off and then removed the undershirt he had on. Her blood rushed against his length as her lips swelled with heat and desire.

She braided her hands in his hair and pulled his mouth back to hers. He angled his head and consumed her lips with greed. He kneaded her backside and pulled her into him as he gave a thrust. He mimicked taking her as he watched the thin cotton between her legs turn translucent. Her body eagerly prepared her for him.

She bucked against him and pushed him back. She landed on her feet as she gracefully slid off the counter and took his hand.

"Come here," the cooed command fell heavily from her kiss-swollen lips. He followed her and let her take the lead for the moment. That was what she clearly wanted.

She crawled onto the large bed and situated herself on the edge. She folded her legs underneath her and sat on her adorable feet. Grabbing two of his belt loops, she jerked him forward.

He ran his hands over her breasts and spun his thumbs over her nipples. They were swollen, pert, and vying for his attention. He rewarded their effort.

With a few quick movements, she unbuckled his belt and unzipped his pants. Then, with a great deal of finesse, she shoved his pants and boxers down, and located what she was craving.

He watched her ardently as an excited moan escaped her lungs. She lightly traced her fingers up his length, and he prayed she was about to do what he was fairly certain was on her mind. Every cell in his body quaked with need as she licked her lips seductively.

"You thirsty, baby?" He laced his right hand in her hair and pulled it tight around his fist. "I want you thirsty for my cum. I want to see it in your mouth. Suck it like my good girl," he demanded.

Her rhythms spiked wildly. Her entire body tensed as she gave him a sultry grin and then let her tongue dance from his sac to his head. A hungry growl thundered from his chest, and his head fell back from the exquisite sensation.

A moment later, she drowned him in her mouth. She sucked him hard and moaned against him as she drew all of the tension, irritation, confusion, and shame from his body. She filled him with her healing love. Dan carefully guided her head to his strain. He wanted her to take more.

She arched her back and brushed his sac with her breasts. A

deafening, guttural growl thundered from him. She pulled back with a slight smile.

"Shh," she reminded him before she began her work again. Her energy flooded around him as her arousal increased with what she was giving him.

He could feel it. He could feel what she wanted. He felt the rebellion and the ardent desire. He felt the thirst. He leaked into her mouth, and her satisfied moan made him shudder and groan in elation.

He didn't want her to do anything she didn't want to do, but it was there. He could feel it, and the need built readily as she worked. She continued to suck and lick him. She spun her tongue hypnotically over his head, and then flicked it deliciously over his shaft.

He cupped her cheek tenderly and watched her pull him into her mouth more deeply. His head slipped to her throat, and he was certain he'd died and gone to heaven.

"You're gonna drink it like a good girl for me, aren't you, baby doll? You're about to make me explode, and you're gonna swallow it all," he warned her but was still unable to believe how utterly incredible it was that she wanted to drink him.

It was indescribable perfection. She drowned him in her mouth and pulled. Her cheeks hollowed and she sucked hard. He was unable to stop the release as he flooded her mouth. She continued to draw from him as she swallowed him down, and he convulsed from the delicious sight.

When she'd sucked him dry, she pulled away with a seductive smile as he panted and his muscles quaked from his release.

"You are the most incredible women in the world. Now, I want you to lie back, honey, 'cause I'm about to take good care of you." Her satisfaction turned instantly back into voracious hunger.

He threw the many varied throw pillows off of the bed and situated her against the ones he left.

He'd show her exactly what he could do with his Double-Predilected energy bands. *You haven't been able to do this with anyone but Amelia.* His brain cleared from his first release enough to form the badgering taunt, but Dan knew he could. When a Double-

Predilect was with the right person, they could come more than once.

"That's what you need, isn't it, baby doll?" he urged as she let her head fall back and moaned in desperation. "Spread your legs for me. Show me where you're hot and wet. Show me where that needy little ache is so I can fuck it out of you."

She bucked as she did as she was told. He grasped one of her calves and pulled her legs open around him. Dan remained up on his knees over her. He held her legs apart and traced his index finger tenderly over her mound and then down her slit as her breath stuttered deliciously.

He caught the thinnest part of the panties and hooked his finger through the fabric. With one quick move, he jerked it off of her as she cried out loudly.

He spread her legs farther and traced delicate patterns up the most sensitive parts of her inner thighs and then over her swollen lips. "Is it right here, baby?"

"Oh, yes. Please," she begged and bucked. She grabbed his hand as he traced and tried to force the issue. Her desperation drove him wild.

"All right, honey. Just relax. I'm gonna give you what you want, but not yet."

She begged and called out his name in heated need.

He leaned down and separated her slightly as she panted and her body flushed. He blew cold breath into the fevered heart of her and watched as hot sex dripped from her lips. He slowly dragged his tongue over her. Her energy seeped from her slit. He listened as she pled for more.

He turned his head and sucked her right lip and then her left. He dipped his tongue between her folds and lapped over her. He moved closer to her clit with each and every pass.

She went wild. Her energy swirled around him in erotic spirals of ecstasy. He bathed her with his tongue until he reached the delicate pearl that was throbbing so hungry for his tongue. He held her lips apart and teased her clit. She trembled. He blew cold air over her and watched it pulsate.

"That's my good girl. That aches, doesn't it, baby? It's sensitive for me." He tenderly touched it with his index finger. She panted and shook. Then he leaned and began to suck and drown it with his tongue. She broke and filled his mouth with all of her. He drank her dry.

He let her orgasm wash through her as he dipped his fingers between her folds as she tried to regain the ability to breathe.

That was it. He was ready. He'd recovered fully and wanted more of her. Her body, her energy, his longing to join her, and his love had restored him.

He continued to spin his fingers over the spots that made her scream out his name, and he leaned closer to her.

"I'm going to cast you, and then I'm going to take you hard, baby doll. I want some more. I'll never get enough of you."

Her eyes flashed open in delighted shock as she continued to writhe under his touch. Her low moan urged him on.

He pulled his hand away and used her energy to summon as he added his own and then sealed her off. He soothed her as he went and made certain that she felt nothing but pleasure at his hands.

Deep carnal need overtook him as he lay out over her and plunged her throbbing depths without warning. Her tight little pussy trembled from his sheer size as he filled her to overflowing. Her muscles cinched around him as he growled in heated need and ground his body into hers.

He pumped her full. He opened her to his hilt and drove her hard.

"That's my good girl. Open up for me and take a little more. You're all mine. Every inch belongs to me," he commanded as she called out his name like a prayer she needed answered.

Her body begged for more. Her energy consumed him as he took all of her for himself. The ecstasy was intoxicating. He gripped her waist as her calves fell over his forearms. He pounded rough and ragged. She clawed at the bedsheets.

Dan felt whole, complete, and healed as he drove into her. She arched her back and swelled around him. Her luscious tits swayed in a hypnotic dance to the rhythm of his force. The first hungry pulse of her release seared through him, and he buried himself inside her.

They came together. He filled her full yet again, and he reveled in their energy mixing in their releases deep inside of her. He fell to his side, panted, and gasped for breath as he pulled her on his chest and held her tight. She continued to tremble and pant.

When she regained the ability to breathe normally, she smiled against his chest. "Okay, that was…"

"Not something that's happened to me in a very, very long time." He was awash in the ecstasy of it all and in the remembrances.

"Oh." Fionna nodded her understanding. Her adoring grin told him that she was both honored and not in any way jealous of Amelia.

"Fi, honey, I told you, everything about you, everything about us together, is new and different for me. I just hope you think it's as incredible as I do."

She was quiet and introspective for a long moment. "I really do."

He cradled her tenderly and wrapped her up in the sheets and blankets on the vast bed and then in his body.

"Can I ask you something?" she whispered in the darkness. The tantric spirals of erotic energy still filled the air around them. They watched the light as it danced.

"Anything." The exhaustion of his double release began to take hold. He'd forgotten how well he always slept after that happened.

"I know we're not ready to say it yet…"—she hesitated, and he willed his body not to recoil—"and I know we kind of talked about it before, but it's so much stronger now. I hope this doesn't freak you out, but I feel it even stronger now when we're together. It feels incredible." Her tentative energy bordered on panic.

He tried to soothe her, but he had very little left to offer her.

"I guess I was just wondering if it would be all right if, when I'm ready to say it, I tell you, even if you're not ready yet. And you don't ever have to be okay with saying it. I completely understand."

Dan was certain he was being rent in two. His heart ached and stuttered. "I do feel it. I swear. I want to say it. I just don't think I can yet," he choked.

"I know." She casted him. The intoxicating, healing warmth of her flowed through his veins. "I told you, I know the last person you said that to was Amelia, and I know you still love her. I want you to always,

always love her," she insisted as he tried to swallow back the boulder in his throat.

"But I've never said that to anyone. I've never felt this way about anyone before, so I guess I just wanted to tell you that."

Fear seized her rhythms. Fear that he would reject her, fear that he didn't believe that she understood his feelings for Amelia, fear that she was going to give him her heart and he was going to shatter it.

"How about this…" Dan was still grappling with emotion that had him in a chokehold. "When I was a teenager,"—he was embarrassed to share this story, but he wanted her to know him, and she listened intently—"my dad would take Kara and me to school, and my mom would take Meredith and Lindley. Anyway, we would drop Kara off at school and then Dad and I would drive to Langley before he went to the Senate. So, we would talk all the way there. When I would get out of the car, Dad would tell me that he loved me, but I didn't want to say that back right there. Amelia, Will, and Garrett would always be waiting on me at the drop-off. I know I was a prick." He took solace in her giggle.

"Anyway, when Dad figured out that I didn't want to say it, he came up with a plan. Dad would say, 'the Panthers might make the playoffs this year,' and then I would say 'never happen.'" He laughed at his own story. He hadn't thought about that in years, and he had no idea why he wanted her to know that.

Fionna smiled against him and kissed his chest. His heart beat disjointedly for a moment.

She gazed up at him in the moonlit room and the light of their passionate love. "Okay, but I kind of really want to say the words, so how about if when I'm ready, I say it, and then whenever you're ready, and you don't have to be ready when I'm ready, maybe you could just say 'me too,'" she offered hopefully.

Every muscle in his body clenched in terror, desperation, and in all-consuming emotion for the woman he held in his arms.

"Fi," he whispered as she gazed at him, "me too."

CHAPTER 23

COFFEE AND CONVERSATION

LOGAN HAYDENSHIRE

A smile formed on his lips, but Logan kept his eyes closed. He reveled in Adeline curled up tenderly beside him sleeping peacefully.

He wondered what the chances were that Lucas had the necessary equipment to make her some coffee without the aid of anyone in uniform. Logan shuddered at the thought of ordering someone to make them coffee.

He didn't want to awaken Adeline. The day before had thoroughly worn her out, and she looked so tiny and fragile lying in his long, muscular arms.

He wanted her to sleep. He wanted her mind and her body to rest. The next few weeks weren't going to be easy. The trial was coming up, and Lucas would be visiting.

Logan slid out from under her as gently as he was able. He covered her and sealed heat into the fibers of the blankets as he nestled them around her.

She'd pulled on one of his T-shirts but wasn't wearing anything else. The thought had Logan's groin on high alert as he moved silently to the bathroom.

When he returned, she was still sleeping soundly. He pulled on a pair of jeans and eased the door open and closed it silently as he exited.

He was pleased when he made it all the way to the kitchen without running into a maid, butler, or Lucas.

He began poking around. There was a canister of coffee by the extremely elaborate coffee maker, but he needed to find the filters and spoons.

After pausing a moment to listen, he didn't hear anyone else in the apartment, so he began opening drawers. He located the filters in the drawer under the coffeemaker, and then found the silverware a few drawers down.

As he studied the appliance, Logan tried to figure out how to make a simple cup of coffee in the dual spout contraption. He decided to just cast it and make it work according to his own design.

"Logan." He heard his name and spun around to find Lucas staring him down. He was wearing a pair of monogrammed silk pajamas and matching slippers, the kind that Logan and his brothers would beat a guy up for wearing. He tried not to chuckle at the thought.

"Oh, sorry. I was just trying to make Ad some coffee." He held up the spoon and gestured to the coffeemaker.

Lucas nodded and gave Logan a forced smile. "I can get Marta to do that for her."

"I'm sure." Logan nodded. "I just usually make her coffee for her so I thought I would." He studied Adeline's father. The resemblance still overwhelmed him.

"Where is Adeline?" There was more than a hint of inquisition in his tone.

"She's still sleeping. Yesterday was pretty tough for her."

"I'm sure," Lucas quoted back the phrase. "Do her friends call her Ad or just you?"

"Only I do that. No one else does."

"Did you sleep all right?" Lucas's next question held a note of disdain.

Logan tried not to smirk as he assumed he knew the reason for the discomfort. "Yes, sir. We slept great. Thank you again for letting us stay here."

"Of course. She's my daughter. I hope you'll visit often and stay here whenever you're in the country."

Uncomfortable silence filled the room, and Logan tried to think of what to say. "Would it be all right if I…?" He gestured back to the coffeemaker.

"Oh, certainly."

With a smile, Logan moved back to the machine and began to discern how it worked without the use of his cast.

"She feels very safe with you." Lucas seemed intrigued with Logan's work. While he considered, he started to speak but then Lucas added, "Her energy soothes as soon as you enter the room. She seems delighted when you're near her, but she's afraid when you aren't."

"Well,"—Logan forced the basket for the coffee filter out of the maker by sheer strength—"I don't want her to be afraid when I'm not there, but shouldn't her energy soothe when I'm near her? I'm her husband."

As he made his statement, Logan considered how Lucas was able to read Adeline so well. To his knowledge, her father had never even come in contact with her skin.

He thought of his own parents with a sting of homesickness. Because they were both Gifted, Logan and all of his siblings held a mix of both of their energies, but Candy wasn't Gifted.

Gifted DNA would always be dominant, especially from a bloodline as strong as the Nguyens'. Adeline's Gifted energies and Lucas's would be an almost perfect match. That was why Logan felt such a strong reading when he'd shaken Ethan's hand at his father's inaugural ball. Her uncle's rhythms were also very close to Adeline's.

As Logan began brewing a pot of coffee, he turned to the sink to rinse off the spoon he'd used.

"You don't have to do dishes," Lucas scoffed. Logan shrugged as he laid the spoon in the basin. "Might I ask that you have a cup of coffee with me just until Adeline awakens? I'd really like to know you better as well."

Having coffee with his father-in-law hadn't been his plan, but he saw no other polite options.

"Uh sure, just let me go check on her. I need to make sure she didn't wake up when I left and isn't wondering where I am."

Lucas nodded as Logan made his exit and headed back up the stairs.

He eased open the bedroom door and scooted inside. Adeline was still sound asleep, tucked up in the huge bed and clinging to the pillow Logan had slept on.

With a tender smile, he moved to her. He sealed more heat into the fibers of the coverings. As he brushed a hesitant kiss across her cheek, he added his own soothing energies to hers. The tension and terror of the day before had exhausted her, and he stared at her adoringly as he watched her body try to recuperate.

An idea formed in his mind as his eyes landed on a stack of expensive stationery situated neatly on a desk in the corner of the room. He pulled a sheet of the paper and one of the pens from the desk.

Dear Mrs. Haydenshire,

Lucas asked me to have coffee with him downstairs. Text me when you get up. I'll bring up your coffee and give you your good morning kiss.

I love you so much,

Logan

With that, he grabbed his cell, stowed it in his pocket, pulled on a T-shirt, and set Adeline's cell phone on top of the note on the pillow beside her.

When he returned to the kitchen, Logan found it empty. Some form of ridiculous hopefulness tried to emerge in his gut. Perhaps Lucas had changed his mind, and he could return to bed with his wife and be left alone.

He spun and almost ran into a maid whom he assumed must be Marta.

"Mr. Haydenshire, sir, the prince asked to have your coffee on the balcony. I've arranged everything."

She gestured through what appeared to be a library, onto a balcony that overlooked the Nguyens' property. He noted Lucas seated at a wrought iron table, glancing at a Gifted newspaper. There was a tray on the table that held a silver coffee service. The table was set with several delicate china coffee cups. There were also platters with fruit and pastries.

With a sigh, he headed toward the small balcony. *Apparently, even coffee is an event here.*

"Thank you." He turned back to the maid and remembered his manners with a smile.

"Certainly, sir." The woman curtsied. Logan cringed. "Please there's not need to bow to me."

Confusion tensed her brow as she nodded.

Logan slid out the glass door and offered a forced smile to Lucas.

"I didn't know I needed to dress up for coffee," he offered as a slight apology.

"You're fine. Have a seat. How do you take your coffee?" Lucas turned back into the consummate host. "Shall I pour Adeline a cup?"

"She's still asleep…sir." Logan added cream and sugar to the warm, soothing liquid. He tried to hide his slight disdain that the cup held approximately two sips of coffee.

"I'm so pleased that she's comfortable," Lucas commented as he set the paper down on an adjoining table.

Logan smiled and nodded as he drew a sip. He'd had coffee every morning that they'd been in Australia. It was quite good. Adeline loved it, and Logan had purchased a fair amount to take back to the States.

"Although, I get the impression she's comfortable anywhere that you are," Lucas stated pointedly.

As this was the second time Lucas had made a remark along those lines, it didn't take long for Logan's law enforcement training to kick in with the caffeine. "I assume that bothers you."

"No, not at all. I just hope someday she'll be comfortable with me."

"She's been hurt a great deal, mostly at the hands of her mother. She's very guarded. She doesn't let people in easily. You're going to have to give her some time."

"Yes, I'm sure. I suppose patience never was my virtue." Before Logan could respond, Lucas continued, "Tell me how you two met."

Logan wondered which story he wanted to tell.

"Well,"—he accepted a fruit pastry as Lucas offered it—"we saw each other at sub-freshman orientation at Venton Academy just before we both started our Gifted educations."

Lucas seemed to soak up the story.

"Just ask Rainer. I was sold right then and there, but I took some time and got to know her. She was different, serious, guarded, like I said. A lot of the kids we went to school with weren't particularly kind. I asked her to eat lunch with Rainer and me and a few of our friends. The next year, when Emily started, they got really close. I worked up the courage to ask her out, and I guess the rest is history."

"Yes, I was informed last night that you and Rainer Lawson have been friends, I believe the words used were, quite literally since birth." Logan grinned. "He's very protective of you as well," Lucas narrowed his eyes as he studied Logan.

While thinking that Lucas seemed to enjoy pointing out the obvious, Logan shrugged. "He's my best friend. We're both Ioses Preds. We've been through it all together. He's lived on our farm since he was fourteen. We shared a room. He's my partner at Iodex. He's marrying my sister, and truthfully, he's the best guy I've ever known. If you pick a fight with one of us, you're getting both," he concluded firmly.

"And Rainer's father was the American Crown before your father, correct?"

"Yes, sir. Regis Carrington became Crown after Rainer's dad was assassinated, but yeah." He nodded but somehow felt that none of his answers were deemed correct.

"And Rainer was all right with your dating Adeline, even though she didn't have a name or a crest?"

"Hell yeah," Logan scoffed. "Of course. If she was who I wanted, he was on board. He defended her long before we ever even started dating officially. Like I told you, some of the idiots we went to school with weren't very nice."

"What can I do?" Lucas finally leaned across the table to make his plea. "I want to have a relationship with Adeline. I want to make up for not being there when she was growing up, but all she seems to want is you." Irritation perforated his tone.

Logan nodded and drew a deep breath. "I really appreciate all you've already agreed to do for her, with the trial and everything, and so does she. You're going to have to give her some time, sir. By the time we got in that limo last night, she'd convinced herself you were going to reject her instantly, that you would be a male version of her mother.

"She was terrified. She didn't want to be hurt again, and quite honestly, if we hadn't needed you so badly to testify at the trial so she can keep doing what she loves, I wouldn't have ever agreed to put her through even the potential of being rejected again. I just love her too much for that," Logan choked over the emotion that had come on him suddenly. "But this,"—Logan lifted the china coffee cup—"this just isn't her, sir, and I know, had things been different, it might have been. She's uncomfortable with seven-course meals, and maids, and butlers, and quite honestly, your family makes her nervous.

"She didn't know how to react, so she clung to me. Because, although I've certainly screwed up a few times on her account, she knows I love her. She knows I would never reject her and that nothing makes me happier than being with her. It doesn't even matter what we're doing.

"So, I guess what I'm trying to say is that you're going to have to prove yourself. Prove to her that you won't shut her out when the press has a field day with the story. Prove to her that you're going to be there when she needs you." Logan slumped back in his chair and hoped he'd helped Lucas understand Adeline at least a little.

Lucas was quiet for several minutes as he considered Logan's words. "I need your help then. I have no intention of rejecting her, ever. I was certainly shocked to meet her, obviously, but I'm also thrilled. I want to be a part of her life, but she'll never let me in unless you do. That much is painfully obvious."

Logan stared Lucas down. "No, she won't," he agreed, "and don't ever think that I don't think about that whenever I decide to let someone in. I'm certain being an Ioses Predilect plays into this, but I'll tell you right now I'm extremely protective of her. She's been hurt more than anyone ever should be, and I won't allow it to ever happen again.

"She is everything to me. I love her more than anything in the world, and I've worked patiently and diligently to prove that to her over the past six years. Convincing her that I love her wasn't easy, but it can be done. You're just going to have to play on her terms. Let her decide to let you in, and if you're concerned that something might make her back away, ask me. I want you to have a relationship with her. I will help you, but you can't throw money at her or buy her things to prove your love. Believe me, I tried that gig years ago."

With that, Logan's cell chirped, and he smiled involuntarily as he pulled it from his pocket.

'I'm up, and I miss you'

was Adeline's text.

His smile widened. He missed her, too.

"She wants you to come back upstairs," Lucas stated knowingly as Logan nodded. Her father's annoyance wasn't well hidden. "Will she come down and join us?" Lucas stood. "Here, we could take the tray up to your room."

"Oh, most definitely not." Logan shook his head. "I worked hard to make certain she felt safe in that room last night. She's wearing one of my T-shirts that she sleeps in at home, and she won't want you to see her in her pajamas without makeup and the whole deal. She'll come down here for coffee if she knows you want her to, but you'll have to give her a few minutes. She probably won't say much, but she'll listen."

Lucas nodded his defeat, and Logan tried to prove that he was helping Lucas and not hindering his efforts.

"Hey, at some point, maybe you could invite Emily to come over and hang out with us. Em's one of her favorite people in the entire world. They adore each other." Logan tried to think of ways to get Adeline to open up for her father. He hesitated but then went on with, "She doesn't have to explain how she feels to Emily. She's a Receiver. She always knows and she makes Adeline feel better."

"Any of Adeline's friends are welcome here anytime," Lucas

assured. "I was hoping to join you and your friends today wherever you'd like to go, get to know all of you better. I think Arlo would like to come along as well."

"That would probably be good, but let me go get her up. We'll be back down here in a little while. Just give her some time."

"I'll be waiting," Lucas vowed, though, true to his word, patience didn't seem to be his forte. He sighed. "How does she like her coffee? You could take some to her. I got the impression when you were stalking around my kitchen that she must like it when she first wakes up. I'll have Marta make it before you awaken tomorrow."

"Sorry about that. Taking care of her is kind of my job, and I love doing it. I didn't mean to wake you up."

"You didn't," Lucas assured. "I didn't sleep very well."

Logan nodded his understanding. "She likes her coffee with lots of cream and no sugar. She's sweet enough." The end of the statement fell involuntarily from Logan's lips. He always said it to her whenever he fixed her a mug.

Lucas gave him a genuine smile. "You must say that to her."

Logan nodded and chuckled.

"I'll do this right," Lucas promised as Logan poured Adeline's coffee and casted it to stay warm. "I'll play by your rules. You just set the bounds. I'll do anything you say, but I want a relationship with my daughter." Lucas's vow came with more than a note of a command. He didn't look particularly happy about Logan's instructions on Adeline's behalf, but he seemed to realize he didn't have much choice.

"I'll tell her that," Logan offered.

Lucas gestured back toward the house. "I'll wait here for both of you."

CHAPTER 24

HER FATHER'S DAUGHTER

Adeline was pacing when Logan opened the bedroom door.

"Sorry, baby. I was talking to Lucas." He set the cup and saucer on the nearest piece of furniture and wrapped her up in his arms. She clung to him.

"About me." She sighed.

Logan kissed the top of her head. "He really wants to get to know you. He really wants to be a part of your life, and I think he got the impression last night that he's going to have to go through me to do that."

Adeline nodded against Logan's chest. "He does," she whispered.

Logan squeezed her tighter. "I know, and I won't let you down."

Adeline pulled away from him slightly. "I know you won't. You never have." Her beautiful smile returned.

"Lucas was hoping you'd come downstairs and have coffee with him." Logan concentrated and slipped his hands up the T-shirt she was wearing. He caressed her backside and then laid his hands on her skin. He wanted to read her.

"You're coming too, right?"

"Of course."

"Okay." Adeline drew an audible breath. "What am I supposed to wear for coffee here?"

"I had coffee with him in this, so why don't you just put on some jeans, or sweats, or something?"

If she agreed, then they were off to a good start. If she put on a dress or skirt and did the full-blown makeup routine, then it was going to be a long, drawn-out process of getting her to let her father know her.

"He's wearing pajamas," Logan added hopefully.

"Are you sure?"

"He's your father. You're beautiful no matter what you're wearing."

"Only to you."

"No, not only to me. I'm pretty sure your dad thinks you're almost as beautiful as I do."

After drawing on deep resolve, Adeline nodded. "Okay, I guess." She located a pair of jeans. She did pull her brush through her hair and put on a matching set of bra and panties, then she grimaced as she took in her face in the mirror. Logan bit back his irritation as she did this, but a few minutes later, she picked up the coffee cup and waited on him to lead her down the stairs.

Lucas looked delighted when Logan pulled Adeline's chair out for her and seated himself beside her. He held her left hand so she could drink her coffee but made certain she could draw from him.

Lucas noted Adeline's tight grasp on Logan as he took in the Ioses T-shirt that was much too big for her, but he didn't comment.

"Is there anything in particular you'd like to do today? I'd love to show you some of Sydney's highlights." Lucas offered Adeline the trays of pastries and fruits.

"Oh, it doesn't matter to me," she assured quickly. Logan squeezed her hand and winked at her as she glanced at him. "Whatever you want to do is fine."

Lucas smiled and nodded. "Tell me what you like to do at home for fun, and I'll see what we can find here."

Logan gave him a slight nod. It was a good approach.

"I work as much as I can, and there's a lot of studying because I want to be really good at what I do. When I'm not doing that, I just like hanging out with Logan or Rainer and Emily."

She pulled a tiny bite of a strawberry muffin off and ate it quickly.

Logan and Lucas were both aware that she hadn't really given much away, but Lucas wasn't giving up.

"Okay," he replied. "What do you do when you're alone?"

Logan felt genuinely sorry for Lucas. He had a great deal to learn.

"Read, but I don't like to be all alone. It scares me." Her face colored rapidly, but she forced herself to go on. "If Logan has to work late, I usually go up to the farmhouse and play with the twins or help Mrs. Haydenshire. She's teaching me to cook and to sew, so that's been fun." Adeline's expression said she hoped she'd given the correct answer.

Her response visibly disturbed Lucas, but he didn't probe further into why Adeline was afraid to be alone. He clenched his jaw. Logan smiled as he watched Lucas begin to put together the intricate pieces of Adeline.

"Did you have a maid of honor in your wedding, dear?"

"Emily," Adeline announced with a grin and more volume than she'd answered with thus far. Her smile brought a duplicate reaction from her father.

"Okay, and what do you and Emily do when Rainer and Logan are working or being irritating blokes?"

Adeline's sweet giggle melted both of the men seated at the table with her. Lucas beamed at her, and Logan gave him an impressed smile.

"Emily loves to shop," Adeline stated with another smile, "and since I have a job now, it is a lot of fun. I didn't really do that much growing up."

Lucas covered his pain well, but Adeline saw it in his eyes. Logan felt her regret. She didn't want to make him feel bad about her childhood.

"I would really like it if you'd let me make up for that just a little," Lucas pled fervently. Logan tensed. He wasn't certain how she would react to the request.

"You don't have to do that."

Logan offered Lucas a sorrowful glance and a minute headshake, but Lucas advanced.

"I know, love."

Logan braced as Adeline's eyes goggled. She recoiled visibly.

"You don't have to call me things like that. Only Logan does that and Governor Haydenshire."

Lucas nodded as he accepted the answer to his test.

"You'll find as we get to know each other, that I do very few things simply because I think that I should. So, unless you don't want me to use terms of endearment for my own daughter, then I'm going to continue to call you things like that, all right? I noticed last night that Logan called you baby a few times. It seemed to make you quite happy, so I also assume it must be a special name he has for you. I certainly won't call you that."

Adeline blushed violently, and Logan was impressed.

"Okay. If you want to, it's fine."

"I want to, and I would love nothing more than to take you and your friends shopping to your heart's content. I understand that you don't feel that I have twenty-one years to make up for, but I do. Perhaps we could take in a show at the opera house this evening and enjoy all that it has to offer. It is quite impressive."

Adeline drew from Logan's hand.

"I've never seen an opera," she admitted as Logan supplied her with soothing strength.

Lucas smiled and nodded. He ignored Adeline's momentary tremble as Logan forced too much energy in at once.

"There are numerous kinds of shows at the opera house. I'm not really certain what's playing tonight, but we have passes for everything. If it's not something that would make you smile, then we can have dinner there and then take in the views."

"That sounds nice," Adeline managed. "Thank you."

"Certainly, dear. If there's anything else you'd like to do, I trust you'll let Logan know and that he'll let me know."

Adeline blushed again. "Probably," she admitted as Logan chuckled and kissed her cheek.

"My entire family will join us tonight at the Opera House for dinner. You'll get to meet Liam, my oldest brother, and his family. He has children a little younger than you, so you can meet your cousins."

Adeline nodded, but her rhythms tensed again. Logan understood that the plans had been made before Adeline had ever agreed to them.

He took over as Adeline finished the pastry she'd started and swallowed down the last of her coffee.

"Do you wanna get ready and go see what Em and Rainer are up to?"

"Yes." Relief and exuberance fought for dominance in her rhythm strains.

She turned back to Lucas with a slight grimace. "If it's all right with you. I don't want to be any trouble."

Pain etched Lucas's face once again. "I'm not holding you prisoner here, love. How could my daughter going to see her best friend be any trouble at all? You're welcome to invite Rainer and Emily back with you, along with Officer Vindico and Ms. Styler. Just tell me when you're ready to begin our day, and I'll phone the drivers."

Adeline nodded, though Logan noted she was uncomfortable with there being drivers.

"Why don't you go get ready, baby? I'll text Rainer and tell him we're coming out," Logan eased. There were a few things he needed to tell Lucas.

Adeline gave Lucas a genuine smile. "Thank you for breakfast. It was very good."

With an adoring grin, Lucas nodded.

"If you'll tell me what you like to eat, I'll make arrangements for lunch, and I can have Marta fix whatever you might like for breakfast tomorrow."

"Oh, anything's fine," Adeline gave her customary response, but Logan squeezed her hand and tried to encourage her to let her guard down just a little. "Maybe not sushi if it's okay."

"Now we're getting somewhere." Lucas seemed pleased.

After giving her a wry grin, Logan stepped in. "Her favorite foods are probably my mom's pot roast and potatoes, and she loves her chicken and dumplings. Ad makes amazing nachos and these chicken tacos that are to die for."

Adeline shook her head. "That's only because your mom taught me to make Mexican food first."

Logan rolled his eyes and continued, "Her favorite thing to drink is Dr Pepper, but you don't have it here."

"Well, most of Australia doesn't have Dr Pepper from the States, but I do happen to have it here," Lucas corrected with a grin.

"You do?" Adeline marveled. She and Logan had discussed how much they missed American Dr Pepper a few times since they'd arrived.

"It seems we have more in common than our eyes and our rhythms. It's my favorite as well. I ship it in by the case."

The grin on Adeline's face delighted both of the men gazing at her.

"Can I make you some?"

"She likes it chilled in the can," Logan supplied.

"Easy enough." Lucas gestured back inside the apartment. He followed Logan and Adeline inside and moved to the kitchen. He pulled two Dr Pepper cans from the cabinet and chilled them with his hand.

"Thank you." Adeline reacted to the soft drink like her father had just handed her gold bricks.

"You're very welcome." Lucas seemed taken aback.

"Is it all right if I take it upstairs?"

"Of course."

"You go on up. I'll be right there, baby." Logan kissed her cheek and willed her to go without him. She nodded, but disappointment cast her features as she headed toward the stairs.

"Okay, you said you wanted my help," was Logan's opening line as he heard the door close to the room he and Adeline were sharing. Lucas listened intently. "Don't call her honey, or any form of the word, and sure as hell don't call her sugar. I think it's good that you're calling her dear, or love, or whatever, but I'd been telling her for two years that I loved her before she was capable of saying it back to me."

Lucas shook his head with a sigh. "You're a very patient man, Logan."

"I didn't want her to say it until she was ready, but I wanted her to know how I felt."

"Well, certainly you must have felt that when you"—Lucas choked

as he considered the implications of his argument—"were with her."
He finally managed through his tightly clenched jaw.

With a concerted effort not to glare at Lucas, Logan hemmed. His
and Adeline's physical relationship wasn't anyone else's business, not
even her father's.

"That isn't something we did for quite some time." Logan refused
to say more on the topic.

Lucas was visibly impressed. "Okay, I won't call her hun, or honey,
and I can't fathom calling anyone, much less my daughter, sugar." He
scowled. "Any other advice?" He wanted a subject change as well.

"No, I thought that went really well." He gestured back toward the
deck. Lucas seemed pleased with the assessment.

"May I ask you a few more questions before you go up and join my
daughter in the shower?" he requested wryly.

Logan smirked but refused to agree.

"She said she's afraid to be alone." Lucas immediately moved on
from his quip. "You told me yesterday that you share a house with
Rainer and Emily on your family's property. Will she stay alone with
your friend Rainer?"

Logan's brow furrowed. "Of course. She and Rainer are friends.
She knows he'd keep her safe no matter what. They get along great."
Logan wondered where that particular question had come from.

"And all of your brothers, what about them?"

Logan shrugged. "Most of my brothers are grown and have their
own places, so it doesn't happen often, but yeah, same deal. She knows
any of my brothers would keep her safe. She knows they love her.
She's worked on half of them when they got hurt, and she sure as hell
knows no one in my family would ever hurt her."

"And your father?"

"My dad adores Adeline, and she loves him. My parents even hung
her report cards up on the fridge when we were in school. He used to
help her with all of the Adminis classes she had to take to graduate."
Logan tried to explain the depth of his parents' love for Adeline and
her unwavering adoration of them.

Lucas sighed. "So, it's not all men she's afraid of, it's just me."

Understanding lit Logan's features. "I don't think she's afraid of you. She's afraid you're going to hurt her, like I said. This all makes her nervous." He gestured around the apartment. "She's worried she's going to upset you, like taking the Dr Pepper upstairs. She's afraid she's going to offend you inadvertently. She'll loosen up the more time she spends with you. Being with Rainer and Em will help. You'll see."

"Do you think they might be willing to come here, instead of you and Adeline holing up with them in the guesthouse?"

"I'll ask, but you need to give her a little space. Let her relax with Emily. Then I'll see if I can get them back over here."

"I really do appreciate your help."

"No problem." Logan smiled as he turned to follow Adeline's path up the stairs and into the shower.

CHAPTER 25

GOOD MORNINGS

DAN VINDICO

A loud banging awoke Dan from his deep slumber.

"Damn it," he growled. He'd been enjoying having Fionna's naked body curled up beside his as he kept her back tucked to his chest and his arm wrapped over her protectively.

The noise blared again, and Fionna whimpered. He moved away from her and threw back the covers.

"Come back," she fussed. Her voice was rough from sleep.

Dan kissed her cheek as he pulled on a pair of basketball shorts.

"I'll be right back, honey. Clearly, someone wants our attention." He gestured to the door as he heard the next round of knocking.

"Make Rainer get it. I want you to stay with me."

Dan considered that for a moment. "Since I don't know what Ms. Haydenshire might be wearing, let me get it and then I'll harass Lawson for not waking up."

Fionna giggled as he opened the door just enough to squeeze out without revealing her luscious body in the bed.

Rainer met him on the stairs in a pair of boxers. He rubbed his eyes and yawned. "It's probably Logan and Adeline."

They both stalked to the door. Dan threw it open with a hateful glare for a butler. He was carrying a large platter of breakfast foods.

"The Lady sent breakfast and coffee for you. You'll let us know if you need anything else?"

"Uh, thank you," Rainer managed. The butler nodded once as he forced himself inside.

"And I'll just be tidying up for you, changing your sheets, and cleaning up your dishes when you've finished your meal. May I set the table for you?"

"Ms. Styler is currently still using our sheets, and I intend to go back and join her. Perhaps you could come back later," Dan commanded. *Who did these people think they were?*

The butler looked concerned. "The prince has several activities planned for you today. She should get up."

Before Dan could utter any of the phrases that pulsed acridly through his mind, Rainer cringed and shook his head.

"It's not even seven o'clock, and Ms. Haydenshire is also still asleep. So, we'll let them be. We'll take the breakfast, which looks delicious, thank you. Then we'll be ready whenever Logan and Adeline are," he mimicked the tone that Dan used when he made a suggestion that was actually an order.

Dan smiled at him as the butler sighed and turned to leave.

"Very nice, Lawson," Dan complimented.

"I've been paying attention." Rainer laughed as he set the large platter on the kitchen counter and headed back up the stairs. Dan followed him.

Fionna was exiting the bathroom when he returned. "Was that Logan and Adeline? Is she okay?"

Dan gazed at her tenderly. Her love and caring for Adeline made his heart swell. He shook his head. "No, it was yet another butler delivering breakfast and informing us that perhaps we should get up so he can change the sheets."

Dan seated himself on the bed before he took Fionna's hand and pulled her to him. "But I don't want you to get up. I want to hold you against me just like I was before we were so rudely interrupted." The truthfulness of his vow perforated his tone.

Fionna beamed and immediately crawled back in bed.

Dan was woefully unable to take his eyes off of her gorgeous ass as she crawled in.

"Now I'm cold and lonely." She pulled her lush lips into a delicious pout.

"Can't have that." He lay on his side and scooted her closer. "Come here to me. Let me keep you warm."

"Dan," she whispered, and he immediately felt her energy spin in nervous twists.

"What's wrong, baby?"

"I did something kind of not nice, and I'm afraid you'll be mad at me, or think I'm completely insane, which I probably am." Her confession had him trying to hide his chuckle.

"I don't think you're insane. Just tell me what you did. You're so damn sweet it can't be too bad. I assume by kind of not nice you don't mean kind of illegal."

Fionna giggled. Dan let the sound soothe his soul.

"No." She shook her head and then got distracted. "But Garrett told me in the Non-Gifted Realm, it's illegal to have oral sex or sex in general in Virginia if you're not married. So, we might have to arrest each other." She cracked herself up. Dan laughed at how cute she was.

"The Non-Gifted love to make up asinine laws involving what goes on in other people's bedrooms. I can't for the life of me figure out why they care, but that's good to know. If Officer Haydenshire really gets on my nerves, I'll just arrest him. I'm beyond certain he's been breaking those laws on a daily basis for the last fifteen years or so." He brought on another round of laughter from Fionna as she nodded her agreement. "Tell me what's got my girl so worried." Dan guided her back to their original conversation.

"Promise you won't be mad. I'll get you more if you want me to."

Whatever it was that she was going to get more of it had devastation coursing through her veins.

The only thing Dan could come up with was that she must've spilled something on some of his clothes. He kissed her head sweetly.

"I'm not going to be mad. Just tell me."

"Okay," she forced herself to go on. Her body tensed and she coiled up into a tight ball. She hid her face, and Dan had to lean to hear her.

"Yesterday, while you were in the shower..." she began.

Dan set his shield over her. He tried to soothe her while wondering what on earth she might've ruined that had her reacting like this. She stopped talking abruptly.

"Yesterday, I was in the shower and you…?"

"And I kind of went crazy, and I don't know what got into me," she whimpered.

Dan had never seen her cheeks blaze crimson before that moment.

Now insanely curious, he tried to will patience. "Fi, honey, come on. It can't be this bad."

"I'm not a crazy, clingy girlfriend, I swear. Just please don't freak."

"I don't mind you being clingy. I kind of like it especially if you need me. Please just tell me what happened." Dan tried to force his tone off of the demanding plateau it had landed on.

"I threw away all of the condoms in your wallet." She cringed. Her entire body braced for rejection. "I swear I didn't look at anything else in there. I just pulled them out, nothing else. I'm so sorry," she pled in absolute desperation.

Though he tried hard not to, Dan cracked up. He couldn't recall the last time he'd laughed that hard, and his reaction shocked Fionna.

"Okay, so, now I'm an insane girlfriend, and you're laughing at me." She pulled the covers over her head and hid from him.

"Baby." Dan choked back more laughter as he pulled her to him. He eased the sheets and blankets away from her beautiful face. "You're not insane. You're adorable, and I'm not upset at all. I'm really hoping I won't need them any time soon." He didn't want to have that conversation just yet, so he moved on quickly. "And you're welcome to go through my wallet any time you'd like. Wallet, phone, anything. I don't care."

She was drowning in a sea of confusion and insecurity. Dan's laughter ended as soon as he felt the emotions flood through her. Maybe he needed to go on with at least some of the conversation he'd been piecing together in his mind since their flight to Sydney several days before.

"Just listen to me, and please really believe what I'm saying to you."

She studied him and tried to manage her own emotions. Her rhythms tensed.

"I haven't been in a serious relationship for a long, long time, but that doesn't mean I don't understand the concept. I just didn't want to have anything to do with them until I was with you." He cradled her face in his hands as she blinked back tears. He leaned and brushed a tender kiss on her forehead.

"I'm not sure if you've noticed this, Miss Styler, but things are moving kind of fast here. I hadn't gotten a chance to clean out my wallet, so you just took something off my to-do list for me."

She grinned, but she stared down at the bed. She wouldn't hold his gaze.

"Like I told you, I'm out of practice on some of the finer points of being a boyfriend, but the major concepts I have. I need you to know I'm not going to hide things from you. If you're sure you want to keep this going at home, I would never cheat on you, ever."

He brushed his thumb over her cheek and tried with all of his strength to read her mind at that moment. "I'm sorry I laughed, but your confession was adorable. You had me thinking I was going to have to help you hide a body. I'm not sure I've ever seen something so cute except maybe you informing me that the spider chased you."

She giggled and rolled her eyes, but she quieted quickly. She was still studying him.

"What, baby?" He could see the doubt and the questions swirl in her beautiful eyes.

"You won't tell me why you got suspended, and there are a lot of other things you keep not telling me. I can feel it. You can't lie to me." The pain was evident in her tone.

Deep regret pierced through him. Of all the people who'd heard the tale, he hadn't told the one person who deserved the truth.

"I didn't tell you about Russia because I've been trying to keep you from knowing how much of absolute asshole I can be. I kept telling myself I could be better for you, and I know I keep saying that being with me will be complicated. You don't really seem to respond. I don't know what you're thinking. That scares the shit out of me because I've already fallen for you. I just wanted to have this one week to be together before we decide if we can make this work at home."

She stared him down. "I don't want you to be better for me. I want you to be *you* for me, and I can feel that you don't want to talk about us yet. That's why I don't say anything. I keep trying to wait until you do want to talk about it." She shocked him yet again. "And I don't care what you did, or said, or whatever, in Russia. I'm glad you did it. I think everything happens for a reason and in its own time in its own place. If you hadn't gotten in trouble, Governor Haydenshire wouldn't have made you go to the Angels after-party, and I wouldn't be here lying in bed with you naked." She glanced down at her beautiful body. She was uncomfortable suddenly. She stood to find something to wear.

Dan caught her hands. "Please don't get dressed yet," he begged. "Please, I really do want to go back to bed with you. I just want to hold you, please."

She settled back down beside him and waited patiently.

"I've always had a terrible temper," he confessed with a regret-filled sigh. "After Amelia died, it got worse—much, much worse."

"Did it get worse, or did it just get direction?" The knowledge inside her question astounded him. She'd once again read him like a book.

He nodded his admittance. "Both." With a deep breath, he went on with it. "When I tell you this story, just please promise you won't be afraid of me, or think that I would ever hurt you or yell at you because I never would." Terror filled his soul. This was why he didn't want to tell her. Shame slithered over him and threatened to drag him back to the drowning abyss he'd barely existed in for the last decade.

How could he have used his hands to hurt people who didn't deserve to be hurt and then used them to make love with her? How could she ever accept him like that?

Fionna grasped his arms. "I'm not afraid of you. I don't think I've ever felt safer in my whole life than when I'm wrapped up in your arms or when I'm in your shield." Her words jerked his heart back to life.

The words formed on his tongue, but he couldn't seem to make them reach his lips. Overwhelming love for her filled his entire being.

She smiled. Tears of joy pricked her eyes. She was holding his hands. She'd felt the love he couldn't verbalize.

After allowing himself to draw from her, Dan swallowed. "Wretchkinsides bribed the governing board. He blackmailed the Crown with photographs of him and one of his many mistresses."

Fionna shook her head in disgust. "What did he want?"

"His right-hand man, Candor Pendergrath, was up for parole. He wanted him released." Dan shuddered involuntarily. "He helped Cascavel take Amelia." He tried feebly to paint her the whole picture.

Fionna looked morose. She shook her head and blinked back tears.

"Anyway," he made himself go on, "they released him, of course. And I let them know just what I thought of that. I cussed out the Crown and the board. I said some really vile, filthy things, and then I knocked out several court guards and a few members of Russian Iodex before I fled the country. One of my best friends is the Captain of French Iodex, so I escaped to his house in Paris." He stared at her, desperate to see how she was going to react.

She didn't say anything so he continued, "I'm praying that you don't want to break up with me now, and that if you do decide to stick with me, you don't have a deep desire to spend time in Moscow. I'm fairly certain I'll never be allowed on Russian soil ever again." He tried for a joke, but desperation filled his plea.

She chuckled, but concern was her predominant expression.

"Gosh, and Moscow is really where I had my heart set on going this Christmas."

Dan leaned and kissed her cheek. He needed to feel more of her.

"Governor Haydenshire made me call all of them and apologize," he whined as Fionna wrinkled her nose adorably, "from his office, in front of him." The disgust he'd felt as he'd worked his way through the calls settled on him once again.

"That's awful." She shuddered.

"I guess I kind of deserved it."

"Because it pissed you off that a corrupt board set a kidnapping murderer free? I don't think so." Fionna adamantly defended his actions, and Dan was overwhelmed.

His heart beat disjointedly as he stared at the most beautiful angel in the world gazing up at him. She accepted him with all of his hideous, gaping flaws. She was sitting there telling him it was going to be okay because she was the angel sent to pull him out of the cavernous pits of hell that had him ensnared.

"I, uh…" he tried. He fought with every fiber of his being. "Fionna, I…" he forced, but his mouth waged war against his mind.

She smiled at him sweetly and crawled in his lap.

"I love you," she whispered as he nodded.

"Me too, so much," he choked.

"And I don't think you did anything wrong. Like I said, I think everything happens for a reason. If you want to wait to talk about us at home, then I want to wait too. I'm glad you got into trouble, because there is nowhere else on earth I want to be other than right here, right now with you."

To ice the cake of perfection she'd just created, she gave him a mischievous grin. "Except, maybe underneath you while you feel me up." She giggled and waggled her eyebrows.

With a delighted groan, Dan chuckled. "If I weren't such a tremendous coward, I would've said it a million times just this morning." He cradled her to him and turned her. He laid her back on the pillows and positioned himself over her as he slid his hands up her sides. He taunted her slightly. He wasn't going to give her what she wanted just yet.

"Why did the butler want to change the sheets? We've only slept here one night," she quizzed offhandedly as she arched her back and pushed her breasts to his face. He gave her a hungry grin.

"He must know you like it dirty, sweetheart."

Her mouth fell open in mock surprise. Dan laughed.

"I do not." That same mix of heat and embarrassment settled in her cheeks. He wasn't letting her get away with her lie, however.

Dan leaned and swirled his tongue over her nipple. She gasped suddenly.

"Really?" He feigned heartbreak. "And here I was thinking you were perfect for me."

She giggled as her blush became more pronounced. "Okay, maybe I'm just a little bit dirty."

"In all the best ways." He winked at her as she beamed.

"But only for you."

"Oh, it better only be for me. Going back to my horrendous temper, I'll kill any guy who tries to get you to be dirty for him."

Dan let his hands slip to her breasts. He began to grope and ply them. He watched her nipples darken and pull taut for him. Her chest rose and fell in waves of anticipation.

"Tell me what you want," he commanded as she trembled. Fire lit in her eyes as she writhed underneath him.

"Make me wet," she begged.

Dan growled as desire seared through his veins. It lit him on scorching fire that only she could douse.

"If I make you drip for me baby, I'm gonna make you take it hard and rough," he informed her as her entire body shuddered in need. A loud moan echoed from the desperation and ardent desire arcing between them. "And I'm gonna mark you, honey, because you're all mine, and I want everyone to know it."

Her abdomen tensed, and she began begging for his mark and begging for release. He slipped his fingers between her folds. She didn't need much. He knew. He could feel her rhythms as they craved his shield.

Dan leaned and pulled her left nipple into his mouth. He dragged his teeth over the puckered mound and then moved up her chest. He halted at the delicate skin just under her collarbone. Dan sucked hard as she went wild. She fucked herself on his fingers.

"That feels good, doesn't it? You're swollen nice and wet for me already, baby doll. I'm about to take you for a ride."

Fionna's entire body rolled under his as she groaned out his name.

"That's right. My good girl knows who owns this pussy," he growled. Her energy spiked hard just like it did when he brought her.

With that, Dan flipped to his back and continued his commands.

"Mount me," he ordered as loud moans seared from her in desperate need. She straddled him as he separated her lips.

"I'm gonna fill you full. Are you ready for me?" he warned as her head fell back in a heated pant, and liquid heat dripped over his length. He growled out his adamant approval.

"Hold on tight, baby doll."

Before he could thrust hard and penetrate her, a loud, invasive knock shook their bedroom door.

A loud string of expletives erupted from Dan's mouth as his eyes flashed in fury.

"Dan." Fionna panicked. She tried to calm him down as she climbed off of him and threw on a robe. He pulled the basketball shorts back on. His acrimony made him lose the straining erection he'd just had.

"What!" he shouted in a boom of fury as he flung the door open.

"Dan, please don't hit him," Fionna begged as she pulled the robe up to her neck to cover the mark he'd left on her chest.

The same butler who'd been informed, not a half hour before, to go away, had returned and looked quite put out. Fionna's terror that the man might've seen the mark only added to Dan's infuriated rage.

"What the hell do you want? Officer Lawson told you to leave!"

Rainer was standing in the hallway. His jaw was clenched tight, and his arms were folded over his chest. He looked just as furious as Dan.

"I knocked numerous times on the door downstairs, but no one answered," the butler stated rather pompously.

"We were busy," Rainer seethed.

Apparently, everyone in the guesthouse had been having a very nice morning.

With his fury that Fionna would somehow be ashamed of her own desires coursing through him viciously, Dan stepped into the hallway and closed the door to their room.

"Which brings me back to the question of why the hell you're here for the second time when it isn't even seven in the fucking morning," Dan roared.

"Sir, there's really no reason to be so rude. Arlo would like to extend an invitation to you and Ms. Styler to join him in his apartment for brunch. Lucas asked me to inform you that Mr. Logan and Ms. Adeline might like your company in his apartment before your shopping excursion. He'd like you to be ready to leave whenever Adeline is ready to go. And Lady Nguyen is quite insistent that I tidy up the guesthouse and change your linens."

Dan stomped toward the man whose eyes goggled as he backed away.

"You can tell Arlo…" Dan seethed, but Rainer stepped in.

"I'm going to go with Chief Vindico and Ms. Styler will not be joining Arlo in his apartment for any reason ever. As I mentioned before, whenever Logan and Adeline want us, they know where we are, or if they want us to come to them, they both have our cell numbers." Rainer knew perfectly well that Lucas was behind the invitation, not Logan.

"Now, our sheets do not need to be changed, and judging by the expression on his face,"—Rainer gestured to Dan—"I'd say if you take one step into their bedroom, it might just be the last step you ever take. So, I'm asking you nicely to leave, and please tell Logan that if he needs me, to call me." He lifted his cell phone. "On a phone."

"This is really quite rude," was the butler's rebuttal.

"Oh, I don't know," Dan spat, "he was a hell of a lot nicer than I would've been."

Rainer's cell chirped, and he looked momentarily surprised.

"See, Logan says *Hey, man. Ad misses you guys. We're coming out in a few, but Lucas really wants you to come back over here later.*"

Rainer put the phone away so the butler couldn't read the rest of the text that Dan assumed was Logan's complaining about Lucas's insistent invitation.

"This is all it takes," Rainer huffed.

"Are you ready for me to take the breakfast tray then?" the butler asked.

"No," Dan and Rainer spat simultaneously.

"Well…" The butler stomped back down the stairs and out the front door.

"Let me see Logan's text." Dan shook his head over their morning and what had been interrupted. "Believe me, I feel your pain."

"Yeah, I heard," Rainer informed wryly.

Dan chose to ignore that information as he read Logan's text. With a smile, he replied on Rainer's phone, letting Rainer see what he was typing.

Rainer grinned as Dan hit send. "Very cool, man."

"Yeah, well, you might want to work out with me because I might need some help if I decide to let Arlo know just what I think of him making a play for Fionna."

Rainer laughed and shook his head. "Come on. He's an international playboy. You could take him in your sleep." Rainer's admiration made Dan chuckle.

"Yeah, well, the international playboy is humping my last nerve and that's a very dangerous thing to do." His mind immediately went back to Fionna holed up in their room. He knew she was regretting what he'd done.

Rainer's phone chirped again, and he smiled.

"Logan says, *you are awesome*."

"I do what I can." Dan waved to Rainer and returned to Fionna. He tried to think of what to say to take away her self-imposed shame.

Fionna was pacing. She looked morose as Dan entered the room.

"Okay, that was not at all how that was supposed to end. Come here, sweetheart." He wrapped his arms around her and let her feel his powerful, protective embrace as he pushed his shield out from his body with ease. He moved his hand to her chest and healed the rather large mark in a matter of seconds.

"Do you think he saw it?"

All Dan could feel in her energy was shame, and it infuriated him all over again.

"No, I don't, and you know what? He had no business being up here. I may kill Arlo Nguyen. I'm beyond certain he's the one who pressed the issue and sent him back."

Before Fionna could ask how Dan knew that, he went on. "Baby, what we share, what happens in our bedroom, is for you and me and no one else. I will never share anything that we do with anyone. That is sacred between the two of us. I will guard that with my life, and I don't ever want you to feel ashamed because you want something, okay?" She nodded against him and let him soothe her regret-filled rhythms.

"Why do you think Arlo did that?"

"Because, Rainer and I eavesdropped on a conversation between Lucas, his brothers, and his dad last night. I wanted to know what they really thought about Adeline." He knew he should feel bad for listening in, but he couldn't locate any remorse anywhere in his body.

"Oh, good. I was hoping you'd get to do something like that. That's why I wanted you to go play." Fionna seemed eager to let her shame and disappointment go. "What did they say? Please tell me that all of that about having a relationship with Adeline wasn't just a line. He didn't feel like he was lying to me."

"No." Dan shook his head. "Lucas seems very genuine, like you told me last night. He said basically the same things to his brothers that he said at dinner. Arlo, however, made an extremely lewd comment about you, and I'm pretty sure he'd like nothing more than for you to be a notch in his bedpost." Fury pulsed through Dan. "So, maybe you're the antidote to my temper because I didn't beat the piss out of him last night, even though I wanted to. But if he keeps this up, I will."

Fionna smiled against him. "Tell me what he said, and I'll decide if I want you to just go ahead and beat him up, or if I want to rub it in his face all day and then let you beat him up."

Dan's heart swelled, but he shook his head. "I don't talk like that ever, and I most certainly don't say things like that in front of women, most especially you."

"Wow, it must've been bad." She considered. "Okay, I'll get Emily to get Rainer to tell her, and then she'll tell me."

"Fi." He raised his left eyebrow.

"Just tell me."

Dan sighed. "He said he'd be up you like a rat up a drain pipe."

Fionna scowled in disgust. She gagged. "Oh, gross."

Dan held up his hands. "I told you."

She narrowed her eyes. "Well, I think we'll treat Arlo to a little show today. He's probably going with us, right?"

"I have no doubt." Dan wondered what she was up to. "I'm pretty sure he thinks being in the Australian Royal Family, with more money than a televangelist preacher, will have you jumping at the chance to climb into his bed, as compared to a lowly Iodex officer with a bad temper."

Fionna looked highly insulted. "Then he doesn't know the first thing about me, does he? I don't jump into anyone's bed, and more importantly, I'm your girlfriend. I made a commitment to you, even if we haven't worked out all the details. I'm in love with you, even if it has only been a week." She looked momentarily shocked by the revelation.

Renewed breath cleansed Dan's lungs. His heart located a healthy cadence. Life itself washed through his veins. He wrapped his arms around her. He just had to keep her safe. It was as easy and as painstakingly, gut-wrenchingly difficult as that.

"And Arlo can stuff it," she declared. "I plan to show him precisely where my loyalties lie."

"You just keep blowing my mind," Dan stole her line for him as he pulled her back to him. "And tonight, when we get back here, I'm taking you for that ride, baby doll."

CHAPTER 26

AN ADELINE OUT OF WATER

Dan used every piece of equipment in the well-equipped gym in the guesthouse. Rainer and Logan joined him. They both seemed to have a fair amount of tension and testosterone to sweat out.

Two and a half hours later, Dan reentered the living room to find the ladies lying on the couches talking and laughing. Adeline looked vastly more relaxed than she had when she'd arrived. Fionna wrinkled her nose as Dan neared.

"What? I don't get a hug, baby doll? I've been gone for two hours. I missed you." His teasing elicited her infectious giggle as he ran a towel over his face.

Rainer and Logan followed Dan in a few minutes later. He'd finished his two mile cool-down run several minutes before them.

"I am so sorry." Adeline shook her head. "I cannot believe they sent that guy out here twice. The whole thing is completely crazy. I will never get used to this."

"You don't have to get used to it. Just get to know your dad while we're here. Then I'll take you back to the ho-hum life we live where if you want to hang with Emily you text her and say, 'hey Em, get over here and bring me a Dr Pepper.' You don't send your butler out to give her an engraved invitation to request her company and that she bring a fizzy refreshment." Logan made everyone laugh.

"I can't wait," Adeline vowed. Everyone grinned at her sweet concern and the bewilderment she'd been living for the past several hours. "He really does want you all to come back over for a little while. Do you mind?" She looked like she was asking her friends to commit some sort of heinous crime.

"Of course we'll go," Fionna assured her. "We want to help you with all of this, as crazy as it kind of is," she admitted with another giggle that Dan found to be adorable.

After the men showered, they changed into polo shirts and slacks. The girls all donned skirts and heels as Lucas's maid had informed them that the dress of the day would be business casual.

They headed back into the palace toward Lucas's apartment. The maid, who'd also made them refreshments, welcomed them in. Lucas seemed pleased they were all there. Dan thanked Lucas for the Dr Pepper that he was providing rather insistently.

"Adeline thought you might all like to go shopping today. Any particular stores that are your favorites?" Lucas asked the ladies, who all looked uncomfortable being singled out.

Dan draped his arm over Fionna. She seemed to want to be tucked away, and he wanted nothing more than to be her Shield. "We did a little shopping the other day, but I don't think we really know what might be around Sydney. Maybe you have a few suggestions," she urged.

Lucas considered for a moment. "My ex-wife preferred Brenthaven—La Perla, Armani, IM, Chanel, Tiffany, things like that, but there's also World Square. It has L'Occitane, Lorna Jane, Peter Alexander."

"There's a La Perla and an IM?" Fionna was almost drooling.

Dan stifled a chuckle. "I think that means she'd like to go to Westerview," he interpreted for her as Lucas offered a nod.

"Excellent."

Marta made another appearance. "Sir, Edward Davies is calling. He says it's urgent," she offered apologetically.

Lucas scoffed. "A friend of mine from New Zealand. He wants to play golf. Will you excuse me for just a moment?"

Everyone assured him that they would. Marta followed Lucas out.

"Hey, Ad, I think we should ask Lucas if we could get you a maid outfit like that to wear for me," Logan teased. Everyone cracked up, and Adeline blushed violently.

"You wish." She shook her head at him.

"Yeah, Haydenshire, why don't you ask her *dad* about that?" Dan goaded. He was astonished at how different Adeline was when she was only with Logan and her friends. She clammed up immediately when Lucas entered the room.

Rainer leaned to set his Dr Pepper on a nearby side table.

Emily gasped, "Don't set that there. That table probably cost more than your Porsche."

Logan kept the laughter going. "Don't worry. I'm sure a plethora of maids will be by to wipe off the tables and probably Rainer's chin if you want them to."

"Nah, I only let Em wipe my chin." Rainer winked at Emily, whose mouth hung open as everyone laughed at the dirty quip.

"You are in so much trouble." Emily shot Rainer a mischievous glare.

"I'm hoping."

"Okay, but she's probably right about that table. This is all so crazy." Adeline seemed to be coming out of her shell before everyone's eyes. She gestured around the sitting room. They all took in the grand room, with its high-back, inlaid silk, woven settees, uncomfortable Queen Anne chairs, and heavy wooden furnishings. "And you should see the room we're staying in. I can't even get in the bed without a stool." Adeline sounded thoroughly unimpressed.

"Oh now, I bet Logan can get you into bed, Miss Adeline," Rainer teased her.

Dan smirked. "Haydenshire, what is wrong with you? Pick her up." He extended his arms in front of him and simulated lifting a woman into a bed.

Logan shook his head. He seemed to thoroughly enjoy cutting up with his friends. "Yeah, I thought about that, but I figured if I just lay there, a maid would bring her to me on a silver platter."

Everyone guffawed, but as the laughter died down, Dan and Logan glanced toward the door just in time to see Lucas's coattails as he made a quick exit.

While wondering just how much he'd overheard, Dan and Logan shared an ominous expression.

CHAPTER 27
LATITUDE

A few minutes later, Lucas made another appearance. He did a decent job of pretending he hadn't heard Adeline and her friends making fun of the palace and the serving staff. But both Fionna and Emily seemed to pick up on his deception.

"Are we ready to begin our day?"

No one looked like they were overly excited to spend the day with Lucas and Arlo and then to have to endure another formal meal with the Nguyens at the Opera House, but they all nodded politely.

Dan pulled Logan to the side as they entered the shopping mall. "Why don't I go with you to apologize?" Dan thought Logan really should offer an apology to Lucas, and he should as well. He was certainly old enough to know better.

"Thanks. I really appreciate it. I don't want to tell Rainer. I'm scared Emily might tell Adeline."

Dan nodded his understanding. Emily and Adeline followed Fionna into a makeup boutique while Arlo cornered Rainer to discuss his Porsche.

It appeared to be a perfect time, so Dan and Logan made their approach.

"Hey Lucas, I'm really sorry about what you overheard. I was just trying to let her blow off a little steam. I shouldn't have said anything," Logan offered sincerely.

Lucas looked highly put out. "Did you not tell me, this very morning, that you would help me establish a relationship with Adeline?"

Dan didn't like his tone, but he said nothing.

"I did, and that's why I'm apologizing."

"I don't really find making fun of the way I live to be very helpful. Do you?"

"I said I was sorry," Logan came right back. He reached the end of his rope rather quickly. Dan bit back a chuckle.

"And you, Officer Vindico, do you always require your officers to work out for hours while they're on holiday and that their wives remain with them while they're in the gym?" Lucas turned his disdain on Dan.

"That's Chief Vindico," Dan spat. "And I did request that Logan work out today. We have to stay in top physical form, and since we'll be back at work next week, I thought he could use a good workout. He's been here for several days vacationing." Dan dared Lucas to debate his reasoning. "I'm sorry if that took your time away from Adeline." He tried to remember that they needed Lucas's help if Adeline was going to keep her job, which was the entire mission of the trip.

Logan seemed to remember the same thing at the same moment.

While drawing a deep breath, Logan visibly swallowed his pride. "I told you she needed a little time with Emily. Look at her. She's smiling again. She's happy." He gestured to the makeup shop. Adeline was standing beside Fionna. They were sampling perfumes, and Adeline looked almost as thrilled to be talking with Fionna as Dan always felt.

"Again, I am really sorry. What I said was stupid and childish, but you've gotta give us a little latitude. This is all really new to us. I'm not saying our way of life is right and yours is wrong, but maids and butlers don't wake us up, alarms do. If we want coffee, we go to the kitchen and fix it, in our pajamas and then cuddle up on our ancient sofa and drink it. If we want something to eat, we fix it ourselves and generally serve it up on paper plates unless we're eating at my parents' house.

"If the toilets need to be cleaned, we clean them. Our house has six rooms, not six hundred. My family owns a huge farm, and if my mom needs the garden tilled or weeded, guess who does that?" Logan pointed to himself. "We're not accustomed to being waited on or having our sheets changed every day." Logan gestured to Dan, who was still irritated about their morning. He nodded his agreement.

Lucas seemed to consider Logan's diatribe. "But your father is the Crown Governor."

"Yes." Logan clearly hoped Lucas would see the point on his own.

"I came to the guesthouse to see what was keeping you," Lucas admitted. Logan furrowed his brow. "I heard Adeline tell you that she couldn't wait to go back home."

With a sigh, Logan nodded. "I told you this is stressful for her. We don't want to be rude or disrespectful. We really do appreciate all of your generosity and your willingness to help us, but"—Logan seemed to draw on deep resolve—"I guess I just hope you can forgive us, forgive her. We really don't know how to act, but I swear we'll try harder."

Lucas stared Logan down. "It seems that you want a great deal of latitude, but you aren't willing to extend any to me or my family. My mother and brother sent you breakfast this morning and an invitation for coffee. You were extremely rude to the butler," he threw at Dan.

"We rise at six and are served coffee. On Sundays, we eat breakfast together as a family. We feel it's just a little more civil to extend an invitation via a member of our staff rather than via a text message. We would also not send a text to our husband from one floor above, requesting that he come and rescue us from the bed she apparently finds too high for her liking.

"We would not stalk around in someone else's kitchen, half-dressed, in effort to make coffee without their permission or help. Nor would I ever make fun of a member of your family's staff or indicate that their uniform is lascivious in nature. And just for your information, my end tables certainly do not cost more than your friend's Porsche," Lucas continued.

Dan shook his head. "You didn't get a phone call at all. You wanted to know what she would say when she was with us and you weren't there."

"Yes, well, I suppose I took a page from your book," Lucas drawled. "I noticed you last night when you started to walk in to presumably strangle my brother for his lewd comment about your girlfriend when Mr. Lawson stopped you.

"I did not tell either of my brothers or my father of your eavesdropping. Because, you see, gentlemen, I am perfectly willing to forgive you, or overlook your lack of breeding and polish, because you, Logan, have something that I want very badly." Lucas turned his haughty glare on Logan. "You have the heart of my daughter, and I can't even have a little piece of it without your help, which I thought I had until I took it upon myself to do a little investigative work."

"All right, fine." Incensed fury blazed in Logan's shield. "We will make a concerted effort to be better guests, and I will help you. Like I told you, I really, truly do want you to have a relationship with Adeline. But, how about you keep your brother from ogling his girlfriend?" He gestured to Arlo who was staring lustfully at Fionna as she investigated a makeup brush display.

Dan clenched his jaw and narrowed his eyes hatefully. He stared at Arlo until he noticed Dan and then immediately turned his gaze from Fionna.

Lucas rolled his eyes. He seemed equally as disgusted with his brother.

Logan continued. "And do you really want Adeline to be herself or do you want to try to cram her into some version of someone you want her to be? I told you she needed to spend time with her friends. I didn't mean for you to spy on her while she did that." He gestured back to Adeline who was now with Emily. They were both smiling as Emily rubbed a sample of something on Adeline's wrist and nodded her encouragement.

"I will accept your apology if you'll perhaps stop pointing out the differences in our lifestyles to Adeline and start helping me really connect with her." Lucas drove a hard bargain.

"Fine." Logan offered Lucas his hand, and Lucas accepted it. "But you don't connect with Adeline, sir. I keep trying to tell you. She connects with you." Logan looked truly defeated.

Dan stepped in, still furious with Arlo and irritated with Lucas's private investigation tactics.

"If you want to connect with your daughter, stop blaming Logan for being who he is and for who you are. Go shop with her and her friends. Just be there with her. You don't have to know anything about what they're doing, but show her that you're interested in what she's interested in. Get to know her friends. As you just pointed out, there are a few people here who already have Adeline's heart."

"He's right," Logan agreed as the three of them went into the store and effectively invaded the ladies' conversations.

CHAPTER 28
WIND INSTRUMENTS

The afternoon went by rather well, Dan thought. Lucas did make a concerted effort to try and connect with Adeline. He purchased several things she admired, but that seemed to make her uncomfortable so eventually he stopped.

Fionna put on quite the show of hanging all over Dan whenever Arlo was watching. This included eating lunch in his lap. The look on Arlo's face thoroughly delighted Dan.

The men were told to go away when the girls spied the vast La Perla boutique. More than ready for a shopping reprieve, the men returned to the food court.

Lucas was visibly uncomfortable with Adeline purchasing lingerie presumably to wear for Logan.

"What time do we need to be at the Opera House?" Logan asked, in an obvious attempt to distract Lucas from what Adeline was doing.

"Oh, yes, I'd nearly forgotten. There's a lecture this evening on wind instruments and then a concert afterwards by the lecture staff. Should be quite a show." Lucas sounded thrilled. "We have private reservations at Bennelong at five thirty, so we can make the nine o'clock show."

"Great." Logan forced a smile. Dan was fairly certain only he and Rainer knew it was a fake.

"How riveting," Rainer huffed to Dan who tried hard not to laugh his agreement.

Lucas and Arlo offered to get beers for everyone. As they left, Dan responded to Rainer's quip.

"Yeah, and the ladies are all in there loading up on La Perla lingerie which, trust me, will make you melt when you see her in it, and you'll be stuck in an opera house listening to a lecture on wind instruments."

Rainer and Logan whimpered.

"Why did I say we'd be better guests?" Logan whined.

Fionna looked extremely pleased as Dan met her outside the lingerie shop over an hour later. She was carrying three large bags and giving Dan a broad grin. "So, funny thing happened," she quipped.

Dan awaited his lecture. "Oh, really?"

"Yes, uh-huh." She giggled and tried her best to feign irritation. "It seems my boyfriend attacked the saleswoman while I was in the dressing room and instructed her to put all of my purchases on his credit card."

"Wow," Dan mocked impression. "What a great guy."

Fionna doubled over with laughter. "You are in big trouble, Chief Vindico." She handed him the card he'd left with the saleswoman. Dan leaned and took the bags and the card from her hands as he growled in her ear, "I really should be punished."

"I'm planning on taking you captive," she replied with a naughty glint in her innocent eyes.

"Believe me, honey, your wish is my command."

"Vindico?" Arlo had sauntered up and presumably overheard Fionna call Dan by his last name. Dan ground his teeth as he turned to Arlo. "You're not related to Lindley Vindico by any chance are you?" Arlo sounded genuinely curious.

"She's my little sister. Why?"

Arlo choked. His eyes goggled. "She's your sister?" he gasped.

"Yes, why?"

"Cannot be the same girl. Maybe your distant cousin or something." Arlo pulled a cell phone from his pocket. "Oh, no, not that one." He grimaced as he flipped through pictures. Dan's stomach churned. "I met her at Governor Haydenshire's inaugural ball, but she's nothing like you," Arlo drawled stupidly. "Here," he landed on a picture of Lindley fully clothed and showed it to Dan and Fionna.

"Yes, that's my sister."

"Wow, well," he chuckled, "she's a real screamer. We had a ball."

Dan fought back the deep desire to pound Arlo into oblivion.

Fionna wrapped her arm around Dan's forearm and willed calm into him. She gave him a sympathetic gaze.

Lucas sent the girls' purchases back to the palace with one of the drivers as the other drove the crowd to the Opera House.

"Wind instruments?" Emily whined as Rainer informed her of their evening plans. Rainer gave her a weary nod.

Dan slapped him on the back as they exited the limo and entered the restaurant that did have gorgeous views of the bay. Apparently private reservations for the ruling family meant they traveled down a long dark corridor to a private dining room. No one else was in sight.

The rest of the Nguyen family was just being seated, and they were all introduced to Liam, his wife, Sophie, and their children, Joshua and Jessica. They were both in their early teens. The entire family all wore identical, derisive sneers.

When Lucas introduced Adeline as his daughter, Liam scowled. "Must you say that so loudly?" The entire table tensed. Adeline looked crushed. "Of course, I don't suppose you can deny her." He gestured to Adeline indignantly.

"Liam, if you have a problem with my daughter, perhaps you should leave. Otherwise, you can keep your demeaning and abusive comments to yourself, because I will not allow you to bully my child." Lucas glared hatefully at his older brother.

Liam scoffed, "So, you're going to choose this girl, the daughter of a whore, over your family? Dad says you're giving her your inheritance. Are you completely mad?"

Lucas shook his head and glowered at Liam.

"No, I'm not choosing my daughter over my family, although I certainly would if need be. I am choosing her over you. So leave."

"No!" Adeline was distraught. "No." She stood and scooted out of her chair quickly. "I don't want you to choose me over anyone." She managed to get out of the restaurant before her tears began to fall.

"Adeline!" Logan was furious as he raced after her. Lucas followed after him.

CHAPTER 29

TAKE IT FROM ME

LOGAN HAYDENSHIRE

"Adeline!" Logan called as he raced out into the private corridor. He searched the numerous darkened hallways frantically. He didn't have to go far before he heard her trembling, tear-filled plea coming from his left.

Her father was right behind him, and Logan bit back the urge to tell him precisely what he thought of his family.

"Yes, sir," he heard Adeline say. "I just want to come home, please," she begged. Logan listened intently to try to locate her. The darkened area seemed to have engulfed his wife. "Yes, sir. No, you don't need to come get me. I was just wondering if it would be all right if I came home tonight. Please, I don't want to stay here anymore."

Logan glared at Lucas. "That's my dad she's on the phone with. If you think I'm overprotective, you haven't seen anything yet."

"No, I'll be all right. I just want to come home," her voice fractured. "Please," she begged again.

"My dad and at least half of my brothers are going to be on the next flight to Sydney. You'd better fix this," Logan demanded. Lucas looked utterly heartbroken.

"I don't know where Logan is right now. I don't really know where I am. It's dark everywhere." They heard her begin to sob.

"Oh, shit." Logan sprinted toward her voice and searched frantically.

"I'm right here, baby." He finally saw the light from her phone. She'd tucked herself into a cutout cove in the wall. In one fluid movement, Logan pulled her cell phone from her grasp and wrapped his arms around her. She buried her face in his chest.

"I'm here, Dad. I just found her." Logan shuddered as his father began shouting. "Dad," Logan attempted to interrupt, but that was going to be impossible He decided to let Lucas in on the infuriated lecture. He casted Adeline's phone and raised the speaker volume.

"If one of my girls wants to come home, then that is precisely where she is coming! You get off of your ass and get her to the airport, Logan Haydenshire! Do you understand what I am saying to you? She is your wife! When she wants to leave, I don't give a damn where you are, you get her out of there, and you do it now," Governor Haydenshire roared furiously.

"It took me a minute to find her. I'll take her to the airport now. I have to call a cab, but I'll bring her home tonight."

"Where is Adeline now?" Governor Haydenshire seethed.

"She's in my arms crying. I'm holding her."

"You'd better be," was his father's next command. "And you tell my sweet girl that I will be there when that plane lands and that she never has to go back. You understand me? You know, maybe I should just come there and get her. There are several things I'd like to say to the Premier's sons."

Logan cringed. "Dad, I'll bring her home. I will take care of her. Please stop yelling at me. I didn't do this."

"Well sometimes, other people upset our wives and guess whose job it is to make that right?" Governor Haydenshire snarled. "Now, I understand that things turned bad a few minutes ago, but she sounds exhausted. It sounds like she's been upset for a long while. It is your job to take care of her, so start acting like a husband and like the man I raised."

Logan's jaw clenched as he held Adeline. "Yes, sir." There wasn't anything else to say. His father was right.

"Your tickets will be at Kingsford Smith as soon as I get off the phone with you, and I will see you at Ronald Reagan tomorrow, and you tell Adeline we love her."

Logan ended the call and tried to soothe Adeline.

"I…didn't…mean for him…to yell… at you," she stuttered through her convulsive tears.

"I deserved it. He's absolutely right, and he loves you, by the way. And so do I." Logan remembered his father's command. Adeline nodded into Logan's shirt.

"I know, and I love him and you too."

In the midst of being on the receiving end of one of his father's notoriously harrowing lectures, Logan had forgotten that Lucas was standing there listening.

Logan's cell phone chirped. He read the text.

I've changed my mind. Garrett wants to come check on Fionna. Will and Connor are coming as well. We're flying out as soon as the pilots get the jet ready. Take Adeline somewhere she feels safe and content. Get her something to eat and try to get her to sleep. Do nothing else! We can all fly back together a little while after I arrive.

With a defeated sigh, Logan shuddered. "So, Dad's on his way here, and Will, Garrett, and Connor are coming as well."

"Really?" Adeline looked concerned, but Logan saw the hopeful serenity there behind the worry that she'd caused the governor trouble.

She wanted him to be there. She was desperate for any piece of home, and Logan lambasted himself. How could he have let her be so miserable on his watch?

"The Crown Governor is coming here?" Lucas still looked shocked by the turn of events.

"No." Logan rolled his eyes. "My dad is coming here because he's worried about her, and he loves her, and he doesn't think I'm taking care of her. He isn't coming as Crown Governor Haydenshire. He's coming as my dad, and if one of his kids, whether they gave birth to them or not, needs him, he's there. That's what he does. And if my mother wasn't five months pregnant and staying home to take care of all of the rest of us, she'd be coming as well."

Lucas sighed and gazed at Adeline. "Love, please, just listen to me. Liam has never gotten on with the rest of the family. That's why he doesn't live at the palace anymore. We see him on big occasions. I'd hoped he'd be civil tonight and that we might mend some things in light of your arrival. This kind of rudeness is nothing new, and it's not on your account. I really don't want you to leave. I'll demand that Liam go. No one wants him here anyway."

Adeline trembled in Logan's arms, but he felt it. That same spark that ignited in her in that supply closet at the hospital made a hesitant return. She drew a deep breath and turned to her father.

"I don't want to be a rift in your family. I don't want your inheritance or for you to try and do things for me now. I appreciate that you want to try to make something up to me, but I'm proud of who I've become. All I want is to keep my job."

With that, her resolve gave out, and Adeline dissolved into a puddle of exhausted tears. Logan cast his shield around her.

Rainer, Emily, Dan, and Fionna, who Logan assumed must've been looking for them for some time, saw Logan's cast light the darkened corridors. They sprinted to them.

"Adeline, are you okay?" Emily soothed. She and Fionna were immediately on the verge of tears. Neither of them was able to get to Adeline though. She was in Logan's orb.

"Dad's on his way, along with Will, Garrett, and Connor," Logan explained.

"Oh man, he let you have it, didn't he?" Rainer grimaced.

Logan was thankful someone in the crowd understood what was actually happening.

"Why is Garrett coming?" Fionna quizzed.

"To check on you and to defend her. They're all coming because they're worried about her. Dad doesn't think I've been taking care of my wife, which judging from the fact that she's sobbing, I'd say he's right."

Lucas stepped up. "No, I'll tell him that you were doing the best you could under the circumstances. I put a tremendous amount of pressure on you. I had no idea your father had such high expectations for his children."

Adeline turned back to Lucas as Logan lowered his cast. "You would do that?"

"Of course. This is entirely my fault. I wanted so badly to show you all of the power, money, and things you can do and have when you're the Premier's granddaughter in the hopes that you'd fall in love with the lifestyle. May I?" Lucas held his hand out for Adeline's phone.

With a shrug, Logan handed it to him. He continued to tenderly rub Adeline's back.

"I'm on my way, sweetheart. I'll be there as fast as the jet can get me there," was the governor's soothing answer when he saw that Adeline was calling him back.

Logan was surprised that Lucas casted the phone as well so that everyone could hear.

"Crown Governor Haydenshire, sir, this is Lucas Nguyen, Adeline's father."

"And what can I do for you, Mr. Nguyen?" Governor Haydenshire drawled though everyone was painfully aware he was not being kind.

"I want to apologize on my brother's behalf. I was just trying to explain to Logan and Adeline the tenuous relationship between Liam and the rest of the family," Lucas offered rather feebly.

Logan braced. He wasn't certain how his father would respond.

The governor was silent for the length of one heartbeat. "I have a plane to catch, Mr. Nguyen. I assume there is a point to this phone call."

Rainer, Logan, Emily, and Dan all grimaced from his tone.

Lucas looked thoroughly shocked. Anger broadcast from his rhythms, but he managed to regain his composure before he responded.

"Sir, I wanted to call and tell you that Logan has been nothing but a consummate husband to my daughter. Please don't blame him for Adeline wanting to return to the States. This is entirely my fault." A modicum of hope played in Lucas's eyes as he took in Adeline who was listening intently. "Logan has done everything in his power to make certain that she was taken care of to the point of rather rudely turning down an invitation from my father to play billiards so that he could stay and make certain Adeline knew he wouldn't leave her. He went so far as to refuse me entry into a room of my own home to make certain she felt secure.

"I forced the issue of them staying with me. She would've been more comfortable if I'd allowed them to stay at the hotel where you'd arranged. I simply pushed too hard." Lucas appeared deeply pained and remiss. "Logan tried to tell me to give her some time and some space, and I feel I have so much to make up for that I stifled all of his attempts to care for her, including getting angry with him for making her laugh, even if it was at my expense.

"Truthfully, sir, I suppose I'm deeply envious of Logan and Adeline's relationship and of the way he cares for her. He has discerned more about the way to care for the woman he loves and the way to tend his marriage in a week than I knew in fifteen years of being married, which I suppose is one of the reasons I'm divorced.

"I'm certain you've heard that my father named Ethan his successor, and Liam was naturally put out when he was skipped for the throne. My family and I hoped that perhaps this evening, with Adeline being here, we might have a civil dinner as a family, but that was merely a fantasy. I suppose I have a great deal to learn about being a father."

"I'd have to agree with that last statement," Governor Haydenshire stated firmly. "That sounds like a tremendous amount of pressure to put on Adeline. Your father named Ethan his successor well over a year ago, and the entire world knows of the rift in your family. Yet, you decided to take my sweet girl and try to force her to heal a wound she had nothing to do with inflicting when she was simply trying to find you and heal wounds of her own."

"Please understand, Crown Governor, I'm so thrilled to meet Adeline and Logan. I truly want a relationship with my daughter, and I will never be able to repay you for the kindness you and your family have shown her. I did want to assure you that Logan has done everything in his power to be the son you raised. The reason Adeline sounds exhausted and distressed was all my doing. I truly am in awe of the man my daughter married. You should be very proud of your son, Governor." He choked back emotion before continuing.

"And sir, as you certainly have more claim on her than I do, if you want her to return home to you, then I understand. I'll fly all of them back on one of our private jets. You don't have to make the trip, although I do appreciate your willingness to do so on her behalf."

Another round of silence fell over the group.

"Well, I appreciate your frankness, Mr. Nguyen. I understand this has been a trying experience for everyone involved, not just for Logan and Adeline. I'm certain you understand that if my daughter-in-law calls me in tears and asks me to bring her home, then that is precisely what I'm going to do if I have to move heaven and earth to do so."

"Yes, and I assure you that Logan would've done the same if he'd been the one she'd made the request of and so would I."

Adeline offered her father a sweet smile.

"I'm pleased to hear that," Governor Haydenshire offered sincerely. "Although she instructed me not to, I did note that Adeline sounded relieved when I offered to come to Sydney to get her. That's ultimately why I changed my mind, so I'll leave it up to her as to whether or not I make the flight out...which let me assure everyone listening, I am only too happy to do.

"But let me offer you a little advice if I may," the governor requested, though he didn't give Lucas time for refusal. "As you yourself said, Adeline would've been much more comfortable at the hotel with Logan, who I am well aware is an extraordinary young man who will always do right by Adeline and who I could not be more proud of. But I also know that Logan might be trying to serve too many masters, to please you and your family, along with Adeline and his friends. I thought perhaps he might need to be reminded that when he said I do and put that ring on her finger, his loyalties are to Adeline alone.

"That might mean pissing you off by refusing to allow her to stay in the palace where she is uncomfortable or standing up to your family for any reason at all. As you've assured me that Logan has, in fact, been the best husband he knew how to be under the circumstances, allow me to step in on my son's behalf.

"If they choose to stay in Sydney, they will be going back to the hotel where I booked their rooms. This is their honeymoon, first of all. Second, Logan was absolutely right. You are going to have to give Adeline a little space if you want to begin a relationship with her. Take it from me, a man who is well on his way to raising thirteen children, you need to measure your time with your daughter by its quality not by its quantity."

Lucas listened intently.

"Perhaps it would be better if you got to know Adeline where she feels comfortable, here on our farm, with Logan, or with Rainer and Emily, or my wife and me. Perhaps if you visit, you could see her at the hospital, where she is quickly gaining a reputation of being one of the top medios in her field. Wherever it may be, stop trying to force her into a place where you are comfortable at her misery." Fury spilled into Governor Haydenshire's tone again.

"Let me be the first to assure you that as Adeline's father, you are welcome on Haydenshire Farm any time you choose to be here, as long as Adeline wants you to be here. But let me also remind you that this is her home. Should Logan, any of my family, or I feel that Adeline is in some kind of distress because of your presence, you will be asked to leave," the governor offered his hesitant invitation before moving on.

"If Adeline does want to stay in Sydney for the next few days, then I'm going to demand that you let her set the schedule for when you are in her and Logan's company. I'm also going to insist that you leave her time with Logan and time with her friends. She's twenty-one years old and thus far has been through hell at the hands of her mother.

"I don't really feel I'm asking for much for you to allow her time to be with the people who not only love and adore her but who have been there for her and have proven themselves true."

Lucas appeared to be growing weary of the governor's commands. "I want to do that as well. I want to be there for her. That's what I was trying to do."

"You cannot make up for twenty-one years in a few days' time. Since my children arrived at your palace last night, I've received two phone calls from Emily and one from Rainer. That doesn't include the numerous calls made to my wife. My son, Garrett, has received an endless number of texts from Fionna, and my eldest son, Will, received three phone calls from Dan. They were all extremely worried about Adeline and the demands you've heaped on her.

"Then I get a call from Adeline a few minutes ago, in tears asking me to come get her or to fly her home. Let me reiterate my shock by saying the only thing that precious child has ever asked of me is that I walk her down the aisle so she could marry my son." Governor Haydenshire's acrimony shattered his voice. Rage spilled from the fissures.

"So, let me say it the only way I can really think of at this point, Mr. Nguyen—back off!" Governor Haydenshire roared.

Defeat etched Lucas's face as he nodded. "Yes, you're absolutely right. Trying to make up for twenty-one years in the next few days was precisely my plan. I do need to back off, as you said, and give Adeline and myself a little time to process all of this. I would very much like to get to know Adeline at your home. I suppose I just want so badly to make certain that this works out. I don't want to lose her now that I've just found her." Desperation perforated his tone.

"You can only lead a horse to water," Governor Haydenshire reminded Lucas, who looked thoroughly confused.

Logan assumed the expression wasn't prevalent in Australia. "I'll explain it later," he mouthed to Lucas.

"Put my son back on the phone," was Governor Haydenshire's next command.

As Lucas handed the phone to Logan, Adeline edged toward her father. She put her arms around him, thoroughly shocking both Lucas and Logan.

"Logan?" the governor's gruff voice shook Logan from his reverie.

"Uh, yeah, Dad, I'm here." Logan was still staring at Adeline and Lucas who were both hugging and crying.

"Drop the cast on the phone."

"I already did."

"Now, would Adeline feel better if I were there? Do you think she should stay? Most importantly, what does Adeline want me to do?"

"Uh, well…" Logan considered as Lucas pulled away from Adeline and gazed at her adoringly.

"You do whatever you want, dear. I'll stop interfering, and I am sorry for my overdoing things," Lucas apologized.

"I didn't know you called Dad," Emily whispered to Rainer, who smiled.

"I was worried about them. I didn't know you'd already called. I wasn't sure what to do," Rainer admitted.

Logan thought about how truly blessed he was to be in a family who was willing to fly to the other side of the world for the woman he loved.

"I'm leaving this up to you," Governor Haydenshire offered.

"We're sure as hell not eating with Liam or anyone else."

"Good, all right, what else? Do you think Adeline might feel more secure if I was there, or are you going to step up for her?"

"I'll take care of her." Logan began thinking over everything that had happened. "Let me take her back to the Kingsford. I'll let her eat and get a good night's sleep, and nothing else," Logan quoted his father's text and listened to him chuckle. "She'll feel better if it's just us. No expectations from anyone else. If she wants to come home in the morning, we'll take the earliest flight, and if she wants to stay then that's what we'll do." He could almost hear his father's smile from ten thousand miles away.

"Adeline's going to insist that she's fine and wants to stay for dinner and whatever it is you're seeing tonight at the Opera House. She won't want to hurt Lucas's feelings," Governor Haydenshire pointed out. "Are you going to let her walk that rope bridge, because, let me tell you, it's hanging by a thread."

"No, sir, we're leaving as soon as I get off the phone with you." His father's warning strengthened his resolve.

"Good man. And welcome to the marvelous, albeit occasionally treacherous but always rewarding world of being the kind of husband Adeline deserves. In turn, son, you'll have a wife who is so wonderful, you'll never deserve her, but you'll also never be able to live without her."

"Yeah, I already knew that last part," Logan assured his father.

"And Logan," the governor soothed, "if you need me, I'll be there, at a moment's notice."

"I know, Dad. Thank you."

"Anytime. Now give the phone to your wife and then you can inform her father of your decisions." Everyone watched as Adeline took the phone and listened to the governor.

Whatever he said, Adeline beamed as tears leaked from her eyes. She took Emily's hand and guided her and Fionna to the women's restroom. Logan understood that his father wanted to talk to her without influence of either Logan or Lucas.

Logan turned to Lucas. "I'm taking her back to the Kingsford. We'll decide where to go from there in the morning."

Lucas nodded. Disappointment colored his features.

"I don't guess I could convince you to stay after that," Lucas tried feebly.

Logan, Rainer, and Dan all chuckled. Clearly, Lucas needed to spend a little more time with Governor Haydenshire.

"There's not a chance in hell, sir."

"My parents and family will see your leaving as very rude. You were invited guests of the Premier. I'll have to stretch to come up with reasoning for your absence."

Dan rolled his eyes. "Welcome to fatherhood, Mr. Nguyen. You regret not taking care of her for the past twenty-one years? Take care of her now. It seems to me your family's got things just a little screwed up. Maybe work on your priorities before your etiquette."

Lucas looked momentarily startled as he gave a hesitant nod. The ladies returned from the bathroom. Adeline was smiling, and Logan's heart tripped over its next beat. "So, the hotel or are we heading to the airport?"

Adeline threw her arms around his neck and hugged him with all of her might. Logan beamed as he cradled her closely.

"I'm sorry, Lucas. I really do want to spend more time with you, but Governor Haydenshire is sending his plane now. I want to spend the night at the hotel with Logan. Then maybe we could see you tomorrow morning before we go home."

"It's fine if that's what you want." Lucas spoke the words, though the expression on his face said they tasted bitter. "I'll have the drivers take you back to the palace, and I'll have Marta and Fred gather your things."

Adeline looked like she was being physically rent in two before Logan's very eyes.

"If you want, you could have breakfast with Logan and me at the restaurant in the hotel tomorrow. I don't want to lose you, either."

A broad grin formed on her father's face as he nodded. "You just tell me what time and I'll be there."

"Not six," Adeline insisted. Logan chuckled as he brushed a kiss across her cheek. "I don't know, maybe nine?"

Logan raised his eyebrows and gave Lucas a look that said take it or leave it but whatever Adeline said, went.

"I'll be there," Lucas pledged.

"I really am sorry."

"Love, as your father-in-law so eloquently pointed out, I truly have set out about this with very little consideration for your feelings. I wanted to right a wrong instantly. That's what I'm accustomed to doing, I suppose, but this is going to take a great deal of time and effort on both of our parts. I just want you to know that I'm more than willing to put in both if you are."

Adeline nodded. She seemed to force herself to give Lucas another hug. "I am. I promise."

Lucas squeezed her tightly. "Then I'll see you both in the morning."

"Come on, baby." Logan took Adeline's hand and guided her out of the Opera House.

He noted the morose expression on Dan and Fionna's faces as they returned to the palace, but his concern and his responsibility were only for his wife.

Logan carried their luggage back into the honeymoon suite of the Kingsford Wellborn.

"Well, it's not a palace, but it's pretty nice," Logan commented as he locked the door behind them and set their suitcases on the stands.

Adeline smiled up at him sweetly. The moon reflected her peace.

"No, it's not a palace. But you're here, and we're all alone, so it's perfect." She laid her face against his chest and wound her arms around his waist.

While keeping the promise he'd made to his father in the forefront of his mind, Logan cradled her in his arms.

"Why don't you get changed, and I'll order us some dinner?"

Adeline smiled and moved to her suitcase.

Logan settled on the bed and flipped through the room service menu. Adeline shut the bathroom door before he could ask her what she might like to eat.

He decided on several things he knew she'd like, and picked up the phone to order. The receiver fell from Logan's grasp as his mouth dropped open a moment later.

His reaction thoroughly delighted his bride. His heart thundered in his chest as he took her in.

She was dressed in a red satin and black lace flyaway top that tied with a seductive black bow at her cleavage. Her breasts were only obscured by black lace. Her nipples were already strained and pulled taut. Her slender waist was revealed. She was wearing red satin shorts with black lace sides. They were so short he could see the very bottom of her curves perfectly, and he longed to see more.

"You are the most beautiful thing I've ever laid eyes on." He stood up off the bed and moved to her.

"I promise not to tell your dad we did more than eat and sleep." She laughed as Logan scooped her up and laid her on the bed.

"Good," he panted. "My dad doesn't need to know what I'm about to do to you." His vow made her eyes flash as a seductive grin spread across her face.

"I love you, and I'm about to untie that bow and have my way with you."

She whispered his name and arched her back as Logan reached and untied the black ribbon. He watched the satin and lace fall away from her and set to make his claim.

CHAPTER 30
THE TRUTH MAY GET YOU KILLED

DAN VINDICO

The absence of her was physical. Dan's heart ached. He'd held her hand throughout the ride over, but they were leaving the next day.

This was it. He had to explain everything to her, and he had no idea where that would leave them. The euphoria and the lust had to come to an end.

Was their time together enough to make her believe in him and trust him? Did she want to be with him at all? Could he really keep her happy, and could he keep her fate from leading her to a grave all because of him? That damn tomb seared through his mind. Fionna forced a smile, but forlorn was the only emotion that existed in her energy.

"I still don't think you should've had to apologize to Russian governors, who are clearly all low-life, two-timing thugs, but Garrett's dad is kind of amazing."

Dan forced a chuckle. "Yeah," he agreed as he unlocked the door to their suite. "I guess he is."

He brushed a kiss across Fionna's cheek. They still had one night, his mind argued vehemently. Maybe he could put off the conversation. Maybe he could have her one more time before the world intruded again.

"So," he drawled, "how about I order us some dinner and then after we eat maybe I could see some of the purchases you made today?" *Just keep your head in the game. Make this everything she deserves. You don't have to talk yet.*

Fionna chuckled. Her mind seemed to be waging a war of its own. "Actually, you purchased them, and one of them is one of your Christmas presents. I have to decide how exactly I'm going to punish you for that." She tried so hard to flirt. With a great deal of effort, she modulated her voice to a low and seductive tone.

Dan shut down the swirl of grief and confusion in his mind. He growled and wrapped his arms around her. He devoured her mouth until she was panting for breath.

"All I want for Christmas is you naked in my bed."

He let his hands work their way up her skirt and began massaging her backside. He guided her body in rhythmic circles around what should have been a throbbing erection.

"Is that an invitation?" She couldn't do it either. They just couldn't ignore the next day. They had to figure out how or if this was going to work at all. She'd just shut him down cold.

He despised Christmas and everything that went with it. It was generally his policy not to be involved with anyone from Thanksgiving until well after Valentine's Day.

She felt his energy deflate. Dan caught her hands as she fumbled with his belt. She tried to keep up the act, but tears were imminent.

"I think we'd better talk," he choked.

She turned away from him and drew a deep breath. He called himself every horrible name he could come up with in that endless moment of selfish frustration.

"I swear I'm not trying to be as big of an asshole as I'm doing a hell of a job of being right now. Honestly, I'm trying to do this right."

She nodded and gave him her sweet smile.

"I know. You're not being an asshole. I shouldn't have said anything about Christmas or anything at home." Pain shadowed her beautiful face.

"No, you should have. We can't put this off anymore. We need to talk. Please, just let me get us some food. Let's really talk about this because I do want to spend the holidays with you, and trust me, that is not something I've ever said. I want to spend every moment with you, but I can't, and I don't know how to make this work."

She managed a slight nod. Her chin trembled.

"I don't care what we eat. I'm gonna take a quick shower, okay?"

She made a valiant effort not to show him how terrified she was. She was about to come unglued, and she thought the shower would make a good cover.

You earned this, he told himself. *This is what living like a rat bastard for the past decade has gotten you. The most beautiful woman in the world, the one who means more to you than anyone or anything else, is standing in your hotel room fighting tears she doesn't want you to see. One week wasn't enough to do anything at all.*

The thought made him sick. He swallowed down bile as it shot violently from his stomach to his throat.

"Hey,"—he caught her hand as she grabbed sweat pants and an Angels T-shirt and spun toward the bathroom—"please, baby, don't do this. Please, I'm begging you. Don't get in that shower and sob and convince yourself that you should never have gotten involved with me, and make yourself believe that I'm going to do you just like I've done all the others because I'm not. I want to be in this relationship. As fucking terrified as I am, I want this. I am fully committed to you. We have to talk about what that means for both of us if that's what you want too."

She clenched her jaw and shuddered from the effort of halting the emotions that threatened to consume her. Her rhythms tensed in jagged arcs from the effort.

"No," he demanded, "I won't let you." He would fight. He would fight her doubt. He would fight her apprehension and incredulity. He would fight his own reputation. His vehemence shocked her.

Good, because I'm going to make her believe me if it's the last thing I do.

"If you want to take a shower, you can take one with me. If you want to cry or need to cry, then I will stand there and hold you and let you cry. I will wipe away every single tear, and I will still be standing there when you're finished. And I will still be in love with you, Fionna." His own shock over his ability to use the word was no more than hers.

She couldn't quite believe what she'd heard with her own ears any more than she could continue to wage war against her tears. She broke down, and he held her just like he'd promised he would.

He was going to do this. It had just been too damn long. He prayed as she cried. Prayed for help, prayed that he'd be able to keep her safe, prayed that she would somehow find him worthy to be loved. He needed her. He couldn't go on without her.

He needed to stop killing himself slowly, needed to stop drowning his sorrow in a myriad of women who meant nothing to him at all. He needed to stop self-destructing, and he held the only thing that could save him from himself sobbing in his arms.

"Shh, baby. It's okay. I'm right here."

He wiped away the first of what he knew would be hours of tears. He unbuttoned her blouse and unclasped her bra.

While carefully guiding her with him, he edged the few steps toward his suitcase. He pulled out one of his Iodex T-shirts and swathed her body in it. He unzipped her skirt and slid it down her curves. Dan was unable to recall another time, in the dozens of skirts he'd unzipped, he'd had no ulterior motive.

He released her only long enough to remove his shirt, and he moved her to the bed. She was still shuddering with tears.

He lay back and pulled her onto his chest. He cradled her tenderly and let her cry. Her tears cut like knives. He let her sob. He'd earned every jagged, piercing tear that beaded and burned his skin.

She was terrified, but so was he. She didn't trust him. He didn't trust himself. The road they were trying to navigate would be treacherous and fraught with every kind of pitfall there could possibly be. He didn't care.

He let her cry herself out. He deserved the agony and the suffering that watching her brought on in heavy doses. He wiped away tear after tear and handed her tissues until the box on the bedside table was empty. He left her only long enough to race to the bathroom for another box.

"I'm sorry," were the first convulsive words she managed.

"Shh," he soothed, "you have nothing to be sorry for."

"I don't even know what happened." She shuddered against him.

Dan nodded. "I know you're hungry, baby. We have a whole lot of time to talk about what happened and what we want to happen."

He wasn't going anywhere. If he had to stay up with her all night long, so be it. He wasn't walking away. "Shh, shh." He pulled her back to him. She tried to move away as he reached for the phone. "You stay right here."

Relief flooded through her as she nodded against him. He quickly ordered sandwiches he knew she'd liked from their picnic several nights before on the beach. He informed the attendant he'd tip well if they didn't have to wait. Less than five minutes later, there was a knock on their door.

She was a mess—a sobbing, convulsive, swollen, red-eyed, beautiful disaster. He caressed her face and soothed her with his body.

"Baby, I'm going to lay you down and walk from here to the door to get our food. Then I'm coming right back, and I'm going to feed you, okay?" He kissed her forehead as she nodded.

She sat up off of him and attempted to wipe away her tears and her extreme embarrassment. Dan moved quickly. He grabbed several Australian twenties from his wallet, and edged the door open enough to get the tray inside. He blocked the attendant from entering.

No one else was seeing her like this. Those tears were his, just like the perfect swell of her breasts, and the arch of her back, the curve of her gorgeous ass, her long luscious legs, and the tender, delicate, lips between them. They were all his and no one else's.

He folded the money and handed it to the pimple-faced teenager that held the tray.

"Hey, thanks, mate." The kid flipped excitedly through the twenties. "You need anything else just ask for me. I'm Derrick."

Quite shocked that he was able to chuckle, Dan nodded. "Will do." Derrick continued to stand and stare at Dan. He didn't move. "Thanks," Dan added as Derrick continued to stare into the room. "Go away," he finally ordered.

Derrick looked momentarily shocked. "Oh, right, sorry." He sped from the door.

Dan carried the tray into the room and shook his head. Fionna was laughing at the exchange. He positioned the tray carefully on the end of the bed and kissed her head.

"So, Derrick can make you smile and laugh, but I just make you cry."

Pain etched her swollen face. "Dan." She shook her head and stared at the bed.

"I got you a surprise." He changed tactics quickly.

She furrowed her brow. "Why?"

Dan chuckled at the question. "I don't know, because I like to make you smile, and I thought you'd like this, and I want to make you happy."

She waited as he moved back to his suitcase.

"When I helped Logan carry out their stuff to keep him from screeching at his father-in-law's butler for attempting to repack Adeline's suitcase, I might've swiped several of these from the cabinet."

He pulled two cans of Dr Pepper from his suitcase and chilled them. He handed her one. Her mouth fell open and then pulled into a delighted grin.

"I'm pretty sure that's against the law, Chief Vindico." She sounded much more like herself.

Dan joined her on the bed. "It's a misdemeanor at best. I'm pretty sure I could get off with the whole 'he offered me several earlier and I thought it was a standing offer' routine. And I would do absolutely anything for you," he informed her and then watched as his vow settled on her. "Plus, the soda here sucks."

"I love you," she vowed suddenly. All traces of laughter evaporated. It was a test to see if he was going to do what he'd said and still be there now that the tears were gone.

"Me too," he assured her. "Now, how about if you eat, and I talk?"

She drew a long sip of the Dr Pepper he'd given her and swallowed down an infinitesimal bite of her sandwich. She stared up at him. "Will you please just be honest with me, completely honest? Because I know when you hide things or you try to cover something up. I'm a pretty damn strong Receiver." All the pretenses were gone. He'd drawn the final ace.

Dan rubbed his hands over his face and tried to determine where to begin.

"Completely honest, huh?" He bought just a little more time.

She nodded and set the sandwich back on her plate.

"Fine." He drew a deep breath. "Fionna, I'm the biggest asshole you'll ever meet. I'm a selfish bastard, but even I can't really believe that I'm about to say what I'm about to say to you. Being in a relationship with me is extremely dangerous, and it's the very last thing you should ever do. I know all of this, and yet I can't seem to talk myself out of begging you to be with me and only me. I'm rude, pompous, egotistical, and self-absorbed. I want you only for myself, but I can never be seen anywhere with you.

"I can't take you places. I can't even take you out for dinner. I can't go to the grocery store with you and buy you Karamel Sutra ice cream. I can't go fill your car up with gas. I can't take you to see your favorite band play in concert. I can't threaten pricks who hit on you. I can't sit in the Angels box and whistle when you run on the field. I can't take care of you the way I want to or the way you should be taken care of. I can't spoil you, but baby, I wish more than anything in this world or the next one that I could.

"I'm going to sit here and tell you that if you want to be in this relationship, you're going to have to go out and be seen with your friends and with other guys. And that it's going to piss me the fuck off, and then I'm probably going to be a royal asshole to you because I'll be so damn jealous I won't be able to see straight. And the very worst part of all is that we have to do all of this because, if anyone ever finds out about us, Wretchkinsides will kill you too."

He choked and blinked back tears of his own. "There, that's the whole truth." He threw his hands out in defeat. "All I can really offer you is that if you'll stick this out with me, when I end him, baby, I will skywrite how in love with you I am over every single city, in every country, on every continent on this planet."

Dan's heart refused him the next beat. Air seized in his lungs. It burned as his body begged for more, but he was unable to provide any.

He stared at her and willed her to say anything at all. The silence beat against his eardrums and ricocheted in his restless mind.

CHAPTER 31
QUESTIONS AND ANSWERS

"Okay." She nodded and a grin played on her beautiful lips. He swallowed harshly. He wasn't certain what she was telling him.

"Okay?" he finally begged.

"You told me everything we couldn't do, and I'm okay with all of that, but I'd like to know what we can do."

A riptide of confusion drowned him. He'd been far too focused on everything he couldn't give her to try and see any glimmer of hope, but she was the light in his darkness yet again.

"Uh, I don't really know," he admitted.

Her grin turned into her smile, the one she'd been reserving for him. "Can you come over to my house and have pizza with me if I order it before you get there?"

"Yes, as long as no one sees my bike there or sees me going in or out."

"I have a garage with a door into my kitchen, and none of my neighbors are Gifted," she pointed out. "Can I go to your house and maybe stay over?"

"You can come to my house whenever you want. My house is about as hidden as a house in the middle of Arlington can be. No one knows where I live and, baby, if you're willing to do this, I don't plan on ever not spending the night with you somewhere, anywhere."

His heart sent blood surging through his veins. He felt faint from the heady sensation. It was like being burned and then drenched in an icy river.

She grinned and crawled back into his lap. "Will your Iodex guys know about us?"

"Are you kidding me? Baby doll, I may hire a team of people just for the purposes of keeping you safe when I'm not there."

"Will you be there if I get scared?" She swallowed down the mounting emotions.

"Yes, always. I'll stop working all day and night. I'll do anything. If you need me or you want me, I'll be there."

She nodded. "I know this is going to be really hard, but I love you. You're worth fighting for. We're worth all of the precautions. And…" she paused and drew a deep breath, "I can feel how scared you are. You're not an asshole, Dan. You're terrified. But I'm not Amelia. I hate that she couldn't do what I can do, but I can feel them a long way away. I can feel them coming. I can feel them lying. I can feel their darkness. I can tell when I'm in danger. I know when something bad is going to happen a long time before it happens. I'm pretty powerful, like I said. I can help you take care of me."

"I know how powerful you are, but he's a monster." Dan's gut clenched. He squeezed his eyes shut.

"I know." She unleashed the full power of her Receiver's cast. It flooded through him, righting every wrong, healing every wound, restoring him, calming him, and letting him feel the intensity of her love. The unending depths of her power overwhelmed him. "Can I keep asking you questions?"

Dan didn't understand how she could be okay with this, or how she could sound excited about the parameters of their relationship.

"Of course." He was desperate for her to keep going. With every question he answered, hope resurrected in his soul.

"Will you watch old movies with me when you come to my house?"

Dan grinned. "Can I get you naked when they're over?" He

couldn't believe he was able to joke, but when he looked up into those intoxicating eyes, he saw life. He saw light, and he moved toward it.

"Yes." She giggled, and he tried to memorize the sound. Another question formed on her features, but she didn't ask.

"What, baby? Just ask me."

"Can I meet your parents?" Fear tensed in her rhythms. Dan grimaced. "It's okay. Never mind." She dropped her gaze.

He shook his head. If he wanted her, then he had to give her all of him as well.

"Several things you need to understand before I say yes to that." She looked wary, so he picked up speed. "First of all, my mother is nuts."

Her grin returned along with an incredulous eye roll.

"No, I'm serious. I'm about to invite you to come to my parents' house on Christmas Eve, for the Vindico Christmas revue, and before you agree, you need to understand that my mother is batshit crazy."

"That's what you said about Lindley." She didn't appear to believe him on either count.

"Uh no, Lindley has a very significant undiagnosed personality disorder that desperately needs to be treated. My mother is just your well-above-average kind of crazy."

"I still want to come, but I kind of don't want the first time I meet your parents to be on Christmas Eve. That's a lot of pressure for everyone." She wrinkled her nose.

Determined to prove himself, Dan considered. He rolled his wrist, checked his watch, and pulled his cell phone from his pocket.

Fionna began slowly picking at her sandwich as she watched him.

"Are you okay, son?" Governor Vindico gave a concerned greeting on the first ring.

"I'm fine, Dad. I just had a quick question."

"Okay?"

"I was wondering if I could bring Fionna over Sunday night for dinner with you and Mom," he said nonchalantly, then listened to the stunned silence from ten thousand miles away. The broad, delighted grin on Fionna's face made all of the impending discomfort worth it.

"Of course. Your sisters will want to be here," Governor Vindico warned.

"Yeah, I figured."

"Your mother will be thrilled, so I don't really want her to get attached if that's going to pressure you in any way or going to cause her heartbreak in a few weeks' time."

Dan's head dropped in defeat. "No worries, Dad. Can we come?" He was suddenly desperate to end the conversation.

"Ask if I can bring anything," Fionna whispered.

"You can come to dinner and bring Ms. Styler anytime—you know that. We'd be honored to meet her."

"Fi wants to know if you'd like her to bring anything." Dan's brain mocked him, and his heart hammered out an SOS as he tried to envision his mother's reaction to a woman offering to bring something to dinner. She'd have chapels booked all over the freaking Realm in a week's time. Dan's stomach churned.

"I'll have to check with your mom, but tell her that's very kind." Governor Vindico sounded like he was concerned he might be dreaming.

"You know no one can know we're dating." Dan's voice shook disconcertingly.

"Yes, I think we, of all people, understand that. We'll help you keep her safe. The entire governing board wants to help you, son. We want you to heal. If she's a path toward that, then I will use all of the power I wield to make certain no one knows about the two of you."

"Thanks, Dad, really." He sincerely hoped his father understood he was thankful for more than Sunday dinner.

"You're very welcome. We'll see you Sunday."

Dan ended the call and tossed his phone on the bed. "So, you just made their Christmases for the next ten years."

Fionna laughed again but then became introspective as she studied Dan. "Does your mom being crazy have to do with the fact that she wants you to settle down?"

"That's some of it, but I've never gotten along with my mother. Ever. We've been arguing since I was old enough to talk. I honestly can't stand her."

"Can I ask you something else?" Fionna had worked up the courage to ask whatever she was about to ask him.

"Anything."

"Do Amelia's parents still live next door to your parents?" Her voice lost its tonality. The question was made in a forced whisper.

"Yeah." Dan nodded.

"I know I just completely freaked out, and now I'm going to meet your parents, which will bring on another round of hysteria, so fair warning." He grinned at her. "And I know we have to keep everything hidden, and we're probably not ready for this yet, but at some point I'd really like to meet them."

She took his breath away. His blood seized in his veins. Dan forced his head to nod. "You're gonna have to give me a little time on that one, okay?"

"I know." Fionna brushed a tender kiss on his cheek. "So, do you do the whole go back and stay at your parents' house on Christmas Eve? You know, sleep in your old bedroom and everything?"

Dan fought not to cringe. He would never ever stay in his old bedroom, not ever. His body recoiled from the very thought. Far, far too many things had happened in his bedroom in that bed. He usually refused to even enter the room.

"No," he stated firmly. She felt his revulsion, but his tone surprised her.

"Oh." As she took in his expression, she understood. "Sorry."

He tried to modulate his voice. She wanted the truth. "Uh, no, I do the whole Christmas Eve dinner thing, occasionally go to church with my folks to keep my mother happy, and then I usually go back to the office and work in peaceful solitude until New Year's when the Senate reopens."

Fionna looked horrified as Dan bared his soul. "You work on Christmas?" Her voice held a deep sadness.

He grimaced. He wasn't certain what to say. Quickly deciding to go on with it, he drew a deep breath. "Christmas was Amelia's favorite holiday. She loved the whole deal. I gave her an engagement ring the Christmas before she was killed, so I don't really care for it."

"I'm so sorry."

"Can we talk about something else?"

"Is there anything else I need to do or not do so that we can make this work? I just want this to work so badly." Her voice shook, and his heart fissured.

"I don't think so, sweetheart. Just always remember that the fewer people who know about us the safer you are." He sighed his regret.

"Are you going to cheat on me? Is this going to freak you out?"

"I would never, ever cheat on you." He took her hands and stared into the depths of her eyes. "Never, and I was worried after I told you all the rules that you would freak and leave me here to finish drowning in my own hell."

This seemed to shock Fionna. "I'm not going anywhere. I told you I'm head over heels. Why do you think I cried so hard which is not something anyone has ever seen before except Garrett."

He studied her and tried to come up with an answer that might not bring on more tears. "I don't really know what exactly made you cry like that, baby. I just know I never want to be the reason you cry like that ever again."

"I cried because I don't want to think about not being with you," she fretted. "I don't want to think about sleeping all alone in my bed without you, but I don't want to freak you out. We went on for all these days, and I didn't know what you were going to say. You felt so many horrible emotions. I couldn't work through them all."

"I don't want to sleep without you either, and believe me, nothing has ever made me not want to be at work until you. I think I'm gonna rent several cars when we get back, or maybe I'll just take one of the Iodex Expeditions. I need something that isn't my bike. I hope it's all right that after we spend the weekend together, on Monday I was going to invite myself over after work and then forget to leave until Tuesday morning."

The abject relief that flooded through her rhythms soothed his soul.

She grimaced a moment later. "Okay, but Monday…"

Dan tried to remind himself that if she had plans for Monday that didn't involve him, it would be a good thing. He tried to quell the jealousy that was threatening to tense in his double rhythm strains.

266

"You might want to bring that pizza and ice cream," she concluded.

"Ah." Dan watched her blush. She looked terrified that the fact that she menstruated was going to make him suddenly bolt. "Gotcha." He continued rubbing her back.

"You don't have to stay over." She looked like the offer was costing her a great deal.

He furrowed his brow. "I won't if you really don't want me to, but I was just going to say that if you'd like, after we eat with my parents Sunday night and I invite you to stay at my place, you could bring a box of tampons or pads or whatever you might want to keep there. My closet is half empty, and if it means you'll stay over more, you can keep whatever you want in my bathroom."

Fionna's mouth hung open in shock. "Really?"

Dan laughed at her expression. "I was sort of assuming this might be a monthly occurrence."

Defiant disbelief wiped the smile from her face. She stared him down. "You're sure you want to do this, even at home, even when we have to go to work, and we have bad days? You want me there if I lie on the couch and watch old movies in sweats and feel like hell? When I get sick, you want to be there for all of that?"

It seemed she still didn't really believe him, but he'd prove her wrong. He was determined.

"All of it. Please just give me a chance. Just believe me. If you're willing to do all of this in secret, I will do everything in my power to take care of every single thing you want or need."

She swallowed down the emotion that had come on suddenly.

"And," he soothed, "if you don't feel well or you're sick for any reason, if you should decide to lie around on my couch and watch old movies, then I could come home at lunch and check on you. I could pick you up a pizza on my way. Anything that might make you smile for me." He tousled her hair which made her grin.

"Okay," she agreed. "Okay, I'll believe you, but if you freak out because someone finds out about us, or for some other reason, and you leave, what you just saw will only be the very beginning. I'll have to buy Garrett an entirely new wardrobe because I'll ruin all of his clothes with tears." She willed him to understand that she was going to allow him to hold her precious, fragile heart in his extremely callused hands.

The way her sobs had made him ache physically seared through him. He would never, ever be the reason she did that again.

"The only reason I would ever leave you is to keep you safe, and that is the only vow I can make to you." He needed her to understand as well.

She gave a begrudging nod.

Dan studied her closely. Her eyes were still red, though most of the swelling had gone down. She'd cried off all of her makeup. He thought she was prettier without it.

CHAPTER 32
CHRISTMAS

"So, what do you like to do for Christmas, Ms. Styler?" He changed the subject and shattered the silence before she could vow that she would be safe even if someone found out about them.

"Garrett usually puts my tree up for me if I agree to feed him." She laughed.

Dan tried not to feel the annoyance he'd felt for the past few days every single time she mentioned Garrett's name. They were clearly very close. He'd always known that. It just hadn't irritated him quite so much until now.

"I spend most of the days right up until Christmas Eve at Mom and Dad's bakery. I help them with Christmas orders, and then I bake a bunch of cookies, bread, and stuff and take it to the homeless shelters and orphanages around town. Emily's going to help me this year." Fionna beamed. Her charity work meant a great deal to her. Dan's heart swelled at her exuberance.

"Then I usually do the whole stay in my old room thing on Christmas Eve at my parents' house. It makes them happy, but this year they're going to Monterrey to see my grandmother. Well," she hemmed, "I mean, Gretta's mother. She's been kind of sick lately, so they're going to check on her."

Dan wondered how sick Fionna's grandmother was. "Were you planning on going with them to Mexico, honey?"

Fionna shook her head. "No, I can't. The Angels are challenging in the big exhibition in Vegas the day after Christmas. We do every year." Disappointment colored her olive skin. "I don't guess you could come. A lot of people who aren't dating a player come. It's a huge event. There will be thousands and thousands of people there." Her head lowered as she awaited the expected no.

"I'd love to go, and I think we could make that work. We'd have to be very, very careful, but I'm not saying no, okay? Just let me think about it and figure everything out."

Her eyes, still red from her tears, danced in elation. "Okay." She threw her arms around him. He hugged her fiercely. The weight of their words and their vows turned to hunger as their energy pulsed in the love between them.

They needed to unite. They needed to seal their love inside the heat and passion between them. The only thing that made sense to him in that moment was to own her fully.

"You know, I promised you a ride this morning," he teased as her breaths quickened.

"I thought you wanted to talk about Christmas." Her voice was low and breathy as Dan laid her under him on the bed.

"Can I put your tree up this year and spend Christmas Eve and Christmas Day at your house just the two of us?"

She nodded as he let his fingers gently glide over the satin crotch of the panties she was wearing.

"Good. Anything else we need to decide tonight?"

She shook her head. Her body began to writhe from the sensations he was bringing her. A low moan reverberated from her as she gasped for breath.

"Be a good girl for me and take that shirt off nice and slow." Her energy spiked rapidly. That delicious little submissive praise kink she had made him ache. It drove him wild. She was perfection.

Her eyes were voracious and her lips swollen in need. She sat up and edged the shirt up for him.

"Nice and slow," he demanded. "I want to see your gorgeous body. It's all mine. Show it to me."

She eased the shirt over her head, and her breasts swayed in swollen mounds. She arched her back and moaned from his knowledge of her kinks. "Good girl."

Dan dragged one finger over her slit, still hidden behind the satin. He leaned down and kissed her through the slick fabric as she cried out for him.

He slid one hand up her body and plied her right breast as he licked the satin between her legs.

He began a slow trek upward with his mouth. He kissed all the way up the slight panties, and then spun his tongue over her adorable navel as it clenched in need.

He groped her breasts as he moved his mouth northward. He cradled her face in his hands as he sucked her left breast fervently. He listened to her beg for more.

He swirled his tongue over her nipple, the dark brown tip drawn so tightly it made him ache. She leaned her head to the side and kissed his fingers as he caressed her lips. She pulled two in her mouth and began sucking and licking them. Savage need shot through his shield.

He pulled his hand away from her mouth and devoured her. He pushed his tongue to hers and pulled the intoxicating energy from her mouth.

"Show me where you want me to lick," he commanded.

Her entire body bucked in need. Her eyes flashed heatedly as she reached and pulled the crotch of her panties to the side. Her rhythms stuttered in desperation.

"Right here, baby?" He swirled his index finger over her lips. He barely touched her. He teased, and tempted, and watched her begin to swell and glisten all for him.

"Tell me. Tell me you need to be licked and sucked. Tell me you want to come in my mouth," he ordered in a lust-driven growl.

"Lick me." She spread her legs farther, while keeping her panties pulled to the side. His body ached as he stared at the provocative display. He dragged his tongue up her slit. He spun it over her clit and then moved away. He built her slowly.

He dipped it low, and then went back for more as she cried out his name. She laced her left hand in his hair and pushed him deeper. He groaned against her.

A moment later, her energy was spun too tightly for her to remain still. She writhed and arched her back. She threw her hands to the bed.

Dan continued to lick and kiss. He held the panties for her now. As she rolled under him, he moved the slick fabric back over her and slid his teeth tenderly over the satin crotch. He watched her entire body contort from the erotic sensation.

Her fear, the tears, and the trepidation of deciding to trust him and to be with him had her bound. It was going to take more to set her free.

He pulled away and stood by the bed long enough to remove his trousers and boxers. He gazed at her with hunger and love coursing through his veins.

She watched him slowly ease her panties off of her. Her eyes were heavy and eager, her lips kiss-swollen. Her breasts throbbed, pert and vying for his hands and his mouth to soothe their need.

Her stomach was clenched tight in anticipation. He traced over his favorite tattoo that led to her lips, flushed the color of a rose, swollen wet with yearning.

"You are so damn beautiful." He took her hand and pulled her forward. Her brow furrowed as he positioned himself behind her on the bed.

"Lie back against me, honey. Feel what you do to me."

She quaked and moaned. He positioned her so the top of her backside was against his fierce strain.

"Now, watch what I do to you." He gestured to the mirror on the dresser directly across from the bed. She gazed in the mirror but then turned away. She couldn't see the beauty, the grace, and the allure that everyone else saw when they looked at her.

Dan was astonished. How could she see the good in everyone around her but only see nonexistent flaws in herself?

"Watch me, Fionna," he commanded. "Watch me get your gorgeous body ready for me."

She trembled and writhed in front of him. He let his hands ply her breasts. They both watched in the mirror as he massaged.

He added to the intensity in slow waves until he was giving her nipples light twists, and she was going wild. She arched her back against him and let her head fall on his shoulder.

"Watch me, baby doll. Watch me touch you." He kept his voice low and smooth. His left hand groped her breast as he slid his right to her mound. The tempting rise of nerve endings, raw in their hunger, pulsated under his caress.

"You are perfect, so fucking beautiful," he urged as she begged for his touch. "Such a good girl for me."

"Please, Dan, please."

"Watch yourself drip all for me." He pulled her apart, and watched in the mirror as liquid sex coursed around his fingers.

"Please." She watched now as well. He dipped his fingers between her lips, and she grasped his thighs. She clung to him as he slowly moved his fingers over her. Her muscles clenched tightly around his fingers.

He kept his strokes seeking and smooth. She was unable to keep still. Her energy arced in higher pitches. She was on the edge.

"That feels good, doesn't it, honey? It makes you want more."

Her entire body tensed.

"But it just doesn't feel as good as when it's full does it, baby doll? You need more, don't you? You need to be taken hard. You need to be owned." He had her.

She screamed out his name, threw her head back, and quaked against him. Her fingernails dug into the hardened muscles of his thighs. He throbbed and growled from watching her entire body orgasm in the mirror. It was the most stunning thing he'd ever seen.

"There is nothing more beautiful than watching you come undone for me," he groaned in ardent desire as she gasped for breath.

"I'm gonna set the cast, honey." He cupped the hand that had been inside her moments before.

"You did it this morning. Just take me," she begged as he dropped the orb of erotic energy.

"Mount me," he commanded as he slid down the bed and straddled her over him.

She grasped his strain as he groaned and watched her hands on his cock. She traced the throbbing veins and rubbed him between her folds, drenching him in her liquid silk.

Unable to wait any longer, he wrapped his hands around her waist and thrust hard. He lowered her onto him and filled her. She gasped and moaned her approval.

"Ride me," he ordered as she rocked her body back and forth over his. "That's it. There's my greedy girl." He formed his right hand in a fist and pressed it to her mound. He made certain all of her hot spots got the attention they needed.

"Oh, yes!" she gasped from the sensation of rocking on top of him and against him as she rode harder. He thrust deeply into her as she began to scream for another release.

"Take it, honey. Take it deep. Drown my cock in that sweet cum."

She quaked and writhed on top of him. As she lost it all, she stopped moving. It washed through her, and he eased his thrusts. He let it develop fully around him. The tender, trembling pulls of her body, coupled with the exquisite sensation of their energies combining and rolling in tantric spirals, was blissful perfection.

"I'm not finished with you. Tell me you want more," he demanded as she began to rock faster this time. She wanted it badly.

"More, please. It feels so good!" she cried out, unable to stop the hungry plea.

He kept his fist against her and fought his own release as it gathered fiercely in his groin. His body drew tight. His vision clouded. She'd been through too much. She was too tired for an extended session. This was it, and it was all they needed.

She shuddered, and as he felt the first pulse of her next climax, this one much stronger than the last, he exploded inside of her. He drove himself deep into her as she unfurled around him.

Her energy seared through his veins. It bound and healed him. It made him whole.

She collapsed on top of him, and he wrapped his arms around her as he continued to fill her with his potent release. They both shuddered and gasped until their bodies stilled.

Dan turned to his side, while keeping Fionna pressed against him. He withdrew begrudgingly.

"I don't want to go home," she fussed as Dan tucked her into his protective embrace. "I want to stay here and do that forever."

"If it's all right with you, I thought maybe we could do that at home as well." He listened to her giggle. Her energy began lolling in languid rolls all around him. It soothed him and brought him peace.

Fionna yawned and tucked herself closer to Dan. "Go to sleep, baby. I'm right here, and I'm not going anywhere. I'll keep you safe."

He was still trying to allay the fear that was hidden in the recesses of her heart, fear that he was going to break it into irreparable pieces.

As she quieted, he began his analysis. With methodical precision, he made his plans. Dominic Wretchkinsides would never have the opportunity to get near Fionna. He would no longer come between Dan and the life he longed for.

He would no longer stand in his way.

CHAPTER 33
HOSTILE NEGOTIATIONS

With terror shooting through his veins, Dan exited the Crown Governor's jet with Fionna's fingers laced through his own. The fear was overwhelming. The tides of the unknown robbed him of breath.

Nervously, he let his eyes sweep the tarmac in his methodic, well-trained manner. No one was in the Senate. It was early Saturday, and Governor Haydenshire's plane was the only one arriving. Though no one unsavory would be anywhere near the Gifted Senate, Dan couldn't help but beg the ether that he could have her and somehow keep her safe.

Fionna could feel his trepidation in his energy strains. He was scaring her, but he couldn't seem to gain control of his own emotions.

"I just need to grab a few things out of my office, and I'm going to take out one of our Expeditions. I can't be seen with you in your car. The Expeditions are so darkly tinted no one can see who's driving it, and they're unmarked. I can meet you at your house in a little while if that's okay."

This was how it was going to have to be. She'd vowed to him, just a few hours before, that she was fine with all of the precautions, but Dan hated himself for putting her through this.

He hated himself for where his own selfish desires might take them. The weight of Amelia's tomb pierced through his soul. The very soul Fionna had just mended. His entire body, his entire shield, rejected the image with acrid revulsion.

As they made their way toward the Pentagon, headed toward the Gifted Senate, Garrett Haydenshire's scowl greeted them on the parking deck of Iodex. Fionna's brow furrowed, but Garrett didn't seem to notice. His fury was directed squarely at Dan.

The idea of letting off a little infuriated steam was very appealing, so Dan narrowed his eyes and felt his massive biceps flex of their own accord.

Garrett rolled his eyes. It was in the eye roll that Dan realized he'd been about to direct his frustrations toward one of his closest friends. His disdain for Garrett's hold on Fionna kept him chafed and irritated.

"Fionna, go play with Em," Garrett commanded as they made their approach.

"Don't order her around. Who the hell do you think you are?" Dan was furious.

Fionna brushed a kiss across Dan's cheek and shot a spiteful look at Garrett. "Be nice, both of you. I think I will go see Emily while you two talk. Let's see if we can't stop behaving like we're two. And if you can't do that, then when I get back, I'll make you write ten times 'I will be nice to Fionna's boyfriend.'" She slid her beautiful sienna eyes, fixed in a glare, from Garrett to Dan. "And you can write 'I will be nice to Fionna's best friend.' And if that doesn't work, Fionna is not going to be nice to either of you." She sounded angrier than Dan had ever heard her.

"Got it," Garrett assured her.

Fionna moved toward Rainer and Emily, as they all entered the Iodex offices. Garrett followed Dan toward his private office, without invitation.

"Boyfriend, huh?" He let the door slam behind him.

"Yeah, is that okay with you, or did I need to run my relationship updates by you first?"

Garrett's eyes flashed furiously. "Hey, why don't you stop being such a monumental asswipe? I'm not interested in Fionna."

"Good," Dan shot back.

"What is wrong with you?"

"Why are you here?"

"I'm here because she is one of my best friends, someone who's had a thing for you for a long time. I don't want to see her get hurt by you or because of you. And you're an asshole! I've been there. I've been the guy sitting on her couch with her curled up in a ball in my lap sobbing over guys who don't mean half as much to her as you do. Just in case you haven't noticed, you haven't had all that good a track record with women. Fionna is not the kind of girl you fuck and leave. Do you get what I'm saying to you?"

With every bellow, he moved dangerously closer to Dan. The energy of their shields pulsed with their ire. Dan's fists tightened in anticipation. Garrett matched his stance.

"I know that, and I have no intention of leaving her. I plan to be with her until she orders me away. Now, get the hell out of my office, and stay the hell out of my life."

Garrett gave an arrogant, dismissive laugh. "I don't think so, Danny. Because when you freak and break her heart, I'm the guy who's gonna get to clean up that mess."

Dan's jaw clenched as he tried desperately to will away the deep desire to sink his fists into Garrett's face. He settled for shoving him away.

Unmitigated rage flashed in Garrett's eyes. "You keep your fucking hands off me."

"Not that it's any of your business, but I have no intention of breaking her heart, ever."

"Sure." Garrett rolled his eyes. "Sorry if I have a hard time believing that, but I love her. Every bit as much as I love Emily."

"Oh yeah?" Dan menaced. "Well so do I, only a hell of a lot more than I love any of my sisters."

Stunned disbelief washed over Garrett as his mouth hung open. "Are you serious? Are you shitting me? Did you tell her that? Because you can't walk away after that."

Fury surged through Dan's veins as he lunged at Garrett. He

grabbed him by the collar of his shirt, nearly pulling him off the ground.

"How many times do I fucking have to tell you I'm not leaving?"

It took Garrett a full minute to will enough composure not to take a swing at Dan.

"You gonna marry her, then? Because that's what she wants. That's the kind of woman she is. Kids, mortgage, you being home every night for dinner. That's what she deserves." Garrett's frenzied demand did nothing to make Dan believe he wasn't interested in Fionna.

"I am well aware of what kind of woman she is and of what she wants. I may not be getting down on one knee today, but I'm definitely considering it. I have a few things I have to take care of first." Dan gestured to the wall of mugshots behind his desk.

He never dropped his eyes from Garrett's infuriated glare. He allowed himself one millisecond to wonder if Garrett was as shocked by his words as he was.

He ordered himself to release Garrett's collar and to take a step back. He'd just gotten himself suspended for two weeks for losing his temper. Fighting with the Crown Governor's son certainly wouldn't make anyone believe he'd learned his lesson, but Garrett was pushing all of his buttons.

Garrett studied Dan like he was some kind of alien species. "I'm speechless."

"'Bout damn time."

"Not good enough." Garrett shook his head. "What happens when you start to freak or she says or does something that makes your world start to spin off its axis?"

"You're really starting to piss me the fuck off. She's already spun my world off its axis, and it finally feels like it's where it should have been for a long damn time. So, take a walk."

"I'll walk when I'm finished, and when I'm damn sure you're not gonna get my best friend killed. You didn't do so well with that the last time you thought you were in love."

That was it. He'd gone too far. Dan's demons resided too close to the surface for him to handle that blow. In a quick, solid move, he leapt. Every muscle in his body was poised to strike.

Their shields went to war. Fierce, green energy sizzled in the air between them. The office filled with their infuriated rhythms. It fought to pry them apart, as Dan landed a punch in Garrett's chiseled abs. Garrett groaned but took a swing at Dan's face.

Dan tried to spin out of the way, but Garrett's fist clipped his jaw with a nasty pop.

His shield parried Garrett back again, but Dan wanted another impact. Cursed with abject rage, he waged war against his own shield, against the truth of Garrett's statement, against the man who had far too much claim on Fionna, and against the hellish reality that he had no choice but to exist within.

A low, guttural growl burst from Garrett as Dan's fist met his face, but he wasn't going down. Garrett came right back, and Dan crouched into the hardened blow that forced his breath from his lungs. He stumbled backwards and hit the desk.

"Stop it!" Fionna's voice pierced through the throbbing acrimony that had filled the room. "Stop it right now!"

By weight of the demand, they turned away from each other. Dan gripped his busted jaw but refused to give in to the pain. His lungs begged for air he couldn't provide. Garrett's eye and cheekbone were swollen, but he made no attempt to heal them.

Fionna moved between them. Her face was a mix of exasperation and parental bewilderment.

"What on earth? You're friends. You've been friends since you were toddlers. You run Iodex together!"

"I run Iodex…alone," Dan corrected her.

She rolled her eyes and moved to Garrett. She cupped her hand and tenderly cradled his face. Dan swallowed back vomit as he watched her energies heal Garrett Haydenshire. She turned to Dan.

"Are you hurt?" She moved closer to study him. He reveled in the concern.

"I'm fine."

"Uh-huh." She made the same move with her hands and touched his jaw and his gut. She shook her head. "It's cracked. Just stay still for a minute. Let me heal you."

She closed her eyes, and Dan couldn't help but take in her

intoxicating energy with greed. It was the most astounding feeling in the world. She was his.

Their rhythms combined readily, due to the sheer number of times he'd had her in his bed in the last week. His shield lit in delight. Their rhythms spun in a soothing, united, pulsating hunger that, to Dan, said one should never exist without the other.

With an audible huff, Garrett scowled. "If you two'd like to stop fucking in front of me, that'd be great. And I, for one, would love to hear how you plan to keep her safe." He drew a deep breath and lost a great deal of his earlier furor. "I want you to be happy. Well," he amended, "I want *her* to be happy. She's wanted you for as long as I can remember, but how do we keep her safe?"

"You are aware I'm standing right here, right?" Fionna reminded him.

"I'm not an idiot." Dan couldn't quite help but rub his recently mended chin. It still ached. Fionna hadn't been able to finish soothing him before Garrett's remark had embarrassed her. "She knows we can't be seen anywhere together."

"Yeah, that'll work. So, what, you're just never gonna want to go out to eat, or to take him shopping, or to the movies? You're gonna stay holed up at his house and let him fuck you for entertainment?"

"Watch your mouth!" Dan's vengeance reared again.

Fionna shook her head and shot Dan a warning glare. "Stop it now," she commanded before she turned back to Garrett. "I really am in love. I know you're worried about me, but we will find some way to make this work. I don't need fancy dinners or shopping partners. I own all of my favorite movies, and the pizza guy and the Chinese takeout guy know where I live."

"I still get to come over and hang out, right?" Garrett's defeated question spoke volumes.

"Of course. Whenever you want. You will never not be my best friend. You know that. But I need you two not to get in another fistfight in my living room." Fionna turned back to Dan. "Garrett is not interested in dating me. We've been best friends for years. And if you'd take a deep breath, you'd realize I'm probably pretty safe with him. He is only outranked in Elite by you."

Dan did not agree. His mind raged against the very idea, but he forced his head to give a dejected nod.

"What about Eric?" Garrett quizzed.

"What about him?" Fionna sank down in Dan's desk chair and crossed her arms over her chest with a frown.

"Who's Eric?" Dan wasn't certain who to demand the answer from.

"He's been bugging her," Garrett explained. "She went with him to Dad's inaugural ball. He took her home, and she left him on her doorstep without even a good-night kiss. He wants another shot. He's planning on running on an independent ticket for Peterson's open seat on the board, even though he's way too young. He's a prick, and he doesn't like to hear the word no. We may have to do something about him." His statement was an obvious test.

"Still sitting here," Fionna quipped indignantly.

"I'll take care of it," Dan vowed.

"Yeah, well, be careful before you let your fists do the talking, because his dad owns a portion of the Angels. If you let your temper loose again, it could be enough to get her in trouble with the owners."

"I said I'd take care of it." His fury with Garrett began to slip away as concern for Fionna settled in its place.

"Yeah, and how are you gonna do that? I thought no one could know you're together."

With his mind desperate to find an answer, Dan reached and took Fionna's hand. He needed her close. He guided her into his arms. Her sweet grin delighted him as he spun her, pressed her back to his chest, and wrapped his arms around her waist. Just to spite Garrett, he kissed the top of her head and inhaled deeply of her heady island scent.

Garrett rolled his eyes. "It doesn't bother me. At all. Get over yourself. I want you together. If you'd get your head out of your ass, you'd realize I'm offering to help you. Hell, I'd love nothing more than for you two to make this work. I am the one who got you here." He threw his hands out to Dan and Fionna as they cuddled together.

"What are you offering?" Fionna was intrigued.

"Tell everyone you're dating me. As you pointed out a few minutes ago, Dan and I do a lot of stuff together. We can all go out, hang out, you two could semi-date, and no one would ever know. Chloe, Emily, Sasha, whoever you want, can come with. And let me handle Eric. Nothing would make me happier."

"Eric doesn't sound like the type with Interfeci connections. If he decides he'd like to tangle with either of us, I'll take care of it." Dan was loath to agree to Garrett's plan, but he couldn't help but admit it was an excellent suggestion.

"So you, Garrett Haydenshire, who will never allow anyone to claim him, are going to willingly agree to let people think we're dating?" Fionna's disbelief seemed to offend Garrett.

"No one who really knows me will believe it, baby, but it'll be enough for Nic and the boys, and those are the only people I'm worried about."

She spun and turned the full power of her pleading eyes on Dan. "He's right. This is brilliant. This is what we should do. We can be together more this way, and no one would ever suspect." Her tone took on a desperate edge that doused Dan's stubborn defiance.

There were very few times in his life when he'd hated Dominic Wretchkinsides and his band of low-life thugs more than he did in that moment where he was forced to concur with the despicable plan. He allowed his own damned determination to end the Interfeci to nurse the newly inflicted wound.

"Fine, but she's mine, Haydenshire. Don't ever forget that."

Fionna rolled her eyes again, and Garrett laughed at him outright.

"Just don't screw her up, Dan," was Garrett's final threat before he made his exit.

Fionna turned to Dan with disappointment and embarrassment tugging at her rhythms.

"He has no idea how much you mean to me." Fury ignited again in Dan's vow, as he pulled her back into his arms.

"He's worried about me. He loves me, and I love him. I will always love him, and you need to be okay with that. Promise me," she demanded.

As she'd made virtually no demands on the parameters he'd set for this relationship, Dan knew he was going to have to figure out how to be okay with her relationship with Garrett. "I told you I'm an asshole," was the best he could give her at the moment.

She pulled away and glanced around the office that Dan had practically lived in for the last ten years.

Her brow furrowed as she watched him go on with what he'd planned to do before Garrett had interrupted. He moved to the large corkboard he'd erected against the back windows. Resisting the urge to flip off the smug faces of the Interfeci members' mug shots that he'd lined up there, he pulled the tack from Pendergrath's photo.

The black 'X' through Cascavel's face did give him solace, but he wouldn't stop until every face staring back at him was dead and gone.

He tore down the shot of Pendergrath with the green 'X' and replaced it with a new mug shot.

"What do the Xs mean?" Fionna joined him. She touched his hand, and he felt her soothing Receiver's cast work back through him. With an extended blink, his body inhaled the essence of her.

"Uh…" He shuddered and tried to focus. She released him, and his mind re-centered. "Green means they're in prison but don't have a life sentence. Red means they're in prison with a life sentence. Black means they're no longer polluting the earth by exhaling."

She managed a nod. "I thought it was something like that."

Dan glanced back toward the door and tried to find something else to discuss. His eyes landed on an old photo partially obscured under a stack of papers on his desk. Amelia was caught up in his arms the day he'd carried her over the threshold of their brand-new house. Dan quickly used the papers to cover the photo.

Fionna smiled, and he felt the warmth in his soul.

"Don't you miss the sunshine? I mean, you're the Chief of Iodex. This is the nicest office in this wing, right? You covered up your view." The concern she tried so hard to conceal in hope wounded him further.

He shrugged. "If I get to stare into your eyes and hold you in my arms, I don't need the sun."

CHAPTER 34

ERIC

Dan added the file folders on car makes and models he'd been interested in purchasing at one time and the latest updates on the Interfeci to his briefcase.

The drive and determination to end Wretchkinsides had been compounding with every moment he spent with Fionna.

With every sexy sway of her hips, every inhaled breath of her heady scent, every time their lips met, desperation to break free from the hell he'd lived for the past decade brought cold clarity to his mind and to his shield. If Fionna was the prize, he'd stop at nothing to finally win the game.

After grabbing a set of keys to one of the Iodex Expeditions, he led her to the parking deck. To his great irritation, Garrett joined them on their trek.

"Honey, why is your top open?" Dan gestured to the bright yellow MR2 parked where she'd left it a week before.

"Oh no," Fionna sighed. "It's been doing this. I've tried casting it and everything, but sometimes it just opens and I can't get it shut."

Dan scanned the car to make certain nothing more than an electrical problem was to blame.

Garrett joined him. "I was gonna take it to Sam's. I should've done it while you were gone. I meant to go by your house and get the keys."

Dan willed away his irritation that Garrett obviously had a key to Fionna's home. He placed his hands on the steering column, and Fionna watched as he sent a green pulsing orb through the car. The energy took on a yellow tint as he forced massive amounts of electricity through it, but the top still wouldn't close.

"Here, I'll take her home. You can follow us in the Expedition," Garrett offered.

"She can leave the car here. No one can get in here but the governors and Iodex. We're spending the weekend together anyway." He loaded their bags into one of the Expeditions and helped her into the passenger seat.

"I feel like I'm back on the plane," Fionna teased, as she took in the size of the vehicle compared to her convertible. Dan chuckled as he cranked the engine.

"Yeah, but at least I'm not eating my knees when I drive this."

"Do not speak ill of Lola." She clutched her hand to her heart in mock offense.

Dan laughed as he pulled out of the parking deck and headed toward the highway. "Lola? Your car's name is Lola?"

"Yes, and I think she does this thing with the top when she has PMS." Her sassy retort made him love her even more.

"Does your top come down when you have PMS too, honey, or is that just Lola's?"

They joked most of the way to Alexandria. Dan reveled in her laughter and in just being with her. He turned down her street and smiled at her as she kept her gaze fixed on him.

"You wanna have a spend-the-night party?" she teased.

"I thought you'd never ask." His voice took on an eager thrum. Excitement lit her eyes, and Dan's heartbeat sped.

"Are you going to braid my hair and let me tell you about this guy I have a huge crush on?"

"I would definitely like to hear about this guy, but I'm not much with hair."

"You had three little sisters and you can't braid hair?" Her sweet grin was still spread across her beautiful face.

"I was so freaking disgusted with the sheer amount of hair I had to pull out of the shower drain every damn day, I never wanted to get anywhere near their heads."

Fionna dissolved into another fit of giggles.

I could sit and listen to her laugh at my stupid jokes for the rest of my life. The thought caught him off guard again. How could he have fallen so hard so fast? He'd sworn when he'd finally been able to come to grips with the fact that Amelia was gone, he'd never fall in love again.

He turned down the driveway, and all signs of happiness and contentment washed from her face.

"Not again." She suddenly looked frightened. Dan's entire body tensed. His shield pulsed as he crested the slight hill and took in a guy dressed in a designer suit, leaning against his BMW, and gazing at it lustfully.

"I'm guessing this is Eric."

"Yes," Fionna whimpered. "He's such a prick. He keeps showing up here unannounced and demanding that I give him another chance. Like Garrett said, his dad is one of the Angel owners, so I kind of have to be nice. He freaks me out."

She glared at Eric as Dan edged the Expedition into the parking space right beside the house.

"How nice do I have to be?"

Fionna considered. "Not as nice as I have to be but nicer than I would like for you to be."

"I think I can handle that. Why don't you stay in the car for me?" Aware that his request had taken on the tone of a command, he studied her to see how she might react. It didn't seem to bother her, but she also didn't comply.

"No, then he'll make up some crap about you being controlling. I'm telling you he's a massive jerk."

Sizing Eric up didn't take long, so Dan decided to go ahead and scare the shit out of him in hopes that he'd get his thing for Fionna out of his system.

He reached across her seat, popped open the glove box, and pulled out a set of cuffs. He linked them through one of his belt loops and then pulled on a shoulder holster. He slid it over his massive bicep and loaded a Glock into it.

Dan narrowed his eyes, clenched his jaw, and stepped out of the Expedition.

"Hi there,"—he extended his arm, making certain the gun was on full display—"I'm Dan Vindico. Do we know you?" He leveled a hate-filled glare at Eric.

"Eric, what are you doing here?" Fionna crossed her arms over her chest and stayed close to Dan.

"Fionna's seeing me," was Eric's opening line. Dan chuckled but offered no comment.

"No, I'm not! We went out once, months ago. I don't ever want to see you again."

"Where have you been? I've come by every night this week," Eric demanded.

Dan's eyes lit furiously. "I don't really believe that's any of your business." He stepped closer and shot Eric the customary male look that said he could crush him with one hand. "Since Fionna just informed you that she never wants to see you again, I'm going to give you approximately thirty seconds to get inside your car and leave before I arrest you for trespassing."

"I'm not trespassing. There are no private property signs."

This guy was trouble, and he'd been in trouble before. Dan would bet his badge on it.

"Fionna, did you invite this asshole to be here?"

"NO!" Fionna shouted.

"And do you feel threatened?" Dan eased as a broad grin spread across her face. She sidled closer.

"Yes, I've told him over and over again not to come back. I'm really scared." She pouted preciously, and Dan tried hard not to laugh.

"And you can come by my office tomorrow morning to sign a restraining order?"

"Of course."

"Sounds like trespassing to me, and as the Chief of Elite Iodex, I should know. So, would you like to leave now or would you prefer a nice weekend in Felsink? I hear the weather underground is lovely this time of year."

Eric rolled his eyes as he glared at Dan. "Because you think she's yours?"

Dan's fists clenched. They still ached from fighting with Garrett. They'd been back less than an hour and he was already contemplating a second fistfight. This wasn't good.

"I never said that," he corrected Eric and watched disappointment broadcast from Fionna. But he had to do this by the book. He'd make no mistakes when it came to her. "Fionna and I are friends. I was giving her a ride home. She asked you to leave. It tends to piss me off when guys don't do as they're told."

A moment of realization seemed to dawn on Eric as he took in Dan's sheer size and strength. He gave another indignant huff.

"Whatever. Fionna, when this guy leaves, give me a call. Dad and I were talking, and we think some pictures of the two of us on my campaign flyers would look really good for me."

Fury lit Fionna's face as her rhythms tensed violently. "I am not now nor was I ever your girlfriend. I will not have my picture taken with you ever. I am seeing..." She caught herself. Dan gave a minute headshake. "Someone else. Just leave!"

"I'm sure you'll come around." Eric climbed back in his car and backed out of the driveway.

Dan edged Fionna out of the way as he kept his glare fixed on Eric.

"Okay, I was just trying to get to Eric there, but you *are* going to sign a restraining order. He's not going to give up, and I swear I'm not saying this just because I want to spend every waking moment with you, but until I'm sure he isn't going to be a problem anymore, I'm going to be staying with you constantly. I'm also going to beef up the security teams at the arena when you're at work."

To his delight, Fionna beamed. "And I thought Eric wasn't good for anything. Turns out I was wrong."

With a chuckle meant to hide his deep concern, Dan unloaded their bags and followed Fionna into her house.

CHAPTER 35

THE WAYS OF A VINDICO

Sunday evening, after Fionna had fixed a beautiful platter of hors d'oeuvres and changed clothes more times than Dan could count, they stood on the brick front porch ready to enter his parents' mansion.

"I'm so nervous." Fionna looked faint as Dan reached for his parents' house key on his ring.

"They're going to love you. How could they not?"

She seemed far too distressed to listen to reason, so Dan gently guided her inside.

"We're here." He tried not to sound overly irritated about that fact as he took in the home that had raised him.

The entry hall had cornflower-blue and mauve wallpaper along with flagstone flooring in varying shades of gray. His mother had taken to home decorating in the nineties and hadn't updated much.

Dan's senior picture from the academy hung, along with Kara and Meredith's, beside the stiff oak hall tree. It resided next to a picture of his parents' wedding day and of his father being sworn in as a governor of the Realm.

Lindley had refused to sit for her senior portrait unless she could pose provocatively, so Governor Vindico had informed her that she just wouldn't have one taken.

His mother appeared. She looked distressed.

"Daniel." She sighed and wiped her hands on her apron that covered a dress that was much nicer than what she normally wore to a family dinner.

"Hey, Mom." He gave her an awkward, one-armed hug. He was carrying the tray of hors d'oeuvres in his other arm. "This is my girlfriend, Fionna Styler." He introduced his mother, who stared at Fionna as if she was the last drink of lemonade on Satan's sunporch. Dan's stomach churned ominously.

"Fionna, it is such a pleasure to meet you." She dragged Fionna in for an all-encompassing hug. "Obviously we know who you are though. Everyone knows you."

Shocked, Fionna hugged her back with a great deal of trepidation.

Kara, Dan's favorite sister, appeared a moment later.

"Hey Fionna, I haven't seen you since you went off and became a famous Angel." She and Fionna embraced much more naturally.

Kara grinned at Dan as she wrapped her arms around his waist. She was several inches shorter than him.

"Hey, Care Bear." Dan hugged her to him. She seemed surprised at his embrace.

"Fionna, these appetizers look lovely. You shouldn't have gone to so much trouble." Mrs. Vindico directed everyone farther into the house.

"It was no trouble." Fionna threw Dan a threatening glare to make certain that he didn't comment on the two hours it had taken her to prepare them.

With a slight shudder, Dan followed Fionna into his mother's large kitchen. The wallpaper, with pictures of clustered fruit all larger than his head, had always disturbed him. His mother was a horrible cook. Dan never understood the need for the massive kitchen. Surely, she could burn things on a hot plate.

But the travertine tile floor had recently been polished, and the hideous floral backsplash over the oven gleamed. It was obvious his mother had been cleaning for days.

Kara's husband, Zach, and Governor Vindico entered from the garage.

"I'm sorry. I didn't realize you'd arrived." The governor gave Fionna his warm, fatherly smile.

"Fionna, this is my Dad and my brother-in-law Zach."

"We're so glad to have you. Can I get you something to drink?" Governor Vindico slid seamlessly into the role of host. It suited him well.

"I'm fine, sir."

"I was just in the garage helping Zach load up Kara's old crib," the governor stated with a broad grin.

"Oh, really?" Dan raised his eyebrows at Kara who was nodding excitedly. "Congrats, sis." He extended his hand toward Zach, who shook it, though he looked rather bewildered.

"When did you find out?"

"Oh, uh, today," Zach stumbled over the words.

Dan now understood his slight trepidation.

"Now, Fionna, are you interested in starting a family soon?" Mrs. Vindico launched into her interrogation.

Fionna's eyes goggled. Dan ground his teeth. "Mom, could we get through the salad before you start trying to direct her life?"

"You're not getting any younger, Daniel."

Dan let his eyes close in defeat. Fionna reached for his hand. She soothed him, as she tried to recover from the rather personal question.

Desperate for a subject change, Dan turned to Kara. "Is Meredith here?"

"No, she wanted to come, but Tim's sick," Kara announced with a heavy eye roll.

Fionna's brow furrowed.

"Meredith's husband is terminally ill with hypochondria," Dan whispered as he wrapped his arm around her shoulders. "Maybe you can meet them Christmas Eve."

His mother looked thrilled as she instructed the governor on how to cut the ham. Dan glared at the offending ham fresh from the blazing oven. His mother was perpetually terrified of undercooked foods, therefore she had a tendency to cook meats until they resembled products manufactured by Goodyear.

"You've invited Fionna for Christmas dinner?" Mrs. Vindico wore an expression that looked as if someone had just informed her that she was Queen of the Realm.

Dan tried not to grimace as Fionna bit back laughter at his mother's wide-eyed exuberance.

"Yeah, is that okay?"

"Of course, of course, of course."

Kara shook her head and offered Dan and Fionna sympathetic looks.

"You know I've been considering new drapes in the guest rooms. I should just go ahead and order those right now." Mrs. Vindico retrieved a measuring tape from one of the kitchen drawers.

"We're not staying overnight. We'll just be here for dinner. No need to call the decorator." Dan sighed.

Fionna gave Mrs. Vindico a polite smile, but she looked extremely uncomfortable.

"Let me get you a drink, honey." Dan moved toward the refrigerator. His mother nearly back-flipped over the kitchen island after hearing Dan's term of endearment for Fionna.

"What can I make you, Fionna?" The governor stepped in again. He poured Mrs. Vindico a large glass of white wine and handed it to her though she hadn't asked for one.

Fionna smiled. "I'll just have whatever Dan's having."

Dan tightened his arm over her shoulders to try to give her a place to hide. He leaned to whisper in her ear, "If she keeps this up, Dan's going to drink the entire liquor cabinet, so you may have to drive."

He debated just casting his shield over her now and leaving her in it for the duration.

Her adorable giggle calmed him.

"You know, girls, I was just reading an article in *Women of the Realm* that said that red wine not only has positive benefits for your heart, but it's also good for all of your reproductive organs. It ripens your uterus for when a seed is planted," Mrs. Vindico informed Kara and Fionna.

"Oh my God, Mom." Kara cringed.

All of the blood in Dan's head drained quickly to his feet. Fionna's mouth hung open in shock.

"Here." Governor Vindico handed Dan and Fionna glasses of the same wine he'd poured for his wife. "Why don't you show Fionna around? I'll get this ham sliced and then we'll eat," he offered apologetically, as Kara began to argue with her mother about the merits of wine.

Dan guided Fionna out of the kitchen and through the well-appointed dining room, complete with hardwood flooring and wainscoted walls. The family Christmas tree had been erected there and held all of his mother's designer baubles that she insisted on collecting.

He steered her through the living room and tried not to lament the horrible blue carpeting his mother insisted on having in every other room of the house. A ridiculously expensive and horrifically gaudy rug was on top of the carpeting. He kept them walking, trying to escape. It was a sensation he was accustomed to feeling every time he came to his parents' home. He guided her into the music room with an eye roll. They edged around the baby grand piano that no one in the family had any clue how to play.

"Baby, I am so sorry," Dan pled as soon as he'd gotten her out of earshot of his parents. She covered her mouth to hold back hysterical laughter.

"Wow," she whispered when she regained the ability to talk.

"I told you she's insane." Dan knew he'd made a huge mistake bringing her to meet his mother.

"No, it's fine. I just don't seem to know how to respond."

"That's because you are sane." Dan downed the wine quickly.

"Really, it's fine. Please don't be nervous. I'm okay. Don't let your mom freak you out."

"I'm not freaking out." He tried to soothe his own energy so he could soothe her. "I'm just terrified every time she opens her mouth, you're going to run out the front door. I won't blame you. If you decide to bolt, I'm going with you."

With a sweet smile, the one that Dan had fallen head over heels for, Fionna leaned toward him and brushed a tender kiss on his jaw.

"I'm fine." She gazed up at him and calmed him instantly. Dan was mesmerized. The golden flecks in her sienna eyes sparkled like a beacon leading him on.

He gently set his wine glass on a nearby bookshelf and caressed her face with his hand as he guided her lips to his. He needed to taste her. He needed to feel her permeate him. He needed a draw of the heavenly life force she offered him.

He traced her bottom lip with his tongue. Her breath came faster as she opened her mouth. Dan leaned his head to the other side as he plundered her mouth and the energy it held.

All of the pent-up aggravation and stress that had formed when he'd stepped into his parents' home melted away. She gracefully set her full wine glass on the shelf beside his without breaking from the kiss.

He moaned quietly in her mouth, as he wrapped his arms around her. He pulled away as she gasped for breath, but desperate for more, he worked his hungry lips down her slender neck.

"I love you," she whispered as he made his way back and consumed her lips once again.

"Me too."

She edged her fingers into his hair and tugged him toward her. Her insatiable need drove him wild.

"So fucking much," he groaned.

Suddenly, the front door burst open. Dan jerked away and Fionna gasped as they both turned just in time to hear, "Whassup bitches!?" screech from Lindley who'd bounced into the foyer.

Fionna's eyes goggled as they took in Dan's youngest sister. She was wearing a sheer orange skirt that revealed the black thong underneath. Her tank top was also fluorescent orange and had the words *Spank Me* written across her chest in silver letters. She'd completed her ensemble with thigh-high motorcycle boots and a denim jacket. The most jarring thing, in Dan's opinion, was Lindley's normally long blonde hair. It was dyed in varying shades of black and purple. It matched her heavy eye makeup which made her appear that she'd been given two black eyes.

Lindley turned and studied Fionna before she smirked. "Oh, right. I forgot Danny Boy was bringing his new slut-a-hoe to dinner."

Dan's fists clenched as he started toward his sister to threaten her with bodily harm.

Fionna grabbed his forearm and shook her head. "She wants your attention." Somehow she didn't seem to mind the extremely rude comment. She offered Lindley a kind smile.

Dan knew she was right. It was precisely what he told his parents whenever Lindley pulled a stunt like this. Whenever someone else was destined to be the center of attention at a gathering, she pulled out all the stops to make everyone as uncomfortable as possible.

Dan's parents stared at Lindley in full-blown shock.

"Uh…um…well, I thought we could enjoy appetizers in here." In true Marion Vindico form, Dan's mother chose to ignore anything she did not want to see. She refused to look at Lindley for any length of time. "Fionna made them, and they look lovely." She set the tray on the coffee table and went back to open another bottle of wine.

Dan guided Fionna back into the living room. Zach and Kara were both carrying small glass plates and exchanged a simultaneous eye roll as they took in Lindley.

"What's up, Care Bear?" Lindley bound toward Kara.

"Hey Lind, nice outfit," Kara huffed indignantly as she sipped the seltzer water her father had provided her.

"Aww, ya think?" Lindley popped her tongue against the roof of her mouth and then, to Dan's horror, she spun and made the sheer fabric of the skirt flare out. Fionna almost choked, as Dan looked away in disgust.

Zach seated Kara and made her a plate of the appetizers before situating himself between Kara and Dan.

Kara gave Fionna a kind grin. "These are delicious. I think I've had something like this when I've been by your parents' bakery. Do you make them for your dad?" Dan offered her an extremely appreciative smile.

"Dad taught me to make them a long time ago, but I don't make them for the bakery." Fionna accepted the tiny plate of delicious finger sandwiches, made on homemade cheddar cheese baguettes, and homemade macadamia nut hummus with vegetables from Dan.

Lindley scowled as she studied the sandwiches and the vegetables on the tray. Dan ground his teeth.

"You know,"—she held one of the sandwiches precariously between her index finger and thumb and made a rude gagging noise—"milk cows are either raped by bulls or artificially inseminated against their will and forced to have offspring whether they want to or not. Then their babies are taken away from them so that humans can have the milk."

Fionna smiled and handled Lindley beautifully. "I didn't know you were vegan, Lindley, but the dip I made for the vegetables doesn't have any animal byproducts in it, so you should be safe with that."

Dan leaned over and kissed her cheek. He wrapped his arm over her, desperate to protect her from his family. Zach gave him an impressed smile.

His mother beamed over the kiss for a full minute and a half. *She should have been in here earlier,* Dan thought wryly, as he recalled the impassioned kiss they'd shared before his sister's explosive arrival.

Fionna's rebuttal only served to further irritate Lindley though.

"So, Fionna," Lindley drawled her name out into long syllables of disdain, "why don't you tell the fam when you hoed it out for Dan and how you've managed to keep him interested for more than forty-eight hours?"

"Lindley," Governor Vindico roared, "you will be polite to your brother's girlfriend or you can leave."

Dan glared hatefully at his sister as Fionna's jaw clenched. "You do not have to answer anything she asks you or even speak to her at all."

"Uh, well," Fionna began, once she'd regained her equilibrium. "Dan came to a party the Angels threw, and we ended up having dinner and a few drinks that night. He invited me to Sydney with him, and it sort of went from there."

"Oh, so you went down. Yeah, I heard Danny Boy likes that," Lindley announced just for the shock of saying something like that.

Fionna almost dropped her wine glass. Dan reached and took it from her shaking hand. Governor Vindico's eyes closed in defeat as he shook his head.

Mrs. Vindico chose to completely ignore Lindley and turned her full attention on Fionna. "Tell us all about the Angels. Now, how long have you challenged for them? I can't wait to tell a few friends."

"Mother, no one can know we're dating." Panic clouded Dan's already bad mood. Between Lindley and his mother, his heart wasn't going to survive the evening. His parents, of all people, should understand that anyone knowing about their relationship could get Fionna murdered.

"Yes, yes, I know, but when you decide that I can tell people."

Fionna nodded as some of the color began to return to her cheeks.

"I was recruited out of the academy the year Kara and I graduated, so eight seasons now."

"She was the lead Receiver for the Vixens the whole time we were at school, Mom. She's amazing," Kara added helpfully.

Dan decided to send his sister flowers the next day.

"We enjoyed the challenge we went to recently. I really thought that was unfair how they didn't give you more time after you'd already had to do two other transfers." Mrs. Vindico leapt back in for more information.

Fionna smiled, and Dan couldn't quite hide his chuckle.

"Thank you, but unfortunately that's not really the way the challenges go, I guess. It turned out to be a pretty great day though."

"Yeah," Dan agreed as he brushed another kiss across her cheek, "it was an amazing day."

The night they'd sealed their fate as he'd made her all his own would always be qualified as one of the greatest days of his life.

The appetizers disappeared quickly. Kara, Zach, and the governor all raved about them.

Mrs. Vindico seated everyone at the dining room table where she'd arranged fine china plates and the silver.

"I'm really underdressed." Fionna panicked as she took in the display.

"She's trying to impress you so you'll stick around." Dan winked at her.

"Maybe I should tell her it's her son I find so impressive." She somehow always made him feel like a king.

The bowls and trays were passed, and Dan couldn't help but quip as the ham was served, "Gee, Lindley, you're the only vegan I know who eats pig."

"Blow me," Lindley shot back furiously.

Dinner began and Kara sighed. "So, Lindley, you're going to be an aunt again." She braced for whatever the retort everyone knew was coming was going to be.

"Great." Lindley rolled her eyes. "Can't wait to see which of his sperm actually got through. Why don't you just go ahead and name the kid pussy and save his friends the time?" She shot Zach a challenging glare.

Zach scowled, but Kara caught his arm. "Just ignore her."

Zach speared a piece of ham viciously on his fork since that was the only way to force Marion Vindico's ham onto a speared weapon.

"Now, Fionna dear, back to you. How long do you plan on challenging for the Angels? You must be thinking about settling down and starting a family soon," Mrs. Vindico urged.

Dan promptly choked on his water as Fionna looked at him utterly bewildered.

"My God, Mother," Dan spat as soon as he regained the ability to breathe. "As if *she's* not bad enough." He gestured angrily toward Lindley. "Must you give her the third degree?"

"It was my understanding that women who play in Summation Challenges cannot be pregnant. It could be harmful to the baby, so that will be something we need to plan."

Governor Vindico shook his head. "Marion, Dan and Fionna haven't been dating very long. I know that I, for one, would really like for our family not to ruin this for him. I don't think we'll ever need to plan anything on Fionna's account. She seems perfectly capable. Why don't we talk about something else? Anything else."

Dan gave his father an appreciative look, and Fionna withered in her chair.

Mrs. Vindico drew another breath as she offered more mayonnaise for the canned pears, arranged on pieces of soggy lettuce, covered in stale cheese that resided in an oozing concoction on everyone's salad plates.

"Thank you." Fionna accepted the mayonnaise. She added just a little to her still-full plate. As Dan wasn't any more excited about eating the salad than she seemed to be, he leaned in closer. "Don't eat anything you don't like, baby." Dan couldn't fathom why his mother had insisted on making the waterlogged atrocity for the last thirty years.

"Oh no, it's good," Fionna lied as she cut a small piece of the pear, avoiding the mayonnaise and cheese altogether, and choked it down with a large swig of water.

"Daniel, have you taken Fionna to your house yet?" Mrs. Vindico asked.

With a slight eye roll, Dan shook his head. "No, we just got back from Sydney. We're heading there when we leave."

"And I assume that you'll be taking Fionna home after that." In the very odd juxtaposition that was Marion Vindico, she remembered that according to her world rules, the marriage must come before the grandson she so desperately wanted Dan to father.

"No, Mother. I won't."

With a quick purse of her lips to show her disapproval, she went on. "Daniel's home could really use a feminine touch." Mrs. Vindico began passing lumpy, partially-cooked canned potatoes she'd attempted to turn into mashed potatoes and severely overcooked canned English peas around the table insistently. They were both bathing in cloudy, separating water.

Dan whimpered. "Baby, there is a pistol in the glove box of the truck," he whispered as Fionna began to giggle. "I really want you to go outside, get it, and then if you could just shoot me now, that'd be great."

Fionna covered her mouth in an effort to hide her laughter.

"Please," Dan pled, further cracking her up.

"I keep telling Daniel that he'd never get a woman who would make an acceptable daughter-in-law and mother to his sons if he doesn't spruce the place up a little. You know—curtains, throw pillows, knickknacks, pictures on the walls, that kind of thing."

Dan ground his teeth. "If she doesn't leave me after this meal, I think she'll make it through the fact that I don't have curtains, Mom."

Fionna was still trying to quell her laughter as she glanced around the Vindicos' home.

Dan's mother was obsessed with window coverings. Every window in their home had solid wooden blinds, sheers, and multiple layers of curtains sewn of busily patterned fabrics.

Since he was a child, Dan had believed his mother was trying to choke out any fresh air that could possibly be brought into the home before he had a chance to breathe it in.

"Well, I'm certain Fionna's home is well-appointed and that she has draperies."

Lindley wasn't going to let that go. Dan squeezed his eyes shut in defeat.

"It's not her drapes he's interested in, Mom. It's her carpet."

Fionna managed to chew through a bite of the rubberized ham and choke it down before smiling at Mrs. Vindico.

"I've actually been redoing my home since I bought it a couple of years ago." She was clearly hoping to guide the table to a different topic.

Governor Vindico leapt to help. "Is it an older home or did you just not care for the aesthetics?"

"It was built in the early forties. It's a bungalow. I fell in love with the front porch when I first saw it. I've been redoing it a little bit at a time. It's been fun. I love shopping for period pieces and mixing them with newer, more modern things. Garrett told me I should redo the floors, but I just had them resealed. I love all the old markings and scuffs. I think it gives it character. I love to think about how they got there and the people who lived there before me."

The governor nodded. "I agree with you. I hate when people buy these beautiful pieces of architectural history and then gut them. What's the point? Garrett's like his old man. He always has been. Stephen likes a fresh start. Nothing wrong with that, either, I suppose." The governor kept up the conversation easily.

He looked very impressed with Fionna and allowed Dan to breathe for the moment.

"I kind of like my windows uncovered. I made a few little café curtains for my kitchen from some old flour sack cloth I found at a craft fair back in the spring. They don't really cover much, but I love the sunshine too much to cover the windows."

Mrs. Vindico looked deeply distressed, and Dan was quite certain he could never love anything more than the woman seated beside him.

"I had a wall removed between the master bathroom and one of the closets. The bathrooms are kind of tiny." Fionna wrinkled her nose as she continued her descriptions.

Governor Vindico chuckled. "Dan's probably used to that. His mother used to make him share a bathroom with all three of the girls."

Fionna laughed as Dan huffed, "She thought it would help us bond."

"And it did. It was in all of the parenting books, and *Women of the Realm* suggested it," Mrs. Vindico insisted.

Governor Vindico chuckled as he shook his head. "I finally stepped in and added another bathroom upstairs when Dan threatened to build himself an outhouse in the backyard."

Lindley's eyes spun in delight. "He just got his panties in a bunch because Mere and I found his Playboy stash under the bathroom sink. Whatcha doin' in there, Danny?"

Dan wasn't certain which he would've preferred most at that moment, to die or to murder Lindley. Fionna coughed and then drank copious amounts of water and refused to meet anyone's eye.

"Fionna, do you have any sisters or brothers?" Mrs. Vindico didn't care for her husband's teasing or Lindley's remark.

"No, ma'am. It's just me." She glanced at Dan, clearly not certain if this was the right answer.

"You have no idea how lucky you are," Dan spat under his breath as he glared at Lindley.

Mrs. Vindico considered the response with a terse pout. "And do you think you'll only want one child or to have a bigger family?"

Dan shifted his glare to his mother as he rubbed Fionna's leg consolingly. "Do not, under any circumstances, ask her about having children again or we are leaving."

Governor Vindico managed to guide the conversation to more mundane topics like the hopefuls in the upcoming elections for the open seats on the board.

That lasted until his mother served small crocks of soupy microwave bread pudding that Dan abhorred.

It wasn't lost on him, despite the horrific evening, that Fionna hadn't eaten much of her meal—not that anyone blamed her. It was inedible. She'd pushed the slimy, canned English peas around her plate and had hidden them under her severely overcooked ham just like Dan and his sisters had done growing up.

"We'll leave in a minute and go by and pick up something on the way to my house." Dan prayed that after meeting his family she still wanted to have anything to do with him at all.

Fionna tried to smile, but she looked thoroughly worn out. "Would you mind showing me to the powder room?"

With a concerned nod, he stood and showed her the way. In no rush to get back to his family in the dining room, he waited for her in the darkened hallway.

When she emerged, he pulled her to his chest. He just needed her. He needed to know she wasn't wary of him because of his family. "I'm so sorry, honey. This is so much worse than I ever envisioned." He shook his head in disdain.

Fionna chuckled. "It's fine. It's just a lot of emotion to feel. Lindley's very erratic, and your mom is…a lot. I'm a little tired."

"I can't imagine why." He was exhausted from the stress of the evening himself. Fionna laid her head on his shoulder, with her face toward his neck. She hid from the world in him. The motion quelled his terror.

"Why don't we go on?" Dan soothed. "Did you pack everything you need?"

"Are you sure you want me to stay with you tonight? I'm kind of" —she bit her lip—"starting to not feel so good." She gestured to her abdomen.

He cupped his hand and summoned a small amount of heat energy. While keeping her carefully cradled to his chest, he rubbed her lower back. Her energy tensed with her cramps.

She melted into him as he massaged the inflamed muscles. The relief was almost instantaneous.

"I want you to stay with me every night, baby, and if we go now then I can put you to bed, and hold you, and do this until you feel better," he whispered tenderly.

"Are you sure?"

"I'm sure. Let me take care of you."

Governor Vindico turned the corner, clearing his throat loudly. He'd obviously been sent to check on Fionna and Dan but hadn't wanted to interrupt anything.

"Is everything all right?" He took in Fionna trying to back away and Dan keeping a firm hold on her.

"Fi's not feeling all that well. I think we may head out."

"Sure, son. I'm sorry, sweetheart. Can I get you anything before you go?"

Fionna smiled and shook her head. "No, sir, I'm all right, just a little tired."

"We enjoyed meeting you. I'm sorry if Marion came on a little strong. She really does mean well. She worries about Dan. If we haven't scared you off too badly, we'd love to have you as often as you'd like to be here."

Fionna gave the governor her sweet grin. "I had a very nice time. Thank you so much for having me." She turned back to Dan. "We really should stay through dessert and help your mom clean up."

Dan started to argue, but the governor stepped in.

"We're almost through with the pudding. Why don't you just come tell everyone goodbye, and I'll help your mom with the dishes."

Fionna gave Dan a pleading gaze.

"Fine." He knew Fionna's guilt over leaving early would be worse than her discomfort for the next few minutes.

CHAPTER 36
A HOUSE

After he rescued Fionna from yet another round of interrogations about her opinions on breastfeeding and child rearing, Dan helped her into the Expedition and moved quickly to the driver's side.

"Are you okay, sweetheart?" He backed out of his parents' driveway.

"I'm all right. Just a few cramps, but I understand if you'd rather just take me back home." Her words were strangled by her emotions.

Dan studied her for a long moment. "Fi, baby, are you afraid to stay at my house? If the not-having-curtains thing is that disturbing, I guess I'll understand." He allowed her hearty laughter to soothe him, but he wasn't fool enough to believe he'd shattered through her concern.

"Your mom is big on curtains."

"You have no idea. That's just the beginning." Dan let her laughter die down before he urged, "What is it really, baby doll? Why don't you want to stay with me?"

"I do want to stay with you, more than you know. I'm just…" she hemmed, "I really don't want to tell you this." She sank down farther in the seat and accepted her own defeat.

"Just tell me. Whatever it is, we'll figure it out."

"I sometimes, kind of, have...you know...problems with my period."

Dan tried to discern what to ask next. Before he could respond, she went on.

"I've had a few cysts, and everything was fine once they were out. I just don't ever really know how bad it might be. I don't want to completely gross you out and make you never want to see me or let me sleep in your bed again." Her chin trembled, and he understood how terrified she was.

"Baby, first of all, the only thing you just told me that concerns me was the fact that you said you had cysts, which I'm certain must've been painful. It breaks my heart to know you were hurting. But, believe me, I've seen some pretty gruesome things in my line of work. Nothing is going to gross me out. I own a washer and a dryer, although I'm not certain I've used them more than once or twice. And, hell, it's been years since I bought new sheets, so if worse comes to worse you can pick some out for us."

She gave him a weak smile. "Because of the cysts, the medios won't let me do the cast as soon as I start. I have to wait several hours, so it won't be gone as fast as some Gifted girls."

In his complete inexperience with Gifted women, he'd forgotten that they could cast their own uteruses and force their bodies to dispense with the unneeded lining rapidly instead of the week it usually lasted for Non-Gifted women. He couldn't recall how long she'd actually bleed, but that also wasn't important.

Dan took her hand and steered the car with the other. "See? Still not running away."

"I think your mom was right. Sharing a bathroom with your sisters was good for you."

He laughed and shook his head. "Trust me, it wasn't." While trying to dislodge the hazed fog that had formed in his mind from their exhaustive evening, Dan fished his phone from his jacket pocket.

They met the pizza delivery guy at the door. When his dilapidated truck pulled away from the curb, Dan guided Fionna inside. He tried to shut out the freezing night air. It wasn't much warmer in the house. He moved to the thermostat and raised the temperature.

Fionna glanced around, but she didn't move beyond the entryway. Dan entered all of the codes into the intricate alarm systems he'd set up in his house.

"So, this is it." He gestured from the foyer to the living room, and then up the staircase. As Dan was still carrying both pizzas and Fionna's bags, he scooted her farther in. "Make yourself at home. I'm just gonna set this down. You get comfortable."

She followed him into the kitchen and studied the surroundings as she went.

"Wow." She smiled as she entered the kitchen.

"What?"

"You have a great kitchen. I can't believe you don't cook here."

Dan had never really thought much about the kitchen. He'd purchased the house because of its proximity to the Pentagon and because it had great running trails from the backyard through a nearby park that backed up to a large lake, which was a natural barrier.

The fact that it had a decent sized lot, with trees and brush that covered some of the house, had made the decision easy for Dan. It was also in an entirely Non-Gifted neighborhood. Since being concealed was his only concern, he'd never cut back the trees or the bushes. He had numerous security measures in place, including casted electrical lines if anyone should tamper with the electricity, cameras located at every entrance, enhanced shatter-proof glass on all the windows, and casted steel casings on every door. Four alarm systems monitored the entire property constantly. No one was getting in who wasn't supposed to be there.

"Don't say that yet," he teased, "I don't think I've ever turned the ovens on."

Fionna gave him his smile as she began to explore.

"But you have two of them. I would love that. And this island is amazing." She slid her hand along the large island that ran through the center of the kitchen. It contained the cooktop and a bar area.

Dan was pleased she liked it but wasn't certain what to say. "Pizza?" He pointed to the boxes he'd laid on the counter.

Fionna grinned and nodded. "I'm starving."

"Again, I cannot tell you how sorry I am about dinner. Even I couldn't have imagined it would be that bad." He pulled two large pieces of pizza from the box, put them on a paper plate, and handed them to her.

She giggled. "I thought your mom was sweet, but I got the impression she's very interested in you procreating."

"Picked up on that, did you?" They laughed together. It was a sound Dan was quickly becoming addicted to. Certain he owed her some explanation for his mother's insane behavior, he grimaced.

"Okay, now I'm going to ask you not to freak, but she does that because if I don't have kids, I'm the end of the Vindico line. My mother, for some reason I will never understand, is a devoted apostle of the patriarchy." His body repelled the very idea of creating children.

Understanding lit Fionna's beautiful face as she nodded slowly. "Got it." She held her plate and glanced around. "Do you eat in here or in the living room?"

"I don't eat in the house, but you can eat wherever you want."

With a hesitant shrug, she walked through what was supposed to be a dining room, between the kitchen and living room.

Instead of a table or any kind of furniture for the purpose of serving food, it held dozens and dozens of duplicated evidence boxes and investigations he'd done on Wretchkinsides and all of the members of the Interfeci Criminal Organization.

There was a cheap particleboard desk stacked with paperwork, where Dan worked when he couldn't sleep. Two large corkboards hung on the walls. The contents matched the board covering the windows in his office.

"Interesting décor," Fionna commented with a sweet smile.

Dan couldn't seem to decide what he was supposed to feel at the moment. "It's been a process."

She reached back for his hand. He took it and was instantly content. She led him to the well-worn leather couch in the living room. It was a hand-me-down from his father's office. He had a flat-screen TV hung over the mantel of the fireplace that had never been lit. There was a glass-top coffee table and mismatched lamps set on the end tables. There was also a matching leather love seat, but Dan had never used it either.

"So, here's okay?"

"Of course." Dan seated himself and then pulled her down beside him.

She dug into the pizza as he returned for the drinks from his refrigerator that he'd forgotten. He handed her a Dr Pepper and settled himself again. He inhaled the first piece of pizza on his plate.

"This is so good." She looked like she'd never tasted anything better. He chuckled at her exuberance as she licked sauce from her thumb. She finished both pieces and set her plate on the coffee table.

"Do you want some more?" He stood to refill her plate.

"No, thank you, but I kind of think you might have been right about Lindley." She wrinkled her adorable nose. He knew she was worried she'd hurt his feelings.

Dan laughed outright. "I tried to tell you she's certifiable."

Fionna gave him a sorrowful look. She didn't seem to think it was funny. Dan quelled his chuckle.

"Dad wanted to take her to therapy when she was little and then again when she was a teenager. Mom was terrified that people would know something was really wrong with her, and the Realm would talk. She kept telling Dad that Lindley would grow out of it. She refused to admit that Lindley needed help. Then she went wild when she got to the academy, and now..." He threw his hands up and shook his head in abject defeat. "She really does desperately need help, and I don't know how to make that happen."

"I'm so sorry." Fionna sounded truly devastated. Dan finished the last bite of his pizza.

"Yeah, me too." The pain Lindley's antics had caused his family always infuriated him.

Fionna gave him his smile again, mixed with a very appealing, mischievous smirk. "You know, Daniel, if you want to get a suitable woman to have all of your sons, then you're going to need curtains, throw pillows, and pictures on the wall," she quoted his mother, which made him guffaw. She cracked up before she could finish.

"I tell you what, you pose buck naked for me, in a few of my favorite positions, I'll take the pictures, blow them up, and hang them on the walls." He shot her a naughty grin.

"Wouldn't your mother love that?" Fionna came right back as Dan cracked up again as he thought about his mother walking into a room with pictures of a naked Fionna all over the walls.

Fionna tensed suddenly. Her face contorted in pain. Dan stopped laughing. Her breath caught in a sharp inhale, and she began to rub her abdomen.

Her pain affected him physically. Dan took her hand. His heart ached, and his shield tensed in desperation to protect her from the pain.

"Come here, baby." He guided her gently until her head was settled against his chest. He pulled ambient heat from around the room and placed his hand where hers had been.

"I'm really sorry," she fussed.

"For what?"

"It's just so annoying. This is not what I wanted to be doing the first night you let me stay over."

Dan used the hand not soothing the pain in her abdomen to brush her hair behind her shoulders. He began dragging his fingers through the long, chestnut tresses. That always seemed to settle her.

"You can stay over any time you want, and we can do anything you want. But tonight, how about you just come up to my room and get into bed with me? Let me see if I can't get you to sleep, and then in a few days, you can show me what you did want to do on the first night you slept over."

She nodded as she tucked closer to him. "Is your house like Garrett's apartment where if I open a kitchen cabinet there's a pistol, and if I open the medicine cabinet it's full of bullet boxes?"

Dan chuckled. "I do have a very intricate security system that I've already reset for the night. I'll show you how to use it tomorrow. And I do have quite a few firearms in the house, but they're not anywhere you might stumble upon them, except maybe my bedside tables."

314

"With your condoms." She narrowed her eyes at him, catching him off guard.

"Hey now, remember I haven't been back here since I spent the night with you last Sunday night, but you're more than welcome to throw those out as well."

As her moods continued to change more rapidly than Dan was yet accustomed, she blushed. He kept up his massage, but she was clearly exhausted. "Let's go to bed, baby."

She didn't have enough energy to fight it any longer. He hoisted her into his arms.

"You don't have to carry me."

"I like to carry you." He headed up the stairs and drew the light from the lamps into his hand as he went by. "Quick tour." He moved her rapidly down the hallway. "Guest room, guest room, guest room." He gestured his head to the right and the left. "Never had a guest. When Fitz comes, he sleeps on the couch, so no furniture in any of them. Guest bath,"—he gestured to the small room next on his trek— "and my room." He paused as he stepped into the master suite and set her down.

She glanced around as Dan pulled clean sheets from the linen closet in the hall. He set the sheet stack on the bed and raced back down the stairs to retrieve her bags.

When he returned, he found her stripping the bed and remaking it.

"Fi," he scolded, "you get ready for bed. I'll do that."

"I don't mind." She smoothed the fitted sheet, taking far more care than Dan ever did.

"Baby, I know you don't feel well. Please let me take care of you." Dan helped her spread the top sheet, and he sealed heat in its fibers. She smiled and let him finish the task as she grabbed her bags and disappeared behind the bathroom door.

She emerged, several minutes later, wearing a pair of thick period panties that were vastly different from the skimpy underthings she usually preferred. Dan brushed his teeth and crawled into bed.

"Come here to me." He tucked her to his chest and began rubbing her lower back and abdomen with his heated hand again.

"That feels so much better. Why did I never think of that?"

Dan smiled as he kissed her forehead. "Go to sleep, baby. I've got you. I promise."

"I love you," she whispered in the darkness.

"Me too."

A moment later, she was sound asleep safe in his shield.

CHAPTER 37

WHERE THE PAIN RESIDES

Dan gasped for breath. His heart stormed against his rib cage. He blinked away the image of Wretchkinsides's deranged face as he'd murdered Amelia before his eyes. His head shook in a futile effort to remove the image burned in his brain.

He jerked upright and searched the room. Fionna was no longer in the bed. The bathroom door was closed, and the light was on.

He rubbed his face and waited. He willed his pulse and his breathing to steady. *I have to keep her safe,* surged through his mind with every frantic beat of his unsteady heart. He ached to have her back in his arms. He needed to know she was safe and content.

She emerged several minutes later hunched forward. Her face was pale and drawn in the moonlight. Dan's shield sizzled in his palms, desperate to cast her. "What's wrong, sweetheart?" He rushed to her.

She shook her head and began digging through her bags feebly while grasping her abdomen.

"Hey, go lie down. Just tell me what you need."

She eased back to the bed and looked like she had barely enough energy to hold herself upright.

"There are some pain killers in that bag. Will you get me some water?"

"Yeah, of course." Dan took the duffle bag to the bathroom and searched in the light. After locating the pain medication, he raced to the kitchen to get her a glass of water. He handed her the pill bottle and the water before he seated himself beside her. He caressed her body and lovingly tried to soothe any pain.

"I told you I wasn't much fun for a couple of days," she pouted pitifully.

"And I told you I wasn't going anywhere."

Fionna was up several times throughout the night writhing in pain. Dan was a disaster. He'd asked numerous times if she wanted to go to the hospital, but she'd insisted this was normal.

Amelia would get extremely moody for a few days each month. She would eat exorbitant amounts of chocolate and other fatty foods she normally steered clear of, but she was the only other woman Dan had ever been close enough with to have any experience with this kind of thing. She'd certainly never woken up in the night writhing in pain. He didn't feel like he had enough information from other women to know if this was normal or not. He'd seriously considered phoning Rainer and demanding to know if Emily ever had anything like this, but it was three in the morning. That seemed like it might be over-the-top even for him.

"Honey, are you sure you're okay?"

"I told you to just leave me at my house." She was worried she was keeping him up. Not really getting any answers from Fionna, Dan lay back and pulled her onto his chest. He'd pumped heat out every pore of his body as she relaxed against him.

The medicine seemed to kick in around four, and she slept curled up on his chest until six when the alarm on her phone went off. She whimpered as Dan slammed his hand down on top of it.

He kissed the top of her head and tucked it under his chin. "If you'll let me use your phone, I'll call Chloe and tell her you're not coming to practice. You go back to sleep. I'll come home at lunch and check on you. I was going to take your car to Garrett's mechanic, but I can do that tomorrow."

She smiled against him. "I have to go to practice." She drew a deep breath and then timidly traced her fingers down his chiseled abs. Dan was momentarily unable to think.

His brain scrambled from the caress. His cock was already on high alert. He prayed she'd continue her trek downwards, that she'd draw the copious amounts of erotic energy straight from its source, but she explained instead, "It costs too much to miss. I'm not really allowed to be sick."

While willing the blood to return to the head above his waist, Dan recalled the Angel contracts and the sheer amount of money their paychecks were docked for missing practices. *How could I have agreed something like that was legal?* She could feel his worry.

"I'll be okay. The first night is always the worst. By this afternoon, I'll feel better. I'll just be completely exhausted from not sleeping."

After spending several long minutes trying to coax her into staying in his bed where she was finally warm and comfortable, Dan gave up.

She showered, and he tried to find something for her to eat besides cold pizza. That turned out to be a fruitless endeavor. He debated the best way to get her some food.

He moved to the desk in the dining room and dug until he located a blank restraining order form. Coffee was next on the list of things he wanted to make certain she had. He marched to the Mr. Coffee situated on his counter but then remembered that he had no cream. Dan always drank his coffee black.

Of the many things he'd memorized about Fionna Styler in the past week, one was that she loved coffee and preferred it sweetened with honey with lots and lots of cream. He smirked as he let the image of him devouring her own honey cream mixture with his head between her gorgeous thighs form in his mind.

"What's that look for?" She wrapped her arms around his chest. He hadn't heard her come into the kitchen. Her sudden appearance disturbed him. His senses were sharpened from necessity. Iodex officers heard every movement. It was how they remained alive.

He cradled her to him but didn't comment on her question. "I'm gonna go pick us up something for breakfast. I wanted to make sure you were okay for me to leave."

"Oh, Garrett texted and said he'd pick me up and take me to the arena since I don't have a car. We can just get something on the way."

Dan tried to modulate his resentment, but she was far too strong a Receiver to have missed the changing flow of his rhythms.

She stretched up on her tiptoes and brushed her lips along his jawline. "But I would really rather have coffee with you." Certain she was lying to soothe his ego, Dan shook his head.

"Just give me ten minutes, okay?"

She watched him throw on his worn riding jacket, locate his keys and phone, and race out to his most prized possession.

Dan kicked his custom MV Agusta Brutale 575 to life. The powerful bike gave its metallic rumble between his legs, and a broad grin spread across his features.

Three minutes behind his estimated time, he raced back inside his kitchen. The line at Starbucks had held him up, but the delight in her eyes when he handed over the honey-sweetened latte was worth it.

This time they sat at his kitchen table, sipped coffee, and ate the bacon and gouda sandwiches he'd procured. The food wasn't nearly as enthralling as the company, but Dan reveled in the fact that they were having breakfast together.

It was almost as if he could have a normal life. He could have a girlfriend. He could spend time with her outside of one of their houses. He could wrap his arms around her and kiss her in public. The longing sat with a harsh pain in his chest.

Garrett's knock on the front door pounded against the scars his life had left inside him. Dan spent several long minutes making Garrett watch a passionate goodbye between him and Fionna.

Still not certain what to make of Garrett, Dan had to admit he really didn't seem to have minded the long-drawn kiss. He laughed and told Fionna he'd meet her in his Highlander whenever she was finished.

CHAPTER 38
BRAIN NOT BRAWN

When he finally raced into his office, he found the Crown Governor waiting along with the rest of the Elite team.

"Sorry," he offered. He was twenty minutes late for his first day back after suspension. Regret threatened to take chokehold.

"No, no." Governor Haydenshire laughed. "You being late might be the best thing that's happened since I became Crown. Never thought I'd see the day. I just came to say welcome back."

"Yeah, welcome back," Portwood joined in the greeting with a wry grin.

"Thanks," Dan chuckled as he took a moment to revel in sitting in his desk again.

"Good to see you're still smiling. I guess Sydney didn't wear off?" Logan goaded.

Aware that he was being studied, Dan fought not to roll his eyes. He had no intention of swapping locker room banter with any of his officers. He wasn't a seventeen-year-old prick, and he would guard what he shared with Fionna with his life.

"All right, I want to hear about Pendergrath since he was allowed back in the country, but then I want you to pull some information for me."

Everyone nodded as Portwood read off of Pendergrath's current file. Dan clenched his jaw when he got to the fact that an elderly couple in the area was found dead and their children stunned to learn that their fortune had been donated to an unregistered charity.

Logan went over the calls they'd been on during the first week of Dan's absence, and Ramier gave the Internet reports and social media accounts they'd hacked of criminals around the globe.

"We're way backed up on paperwork, and we still need to get everything together for Adeline's trial next month," Logan lamented just as Garrett sauntered in almost an hour late. Since he'd been taking care of Fionna, Dan said nothing.

"Oh, and Adderand and Pravus just made a trip to Brussels. I'm sure they're just visiting family for Christmas." Portwood rolled his eyes at the very idea. Adderand was now Wretchkinsides's top hit man since Dan had taken out Cascavel. Pravus was devil number three in line for the Interfeci throne right behind Pendergrath.

"Did they?" Dan's mind raced with what could be going on in Belgium since Pendergrath's release from prison that would require two of the top dogs to be flown out to Europe.

He began handing out assignments and informing everyone that they would be training and working out after lunch.

"Lawson and Haydenshire," he called as everyone else exited his office. "Since you haven't been here for a week to have any paperwork to catch up on, would you do me a favor?" With the ready compliancy he expected, they agreed. "I want any information you can find on Eric Kent, medium height and build, around thirty years old, black hair, brown eyes. He's trying to run for one of the governor seats. And send this restraining order out with Mercer now."

"No problem," Logan agreed as they took the restraining order and left.

An hour later, they returned to Dan's office.

"We didn't find much." Rainer handed Dan a folder of what they'd located. "He's an Adminis Predilect, went to Hans Bethe, even though his parents live here. There were a few complaints from some girls he dated. They all stated that he badgered them when they broke it off with him, but there were no arrests made."

Logan nodded and picked up the tale. "The headmaster gave him a formal reprimand with threat of expulsion if there were any more complaints. His old man got him out of trouble by promising he'd leave the girls alone. Two years ago, he was brought in on suspicion of voyeurism peeping-tom style." Logan scowled as he read the report. Fury sizzled in Dan's shield. "There were no official charges filed there either. It wouldn't look good if that made it to the political arena though. His dad stepped in again, money changed hands, and that was the end of it."

Dan ground his teeth. He willed himself to stay at his desk, as opposed to driving out to Eric's apartment and beating him within an inch of his life.

"Add this to the file." Dan handed over the yellow and pink carbon copies of the restraining order Fionna had signed that morning at his house.

"He's bothering Fi?" Logan asked. Thirst for justice tensed in both Rainer and Logan's shields.

Dan nodded. "Yeah, but I'll take care of it. Do you mind taking me out to Sam's at lunch? I want to get her car checked out. I don't like the fact that it's suddenly not working when it was sitting in the Iodex parking deck."

"Sure, no problem. I'll call and tell him we're coming," Rainer promised.

"Thanks."

Dan's cell phone rang. He smiled when he saw who was calling.

"Hey, baby doll, are you feeling any better?"

"No...not really," Fionna hesitated. She'd been crying. Her voice was haggard and frightened. Dan panicked. He stood and threw his holster on. His shield tensed with worry.

"What's wrong?"

"They told me to call Iodex, but I decided to just call you. Was that okay?"

"Of course. Tell me what happened."

"Eric's here and he won't leave."

Wrath-fueled fury scorched through Dan like a flame through gasoline.

"Security won't let him in the stadium. He keeps insisting he's my boyfriend and that I told him he could come watch me practice." He heard her breath shudder as she tried hard not to cry again. "I went out to tell him to leave. He just keeps telling me that he's announcing his candidacy tonight and that I need to be there. It's like he can't even hear me talk."

"Is he still there?" Dan was impressed at how calm he sounded despite the fact that he was enraged.

"Yes, he's refusing to leave until I go with him."

"It's all right, sweetheart. I'm on my way. Listen to me. Stay inside the arena. Do not go back and talk to him. Stay as close to Emily as you can. Where's Emily's security team?"

"They're who he's arguing with now. Thank you for coming."

"I told you if you need me, I'm there. I'm bringing a team with me. Just stay inside. I'll be right there. Stay with Emily, okay?"

Emily was the ideal choice due to the ring she was wearing. Dan tried to console himself with the knowledge that the engagement ring Rainer Lawson had given his lifetime love was the Lawson family ring. Imbibed with promethium, the wearer could access a supply of nuclear energy whenever it was needed. Emily Haydenshire, a Receiver with virtually no shielding energies at all, could throw a shield more fierce than Dan's as long as she was wearing that ring. She couldn't maintain it for long, but throwing it generally got the job done.

"Okay…" Fionna sounded timid and weak again. "But I thought I wasn't supposed to call you because no one can know."

The fact that Fionna was exhausted and feeling awful only added fuel to the ferocious fire burning in Dan's gut. "Baby, I will be there. I will take care of Eric. No one who doesn't need to know about us will know about us. I'll make this work. I will always take care of you."

Dan ended the call. Rainer and Logan stared at him, both extremely concerned.

"You wanna go see Emily for a few minutes?" Dan reseated himself and pulled up the information he wanted from his computer.

"Always, but is Fionna okay?" Rainer quizzed.

"It seems Mr. Kent is at the arena and won't leave." Dan copied down the numbers he needed. "Go tell Garrett he's coming along. I want a full team."

Rainer and Logan raced out of the office and returned with Garrett. They all slung on their holsters and pulled on Iodex jackets.

"I knew he was going to be trouble. He just wouldn't quit." Garrett shook his head. Dan grabbed his own Iodex jacket and rushed everyone out to the Expeditions.

"You drive." Dan threw the keys to Rainer, as he climbed in the passenger seat. Rainer cranked the SUV and flew out of the parking deck. Dan dialed his phone.

"This is Thomas Kent," the man answered on the second ring.

"Mr. Kent, this is Dan Vindico, Chief of Elite Iodex. Sir, I just wanted to call and tell you we've had several complaints from the Angels challengers practicing at the arena this morning. It seems your son is there and is refusing to leave." Dan tried to sound as professional and aloof as he could manage.

"What?"

"Yes, sir. Some of the challengers are quite agitated. I'm with a team headed that way right now. He's been asked to leave numerous times by arena security. I'm afraid I'm going to have to arrest him."

"No, don't do that. I'm sure he's just visiting Fionna Styler."

Every ounce of chiseled muscle in Dan's body seized. His shield flared around him in fury. Garrett shot him a concerned glance.

"I'm not certain what Eric has told you, Mr. Kent, but Ms. Styler has filed one of the many complaints this morning. She also filed a restraining order over the weekend against Eric. He's in violation of that already."

"What? I thought they were dating," Kent demanded hotly.

"Not according to Ms. Styler. She's assured me repeatedly that she agreed to go out with Eric once and then never again. She will be pressing charges if I arrest him today. I have to tell you, sir, an arrest for harassment and trespassing, along with the charges for not obeying the restraining order, on top of his previous suspicion of voyeurism, are not going to bode well in the political arena," Dan stated the key to the entire conversation.

Mr. Kent began mumbling furiously. "Who else has filed a complaint?"

Dan fought back a chuckle. "I'm not at liberty to name names. I'm certain you understand that. Several other challengers have phoned Iodex. I'm going to have to call Medio Sawyer and the other team owners. After I make the arrest, there's a conflict of interest with you having a partial share in the team your son is harassing."

"Okay, okay," Kent panicked. "I'm on my way. I'll get him to leave. Just don't arrest him!"

"That depends on whether or not he's there when we arrive. I'll reassess the situation then."

"I'm leaving now. I'm in my car."

"I'll see you soon then." Dan ended the call.

"Very, very well played," Garrett complimented. "I'm impressed. She's good for you."

Dan couldn't quite hide his grin as he instructed Rainer to speed it up.

"Yeah, and just in case it gets brought up again, I feel certain Emily called Iodex to complain." Rainer flipped on the internal blue lights and floored the Expedition. Dan nodded his appreciation.

"Yeah, Chloe as well," Garrett corroborated.

"I figured they did." Dan called the next number on his list.

"Georgetown Hospital," the chipper assistant announced.

"This is Dan Vindico, Chief of Iodex. I need to speak to Medio Sawyer, please. It's very important."

"Uh," the woman stammered. "Medio Sawyer is making rounds."

"Please let him know that Iodex is heading to the Alexandria Arena and that his daughter may be in danger."

"Yes, sir. Chloe has phoned already, but I hadn't given Medio Sawyer his messages yet."

"I need you to do that for me…now."

"Yes, sir." The woman put him on hold, and Dan waited as Rainer slowed down at a red light.

"This is Medio Sawyer," huffed a man's voice.

"Medio Sawyer, this is Dan Vindico."

"Hey, Dan. I haven't heard from you in years, son. Is something wrong?"

"Yes, sir, it seems Eric Kent is at the arena and won't leave. He's threatened Fionna Styler, and I know Chloe's already phoned, but several of the challengers are quite concerned. I'm heading out now with an Elite team. We should be arriving in the next few minutes, but I have to tell you, as the majority owner, in the contract the players sign every year, you guarantee their safety while on Angels' property. With Thomas being an owner, you may have to do something about him and his son."

Medio Sawyer was silent for the length of one heartbeat. "Believe me, he's been nothing but trouble since he bought in. I'd love nothing more than to force him out, but with the new law, I can't buy him out."

A broad grin spread across Dan's face. "I kind of figured. I'll have Chloe phone you when we arrive."

"No, let me find someone to finish my rounds. I'm on my way, and if you need to arrest Eric, please do so."

Perfect, Dan thought with a wry grin, as Rainer pulled into the parking deck of the arena and was waved through by security.

The doors of the Expedition flew open. Dan scowled at the scene before him.

"I didn't know they were sending out the big guns, Dan," Eddie Campton, head of arena security, offered apologetically. A disturbance call would normally be handled by a Non-Elite team.

"It's no problem."

Eric was standing between Eddie and another guard. He had his arms crossed in indignation. "He's only out here because he wants Fionna all for himself." Eric sounded like an overgrown toddler.

"Let's go ahead and get him cuffed," Dan spat to Garrett who looked only too happy to complete the task.

"Yes, sir." Garrett glared hatefully at Eric.

"And him too! They're jealous because Fionna's with me, and they both want her."

With entirely more force than was necessary, Garrett seized Eric's right shoulder and spun him. He shoved him hard into the brick wall outside the arena entrance. In one quick move, he shoved his knee into Eric and grasped his wrists. He slapped the cuffs on and then sealed them with his cast.

"You can't arrest me just because my girlfriend and I had a disagreement," Eric demanded nonsensically.

Acrimony rose in the bile in Dan's throat. "Your father's on his way along with the other team owners," Dan drawled.

Eric spun his head back with a savage look in his eye. "What?" he panicked.

"So, you can hear. You just don't listen. I kind of figured." Dan narrowed his eyes in disdain. "Here's the problem, stud." He moved his face inches from Eric's. "You either listen when I talk, or I'm going to have my officers throw you in the back of that truck, and you can plan your political career from Felsink. Maybe the other inmates will vote you the fucking most gorgeous thing they've ever laid eyes on and then they'll all agree to date you."

Rainer and Logan fought back laughter. They each held a cast containing enough electrical current to stun Eric if Dan needed them to.

"I don't give a damn who Fionna is dating. It isn't me, and it certainly isn't you." The lie blistered Dan's throat. "She thinks you're an asshole. She filed a restraining order against you which you are currently in violation of. But that's why you're here, isn't it? I sent it out a few hours ago with one of my officers. He showed up at your apartment and gave you your copy, and you got mad and came down here."

Eric huffed. He was on the verge of pitching a fit, something Dan wouldn't have minded recording just to show his old man, but he stayed the course. "She wants me. She's just not thinking straight."

Garrett's eyes flashed dangerously as he leaned into Eric and forced the air out of his lungs. "Let me tell you something about women, you prick. They sure as hell know what they want, and it isn't you. Now shut the fuck up and listen."

Just then, a sleek, silver Jaguar slid into the parking lot.

"Figures." Rainer rolled his eyes as Dan tried not to smile at the implication.

A man with slicked hair that appeared to be bulletproof, dressed in an expensive suit, raced from the driver's seat.

"I thought you weren't arresting him," Mr. Kent pled. "Eric, you cannot be arrested. How will that look for the campaign?"

Eric clammed up and pouted as soon as his father arrived.

Dan put on a show of talking about everything that had happened with each of the security guards, the Iodex team assigned to Emily, and then making certain the players were all safe inside the arena.

Medio Sawyer pulled in. Much to Dan's delight, he'd phoned Frank Magnus, one of the partners in Jack Stariff's legal firm, and Anna Eleanor, the head of the Auxiliary Service Department in the Senate, who was also the top pick to fill Governor Haydenshire's previously occupied seat on the board. She'd been backed by all of the current governors.

They'd traveled together from the Pentagon, and they pulled in behind Sawyer. Together with Sawyer they represented seventy-three percent of the shareholders of the Angels. Dan was elated.

"What's going on, Chief Vindico?" Anna demanded.

"We were called out here because Mr. Kent is refusing to leave the arena. He's been harassing Fionna Styler. She filed a restraining order over the weekend."

Anna Eleanor had worked diligently to climb the ranks in the Auxiliary Order of the Senate. As far as Dan was concerned, she was a consummate professional. She was absolutely brilliant. She was occasionally wary of men, him included.

She narrowed her eyes in on Thomas Kent. "As you and your son are both here, with him in handcuffs, it doesn't seem that you have much of a defense, Thomas."

At that moment, Crown Governor Haydenshire's minivan pulled onto the scene, and Dan heard Garrett bellow, "Oh, I do not think so, you little bitch."

Dan turned and saw Eric attempting to summon an electrical charge in effort to release Garrett's shield on the cuffs and to burn Garrett.

"Garrett, move!" Dan shouted. He leapt back as Logan sent a pulse from his own cast. Eric convulsed and hit the ground hard. His body continued to twitch from the cast.

Stunned gasps sounded from all of the onlookers. Shaking his head, Dan sighed. He'd never have bet Eric had the balls to pull something like that.

"I'm sorry, Mr. Kent, but Eric has been belligerent since we arrived. He's in violation of the restraining order, and now he's attempted to injure one of my officers in an effort to resist arrest. I'm going to have to take him in."

"No, wait!" Thomas moved toward Eric who was out cold on the ground. Dan suspected if it hadn't been his big brother Eric had tried to summon against, Logan might not have used quite so much force.

"He'll never come back here. I promise. I'll do anything. He'll never come around Fionna again. I'll sell my shares. I'll sell them at the board meeting Friday night. I won't even let him come to the challenges."

Sawyer and Magnus were both intrigued.

"Where is Emily? And where is Fionna?" Governor Haydenshire's infuriated demand shook everyone from their reverie.

"The entire team is inside, Crown Governor. I wouldn't let them leave for lunch until this was resolved," Eddie explained.

"You can talk to the Crown, Mr. Kent. I don't have the authority to keep him from being arrested after he summoned against Officer Haydenshire," Dan said.

Thomas turned his pleading eyes on Governor Haydenshire who did not appear to be in a very forgiving mood. A slight groan sounded from Eric as he began to come around.

Governor Haydenshire narrowed his eyes. "Dan, load him up. I'd prefer for both Eric and his father to be away from my daughter and her teammates." He turned his glare on Thomas Kent. "That is my son he just summoned against, and my daughter is inside that arena," he snarled.

Thomas paled dramatically.

Dan decided for once to trust someone else's authority instead of trying to exercise his own. "Yes, sir."

She'll make you a better person. Rainer's words, from the hotel in

Sydney, formed in Dan's mind as he watched Garrett and Logan shove Eric into the back of the SUV. He was drooling.

Dan moved to Governor Haydenshire. "Sir, would it be all right if I went in for just a minute?" He gestured his head toward the arena doors as he quietly made his request.

"I appreciate your asking instead of just going on with whatever you'd decided you were going to do. Your new situation, which I highly suspect is what the rest of us might call a real life, is good for you," Governor Haydenshire pointed out. "It's a nice change."

Dan decided against explaining that if he wasn't granted permission, he'd be asking for forgiveness later because he was going.

"Go ahead, but I want this resolved in my office before we go home tonight."

"Yes, sir." Dan sprinted through the metal doors.

CHAPTER 39
RISK AND REGRET

After he scanned the stadium to make certain the field aegis wasn't set to shield, Dan headed down the steps. It seemed Chloe and the coaches had decided to go on with practice since the ladies couldn't leave for lunch.

Fionna and Emily were doing rapid transfers of heat into elastic bandings and then pulling the elastic energy and forcing it toward a piezoelectric disk until it changed shape and produced electricity.

Dan studied Fionna. His heart hammered in his chest. He tried to remember that he was supposed to be talking to her as if she was the victim of a crime, but every fiber of his being wanted to go to her. He wanted to pull her into his fierce embrace and shield her from any foe.

She looked pale and weak. Worry etched her beautiful features. He waited until she dropped her cast. She immediate turned and smiled at him. She must've sensed his nearness.

He moved onto the field but was stopped by Chloe Sawyer.

"What happened?" She gestured out the arena doors.

"We took him in but haven't charged him yet. I need to talk to Fionna for a few minutes. Is that all right?" This bullshit of asking permission was wearing on his last nerve. She was his. The sooner he ended Wretchkinsides, the sooner the world would understand that.

He couldn't keep his eyes off her. "Dan, she's my best friend. I was there the night you chased her home from Anglington's, remember? We all know the deal. We all love her. We'd never let anyone know about you two. We just want her to be happy. She hasn't been happy in a long time. But you listen to me, if you fuck her up, I'll fuck you up. You got that?"

He nodded his understanding. It was odd that he didn't mind the threat. But what did she mean Fionna hadn't been happy in a long time? Why hadn't he known that? He'd spent hours on end with her over the last week sharing secrets they'd never told another soul, or at least he thought they had.

"I know she's not feeling well. She can go home early if she wants. I won't tell Dad," Chloe offered as she glanced Fionna's way.

"Thanks." Dan managed to locate his voice. "She had a rough night."

"Yeah, I know." Chloe chuckled at his concern. "She's done that since we were teenagers." There was more than a note of defiance in her tone. She was less than subtly reminding Dan that she'd been an important part of Fionna's life for a lot longer than he had.

He gave her a forced smile and then moved to Fionna.

"Hey." Her face lit as he neared, and his heart gave a quickening beat. Unable to stop himself from doing another systematic search of the area to make certain no one saw them, he edged closer.

"Hey, baby."

"Can I hug you, please?" Desperation darkened her weary eyes.

"Why don't we go somewhere else and talk?" He couldn't do it. He couldn't put her at risk of someone seeing them even if all the Angels now knew.

She nodded and guided him into the well-appointed Angels locker room.

"I'm really hoping I'm the only guy who's ever been in here." He tried to lighten the mood as he spun her into his arms and his fierce shield formed around her. He let heat spill into the bands of protection, and she sighed contentedly a moment later. She nuzzled her face against his chest, and everything in his world was suddenly right.

"Are you okay?" He began rubbing her back.

"I am now." She attempted a sweet smile, but exhaustion was still her predominant feature. "Can we leave now? We could go to my house and have lunch together. It's only five minutes from here."

With another searing stab of regret, Dan shook his head. "I can't. I have to get back. They've got Eric in the truck, and they're waiting on me. I just wanted to come make sure you were all right."

She tried to hide the disappointment with a forced smile. "Does that mean you arrested him?"

"Not yet. Governor Haydenshire stepped in. We're all heading back to his office. I'm not certain what his plan is, but I have to go along I suppose. He tried to pull an electrical current through the cuffs while Garrett held them, so at this point he could be looking at time."

"Oh, my gosh! Is Garrett okay?"

Jealousy was a weary partner, that was for damn sure. He just had no idea how to rid himself of the emotion.

"He's fine. He saw what he was trying to do. Logan stunned Eric."

"Wow, your job is really dangerous." Fear timed in her rhythms.

"It's not always. A lot of the time I'm at my desk doing paperwork."

She nodded against his chest. She seemed unwilling to let him go anytime in the near future. He held her tight and kissed the top of her head.

"I have to go, sweetheart. But as soon as I'm finished with Eric, I'll head out. Chloe said you could leave early. How about you meet me in the parking deck?" Somehow picking her up from work, even covertly, soothed him.

"Yeah, it's good to be friends with the captain."

Dan chuckled as he lowered his shield and eased away from her. It was like severing his own soul. "I have to go, baby. I'm sorry."

"It's okay." Her beautiful, genuine, dazzling smile formed on her face. His shield had given her the strength she'd needed, and that was enough to heal the abrasions his day had inflicted. He allowed himself one moment of lust as he guided her mouth to his.

"All mine," he breathed the words over her lips, before he turned his head and consumed her with greed. A furtive moan spilled from her, as she laced her fingers through his hair and pulled him in for more.

She sucked his tongue until she'd pulled just a little of his energy. A desperate groan echoed from his lungs, as he envisioned her sucking his cock that begged for her affection. She broke the kiss with panted breath. The passion between them was far too tempting.

"I'll pick you up in a little while."

She slid her bottom lip through her teeth. He knew she could still taste his rhythms there. The motion made his cock tug sharply. He had to get it together. She moved toward the door, and he forced his feet to follow her trek.

"Hey, Fi, baby." He suddenly remembered Chloe's words. "If there's ever anything you want to talk about or that's upsetting you, you'll tell me, right?"

"Of course. I've already told you more than I've ever told anyone." She seemed hurt by his request.

"I know. I just want you to know you can tell me anything, any time. If anything's bothering you, I want to know. I want to make it better."

Confusion furrowed her brow, but she nodded and guided him back to the field.

At four o'clock, Dan, Rainer, Logan, and Garrett emerged from the Crown Governor's office, never having had lunch.

Dan was relatively pleased with the outcome of the exhaustive meeting. Thomas Kent had agreed to sell his shares of Angel Enterprises at the next board meeting in exchange for Eric not being arrested and agreeing to stay away from the players and the arena.

As his only crimes were breaking the restraining order and resisting arrest, which wouldn't bring much in the way of prison time, Dan and Garrett had agreed it was the best possible scenario.

Governor Haydenshire had shouted at Eric for a solid half hour and had warned both him and his father against Eric's running for governor. According to Thomas, Eric was still going to announce his candidacy that evening.

Governor Haydenshire had sent Eric to the holding cells in the Senate while he'd discussed the fact that if Eric continued to provoke Fionna or any of the Angels, criminal action would be taken.

"You can all go on, and tell Sam I'm sorry I didn't make it out there today," Dan instructed Rainer. Everyone nodded their appreciation and agreement.

"Why don't you and I go let Eric out of his cage?" Garrett raised his eyebrows and shot Dan a knowing grin. With a sigh, Dan nodded and grabbed the keys to the holding cells.

"So, you're really okay playing third wheel in all of this?" Dan wanted a better read on Garrett's thoughts and to remind him of his place.

Garrett smirked. "I'm fine with it. You're not, so maybe I should be asking you. I sure as hell wouldn't play boyfriend with anyone else, but I love Fi. But I don't love her like that. I also get that you don't get how anyone can be in her presence and not fall for her. I'm telling myself that's a good thing. But hear me say this, there are far too many women out there for me to ever settle down. But that doesn't mean I won't do whatever needs to be done to help my friends settle down *if* that's what they want."

Dan caught the test in the phrase. Garrett still didn't believe that Dan was as committed to the relationship as he was convinced Fionna was. That was a test Dan had no intention of failing.

He couldn't shake the worry over Chloe's warning that Fionna hadn't been happy. His ego was plagued with badgering questions. Was Fionna really as committed to this as she seemed to be? Did he know her as well as he thought he did? Swallowing down a bitter dose of pride, he drew a deep breath.

"Thank you for doing this. She's the first thing in ten long years that's made me believe this life might actually be worth hanging around for."

Garrett fought his visible shock and studied Dan. He finally managed a nod. "Yeah, I can tell, and you're welcome. You just make sure if that feeling changes anytime soon, you talk to me before you run your mouth to her."

"It's not going to change, but fine."

They turned down the corridor of holding cells. Dan let the keys on the large ring clatter ominously. "Well, Eric, it seems Daddy came through for you again. I guess we're gonna let you go," Dan drawled hatefully.

Garrett turned his typical smirk into a vicious scowl. Eric huffed indignantly as Dan unlocked the cell. He was careful not to touch the enhanced bars.

Dan stepped back and watched realization set on Eric. He was down a long empty hallway with no one but Dan Vindico and Garrett Haydenshire.

"Look a little nervous there, Kent. Something wrong?" Garrett mocked in his face.

"No." Eric attempted to edge by Dan. He stepped minutely to the left and blocked his way. Eric tried the same move on the other side, but Garrett blocked him with ease.

"Let's chat, Eric," Garrett sneered.

"Where's my father?"

Dan laughed derisively. "You need Daddy to come clean up your shit, little boy? Because, believe me, you're in it deep."

Garrett narrowed his hate-filled eyes. "You know I'd hate you for being a prick to women in general, and I would still do everything in my power to make certain you end up in Felsink where you belong no matter which girl you were messing with. But you see, Eric, you decided to go and mess with our girl. That was a really, really stupid decision on your part." He shoved Eric hard up against the concrete wall of the corridor.

"Your girl?" Eric was astounded as he made all of the assumptions Dan and Garrett were implying. His eyes darted from one infuriated glare to the other.

"Look at me." Dan took Eric's jaw in his hand and slammed his head against the wall Garrett had just shoved his body into. He leaned his face inches from Eric and held his head so that he had nowhere to look but into Dan's infuriated eyes.

"If you ever, ever come anywhere near Fionna again, we will make absolutely certain it's the last thing you ever do. We'll break every single bone in your pathetic little body if you so much as think about her again. We already took care of deleting all of her contact information from your phone when we locked you up, but you can go ahead and forget her address as well. Forget whatever the hell it is you convinced yourself you had with her, because if you don't, we will tear you into so many little pieces no one will ever be able to put you back together. We will destroy you. You got it, you motherfucking asshole?"

Eric attempted to nod. His eyes spun as Dan released him.

"Get the hell out of my face, and you better pray we don't ever see you again," Garrett spat.

"Just wait until I'm governor. Fionna was a sweet girl. You've ruined her. When I'm on the board, I'm going to see to it that neither of you is employed by the Senate and that what you're doing with Fionna is illegal."

Dan laughed again as he shoved Eric toward the door.

"Who said we were doing anything with Fionna?" Garrett continued to provoke their prey.

"I've seen her with both of you. You want her all for yourselves, and she's just very inexperienced. That's why she doesn't want to get involved with me. You took advantage of her. Wait 'til I'm a governor."

"You're delusional." Garrett fought not to laugh. Dan did a better job, but he had more to lose. Fionna was far from inexperienced. Quickly shutting those thoughts down, Dan kept his hand on the back of Eric's neck and shoved him through the Iodex office doors.

"Tuttle, would you get Governor Kent," he drawled derisively, "his shit and then get him the hell out of my face?"

Tuttle smirked. "Sure thing, boss, and I'm glad you're back. We missed you."

Dan went back to get his jacket from his office before leaving for the arena. He saw Logan and Rainer beside his door. They were talking to none other than Mitchell O'Ryan. Rainer's face was ghost-white.

"What are you doing here, Mitchell?" Dan demanded.

"I want my dad back out of Felsink." Mitchell's voice faltered in his demand. Dan immediately recognized the fear.

"I talked to your dad two weeks ago. He didn't have anything new for me."

"I know, and he really didn't then, but Uncle Nic came by my house. He asked my mom if Marlisa could stay with us. He said he's going back to Moscow to see Aunt Lucinda for a few weeks or something. Anyway, I grabbed all of the files I found in his briefcase. I switched them with a bunch of paper, and he left before he noticed."

Dan's heart stuttered out of rhythm. His brain flew into overdrive. Elation and terror swelled in his rhythms.

"He will kill you if he finds out what you did," fell from Dan's mouth before he could halt the words.

"I know, but he's coming back tonight to see Marlisa before he flies out. I was thinking if we could copy all this stuff then I could sneak it back in, and he'd never know."

Logan shook his head in utter disbelief. "Good God, Mitchell, are you insane?"

"Just please help me. My dad's really sick. He's got to get out of there."

Dan continued to draw deep breaths as he tried to formulate what to do next. Mitchell was correct. His father wasn't doing well in Felsink. Dan's only concern two weeks before had been that if O'Ryan died in prison, Dan had lost his inside man.

Dan didn't have enough evidence linked to Wretchkinsides directly that would keep him in prison for any length of time, so showing up at the O'Ryans' mansion and arresting him wasn't a good option.

If they took down Wretchkinsides without Pravus and Pendergrath, they would most definitely kill the O'Ryans if they ever figured out how Dan knew where Dominic was going to be and when.

"What time is he coming back?" Dan demanded.

"Mom invited him for dinner at seven."

"Not that you've left me much choice, but I guess we're in it now. Garrett, would you mind..."

"Already on my way. I'll get Emily too. And yes, if she's not feeling well, I'll take her home and stay with her until you get there."

Defeat settled thickly in Dan's throat. He made certain Mitchell was distracted with Rainer and Logan and reminded himself that Garrett hadn't said her name.

Garrett seemed to understand how hard the request had been for Dan to make. He slapped Dan on the shoulder consolingly and turned so no one else could hear him.

"She's not gonna want to go home without you, and it's sure as hell not me who makes her smile like she's been smiling. I might do in a pinch, but I'm not the guy she wants taking care of her when she's sick. Just get over yourself, man."

Dan tried to keep his mind on the task ahead of him.

"Thank you," he managed as Garrett rushed out the door. "All right," he called loudly to every other officer, "I need every piece of information in these files." He lifted the large stack of manila folders from Mitchell's hands. "I need them copied quickly. I will hand you a number when you pick up your stack. For the love of God, don't be stupid and get the documents out of order. Take a stack, take a number, and then go find any available copier and make it fly." Dan held up a pad of sticky notes as he gave his orders.

Everyone moved to him rapidly. Rainer and Logan took the first stack and the number one.

"Let's go use Dad's copier. No one else will," Logan pointed out. Rainer gave a single nod as they sprinted toward the governors' corridor.

Dominic Wretchkinsides was brilliant. He was well aware that everything kept on a computer could be hacked. Despite the system being antiquated, he still did most of his planning on paper. Mitchell had quite literally handed them gold.

CHAPTER 40

HARD EVIDENCE

RAINER LAWSON

"Dad," Logan spluttered as he and Rainer almost ran headlong into the Crown Governor in their sprint. Startled, Governor Haydenshire's eyes goggled momentarily. "Can we use your copier? We need to get this done quickly. It's from Wretchkinsides's briefcase. We need to get it back before he realizes it's gone."

"How on earth...?" Governor Haydenshire reopened his office door and followed Logan and Rainer inside. "Where did this come from?"

"Mitchell," Logan supplied as Rainer casted the copier in the back corner of the plush office and primed it. "Vindico made a deal with Mitch's dad a few months ago that if he coughed up anything he found on Wretchkinsides, he'd get him out of Felsink early," Logan explained, while he began feeding large stacks of paper into the copier. "Mitch apparently decided to take over when his father was sent back to prison."

Governor Haydenshire rubbed his temples as the ramifications visibly settled on him.

"I sincerely hope Daniel has some plan to make certain that Mitchell O'Ryan survives this night." The governor shook his head as he stepped in and cooled the machine for them. Logan slid to the other end of the copier and carefully arranged the pieces back into neat stacks. His mouth fell open with a sudden gasp.

"Rainer!" He stared down at the document copy that had just flown off the machine. The stunned shock that etched Logan's entire face caused Rainer to drop his cast.

"What?" Rainer studied the paper in Logan's hand. His mind rejected the information as his stomach flipped uncomfortably. He jerked the paper from Logan's hands and recalled his flight to Rio, where he'd listened to Pete Namphis talk about his uncle having documents forged to gain custody of Rainer once his father had been killed.

To stare down at the evidence, to hold the script in his hands that had insured his misery and ultimately his uncle's death had Rainer's lungs seizing. His heart thundered in his chest. He couldn't breathe around the pain.

"Here." Logan supplied him with the papers that had fallen underneath the one Rainer had pulled from his grasp. It was a contract signed by his uncle, in his childish, scratching handwriting, that promised his service to the Interfeci organization at any time in the future for the services he'd been provided. Dominic Wretchkinsides's harshly slanting signature was underneath Stan's.

It certainly wouldn't hold up in court, as contracts for illegal actions rarely did, but Rainer stared down at three pieces of paper that had forever altered the course of his life.

The original custody document that Wretchkinsides had managed to get his hands on glared back at him. Wretchkinsides had planned the hit on Rainer's father. He'd known to secure this ahead of time which meant Stan had known as well. Rainer willed the vomit in his gut to remain in place.

At any time that I may not be able to care for my son, Rainer Emory Lawson, I, Crown Governor Joseph Emory Lawson, do hereby give full rights, responsibilities, and duties to Governor Stephen William Haydenshire and Mrs. Lillian Anderson Haydenshire until the time that Rainer comes of age.

"Son, are you all right?" Governor Haydenshire took Rainer's shoulder to steady him, then he pulled him into his protective embrace.

Rainer allowed this for several long seconds, but then he stepped back and flipped the paper again. He saw the near perfect forgery. The Haydenshires' names had been replaced with his uncle's.

"This is the only custody document I ever saw." Governor Haydenshire touched the forgery as if the paper might singe his hands from the evil it held. "If I'd suspected this, I would never have let you live there, even for the few weeks that you had to endure. Tell me you know that."

Rainer managed a haggard nod. "Just finish the copies."

"Logan, mark where these belong and bring the rest when they've finished." Governor Haydenshire guided Rainer out of the office and back to Iodex. "Dan…" Governor Haydenshire opened Dan's door without knocking. Dan and Portwood were making the copier in the office move rapidly, as document after document flew out the other side into a box Dan had placed to catch the evidence.

Vindico spun as soon as he heard the governor's voice. Governor Haydenshire handed the forgeries and the contract to him. His mouth fell open.

"Lawson, I'm…so sorry," he offered sincerely. "I suspected this, but I never thought he would've kept the copies."

Neither of them stated what they knew. The documents were still in Wretchkinsides's briefcase because they'd been used to force his uncle to try to kill Emily just a few weeks before.

Garrett returned just then with Emily and Fionna.

Emily rushed into the office. "What's wrong?" She'd known something was wrong without even having to be near Rainer.

"Rainer, are you okay?" Fionna's voice faltered as she glanced at Dan quizzically. Fionna seemed to also sense Rainer's utter confusion and devastation over what to feel and the desperate ache that seemed to close his throat whenever he longed to talk to his father.

Dan handed the copies to Emily.

"What does this mean?" She studied the custody document. The governor pulled the contract from underneath and pointed to the signatures.

"Oh my gosh," she choked and then threw her arms around Rainer.

"This is enough, Daniel. Let's finally end this," Governor Haydenshire urged. Rainer recognized the tone the governor used when he was testing one of his children.

"Yeah, forging Crown Governor Lawson's will. We can take him from O'Ryan's house," Garrett agreed. "He'll go away for life for this." He pointed to the papers in his little sister's hand.

"He's right, Dan. Forging Joseph's will is enough to put him in Coriolis for the rest of his life."

Dan had to visibly calm himself. He reached for Fionna's hand. "If we arrest him tonight, Pendergrath and Pravus will kill Mitchell and his mother. Maybe now everyone understands why I was rather perturbed that Pendergrath was released from prison a few weeks ago."

"Hey, listen, I'm sorry or whatever, Rainer, but I kinda gotta go." Mitchell's frantic demand shattered the glare Dan was giving the governor.

As Iodex officers began returning with their stacks of documents, he oversaw that they were restacked properly.

"Do you want an Elite team at your house, Mitchell? We will keep you safe," Dan offered.

"No," Mitchell insisted, "he'd see you somehow. He'd know something was up. Just give them to me. I'll get them back in without him knowing. I'll find a way. Whenever Marlisa is involved, he's not as fucked-up as he usually is."

"Are you certain?" Governor Haydenshire's question was laced with deep concern.

"I'll be fine. I gotta go."

"All right, send a text to either Lawson or Haydenshire when he leaves and let us know that you're all right. If I haven't heard from you by eight, we're coming in," Dan warned.

"Okay, fine." Mitchell took the mended stack and raced from the offices.

"So," Fionna soothed sweetly as she laid her head against Dan's bicep. "How about if Emily and I borrow the Highlander and go get everyone some dinner and then we can stay and help you go through all of this?"

Vindico looked surprised at her suggestion. "No, honey. It's okay." He paused and stared longingly at the stack of papers on Rainer's desk. "I need to get you home. We'll work through it tomorrow."

A broad grin spread across Fionna's face. Rainer wasn't certain what she'd just discovered about Vindico, but she was extremely pleased. "How about all of us go to my house, and I'll make us some dinner. We can all go through this." She gestured to the stack of files.

"That sounds more than reasonable," the governor agreed.

"Are you sure?" Dan turned to Fionna so he was staring into her eyes.

"This is huge. I know it. I can feel it." She squeezed his hand to show him how she felt it. "And this is important to you, so it's important to me. I don't mind."

He nodded hesitantly. "Okay, we'll work while we eat, but then you yahoos are out," he goaded as everyone chuckled, thankful that they would all be together to await Mitchell's text. "Everyone else can head home. If we don't hear from O'Ryan by eight, I'll let you know if I need backup."

Lost in a daze and going through the motions from habit alone, Rainer opened the passenger side door of his Porsche for Emily.

"Talk to me. Tell me what you're thinking." She tried to soothe his frantic rhythms with her cast.

"I don't know," he confessed sincerely.

"I know we kind of already knew all of that," she reminded him gently. "But that doesn't make seeing it with your own eyes any less horrible."

Rainer had told Emily about the conversation he'd overheard on his flight to Rio after she'd returned from her trip. He told her everything just as he always did.

She was right. Something about the finality of the concrete evidence had thrown him. He couldn't reason why, and he certainly couldn't explain it to her. He didn't understand it himself. He didn't really see anything in front of him as he drove.

"Do you want to know what I think?" she finally whispered.

Rainer raised his eyebrows and awaited her response. She squeezed the top of his hand on the gearshift. "I don't think you're upset because you had to live with your uncle or for all of the abuse you endured. I think you're upset," she choked back tears, "because when your uncle signed that contract, he signed his own death warrant. He forced you to be the one to do what you had to do to him. He forced you to choose between us. He forced you to kill him," she explained the harrowing reality that lay in the recesses of Rainer's mind. "He not only viciously betrayed you, he betrayed your dad, his own brother."

His conscience was trying so hard to keep it from him. His shield had erected in his mind. Rainer nodded, as he swallowed down the choking realization of the cold, hard truth.

CHAPTER 41

BATTLE BY PROXY

DAN VINDICO

"Fi, baby, we don't need to do this," Dan argued as he opened the door to the Expedition for Fionna and then loaded the box of evidence into the middle seat. He stopped short of buckling it in. He still couldn't believe what he'd been handed. "Let me pick us up some dinner. I planned to take you home, lie on the couch with you, and watch movies. I want to take care of you. You're more important than any evidence."

As the words egressed his mouth, the shock of his own statement dumbfounded him. How could she have changed him so thoroughly in such a short amount of time?

Dan was certain she was exhausted and still rather tender in a few key areas from her cycle, and now she was hosting an impromptu dinner for half of the Elite squadron and their significant others.

Fionna chuckled and leaned across the console to brush a kiss along his jawline. "I somehow doubt that *Casablanca* and *Some Like It Hot* are really going to be able to hold your attention when you have the contents of Wretchkinsides's briefcase in a box at my house."

Not certain if he should just go ahead and apologize for the truthfulness of her statement or deny that it was factual, Dan debated. "I can't believe that kid did this." He jerked his thumb back toward the evidence box.

"That was really brave," Fionna admired.

"Yeah, and that's not usually the O'Ryans' gig. But I'll tell you this, crime families are always brought down by one member they've all overlooked."

"Do you think Rainer's all right?"

"He's had an awful year," Dan admitted. "I think he suspected there'd been a forgery, so I don't think he was shocked. But, you know how his uncle was killed. That takes its toll, trust me. I'd give him another week off, but that wouldn't do any good. It'd only make him more miserable. You can't dictate recovery time for grief. But this will drive him." Dan knew because Rainer reminded him of himself at twenty-one.

"Maybe we can get his mind off of it for tonight anyway."

Dan smiled. She was so incredibly sweet. Her tender care for everyone around her always pierced through the hardened edges he'd fortified around his heart.

"I'm pretty sure Miss Haydenshire has the perfect formula for that."

Fionna giggled and nodded her head.

When they arrived, Dan prepared sodas and beers while Fionna slowly heated some soup she'd made a few weeks before and then frozen. Dan helped her fix sandwiches and grilled them under her instruction.

Garrett spread the documents out on Fionna's living room floor while Rainer checked his phone constantly for the text from Mitchell.

As Dan and Fionna served the plates, everyone pulled a folder to them and began going through the documents. Fionna stayed by Dan and looked over what he was going through. Emily did the same with Rainer. Dan noted that she constantly eased her soothing restorative casts through Rainer's forearm, and he didn't seem to mind.

Logan and Adeline arrived from the hospital and were handed plates, drinks, and another folder. At a quarter to eight, Rainer's cell chirped. Visible relief washed over him.

"Mitchell says, 'He came and didn't stay long. Got the files back in no problem.'" No one believed it had been that easy.

"Are you going to let his dad out?" Fionna asked.

"Yes, tonight." Dan assured her that Mitchell's sacrifice wouldn't go unrewarded. "And I'm not putting him back in."

"What is that?" She pointed to a stack of papers. The word *Angel* must've caught her eye. Dan picked them up and began reading.

All of the heat in his body turned to frigid disbelief. He set down his sandwich carefully as he flipped to the next page and shook his head.

"What is it?" Rainer slid closer. Dan handed him the top sheet as he continued to read the ones underneath. "He can't do this."

Nausea washed over Dan in waves as he realized he'd just forced Thomas Kent to market his stock in the Arlington Angels at the same time Dominic Wretchkinsides was trying to force a hostile takeover.

Emily grabbed the paper Dan had given Rainer as he shook his head in stunned disbelief.

"What does this mean? What's a proxy fight?" she demanded.

"Uh," Rainer stammered, "in this case it means the Interfeci Organization is going to try to convince the owners of the Angels to put the team under new management and to give the controlling interest and the capital you produce to Wretchkinsides." He sounded sickened as he said the words.

"What?!" Emily and Fionna gasped at the same moment.

"He can't buy us. We aren't for sale," Emily determined. Rainer grimaced at her tone.

"Em," Rainer soothed as Dan watched, impressed with how he handled her distress. "Just listen to me for a minute, okay?"

Emily stared up at him with tears in her eyes. Fionna tried not to cry as Dan embraced her.

"The Angels are a business, just like anything else. Remember, we talked about this after Chloe was attacked while we were in Paris. We thought they'd backed off, but clearly they hadn't. The Angels can be bought and sold, but I will not let Wretchkinsides buy out the Angels. I'll buy them myself before I let that happen. The real problem is going to be keeping the majority holders and their families safe until we make certain he can't make the purchase. The next board meeting is Friday night. That's when Kent will sell his shares." Rainer began considering everything Dan had already gone over in his head.

"I won't have a job." Fionna broke down as Dan cradled her against his shoulder. He rubbed her back, sharing heartbreak with Rainer over what this was doing to the women they loved.

Garrett lamented, "They never backed off. Nic focused all his efforts on getting Pendergrath out of prison. That took up his time. He's refocused now." He stood and put his plate and bowl in the sink and threw away his beer bottle. He slapped Logan on the shoulder. "I think I'm gonna go check on Chloe, and I'll see if her father and the other shareholders will meet with us tomorrow. Why don't you and Rainer go talk to Dad?"

Dan began to wonder what it was that Garrett Haydenshire really wanted. They were throwing punches a few days before, and now he was clearly trying to give Fionna and Dan some privacy as she continued to sob onto his shoulder.

"Thank you," Dan said quietly as everyone stood to leave.

"Call me if you need me, okay?" were Garrett's soothing words as he kissed the top of Fionna's head. She stood and threw her arms around him. He embraced her tenderly. "We're not going to let this happen," he vowed. She managed a nod. He gave her another quick squeeze and then followed everyone else out. He locked the door with his key.

CHAPTER 42

GOLD

"This house cost me a lot of money." Fionna shuddered against him. "I used most of my savings for the down payment. I haven't really replenished much since then because I paid for all of the construction work, and I have credit cards." She broke down as Dan cradled her to him and tenderly tried to get a word in between her convulsive sobs. "I don't know how to do anything else."

"Okay, listen to me." He tried to wipe away her endless tears. "First of all, I will not let him do this." He gestured to the document containing the plans for the takeover. "If Lawson doesn't buy out Kent, then I will, and it will take more than those shares to make any changes in the team. My main focus will be making certain the majority holders don't give in to the threats they will certainly be receiving soon. I need them to know I'll keep their families safe, so I can keep the team safe."

She nodded as she tried to still her trembling chin. Her abdomen quivered in her effort to stop crying.

"Baby, it's okay." He brushed a tender kiss on her forehead. "I would never let you lose your home or not be able to pay your bills." He was trying not to be offended that she thought he would allow that.

"But what happens if you can't stop him? What happens if the owners get scared and sell to him? I won't play for him. He's a murderer."

She obviously needed a contingency plan, something concrete that she could cling to. She was coming unglued. He cradled her face in his powerful right hand and gazed into the depths of her tear-filled eyes.

"I will not allow that to happen, but if it does, then I will pay off all of your credit cards. And then I'll just go ahead and ask you to move in with me." He watched her eyes widen in shock as he tried to hide his own. "I'd already been thinking about it. I do think we should wait and see what happens Friday, because I don't want you to do anything you aren't sure about. I know how much you love this house. I'd even be willing to sell and move in here with you, but whatever happens, baby, I'm here. I'm not going anywhere, and you don't have to do this alone."

She needed a steady foundation to cling to that wouldn't let her down. He'd be the buoy that kept her afloat. He would be her Shield. That was all he wanted anyway.

She shook her head. "We just started dating. I can't let you pay off my credit cards. You don't even know how much is on them, but if you go upstairs and look in my shoe closet, trust me, you'll take back that offer." She squeezed out several additional tears as her eyes closed tightly.

Dan chuckled as he shook his head. "Sweetheart, maybe I didn't explain myself well enough when we were in Sydney. When I started at Iodex, I took out multiple substantial life insurance policies worth significant amounts of money for myself and for Amelia. I never thought anything would happen to her," he admitted in a haggard breath, "but I wanted her to be well taken care of if anything happened to me.

"When she was killed, our house was instantly paid for, and I had several million dollars sitting in my bank account. My dad sold the house for me, and I tried desperately to give all the money to her parents, but they refused. So, I used a small portion of the money to buy where I live now, and I bought my bike. I invested the rest. Like I told you, I haven't really spent any money in the last ten years or so, and I make a nice salary." Giving her an adoring smile, he chuckled. "So, it didn't even scare me that you just told me you have a closet just for shoes."

Fionna finally laughed. The sound eased his weary soul. "Do you really think you can stop him?"

"I do, but I've got a lot to do between now and Friday. It might mean I won't get to be here with you as much as I'd like to be. You're welcome to come up to the Senate any time you want though."

She continued drawing deep breaths and running her hands over her eyes.

"How about this…" Dan stood and pulled her up with him. He guided her to her couch, which had several quilts draped on the arms and quite a few large accent pillows. He pulled one of the pillows to the end and guided her down as she furrowed her brow. After unfurling the quilt that was on top, the one that looked the most worn, he gently tucked it around her. "Now," he whispered, "I know you're exhausted and this has been a hell of a day, so…" He summoned to turn on her television and located the on-demand movies. He selected *Some Like It Hot*—a comedy about running from the mob was almost clichéd at that point—and he started it.

"I noticed you didn't say you would move in with me," he pointed out as he restacked the documents from Wretchkinsides's briefcase and piled them on the floor beside Fionna's couch. He seated himself near her head and glanced her way before he began going through all of the paperwork.

"I'm really scared," she admitted in a pained whisper. He set the paperwork down and tenderly brushed her hair behind her ear as he gazed down at her.

"I know." Dan brushed a kiss on her cheek. With all of her other qualities, she was very wise as well. "I'm scared too, but I know I don't want to think about going home and you not being there. So, we'll wait until you're ready. You just let me know. I'll wait. I don't mind being patient if you're the one I am waiting for." He hoped the knowledge that the ball was in her court would help.

She smiled up at him. "Okay," she agreed as he settled back down on the floor. "If I fall asleep, will you tell me what you find when I wake up?"

"I will if I can. Governor Haydenshire really shouldn't have let me show you, Emily, and Adeline any of this. Of course, I'm not supposed to *have* any of this, and our new Crown has never done a very good job of not telling his wife everything that goes on in the Senate. I guess that's why he allowed it."

Fionna seemed to understand. She settled on the couch and began watching one of her favorite movies. The movie wasn't even half over before she was sound asleep.

Dan glanced at his watch with a grimace. He pulled out his cell phone and texted Fitzroy, Captain of Elite Iodex in France and his best friend.

Call me as soon as you get up.

With that, Dan began reading document after document. Abject disgust washed over him the deeper he dug. His cell phone rang, and he raced to the kitchen to talk to the Crown Governor without disturbing Fionna.

When he returned, he continued to slog through the evidence of the Interfeci's vile work. An hour later, a broad grin spread across his face. "Bingo," he whispered.

Dan stared at Fionna as she slept. He allowed himself a moment to think about what the two of them had and how it had come on so suddenly.

To his surprise, he could locate no fear in the recesses of his mind. He sealed more heat into the fibers of the quilt and turned the television down. Love and hope for a future calmed his shield—emotions he hadn't experienced in so long they were barely recognizable to him.

Turning his attention back to the documents, Dan prayed what he'd just uncovered would make him able to save the Angels and prove to Fionna that he would be there no matter what. She never had to be afraid again because he would be her Shield.

At eleven thirty, Fitz called. Dan answered on the first ring and sprinted back to the kitchen. He didn't want to awaken Fionna.

"I haven't even had coffee yet. This better be good." Fitz yawned deeply.

Dan chuckled. "You're not going to believe it when I tell you, but I struck gold."

"Oh yeah?" Fitz goaded. "I thought you were busy showing some new girl all of your skills."

"She's not just some girl. She is *the* girl." He tried to imagine the look on his best friend's face as he made the statement.

"I'm sorry. I thought I'd dialed Dan Vindico's direct cell. To whom am I speaking exactly?" Fitz demanded as Dan continued to laugh quietly.

"I'll tell you about her later. Right now, listen to me."

"I'm listening, but I'm still in shock so speak slowly."

"Wretchkinsides's nephew came through for me. I have copies of all of the documents that were in his briefcase."

"Are you freaking kidding me?" Fitz gasped.

"I'm not, and," he baited, "I just found a list of bank accounts we had no idea existed." Stunned silence rang from Paris to Alexandria.

"What are you talking to me for? Shut them down and see who crawls out of the walls."

"Whoa, there. Not yet. I plan on shutting them down about noon on Friday. I could really use some help this week, and if you come out here, you could meet Fionna."

"Okay, is someone holding you at gunpoint? Just say the words 'Fitz is king' and I'll get your men out there to save your sorry ass."

Dan tried not to guffaw. "Not a chance."

"So, this is *the girl* and you want me to meet her?"

"Yes, in fact, I took her to meet Mom and Dad last night."

"I gotta sit down."

"So, you'll come out?"

"Hell yeah. Are you kidding me? I don't know which I'm more excited to see, the briefcase or the girl. Wait, what time is it there? I'm booking a flight."

"It's a quarter to midnight." Dan could hear the keys on Fitz's laptop click.

"Where are you?" Fitz drawled suspiciously.

"I am in Fionna's kitchen." Dan's face had set in a permanent smirk.

"And where is Fionna?"

"She's asleep on the couch." Dan braced for what he knew was coming.

Fitz chuckled. "Because she already let you play, and you were about to leave."

"'Let me *play*? What are you, twelve?" He leaned out of the kitchen to make certain Fionna was still asleep.

"Hey, it's not even six in the morning here, and so far you've said nothing to convince me I'm not still dreaming, so indulge me."

Dan rolled his eyes. "Fine. No on both counts."

"So, you're telling me you didn't fuck her and that you're staying over?"

"That is precisely what I'm telling you. Now, do you think you could just book your flight and stop asking me about my sex life?"

Fitz drew an audible breath. "All right, I'll fly out at noon here. That'll give me time to buy Maddie something nice for leaving her here alone with the boys."

Dan chuckled at his plan. "Actually, is there a later flight? I won't be back in the office until later tomorrow afternoon."

"Yeah, I can leave here at two. That'd put me there in time for dinner."

"Perfect, and do you mind staying at my house either alone or if Fi and I stay there too?"

Fitz laughed. "I don't know. Is she loud?"

When I get her going, she sure as hell is, Dan thought with a delighted grin, though he avoided any response at all.

"Must be."

"So, when you grow up, you let me know, and I'll see you tonight, asshole," Dan chided as Fitz laughed again.

Suddenly, Fionna's arms wrapped around Dan from behind as her breasts pressed into his back. She laid her cheek against him.

"Hey, baby. I'm sorry, did I wake you up?"

"Nom de dieu," Fitz switched to French to curse. "I don't even know who you are."

Dan spun and wrapped his free arm around Fionna, as she giggled after hearing Fitz's declaration.

"I'm hanging up now," Dan informed him as Fionna laughed harder.

"I'll see you tonight," was Fitz's parting line as Dan ended the call.

"Fitz can stay here," she offered through a deep yawn. Dan beamed at her.

"You don't need to entertain my friends, honey. He can stay at my place. He's coming for work anyway."

"It's fine, and my guest bedrooms actually have furniture. If he stays here, then when we go to sleep we won't be in the room directly over the couch, which you force your friend to sleep on when he comes to see you." She gave him a lusciously naughty smile.

"Does that mean you're worried Fitz might overhear you screaming out my name and telling me you want more?"

She blushed violently. "Something like that."

She was adorable, but Dan didn't allow his mind to dwell on her concerns. The sounds she made for him were far too intoxicating. He'd be hard up with no reprieve.

"I don't want to put you out. I just know we're going to need some help this week to get everything in place for Friday night."

"You're doing this for me and for the Angels. Letting Fitz stay here is the least I can do. I'll even make a big dinner for you both tomorrow night if you'll be home in time."

"Honey, if you want us here for dinner, we'll be here, but I don't want you going to a lot of trouble. And,"—Dan glanced at the clock on Fionna's oven—"I'm either going to get up early and pick up Garrett, then go get you a rental car, or you can come into the office with me. I can bring the rental back home, but either way I need to put you to bed, Ms. Styler." He gently caressed her face with his hand. She let her eyes close blissfully.

He swallowed down the sudden emotion that always came over

him when he considered how sweet and delicate she looked in his arms. She sighed but then drew a deep steadying breath.

"I'll just go in with you and bring Lola back home. You don't need to worry about her too."

Dan shook his head.

"I will get you a rental, honey, and I will take Lola to meet Sam, and I will take care of the Angels and," he drawled pompously, "as soon as you're up to it, I plan on taking excellent care of you as well. So, why don't you just stand back and watch me work?"

"Is that so?"

"Yeah, baby, it definitely is," he flirted shamelessly and reveled in her giggle.

"Well, I look forward to seeing that, Chief Vindico."

CHAPTER 43
THE UNAPPEALING PAST

It was nearing one in the morning when Fionna emerged from a hot shower glowing pink. She blew dry her long hair and crawled into bed beside Dan. "Can I ask you something I already know the answer to, but I just need to hear you say it?"

He smiled down at her as he kissed the top of her head and cradled her closely. "Of course."

"Okay." She drew a deep breath. "I know you're not going to do this, and I'm really excited for your friend to stay here and you two to go out or whatever but…" she hesitated.

Dan leapt. "No." He shook his head, certain he'd figured her out. "I'm not going out and hanging out with Fitzroy and leaving you all alone. Fitz works long hours, but when he isn't working, he's home with Maddie and the boys." Dan pled Fitz's good character. Fionna gave him a goading grin and let him finish.

"That wasn't what I wanted to know, but I guess I'm glad you told me that."

Dan decided to shut up and listen. He'd obviously missed the mark.

"I just sort of wanted to make sure you weren't going to talk about us with Fitz." The pink glow of her face from the shower deepened which was the clue Dan needed.

"Baby, no." He tried not to be offended, but then recalled Fitzroy's question at the end of their phone call. Maybe he did need a reminder. "I'm not fifteen, and I certainly don't kiss and tell. What we do...that's for you and for me. As shocking as this probably sounds coming from someone like me, I don't take that lightly." His past was haunting him yet again. "When I get you like that, when we're together with nothing between us, that's a private show just for me and no one else."

He needed her to trust him. He desperately wanted her to let him have her deepest, darkest fantasies and to believe that he'd not only turn them to reality for her but that he would never betray her.

He longed to learn the deep, seductive secrets that Fionna Styler kept hidden even from herself. He knew they were there. He just had to access them. He'd already uncovered a few, but he wanted to own them all.

"I know." Fionna sounded relieved. "It's just, sometimes guys are guys, and that's all Garrett ever talks about." Realizing that he not only had to combat his own reputation but Garrett Haydenshire's as well had Dan sighing dejectedly.

"Yeah, I do know, but I will never betray you." He cupped his hand and pulled the electricity from the overhead light, leaving only the lamp on the bedside table softly glowing. The last thing he wanted to discuss in bed with her was Garrett.

"So," he teased, "do you think if I spend the week here with you, at some point I might get to see your inner sanctum, Miss Styler?" He tried not to laugh at his own joke as she giggled.

"I've let you see more than any guy ever, and you should be able to see that again tomorrow night. I set the cast last night, remember?" Losing his own battle, Dan laughed outright.

"I'm excited to hear that, but I was talking about the shoe closet."

She giggled hysterically. "It's not just shoes."

"Oh, yeah? Do you have an old boyfriend tied up in there as well?"

"No," she sassed, "but I did threaten to tie Garrett up in there once if he didn't stop making fun of me for..." She abruptly stopped talking.

"Come on, baby doll, you can't do that." Her giggling continued.

She seemed to enjoy torturing him. "I'm dying here, and if you tell me and Garrett makes fun of you again, I'll beat him up for you."

"I do like that idea, but no more fighting with Garrett."

"All right, fine, but tell me."

"Okay, okay. A couple of years ago I *might* have joined a shoe-of-the-month club and a lingerie-of-the-month club for half price because I joined the shoe club...maybe."

Dan cracked up mostly at her adorable reaction to her own confession.

"Stop laughing at me. You're supposed to love me." Fionna smacked his chest with her hand, only serving to make him laugh harder.

"I do," he vowed with a broad grin. "I really do, but I don't think I can beat Garrett up for that."

Fionna feigned irritation as she crossed her arms over her chest and tried to turn her abashed grin into a scowl. "I got some really cute boots and a rainbow-colored G-string," she huffed as he tried not to cry from laughing. "I said, I might've..." she managed just before joining in his laughter.

"You are the sweetest thing I've ever held in my arms, and I've never been happier." Dan finally regained the ability to talk, as he watched her giggle and cover her face.

She immediately forgave him for his teasing laughter.

"I will only let you see my shoe closet if you don't make fun of me, and if you pick some out for me to wear to bed for you."

Dan growled as he pulled her underneath him in one quick move and kissed her heatedly. Her eyes flashed as he pulled away. She'd missed him as much as he'd missed her. The longing danced in her eyes.

"Are you sure you don't want Fitz to just stay at my house, honey, because tomorrow night I want to make you scream." His voice turned deep in his need. She panted as she considered.

"Maybe." She wound her fingers behind his neck and pulled his lips to hers. He consumed her mouth hungrily, sucked her tongue, and let his teeth slide over her bottom lip. He couldn't stop it. He throbbed against her, hard and so damn hungry.

"I could take care of that for you," she offered in a seductive purr.

"No, ma'am." He moved off of her and ordered himself not to beg her to suck him. "I only play if everybody wins."

She stuck her bottom lip out in a delicious pout. He turned back on his side as she wriggled her body closer. His entire being was thrumming and his mind was drowned with her scent, her taste, her energy, and of the heavenly space that wrapped around him so perfectly between her legs. He leaned and whispered in her ear. His hot breath caressed her delicate neck.

"Just wait, baby. Be patient for me." Her body tensed against his. "Keep thinking about how good it feels when we're together. Keep thinking about how bad I crave you, and the things I'm gonna do when we're finally alone in here tomorrow night. All day I want you to think about me sucking you." He slid his hands over her breasts as she panted in deep desire. She trembled and arched her back, forcing them into his firm grasp. "They're tender, aren't they? I know. I'll be gentle. I'll make it all better." He massaged her breasts slowly. They were swollen and fevered. He caught her nipples between his thumb and index finger. With a light squeeze, she shook in his arms.

"Think about me running my hands all over you, tracing you, making you feel me, touching you in all of those sweet, hidden places that all belong to me. I know how to make my girl hot and wet for me. Think about how good it feels when I run my tongue over your body and mark you where no one else will ever see." She moaned as she gasped for breath. He traced his hands down her stomach and slipped them to her lush backside as he continued.

"I want you to think about me leaning you over this bed, driving you wild until you can't stand it anymore. I'm gonna make you scream out my name, make you tell me you want it harder. You just keep thinking about me sucking you and biting you. I want you to let it build inside of you all day until I get here, and I drink you, and spank you for how hard you make me, my naughty girl. I'll punish you, make you take it until you're so full of me you explode in my arms, and then I'm gonna do it all over again," he promised in a lust-filled rasp.

"Stop," Fionna gasped in heated desperation. "I won't make it through the day. I'll crawl naked across the table at dinner and make you take me in your seat."

Dan tried to hide his cocky smirk as he continued to run his hands over her.

"That'd be an interesting way for Fitzroy to meet you, but if you need it, baby, that's what I'm here for." He watched her body react to his promises.

Her lips were hungry and raw for his kiss. Her nipples were hardened and aching. Her swollen curves so needy, and the tender, wet heat he felt gathering against his thigh drove him wild. He wanted her so badly his entire body vibrated in desperation. His shield craved her energy.

"It'll be your own fault if when you get home I'm splayed out on the table in nothing but a pair of heels."

Dan groaned as he let his mind explore the picture she'd drawn for him. "If you lie out on the table in heels for me, baby doll, I'll kick Fitz out so fast his head will fly, and we'll introduce your dining room to some naughty, naughty things." Her energy continued to spin in tight, jagged spirals that needed to be soothed.

"Well, my dining room is a virgin."

"I can take care of that, trust me."

"You promise you'll do everything you said?" Her tone was laced with desperation. Dan clenched his jaw as he pictured himself doing everything he'd promised her.

"Oh, yeah, baby doll, if that's what you need, I'll do each and every thing." Her energy and her heart flew as he held her close.

"And I get all of that just for showing you my shoe closet?"

She didn't seem to want to fully admit to the items that intrigued her most. She never had to tell him. As long as he knew what she wanted, he'd keep finding ways to make her happy. He chuckled, though his mind was still full of her body and what he wanted to do to her.

"Are we talking a Carrie Bradshaw style shoe closet or not something quite so extreme?"

"Oh, my gosh! You watched *Sex and the City*?"

Dan grimaced. He didn't want to dampen their extremely enjoyable bonding, but he nodded. "It was Amelia's favorite show."

"I knew she had excellent taste." Fionna's declaration thoroughly shocked him. How could she be so accepting of Amelia? She didn't mind at all that he'd had an entire life and love before her. "I own the entire pink, leather-bound collector's set of all six seasons, plus both movies. I keep it in my shoe closet." Her entire being seemed to glow as he kissed her forehead and chuckled.

"You mean you don't keep them in some sort of titanium safe with a fusible lock and a retina scanner?"

She dissolved into another round of giggles. "Can you get me one of those?"

"I'll see what I can do."

"I would never ask you to watch them." Her face fell and her laughter drowned. "Besides the remake was absolutely awful."

"It's fine. I will adamantly deny ever saying this if you tell anyone, but it was a pretty good show. I never actually saw how it ended."

She brushed a kiss on Dan's chest, but then a deep yawn overtook her.

Dan had been so thoroughly enjoying their time he'd forgotten how late it was and that she hadn't slept the night before.

"Go to sleep, baby, and really, if you don't want Fitz to stay or to even come over tomorrow, I'll dump him at my house. I'm not one of those jerks who's gonna drop you because an old buddy of his flies into town."

"I want to meet him, and I want him to stay here unless that interferes with you doing all of those deliciously dirty things you just promised to do to me."

"I might just know how to set a cast to block the sound waves from leaving this bed, so you can scream for me and I can tell you exactly what I want and how I want it, and no one else will hear us."

With that exquisite fire still gleaming in her eyes, Fionna grinned at him. "You might've mentioned that before."

Dan smirked. "I like to keep you guessing, Miss Styler."

"I know." She cuddled closer into his embrace. "I love you," she whispered in the darkness.

"Me too." Dan wished, for what must have been the hundredth time, that he could say it to her with such ease.

He put the worries over whatever had made her unhappy before him away for the moment. Whatever Chloe knew about her, she could keep. He wanted her in the here and now. Their pasts were dark and debilitating. He longed to have her in the light.

CHAPTER 44

IT'S COMPLICATED

RAINER LAWSON

"You wanna grab something to eat on our way back?" Rainer asked Dan as they headed to the parking deck at lunch the next day.

"Sure. Did you and Logan get Stariff everything he needed for that case he's working on?"

"Yeah, he has all of the arrest information. I think that was all he was missing from Iodex." Rainer chuckled as Dan shook his head and folded himself up to get inside Fionna's bright yellow Toyota MR2. "That's just cruel, man. You definitely get boyfriend props for this."

Vindico laughed, but he seemed nervous to the point of anger. "I should get something, that's for damn sure."

"I think I'll let Fionna supply you with the rest of your prize, but I'll let you drive the Porsche back if Sam ends up keeping her car at his shop to work on it."

"Thanks. I need to talk to Sam about buying new cars. I'll get her whatever she wants. This is just painful, and it's way too recognizable." He gestured at the dash of the convertible, as he spread his legs for the steering wheel to be able to turn between them.

"Just follow me." A broad smile spread across Rainer's face, the same one he wore whenever he heard the metallic roar and rattle that he'd come to associate with cranking his Boxster.

After several miles on the interstate and a few turns deep in Alexandria, Rainer glanced in his rearview to make certain that Dan saw him turn into the lot. He shut off the Porsche and climbed out. Dan extracted himself from Fionna's car with great difficulty.

Sam was chuckling as he watched the men emerge.

"Rain Man," Sam greeted with a handshake and a smile before turning to Vindico who was stretching his massive body from the rigors of his drive. "Please, please tell me that isn't your car, son?" Sam extended his hand to Dan. "I'm Sam. You can call me Sam."

Vindico laughed and shook his head. "Dan Vindico, sir, and no, this is my girlfriend's." Rainer watched the smile form on his boss's face from just thinking about Fionna. Hopefulness began to swirl inside of Rainer.

Sam walked around the MR2. He studied the car.

"Mmm, mmm, mmm, mmm, mmm." He shook his head.

"The top comes open on its own and then gets locked. I casted it several times and couldn't get it to move. I'm not sure what's wrong with it."

Rainer choked back laughter. No one had to tell Sam what was wrong with the car they'd brought for him to fix. He always knew just by hearing it pull into his lot.

"Uh-huh," Sam drawled, "but judging by the fact that I thought for a minute Rain Man and I were going to have to use axle grease and a rod to get you outta that car, I'd dare say if girlfriend's top came open, you wouldn't have brought her out here for me to see."

"No, definitely not." Vindico smirked. He was clearly trying to figure Sam out. Rainer was enjoying the show. "Well, you're a big boy, son. You either need to lay off the Wheaties, or you're gonna have to trade her Toyota in on a ring. Maybe get you something you can both get in. Maybe have room to enjoy a drive if you know what I mean." Sam reached and popped the hood on the car.

To Rainer's shock, Dan laughed and didn't seem like the idea was that far-fetched.

"I think it may be a little early for a ring just yet, but I'll take you up on a new car."

"And what is it that Dan Vindico drives?" Sam pulled the dipstick out of the oil tank and shook his head.

"I drive a custom MV Agusta Brutale 575," Vindico supplied as he moved to the hood of the car beside Sam.

"And when is the last time girlfriend had the fluids changed on the car you just wedged yourself in to bring down to see me?"

"I don't know."

"She does know that she has to put something else besides gasoline in this thing?"

"Can't really tell you that, either." Vindico tried to determine what Sam was seeing under the hood.

"Rain Man, go in the shop and get me four quarts of oil."

Rainer raced into the shop. He knew precisely where to go. He returned quickly.

"Four quarts?" Dan gasped. "How many does it hold?"

Sam laughed. "Oh, I'd say just about four quarts."

Dan's head lowered, and he cringed.

"Uh-huh." Sam began adding the oil. "Now that I'm gonna let you crank her again, we'll take her in the shop. Some brake fluid, coolant, and washer fluid, then we'll see if we can make her happy. After that, she might let us go a little farther up her skirt."

Dan begrudgingly got back in the car.

Once Fionna's convertible was inside Sam's shop, he refilled all of the fluids and replaced the air filter.

"Now tell me, is girlfriend pretty, Mr. Big Man?" Sam let the hood close and moved to the trunk.

"Hell, yeah," Dan agreed with a cocky grin. Rainer chuckled.

"She cook?" Sam headed to a shelf near the back of the shop.

"Yeah, she's amazing. She's perfect."

"So, how come you're squeezing yourself into her toy car, but you aren't getting down on your knee and asking Miss Amazing Girlfriend to save you from your sorry self? Let me tell ya, boy, there isn't anything better than coming home at the end of the day to a sweet smile and a warm meal. Not too bad cuddling up on some warm curves when you crawl into bed, either." He popped the cap on a reservoir in the trunk and began pouring fluid in it as well.

Vindico smiled as he nodded. "It's complicated."

"Ya know, boy, it's not as complicated as you young folk like to make it. And let me tell ya why," Sam explained as he lowered the trunk gingerly. "You get yourself up in the morning and you kiss her and you tell her you love her, and you decide that she's gonna be your one and only all day and all night. Then the next morning you do the same thing and you just don't stop."

Vindico furrowed his brow as he considered the advice.

"Now." Sam moved back to the driver's side and cranked Fionna's car. "You tell Miss Amazing Girlfriend that she's gonna have to bring this to see me if she wants it to go when she wants to go." He showed Vindico that the top opened and closed with the push of a button again.

"Thanks, I will." Vindico looked thoroughly impressed with Sam's work. As Sam began wiping his hands on an old rag, he leaned against his GTO that Dan was visibly admiring.

"Now, Mr. Dan Vindico, what is it that you're gonna drive? Because you look to me like a guy who's about ready to trade in his bike built for one and Miss Amazing Girlfriend's car built for one-and-a-quarter into a sweet ride that you can put one hand on the steering wheel and one hand cross her shoulders without your arm hanging out the window."

Dan glanced toward Rainer's Boxster. "I'm not trading in my bike," he announced.

Sam shot Rainer a goading grin. "Uh-huh, that's what they all say. They have to keep whatever it is that cranks and rattles real nice for 'em in case they need it because she starts rattling real loud. But ya see, boy, women aren't so different from cars. You tell 'em how pretty they are, you show them you're gonna take care of 'em, listen to 'em when they talk, tell 'em you love 'em, rub 'em just the right way, and occasionally you lube all the right things, make sure her tank's full, she won't rattle on ya."

Rainer cracked up as Dan shook his head with an abashed grin. Sam chuckled as he gestured to the convertible. "Let me tell ya, Big Man, that engine's shot. It's full a sludge and it's going to lock up any moment now. She doesn't need to drive it. So, why don't you and Miss

America come back and see me. We'll see what we can put you in that might make you smile and make her eyes dance just the way you like," Sam instructed with a knowing grin, as Dan visibly began to understand the depth of wisdom standing before him.

"Emily loves her Hummer," Rainer commented, though he was still enjoying the show that was taking place before his eyes.

"Fionna loves this car."

Sam chuckled. "Yeah, well, I happen to know this kid, great guy, little cocky, occasionally wants to save the world but there's not much wrong with that, I s'pose. He's all right far as I'm concerned. Had a sweet '65 Mustang rebuilt by the finest mechanic on the East Coast." He pointed both of his thumbs to his chest as Dan and Rainer laughed. "But life happens, and one day his sweet thing called me up and said, hey Sam, let's get my sweet pookie a Porsche Boxster convertible fresh off the line. And you know, he don't look too sad to me anymore." Sam put his hand on the scruff of Rainer's neck and shook him slightly before slapping his back.

"She did not call me pookie." Rainer shuddered and brought on another round of laughter.

"I'm kinda swamped this week. Do you think I could bring Fionna out here next week to see what you suggest? And I need for no one else to see us here."

That information visibly concerned Sam momentarily, but he spun to Rainer. "What's my rule, Rain Man?"

"If you're bringing a pretty girl with you, you can come anytime you want."

"And where is your pretty girl?" Sam wiped the hood of the MR2 with a rag.

"She's at her parents' house watching the twins while her mom rests. I think they're making Christmas ornaments. She was thinking about going to Fionna's. They're good friends." Rainer gestured to Dan and began wondering what Emily was doing and wishing he was with her. She was still a mess over the attempted Angels takeover.

"And how is Mama Haydenshire doing?"

"She's been put on bed rest again. They're letting her be up and around some, but the baby's scans still aren't showing that she's

Gifted. Adeline's pretty sure there are other things wrong. We'll see in a few months, I guess."

Sam sighed. "Babies don't need to be Gifted. They need to be loved. I know all of those Haydenshires and all of us are going to love her, so it'll be well."

Rainer certainly hoped Sam was right. "But, yes, Big Man, you're welcome to bring yourself and your sweet thing out here. Just call and let me know, and I'll try to see if I can't get something she might like as much as she like you."

"Thanks, I really appreciate your help."

"We better get back, Sam. Thanks." Rainer shook Sam's hand.

"You tell Miss Emily I said hello and to keep you in line."

"I will."

"Thanks again for everything." Dan's vow made Rainer wonder if he was only pleased with the work on the car or if he was thankful for the advice as well.

"Want me to get my crowbar to get you back in there, son?" Sam gestured to the car. Dan pulled out his checkbook.

"Actually, would you mind if I left it here? I don't want her driving it, and I'm worried about someone seeing me drive it."

"Hey, if you wanna leave her here, I won't say anything to the little lady, so long as you don't want to not be seen driving it because you have another honey on the side."

"Oh, no, sir." Vindico's adamancy seemed to convince Sam immediately. "I'm the Chief of Iodex. There are a lot of people who would like to get back at me for what I do. I can't let anyone know how much I care about her."

A warm smile lit Sam's features as he nodded his understanding. "You just tell her my work's just like she likes it, slow and sweet."

Dan grinned. "Thanks again for everything."

They grabbed a quick lunch on the way back.

"It would be a lot easier to tell Fi that she has to get a new car if she weren't terrified she's going to be out of a job." Dan carried a tray with two burgers, a chicken sandwich, a baked potato, a loaded salad, and Dr Pepper to the table with Rainer.

"I will not let him buy the Angels. I don't care what it costs me." Rainer dug into his much smaller meal.

"We have to play it carefully. I don't want Kent getting your inheritance. We need to work together to let Wretchkinsides know he's out, but not pay more than we'll ever get back. And if anyone other than Kent sells, we could be in trouble."

Neither of them wanted to think about the ownership rules of Summation teams, the ones that could throw a major kink in their plans.

They discussed the current value of the Angels stock and what the majority owners' reactions had been that morning at the meeting.

Magnus was the most concerned and wanted to talk to his wife. He was worried for her safety and that of their children. Dan had pled with him to let the other majority owners or him buy Magnus out should he decide to sell.

As Rainer slurped down his Dr Pepper, Vindico's cell chirped. He glanced at it and grimaced. "Fi wants to know what Sam said."

Rainer offered him a sympathetic smile. "Don't tell her that over the phone." He still wanted to help out whenever he could. He'd never seen his boss so happy or relaxed.

"No joke, Lawson." Vindico bristled, not in the mood for advice, it seemed.

After lunch, they headed back to the office to continue working on the information in Wretchkinsides's briefcase.

CHAPTER 45

THINGS HAPPEN

DAN VINDICO

> Heading to meet Fitz's plane. We'll be on our
> way soon

Dan typed quickly, in response to Fionna's text that she missed him and wanted him. He willed away what her text had elicited, and waved to his team before walking toward the landing strip. After checking his watch, he picked up his pace and tried to decide how to break the news about Lola to Fionna.

As the plane taxied down the runway, he tried to envision his best friend's reaction to the dramatically different Dan Vindico. Fitzroy exited, wearing his customary smirk. He yanked his sunglasses off and shot Dan a goading grin.

"I got it," he announced.

"Oh yeah, what's that?" Dan chuckled as they shook hands.

"You're shitting me with the whole new girl thing. You're trying to get me back for that time when we started that special ops training course in San Diego, and I ordered a ton of porn to your room and had the bill sent to your parents."

Dan rolled his eyes. "Yeah, that's it. I'm trying to get you back for a stupid prank you pulled twelve years ago. I've been working on it all this time, and this is the best I've come up with."

"So, you're giving up your love 'em and leave 'em gig for this girl? She's the one?"

"That *is* what I've been trying to tell you. Now, would you get in the car and shut up?"

They drove in amicable silence for a few minutes. "How're the boys?" Dan quizzed.

"A little girl in Alex's class taught him to curse in English, only he doesn't pronounce them correctly. Maddie and I are torn between correcting him and punishing him."

Dan chuckled. His godson was a handful and a half. The boys attended a bilingual school in Paris so they were well versed in both languages.

"Where are we going?" Fitz asked as Dan pulled onto the interstate.

"We're gonna stay with Fionna for the week. She has a bungalow in Alexandria, so you can actually sleep in a bed, but you better be nice."

"Did you move in with her?" Fitz demanded in utter shock.

"Not yet. I'm kind of hoping she'll decide to move in with me. My house is bigger and a hell of a lot closer to the Senate. Hell of a lot safer too."

Fitz stared at him in bewilderment. "Are you gonna marry her?"

Deciding to really throw Fitzroy for a loop, Dan grinned. "Maybe."

A long, impressive string of stunned curse words in both English and French flowed from Fitzroy's mouth.

"Yeah, and if you say any of that in front of her, I'll have to kick you out, so like I said, be good."

"Maddie's gonna flip."

"Fi's amazing. You'll love her."

Fitzroy continued to shake his head in disbelief.

Dan pulled in the driveway. He wasn't terribly thrilled to see Chloe's Corvette parked there as well.

"Hey, before we go in," Dan eased, "I have to give Fionna some bad news tonight."

"Please tell me you aren't breaking up with her while I'm here."

"Did I not just say I was thinking about asking her to marry me?"

"Okay, but you have to give me a little time to get used to all of this. Is it worse news than the fact that Dominic Wretchkinsides is trying to take over the Arlington Angels?"

With a frustrated sigh, Dan explained, "I took Fi's car to the mechanic today and the engine's pretty much fried, so at some point I have to break it to her that the car she adores has to be replaced." Dan wasn't certain what it was he wanted from Fitz exactly.

"Hey, I'll stay out of the way. You two carry on. You want me out, just say the word." Fitz was still studying Dan speculatively.

"Are you gonna stare at me like I've lost my mind all night or will you eventually get over this?" Dan opened the door and moved to get Fitz's suitcases.

Fitzroy relieved him of the bags but gave no answer as they headed up the walkway. There was a Christmas wreath on the door that hadn't been there when Dan had left that morning.

He knocked and tried to determine why he was suddenly so nervous. Chloe swung the door open.

"Hey, Dan. Sorry. I was supposed to be gone before you got here. I'll see you later." She pushed past Dan and Fitz and scooted down the walkway. Fionna appeared a moment later. She was shaking her head and rolling her eyes.

"Bye, Chloe," she called.

"Bye, love you!" Chloe slid into her car.

"Hi." Fionna beamed at Dan. "Come in. It's cold." Her deep sienna eyes sparkled in the setting sun.

Dan was surprised, yet again, when he entered and found a completely decorated Christmas tree in the sitting room and garland on the mantel.

"Uh," he pointed around the room wondering how she'd done all of the decorating in one day's time. Fionna giggled at his expression. "Sorry." Dan shook himself slightly. "Fionna, this is Jean Paul Fitzroy, but you can call him Fitz or my pet name for him, shit head."

Fionna shook her head. "I think I'll go with Fitz." She extended her hand to Fitzroy.

"I swear he just threatened to kick me out if I cursed in front of you." Fitz kissed Fionna's hand and gave Dan an impressed smile.

"Honey, how did you do all of this?" Dan gestured to the tree, standing where the love seat was that morning in front of the living room windows.

Fionna shrugged. "I wanted the decorations up. I love Christmas. I knew you and Garrett were going to be busy this week, so Daddy came over and got it out of the attic for me. He brought me the *pani popo* I wanted to have with dinner. Chloe came over, and Emily brought the boys over, and we decorated. The twins are so adorable."

Dan smiled at her and tried not to be upset that she'd gotten her father over there to do what Dan should already have done. That certainly wasn't going to help win her father over.

"Oh, here." Fionna noticed Fitzroy carrying his bags. "I'll show you to your room."

"I would've done that for you," Dan insisted as they climbed the stairs. Fitzroy chuckled under his breath.

"I know, but now it's up, and we can enjoy it." She was worried he was upset. Dan tried to modulate his emotions. He willed away his irritation.

"This is a great house. How old is it?" Fitzroy attempted to save Dan from himself.

"It was built in the early forties, but I've redone a lot of it. So, is this okay?" She stood back and gestured Fitz into a small guest bedroom complete with an antique wrought iron bed, a writing desk, a chest of drawers, and a suitcase stand.

"Are you kidding me? I usually sleep on an old leather couch with a spring in my back. This is great."

"Oh, good! Just let me know if you need anything else."

Dan wrapped his arm around her shoulders and immediately picked up on the nervous tension pulsing in her rhythms. "The bathroom's here." She gestured to the guest bath across the hall. "I have a basket under the sink with soap, shampoo, toothbrushes, and stuff like that, if you forgot anything." Fitzroy looked very impressed. "I need to go check on the potatoes."

"Thanks again for putting me up for the next few days. Just let me call Maddie, and I'll be down in a few minutes."

Dan followed Fionna down the stairs. He was having a difficult time not envisioning her wearing nothing but the apron she'd pulled on over her sweater and tight jeans.

"Sweetheart, this is way too much. You shouldn't have done all of this." He was still shocked over the changes in the house that happened since he'd left nine hours before.

"I had fun. I love to cook and have people over. Mrs. Haydenshire wanted the boys out of the house so she could rest for a little while. It seemed like a good idea. Keaton did break one of my crystal ornaments. I'm trying not to be devastated over that."

Dan tried to sort through all of the emotions he was feeling. "Okay, I know. Everything looks amazing. I just wish you'd let me help. I feel badly your dad came over. I should have done that."

"But you were taking care of Lola and the Angels. You can't do it all."

"I feel like I let you down." The stinging regret washed over him.

Fionna's brow knitted. "How, exactly?"

Dan drew a steadying breath and caught Fionna's hands as she slid them out of oven mitts. "Hey." He pulled her toward him and wrapped his arms around her. "I'm not trying to start an argument. I just really want to take care of you, always." The warmth of her smile slipped through his shirt.

"You do take care of me. It really wasn't a big deal, and it's nice to have friends over who can know about us."

Dan didn't have time to react to the ache in his chest from her comment before she continued, "I got to help out the Haydenshires and play with the twins. I got to hang out with my friends. Now I get to spend the night with you and get to know one of your closest friends. All in all, it's a pretty great day."

Dan's heart pricked. Telling her about her car was going to ruin her great day.

"Emily asked Chloe and me to be in her wedding." She was visibly thrilled.

"She might want to rethink that." Dan let his eyes scorch over Fionna's beautiful body.

"Why?"

"I just didn't think most brides wanted to have a bridesmaid who's going to upstage her as soon as she enters the room." His tone softened as he held her close.

"Dan, that's not true," she scoffed and pulled away, but he knew she was pleased with the assessment.

He kissed her forehead sweetly. "I know once I see you walk down the aisle, I certainly won't be able to take my eyes off of you, even to watch Lawson and Miss Haydenshire get hitched." Fionna's energy spun in trilling pleasure as she stretched up on her tiptoes and brushed a kiss along Dan's jawline.

"What's for dinner, baby doll? It smells delicious."

"I hope you like it." She pulled a tray of twice-baked potatoes from the oven and set them beside a dish of fresh green beans. "You said you liked potatoes with cheese and scallions, so this is sort of that, with a little extra, plus my own special spin."

"Trust me, I love the way you spin."

Fionna shook her head at him but gave him his smile. The heady sensation made him weak. His groin took immediate notice.

"I thought about making my world-famous crab cakes," she explained as she ran a heat cast from her hands over the roasted chicken in a baking dish on the counter.

"I wasn't aware you were a world-famous chef," Dan teased her as he brushed a kiss in her hair.

"Well, all the Angels love them, so for me that's kind of the whole world." She handed Dan a bottle of wine. Pleased to be doing something helpful, he took the corkscrew from the counter and opened the bottle.

"Wine," Dan offered as Fitz made his reappearance.

"Naturally," Fitz scoffed.

"How's Maddie?" Dan handed Fitz a glass and then one to Fionna.

"She's good. She said I shouldn't stay here because I'm intruding on you two." He tried to gauge Dan and Fionna.

"No, it's fine. We're happy you're here. I really appreciate everything everyone's doing. This is such a mess," Fionna insisted.

"I'll try to stay out of the way. I can get a hotel or stay at Dan's. Just say the word."

They settled at Fionna's dining table. Fitz cut into the juiciest chicken Dan had ever seen. After adding a small bite of the potatoes and the green beans to his fork, he brought it to his mouth. A moment later his eyes goggled.

"Oh my God, marry her now," he demanded, embarrassing both Dan and Fionna.

Dan's cell phone rang in the middle of dinner.

"I'm sorry, honey. I've got officers out everywhere. I have to take this."

Several minutes later, he returned to the table shaking his head.

"What's wrong?" Fionna approached panic quickly.

"Two of my officers just arrested three men trying to break into the Magnuses' home."

"Do we need to go?" Fitz set his fork down.

"No, they've got it, but this will only be the beginning. They know Magnus is the weakest link." Dan sighed, not certain what to do next. "Berl Kibbey was with them. So, Nic didn't send anyone too important. My guys didn't recognize his accomplices. They're taking them to Felsink, and the next team will start their shift soon."

"No one was hurt, right? They didn't get in the house?" Fionna worried.

"Yeah, baby. I'm sorry. I should have started with that. They're fine. I have an Iodex team at their home, and several others keeping up with them and their children. We'll keep them safe."

"But isn't Wretchkinsides going to know that you know what he's trying to do because of all the extra security? What if he hurts Mitchell?"

Fitzroy was visibly impressed with Fionna's question. Dan grinned. She never ceased to amaze him.

Dan took her hand, trying to reassure her. She drew from him as soon as their fingers interlocked. It was exquisite. He had to force himself to keep talking instead of falling back in his chair and reveling in the extraordinary sensation of her pulling his energy into her own. Fitz very politely ignored them though he was sporting quite a smirk.

"Wretchkinsides has shown interest in the Angels before. You remember when Chloe was attacked?"

Fionna nodded and made another draw. Dan fought not to groan and order Fitz from the table. "Uh…"—he shook himself—"he didn't really have the resources to pull it off until Pendergrath was released and brought his teams into the country. I'm hoping he'll be under the impression that we've had the owners under a vast security protocol for a while now. And, as Mitchell said yesterday, he's in Moscow. I saw him on Iodex street cams there."

"He'll know Friday." Fitzroy helped himself to another slice of chicken.

"Hopefully not before the board meeting."

"Isn't he going to be at the meeting with the owners? How do you buy the stock if you aren't there?" Fionna fretted. Dan smiled at her reassuringly.

"I don't think he'll show up, baby. If he does, he'll be arrested for forging Crown Governor Lawson's custody papers which would actually be worse."

"Why?" Fionna's brow knitted. "I thought you wanted to arrest him."

"I do want to arrest him. More than you even know, but the Interfeci needs to be dismantled from the bottom up. Pendergrath and Pravus have to go down at the same time as Wretchkinsides, otherwise they'll be out for blood. The top dogs all have to fall at once. Right now, we're working on the second string. Adderand is the next on my list."

Suddenly, Dan was overcome with the desperate desire to hold her safely in his arms. Thoughts of the newest Interfeci hit man filled him with panic. He'd trained under Cascavel, Wretchkinsides's prizefighter.

Sitting next to her eating wasn't enough. She looked terrified. He wanted to wrap her up in his embrace and whisper his reassurances that he would keep her safe until she believed him and relaxed in his arms.

"Anyway." Dan wished Fitz would get lost for a little while. "He'll probably send one of his financial representatives to attempt to make the purchase. If I had my guess, he'll send Pendergrath. He has no idea if I'll be there or not, but he's hoping someone will mention to me that it was Pendergrath who made the transaction."

"Why can't you arrest him?"

"I don't have anything on him substantial enough to keep him in prison."

"That's so frustrating!" she huffed.

Fitzroy laughed out loud as Dan grinned at her. "Yes, it is."

They finished the delectable meal, and Fionna stood to clear away the dishes.

"No, ma'am." Dan shook his head. "You must've spent hours making all of this, not to mention all of the decorating plus chasing the twins around all day. You go sit down. I'm doing the dishes."

Fionna looked deeply touched by the simple gesture. "Thank you, but I was just gonna get the pani popo. I'll make some coffee and then make you tell me about Lola."

Fitz laughed. "She's got your number, Danny."

"You kept avoiding the questions all day."

Dan and Fitz cleared the table and made coffee, while Fionna unwrapped a pan of what Dan thought looked like biscuits but smelled even better. She sprinkled confectioner's sugar over the pan, getting some on her cheek, which Dan fought not to lick off as he brushed it away.

She carried the pan back into the dining room.

"This is Hawaiian Coconut Bread," she explained as Dan set her coffee down in front of her. "It's so yummy Daddy can't keep it in stock. It's my favorite."

"It smells great!" Fitz exclaimed as Fionna handed him a plateful.

"It's not always a dessert, but it's so sweet and it's so good with coffee. I thought it would be perfect."

She pulled a small piece off and swallowed it down with a sip of her coffee. Her eyes closed in delight, and Dan found himself woefully unable to look away from the contented smile on her face.

With a deep breath, she braced herself. "Now tell me what's wrong with Lola."

"Maybe I should go somewhere else." Fitz glanced around for an out that didn't present itself.

"No," Fionna scoffed. "It can't be that bad. It's just the top."

Fitz and Dan shared a grimace. Dan allowed himself one bite of dessert, which was even better than the meal.

"Baby, it's not just the top," he began hesitantly.

Fitz stood and picked up his plate. "I've got a little work to do on my laptop. Can I put an adapter in your living room?"

"Oh, of course," Fionna agreed but kept her eyes locked on Dan. Once Fitz had made his escape, Dan scooted closer and took both of her hands in his own. "Just tell me."

He tried to determine the best way to start. "Sam is an outstanding mechanic, and he said the engine's not going to last much longer."

"What? Why? Lola's only a few years old. Aren't they supposed to last longer than that?"

Dan nodded. "Yeah…they are."

"So, why is it not working? I know you're not telling me something." She lifted their hands showing him how she knew. Dan prayed the truth really might set him free.

"Honey, when was the last time you had the oil and fluids changed?" He made certain he didn't sound condescending in any way.

"I don't know." Fionna lost a little of her earlier adamancy. "I guess about a year ago, maybe a little more." She cringed. "Maybe almost two years."

Dan had no idea how to explain to her that she'd effectively killed her own car.

"Is that bad?"

"Kind of."

"I kept thinking that I should, but then I kept forgetting. We travel so much."

Dan decided to try a different tactic. "I talked to Sam about getting us new cars. You don't seem that excited about riding on the Agusta."

"It's actually really hot. You know, in that today I want to wear leather and be a bad girl kind of way," she whispered with a vexing grin that had Dan choking on the coffee he'd just sipped. His body seized from the imagery she conjured. "But it's winter time."

"When the weather warms up, I'll take you for a ride any time you want." Dan regained his composure and waggled his eyebrows. "But," he forced himself back to the conversation at hand, "I want something that you want to ride in no matter how cold it is. So, if you want, I could get something, and you can drive it. I'll drive the bike unless we're going somewhere together."

Fionna smiled at him sweetly. "You don't have to buy a car for me. I think I'll wait to decide on all of this until I find out what's going to happen Friday. But I guess a new car," she hemmed and then gave him his smile, "maybe one you actually fit in, wouldn't be such a bad thing as long as I can pay for it."

After gently brushing an errant hair behind her ear, Dan continued, "I am going to buy a car, honey, so we can both get a new car or just I can. You don't have to decide anything right now. The bike is hell in the rain."

His own statements continued to shock him. He used to revel in riding in the driving rain. The water shattered off of his skin like ricochet from a gunfight. He thrived on the pain. He was certain he deserved it. But sitting in the warmth of Fionna's dining room, with the lights of the Christmas tree glowing in her eyes, the self-imposed pain seemed to have existed an entire lifetime ago.

"I really don't want you driving your car without me. I don't want you to get stranded somewhere."

Fionna grinned and wrinkled her nose. "So, Sam's sure it isn't just PMS?"

Dan laughed. "I don't think that was it. And, when you pick out your hot new ride, how about I take it to see Sam every couple of months to make sure this doesn't happen again."

Fionna looked pained as she nodded. "I swear I'm not an idiot. I just kept forgetting."

"I don't think you're an idiot at all. Things happen."

CHAPTER 46
FITZ AND FI

Dan loaded the last dish into the dishwasher. "Want another cup of coffee, sweetheart?" he called into the living room as he listened to Fionna and Fitzroy talk.

"Okay, you have no idea how extremely odd that sounds coming from his mouth." Fitz made Fionna giggle sweetly.

"Sure, thank you," she answered with more tonality before she turned back to Fitz. "People keep saying stuff like that to me." Dan paused to listen. "But he's the best guy I've ever been with. I'm head over heels. I feel like I could be with him forever. I'm really in love."

Fitzroy chuckled and lowered his voice further. "Yeah, well, trust me, so is he. I really can't believe it's him." Fitzroy's awe was apparent in his tone. "I can't tell you how good you are for him."

"I just hope he's really as happy as I am. Sometimes I can't tell," Fionna admitted hesitantly. Dan was shocked by her willingness to say something like that to someone she'd just met. But he knew she'd probably discerned a great deal about Fitz from the flow of his emotions.

Fitz shook his head. "I know Dan Vindico better than anybody, and it's been a long, long time since I've seen him this happy."

Dan rescued Fitz, as he brought Fionna's coffee and sank down on the couch beside her. He wondered if Fitz's vow had soothed her.

They chatted for a while about cars, what Fitz's boys wanted for Christmas, Wretchkinsides, and the takeover. Fitzroy told Fionna a few stories from his and Dan's days in training.

As the conversation waned, Fionna glanced at Dan. With an extremely fake yawn, she pulled away from him. "I think I'll just go get ready for bed. I'm tired." Her profound blush over her lie made Dan grimace, as Fitzroy choked back hysterical laughter.

Fionna stood and picked up her coffee cup before heading out of the room.

"I'll be up in a few minutes, honey." Dan felt truly sorry for her, as her attempt at being coy hadn't gone quite as well as she'd clearly hoped it might.

As soon as her bedroom door closed, laughter burst from Fitz. Dan shot him a warning glare.

"I really think I should go stay at your place."

Dan bit back his own laughter over Fitz's deep smirk. She was the most adorable thing he'd ever seen.

"You're fine. I'll sound-cast the room," Dan offered wryly as Fitz continued his laughter.

"Take it from me, man, a guy who has to work a hell of a lot harder for it than that,"—he pointed toward the stairs—"you should get down on your knee when you get up there and beg her to marry you now."

Remembering his promise that he would not discuss their love life with Fitz, Dan pressed his lips together to keep from informing his best friend that he might get down on his knees, but it wouldn't be to propose.

Dan shook his head and wondered approximately how long it would take Fionna to put on whatever she had planned for the evening.

"She really is amazing. I get it now."

"She really is." Dan was still staring up the stairs after her.

"She doesn't look anything like Amelia."

The statement pulled Dan from his increasingly erotic reverie. He shrugged. "Should she?"

"No, I think I just sort of thought she would."

Another broad grin spread across Fitz's face, as Dan turned his attention back to the stairs. His curiosity was making him edgy. He wanted to see her and then he wanted to feel her. He wanted to give her everything she clearly needed. His hands longed to have a conversation all their own with her skin.

"You know, I think I'm gonna stay down here for a long while and watch TV very loudly."

"There is a reason you're my best friend." Dan handed Fitzroy the remote on his way out.

"Remember all of us poor saps who'll be cold and alone tonight."

"Been cold and alone for ten damn years." Dan's reply effectively shut Fitzroy up as he took the stairs two at a time.

A mix of deep desire and deep concern that Fionna knew she'd given her plans away and was embarrassed swirled rapidly in Dan's shield. He tapped on the door.

She was dressed in a pale-pink satin and black lace bra that tied seductively between her breasts with a black silk ribbon, and a pair of matching lace shorts so short they didn't cover much, but her face was glowing crimson when she opened the door.

"I'm never ever leaving this room ever again." Her hands flew up to her face as Dan edged inside.

"Baby." He wrapped her up in his arms. All thoughts of having wild, dirty sex were instantly replaced with the desire to reassure her, to make certain she knew how much he loved her and what being with her meant to him.

She buried her face in the crook of his neck and let him shield her from the world.

He braced the back of her head in his right hand. "You are so beautiful, and what we have, what I have," he corrected, "when I hold you in my arms is so much more than I could've ever hoped for. And you look phenomenal, baby."

She was blinking back tears. His heart tugged as the scars she'd mended threatened to break from their delicate sutures. "Don't worry about Fitz. I had to endure his relentless courting of Maddie, and trust me, that,"—he gestured his head back down the stairs—"was nothing."

"I'm still so embarrassed, and I'm so upset about Lola." She pulled away from him and fell back on her bed with a dejected huff.

Dan kicked off his boots and trousers. He unbuttoned his shirt before moving to the bed beside her. "Come here, sweetheart." She pulled herself into a tight ball against his chest. "I'm really sorry about Lola. Believe me, I get being a little bit in love with your ride. Maybe," —he thought back on her confessed concern to Fitzroy—"we could get new cars to sort of represent a new chapter in our life." He brushed a tender kiss on her forehead.

She eased her head up to study him. "Are you sure you're really ready to start a new chapter?"

Dan could feel the trepidation, confusion, and angst swirling through her in a volatile combination. "I'm all yours, honey, and I was really hoping you wanted to be all mine."

"I do. I'm just still scared you're going to change your mind."

"Then I'll just have to keep proving to you I'm not."

The takeover, her car, their relationship, sharing her house with Dan and his best friend, her late-night confessions of some of the deep, dark desires she had but didn't like to think about by the light of day—it had all taken a toll.

Her exhausted terror and confusion washed through his strains as she tucked closer into the sanctuary of his embrace.

She no longer felt safe. Dan tried not to feel defeated as he held her close and whispered kisses in her hair.

Just a little over a week before, he'd set out to take her out of that bar and rock her world. Whether it was his fault or not, it was her foundation that had been shaken.

"Fionna," he whispered, "we're going to get through this. I will not let Wretchkinsides take your whole world away from you, baby. I know there's a lot of crap going on right now, but I am right here and I'm not going anywhere."

Fionna nodded against him. "The Angels aren't my whole world," she choked.

He rubbed her back tenderly with his hands. "You told me before dinner that all of the Angels love your cooking and that to you that was the whole world." He wanted her to know that he understood.

"They used to be." She eased her head up to gaze into his eyes. "But they aren't anymore. That's what scares me."

Dan's heart stuttered and then begin to fly. "If I've learned anything from all the hell I've been through for the last decade, most of it at my own hands, it's that this world is a scary place. Sometimes, it's just too damn much to deal with on your own. I wish I could make you believe that I'm here if you need something to hold on to or to hold you tight because you're scared. You don't have to do this alone."

She was silent for the length of one heartbeat as she nodded against him. "I know you are, and you have no idea how much that means to me. It's just been a lot lately. My life was kind of a mess before you came home with me from Anglington's."

"Just hold on to me, baby. I'm right here. You can tell me about your life before that night. Even if you think you somehow screwed it up, I'll never think that, and I'll still be right here."

She shivered in his arms, and Dan immediately reached and pulled the sheets and comforter over them. He tucked her under his chin and forced heat out from his body. She relaxed in his substantial embrace.

"It is kind of weird with Fitz here," she finally confessed what he'd felt from her all evening. She'd hidden it well. Fitzroy would never have known anything at all, but Dan had felt it as soon as he'd touched her. He would have preferred she tell him what was such a mess about her life before him, but he didn't want to pry.

"I mean, Chloe's stayed here tons of times, and Garrett always stays when I need him."

Dan clenched his jaw so tightly his molars ached.

"In another room or on my couch," she giggled. She felt the jealousy as soon as it permeated his energy. "He stayed with me for the month after Cal died." She tried again to explain how much she and Garrett meant to each other.

"I'm sorry, honey. I swear I'm working on it, but I told you I was possessive as hell. I wasn't lying."

A broad grin formed on her face. He was certain her smile could light the entire world.

"I think it's sweet. Just don't go overboard with the whole 'you're mine, and you can't talk to anyone else, and here's what you're going to think, and do, and eat, and wear' thing."

"I said I was possessive, not a whale-sized douchebag with some kind of psychotic disorder."

"Sorry." She let her bottom lip slide between her teeth. "Still occasionally have flashbacks from a guy I dated for a couple of weeks last year. I told you my life was kind of a mess," she admitted hesitantly. "He was super weird, and he really freaked me out."

"I need to never ever meet anyone you dated before me. From the stories I've heard, I want to kill them all very painfully and very slowly."

"Yeah, if you ever met him in a back alley I would be hard pressed to tell you not to." Her entire frame gave a chilling shudder, and Dan's blood boiled as he began considering what this asshole might've done to her.

"See, you can't be mad at Garrett, mainly because you've been friends since you were two, and you work together. But also because that guy attempted to lock me in a room of his house. I threw a shield and knocked him backwards, then I called Garrett and he put him in the hospital for a very, very long time."

Dan leaned up on his elbow. He couldn't believe what he was hearing.

"Honey, where did you find these ball sacs?"

"He wasn't Gifted, but right up until that night at Anglington's when you saved me from that drunk guy, I'd kind of decided all guys were douchebags—or at least the ones I seemed to attract."

Dan hated to agree, but she did attract them. She was just too sweet and too empathetic. She didn't like to look for the bad in people even if it was obvious. She exuded innocence, even if she wasn't exactly innocent. She liked to make people happy because she could feel their happiness with them which meant she wasn't great at boundaries.

He tightened his hold on her. If she was in his arms, she was safe. He was her Shield.

"Since he's not Gifted, the concussion, broken teeth, ribs, jaw, and hipbone took a while to heal. I'm pretty sure the places where they stitched his lips back together will always be scarred. Oh, and trust me, he still hasn't had sex or maybe even peed at this point," she giggled. "But I met him at this gym I joined because I was taking these intense mixed yoga classes. I was going through a Zen period."

"Honey, if you want to do yoga, I'll buy you any DVD you want or, hell, I'll hire you your own personal instructor, but guys who hang out at gyms just to meet women or to watch them work out are eternally douchebags."

"You're not kidding. The guys who hang out outside of the naked yoga classes are super gigantic assholes."

"See, now I'm incredibly turned on and infuriated all at the same time. You're confusing my entire body." Her laughter gave him solace momentarily. "I will definitely be finding out this guy's name from Garrett, and I just think I might call in a few favors from the Non-Gifted police chief. I can fix it so that he gets a ticket every time he opens his car door. After that, I think he might have a very unfortunate encounter with me and a metal baseball bat." Dan rather enjoyed the thought. "But since I'm not a super, gigantic asshole, do you think I might get to see any of these naked yoga moves?"

"I'm not Zenning anymore." She gave him that naughty grin that made him ache. His groin was suddenly on high alert. "I'm in a whole new phase now."

"Oh, yeah, what's that?"

"The *you* phase."

"I was kind of hoping that I'd be more than a phase," he corrected her and felt her energy soar.

"You definitely are." She lost all traces of humor instantly. "I kind of think you could be my whole life." She laid her heart out on the line for him. She stepped off the ledge and then waited in terror to see if he was going to catch her or if he would let her fall.

"Fi, my whole life used to be about catching Wretchkinsides and taking down the Interfeci. That was all that mattered to me, but in one quick night you turned me upside down, baby doll.

"I don't remember ever feeling anything like this before. I never believed anyone could make me feel the way you make me feel. When you walk into the room, I ache for you. When you laugh, my entire world feels right again. And, my God, when you're under me, honey, when I'm deep inside of you, I swear I've never felt anything so incredible.

"When you're not with me, all I can think about is how badly I want you back in my arms. But I do have to finish what I started. I owe it to Amelia and to all of the other people they've destroyed. I owe it to you because I want you to have all of me, and I know I won't be able to give you that if he's still carrying out his heinous crimes. But sweetheart, please know that you're my whole world too. My whole life belongs to you as soon as I finish him."

"I know that, and everything you have given me is more than I ever could've hoped for. I love you so much," she whispered softly. "But someday I would really like all of you."

"That's definitely my plan. I swear."

DEEP

"Can I get a good night kiss, Miss Styler?"

A grin formed on her face that had been thoughtful a moment before. "I was kind of hoping for more than a kiss."

Dan chuckled as he let his hands caress her curves. "You sure, baby? I don't want you to do anything you're uncomfortable with. I'll take Fitz to my house tomorrow night. We can wait. It's fine."

"If that's what you want."

It wasn't what she wanted. The need surfaced like glowing embers that only needed to be stirred to be ignited. It had been there all along, under the worry, embarrassment, trepidation, and stress.

She'd let him erase all of those, at least for the moment, but she needed something more from him. He was only too happy to fulfill her every desire.

This time she didn't need wild, forceful, earth-shaking, bed-breaking sex. She didn't need to be marked, spanked, praised, and commanded, though she did usually prefer that. It was the last thing she needed that night, and it was the last thing Dan wanted. He was shocked by the realizations.

She needed slow and sensuous love, intimate time to be cradled, worshipped, restored, and reassured. He desperately wanted to make her feel his deep love and adoration so much more than he wanted to make her feel him deeply.

He decided to start with an innocent kiss and then to let her take him anywhere she wanted to go. Dan caressed her face tenderly. He moved so that he could stare into the depths of her eyes lit by the moon.

Hesitating for a moment, letting her anticipation build as her breath picked up pace, he closed his eyes and brushed his lips across hers. A slight moan escaped her.

She responded heatedly. A low groan thundered from him as her energy flowed into him. He parted her lips and swept his ravenous tongue into her mouth.

He slid his hands from her face, down her neck, touching her skin tenderly, feeling her energy begin to swirl in need. "You are so beautiful."

He ached, a physical pain only she could soothe. She panted and reached for him. She trailed her fingers up his cock so softly the feeling was pure torture. He wanted more. He shuddered from the overwhelming sensation.

"I'm going to take this off," he whispered his plan as he let his fingers tease her breasts. They were swollen and throbbing under the satin and lace she'd bound them in. She nodded and watched his every move. Her eyes were dark but fearful. "I'm right here, and I'll stop if you want me to."

If she needed a night to cocoon herself away, as long as she'd let him hold her and keep her safe, he was perfectly fine with that. He would only go as far as she was comfortable.

There was a very distinct difference between love and lust. Both certainly held their place in a relationship, but Dan understood the chasm between the two more in that moment than he ever had in his entire life.

"I don't want you to stop," she begged in a desperate whimper.

Dan kept up the gentle mating of their mouths. He dipped his tongue between her lips slowly. He tasted her and explored her mouth, learning every part of the women he loved.

Letting his fingers trace over her breasts, he took his time pulling the ribbon between them. She gasped and arched her back as he watched them spill out, all for him. "You are just so damn gorgeous."

She began to writhe. He cupped her breasts, lifting their weight tenderly as he began his massage. He listened to her moans become frantic and breathy.

Moving over her, he swirled his tongue down her neck as he trailed his fingers over her fevered flesh. "I want to suck you, baby. I know they hurt. I know you're tender. Let me make it better." He kissed and licked fiery trails from her neck to her darkening nipples.

She trembled and her heavy breasts danced before his eyes. He groaned from the seductive show.

"Please," spilled from her lips. He groped her left breast as he spun his tongue over her right, puckered and pleading for his attention. They needed to be tended thoroughly, needed to be sucked and licked until she felt relief.

He drew her right breast into his mouth, drowning it. He began with soft suckles and then took her with more force. A loud moan of deep satisfaction echoed from her.

Dan concentrated. He pulled the erotic energy from her breasts, but used his own to force a sound cast. He locked the sound waves inside of his shield, which he set over them.

Her eyes flashed as she felt him encase her in his love and in his ultimate protection. To his relief, that was all she felt. The very last thing he wanted was to do something that would only add to her unnecessary embarrassment.

He lifted his head away, and she bucked in ardent desire for more. Dan granted her left breast equal attention. She trembled. Her body was unable to remain still. She rolled in rhythmic waves against him.

He let his hands work down her stomach and abdomen, then he reached up the slight shorts she was wearing. He massaged her backside greedily and had to remind himself to take it slow. But she wanted more. She arched her back to push her cheeks into his hands as he plied and groped her.

He pulled his hands away and slipped them up the satin fabric until he reached the tiny, tied waistband. He pulled the ribbon there as well.

"I'm gonna take these off, baby doll." He forced soothing rhythms through his shield, making her drunk with his energy. "Then I want you to let me taste you. I'll make it feel so good. Get you nice and wet so you can take me."

She cried out for him. Her body was starved for his fullness. He pulled the shorts away from her, as a growl thundered from his chest without him meaning for it to escape. "Let me see you." He separated her legs and traced his fingers over her lips, barely touching her. "So damn beautiful." She was swollen, fevered, and just beginning to glisten for him.

He positioned his head between her lush thighs and licked up her slit. He felt her pulse against his lips, as he fought with every fiber of his being not to move over her and push himself between her folds.

He wanted to feel the heavenly pulses she gave him, wanted to feel her clench tightly around him and the rhythmic tugs of her body as he pushed her over the edge.

He dipped his tongue slowly between her lips as she screamed out for him. She reached and grasped his hair. She pushed him deeper. Her hunger drove his own. He separated her with his thumbs and teased her clit with the tip of his tongue. Her entire body trembled. He coaxed and sucked until she was begging for release.

It was elusive. The past few days had taken their toll. She was still tender and tight from forcing her body to rapidly move through her cycle. He pulled his face away and replaced his tongue with his fingers as she continued to plead for relief.

"I'm gonna give it to you, baby. You need to relax for me." He dipped his fingers deep inside her and moved over the spots that would get her where he needed her to be. With his thumb, he spread her nectar up over her clit and rhythmically worked her over. He just had to be patient. She throbbed, and he leaned down to tend her breasts again. Her body began pulling his fingers deeper. He returned his tongue to her now-pulsing clitoris.

"That's it, honey. Just feel it. I'm right here. I'll do this all night if that's what you need. In my hand. Give it to me like my good girl."

He had her. She spilled herself out. The pent-up need, desire, stress, and the voracious hunger dripped down his fingers as she cried out his name. Her body contorted deliciously as she unfurled.

Dan's own energy hit its highest peak as he watched the erotic display. Perhaps she did need him to indulge in just a few of her most delicious kinks.

"Give it to me. I want it." She wrapped her right hand around his steel-hard strain. Dan groaned. He clenched his jaw and ordered himself not to give in to her commands while she pulled his erotic energy straight from its source.

"I don't think you're ready, baby doll. I'm trying to be gentle. You're still so tight. I don't want you to hurt tomorrow." He knew perfectly well what would happen if he surrendered to her wishes.

A whimper of frustration shook through her. "I already set the cast. I don't want you to be gentle. I want to feel it tomorrow. Every time I move I want to feel you."

White-hot fire burned violently from his groin. It was too much. He just wasn't strong enough to fight her desires. She was simply more than he could withstand. No amount of power or energy would ever grant him the ability to turn down such pleasure. He positioned himself over her.

"You're sure you're ready for me?" He forced himself to ask once more.

"Now!" she commanded again.

Moving with delicate precision, Dan separated her lips with his fingers and pushed inside her. A low, hungry moan escaped him. The sensation was blissful ecstasy.

"God, you feel so fucking good." He pushed farther, unable to help himself as he drowned in her exquisite energy. The liquid heat formed around him so tightly he could hardly move as she encased him.

"Yes," she gasped as her eyes flashed and then closed in her pleasure. Their energy joined readily and seemed to bring her elation as he filled her with his love. He began to pump, pushing deeper with each pass, then pulling away, watching himself coated in the heavenly nectar of her. He had to look away, lest he lose it all. Their energy passed back and forth in perfect accord.

"Harder, please."

"There's my greedy girl begging for my cum," growled from his chest, as he reared up on his arms and transitioned until he was pounding into her. All thoughts of being gentle dissolved in the liquid heat inhaling his body.

She was screaming out his name, bucking underneath him, meeting his every thrust, and begging him for more. She trembled suddenly. Her body writhed as she gripped the sheets. Her mouth hung open in a moan that wouldn't come as the climax robbed her of breath.

"That's my good girl. Give it to me. Just let it go for me. It'll feel so much better when you give in. It's mine." His words drove her over. Her body contorted again, and she clenched around him.

The rhythmic shudders that rocked through her were exquisite. Her orgasm pulsed so fiercely he lost it all. He buried himself inside her. He flooded her body with everything he was as she gasped for breath.

Dan moved off of her and cradled her on his chest. He lambasted himself for what he'd just given in to. His cock gave a slight throb as he made his exit. He could have gone again but not after what he'd just done to her. His secondary rhythm strands were desperate to step in, but she wasn't up to that.

She gave him a satisfied sigh. Her energy rolled in languid waves all around him.

"Fi, honey, I'm…" he started to apologize, but she placed her index finger over his lips.

"Perfect," she concluded with an extremely contented smile.

He kissed her finger and then pulled it away from his mouth. "That was too much. I shouldn't have done…"

"That was perfect. I feel amazing. Now cuddle me up so I can go to sleep and dream about it."

He tried not to let her words make him feel like a king. He shouldn't have given in. She was going to be sore. He wrapped her up in the sheets and blankets and then in his arms.

CHAPTER 48
NOISY REACTIONS

At five o'clock, a loud knock sounded on the bedroom door. Dan raised his head, furious at whoever was knocking. He'd been in a deep, dreamless sleep.

Fionna whimpered, "Go away. I'm naked." She fussed almost unintelligibly, still mostly asleep.

Dan chuckled. "Shh, baby. Nobody needs to know that but me." He eased out from under her, crawled out of bed, and located his boxers. He pulled the sheets up to her chin and then opened the door. He blocked her body easily with his own.

"I'm so sorry, man." Fitz had his back to the door and was staring down the hallway.

"It's fine. What's wrong?" Dan slipped out into the hallway and closed the door.

Relieved, Fitz turned back around. "I just shut off her gas valve. She's got a leak. I heard it hissing from my room. I doubt she has any heat."

"Yeah or hot water," Dan sighed. "I'll get somebody out here to fix it. Let me build a fire. Fi can take a shower at the stadium, and we can use the gym at work unless you want to heat your own water."

Fitz shook his head. "That's a pain. I'll use the one at the gym. I could use a good workout anyway. Is that the only fireplace, though? That's not going to keep her warm upstairs."

Dan appreciated the fact that his best friend understood that Fionna's safety and comfort were his top priorities and that he was perfectly willing to help him achieve his goals.

"Yeah, that's the only one. It'll keep the downstairs warm so she can have her coffee and I'll…" Dan paused with a slight grimace.

Fitz gave him his customary smirk. "…keep her warm until she's ready to get up."

Dan nodded as he traipsed down the stairs. He stacked the small logs from the hearth inside the box, cupped his hand, drew in a tremendous amount of heat, and lit the wood. He shield casted the logs to keep them from burning out.

"Oh, and by the way,"—Fitz followed him into the living room— "pretty sure her neighbors now know your name. I think I'll just get a hotel room tonight."

"What the hell are you talking about?" Dan hoped the darkness covered his embarrassment.

"You dropped the cast there near the end, stud. I don't know what happened to you, but she is definitely your weakness."

"Do not say anything to Fionna!"

"Like I would do *that*," Fitz teased with an impish grin.

Dan narrowed his eyes. "I'm not kidding. I will end you."

"I will *try* not to bring it up."

Dan's mind raced. He knew he'd kept his shield over her. That required very little thought or effort. His shield was a part of him, but the sound wave cast required more attention to hold. He'd certainly been giving her all of his attention.

"Sorry," he managed to choke out.

"S'ok, just glad you're happy, I guess. You did sound very, very happy."

Dan ignored that. "You can't get a hotel. She'll know why. We'll keep it down."

"I would really appreciate that." Fitz's laughter turned into a yawn. "I'm gonna try to get a little more sleep."

"You wanna sleep on the couch? It'll be warmer down here."

"Nah, the house will hold the heat for a while."

Dan gestured his thumb up the stairs. "I'm just gonna go check on Fionna." He wished he didn't sound so thoroughly embarrassed.

"You mean your good girl," he continued to harass.

"It would not even tax me to kill you."

He held up his hands in surrender while sporting a deep goading smirk. "I'll keep that little piece of information to myself."

Dan rolled his eyes and rushed back to Fionna's room. He slid in through the smallest space he could allow as he opened the door and shut it firmly. He willed away the information Fitz had just given him before he slipped into bed beside her. Complete contentedness eased his embarrassment as she cuddled up on his chest.

"Why did you leave?" she fussed without even opening her eyes. Dan brushed his thumb over her cheek as he let heat push out of his pores.

"Your heat went out, baby. I was building a fire. You must have a leak. I'll see if I can get somebody out here to fix it."

She leaned up on her elbow and rubbed her eyes.

"Are you kidding me?"

Dan was taken aback by her mood. She normally flowed steady somewhere between happy, thoughtful, or concerned. He hadn't experienced her in a truly bad mood as of yet.

"No," he hesitated, still trying to learn her.

She fell back on his chest after rolling her eyes. "Maybe I should just sell this place. Last year it was the plumbing, and then the roof, plus all of the renovations, but I love all of the projects I've done."

Realizing that in her recently awakened mind he was getting a picture into something she normally kept more guarded, Dan listened.

"We'll do whatever you want, but if you want to move in with me, I'd be thrilled. You can redo my house however you want it. I certainly don't care. I just want you there."

She sighed and wriggled closer to him. "Your dining room looks just like your office at Iodex. It's sad."

Dan had to force himself not to chuckle at her bluntness so early in the morning.

"Okay," he agreed, "but I have three other bedrooms. If you want, we could move the office upstairs to one of those. You can bring your furniture, or we could buy new stuff," he continued to bait her.

"I don't know, maybe."

A maybe was not a no, and she sounded much more open to the possibility than when he'd first brought it up.

"Go back to sleep, honey. I'll keep you warm, but we're going to have to get up a little earlier because you aren't going to have any hot water for a shower unless you want me to cast it for you."

"Or any way to dry clothes or start my oven without a cast," she fussed.

"We may have to stay at my place tonight. I'll cast your pipes so they don't freeze without heat."

She nodded against him. "I really hope this week gets better."

"Me too." Dan prayed fervently that he'd be able to stop the Angels' takeover. Unable to go back to sleep, he let his mind go over everything that needed to happen before Friday evening.

After going through a drive-thru for breakfast, where he only irritated Fionna further by asking her to sit in the back so that no one working at the restaurant would see her, Dan pulled the Expedition into the arena parking deck.

Trying to make up for the drive-thru incident, Dan leapt out of the SUV, opened Fionna's door, and grabbed her duffle bag and extensive toiletry kit for her.

His brow furrowed as he took in Garrett holding Chloe tenderly to his chest. They were leaning against the entrance doors.

Chloe Sawyer was number one on a lengthy list of women Garrett banged on a regular basis. They'd been doing this off and on since the academy.

As long as one of the women Garrett was bedding wasn't Fionna, Dan genuinely didn't care, but something about the situation seemed odd. Though he was visibly trying to tap into his tender emotional side, Garrett looked furious.

He studied Dan and Fionna and then narrowed his eyes. "You know, Fi, if he did something wrong, you can kick him out of your house. You don't have to move into the arena."

Dan rolled his eyes, but after taking in Chloe's tears, he decided against telling Garrett what he could go do to himself.

"She has a gas leak. She's going to shower here." He was curious as to what had caused Chloe Sawyer—who as far as Dan was concerned was a willful, spoiled, wild child—to cry.

Garrett's eyes flashed in sudden understanding. "Really? That's very interesting."

"Chloe, what happened?" Fionna was almost in tears just watching Chloe cry. This only served to make Chloe sob harder into Garrett's chest. Fionna began rubbing Chloe's arm as she shot a quizzical glance at Garrett. "What happened?" she mouthed.

Emily and Rainer arrived before Garrett could answer. "What's wrong?" Emily panicked. Rainer looked as confused as Dan felt.

"You want me to tell them?" Garrett whispered a kiss on Chloe's forehead and continued to rub her back. He was letting her draw from him constantly.

Dan was actually impressed. He very rarely saw Garrett's sensitive side unless he was dealing with his mother or his little sister. She nodded against Garrett's chest as her breath shuddered.

Katie, Dana, and Carys had arrived by this point. They were all deeply concerned, but when Sasha's husband pulled in the stadium and helped her out of the car, Dan's heart raced and stomach seized.

Chloe, Fionna, and Sasha were the three senior players for the Angels and most certainly the ones the team looked to for guidance and leadership. Always being a man of instinct, Dan felt his left shoulder twitch as his Visium Predilected bands shifted his shield away. He pulled his cell from his pocket and called into the office.

"What's up, Dan?" Portwood asked.

"I need a CSU fingerprint team at Fionna Styler's home. I want the gas main outside of her house printed thoroughly, and then I want it gone over with a fine-toothed comb."

Fitz's eyes closed as he shook his head. He'd figured out what must've happened at the same moment.

"I'll send them out now, but there's probably frost all over the metal fixings. I'm not sure what they'll find."

"Humor me."

"You're the boss. I'll tell them to call you if they find any prints."

"The drive belts in her car snapped this morning," Sasha's husband stated concernedly. "Thankfully they snapped in the driveway. I don't think she could turn it without the power steering. I thought they'd just gotten worn out. I haven't had it into the shop in a while."

"You mean somebody did this to Coco on purpose?" Chloe began sobbing again. Dan stared Garrett down.

"Her dog was run over. She was in the house when I got there last night. She can let herself out, but she always waits on Chloe. Someone lured her out."

Vile revulsion washed over Dan, as Fionna and Emily tried to comfort Chloe. Dan let his vast training kick in as he shielded himself from the emotion and the fear around him. This was something he'd learned after Amelia had been killed. It was how he'd survived for so long. He could only exist inside his own shield.

"Is her car still in your driveway?" He turned to Sasha's husband, who nodded. His face held a mix of deep concern and confusion. He wasn't aware of the attempted takeover.

"Why would someone do this?" He appeared fearful to ask Dan too much. Fionna reached and took Dan's hand. She not only wanted to draw from him, but she was trying to soften his scowl.

After realizing what Fionna wanted, Fitz studied Dan. He did know him better than anyone else, and Fitz had been married for eight years, so he understood that Fionna needed Dan. Fitz visibly willed Dan to let her in and seemed to understand how hard that was.

With a deep breath, Dan forced his shield down. He took her hand.

"I'm not sure," Dan lied to Sasha's husband with ease as he supplied Fionna with peace and strength in heavy doses. "But I'd like to get her car fingerprinted and see if we can't figure out what's going on."

"Yeah, sure, no problem." Sasha's husband was still shying away from Dan. Not unaccustomed to other men being intimidated by his sheer strength and foreboding manner, Dan didn't give it much thought. Being intimidating came with the job.

"Chloe, I'm very sorry for your loss, but I would really feel better if we upped security here today. Would there be a conference room or somewhere my Elite team could meet that wouldn't disturb practice?"

Chloe was still wiping away tears as she turned to Dan and nodded. "There are several places you can use for as long as you'd like."

Dan turned to Rainer. "Go back to the office and get the documents we've been working on." Rainer nodded his understanding. "Tell Haydenshire, Portwood, and Ericcson to meet us here. Tell Tuttle and Ramier they're running the office today, and that I want a report on everything going on there every hour on the hour."

"Yes, sir." Rainer kissed Emily's cheek tenderly. "I'll be right back, baby."

CHAPTER 49

EARNED THE TITLE

An hour later, Dan was pacing in one of the banquet rooms in the stadium. "We've been given permission to use the gym here, and it's a hell of a lot nicer than ours so I plan on making good use of it."

Rainer rolled his eyes with a huff. "Who cares about the gym? We need to figure out what we're going to do to keep them safe."

Dan was in no mood for disrespect. Rainer was an excellent officer, and a hell of a guy in general, but he also had a bit of a temper especially when it came to Emily. If he didn't remind Dan so much of himself at twenty-one, he would've been reprimanded for his mouth on several occasions.

"I'm so sorry, Lawson, but last time I checked it was my name on the door right under the words Chief of Iodex, so if you'd do me the honor of shutting your face, I'll tell you what we're gonna do."

Rainer scowled, and Logan immediately shot Dan a look that said *if you want him you can take me too.*

"Just can it. He's in a bad mood." Garrett softened Dan's blow for Rainer and his brother.

Dan rolled his eyes and continued his relentless pace.

"I don't think I have enough Non-Elite officers to keep one at all of the players' homes."

"What if we take three off the list?" Garrett pointed out that Chloe, Emily, and Fionna essentially already had their own personal bodyguards.

"Maybe." Dan ran the figures in his head. He couldn't shake the terror over the fact that one of Wretchkinsides's thugs had been to Fionna's home while he'd been in bed with her.

He tried to order himself out of the suffocating distraction. Fitz and Garrett both eyed him suspiciously. Portwood joined their silent interrogation. They all knew him far too well.

"Dan, chill. So, there was an Expedition in her driveway. I take the SUVs out all the time. I was there. That's the story. They weren't paying any attention to who was at her house. They had to get in and out of her backyard. Let it go," Garrett commanded. The order coupled with the fact that Garrett had read him with such ease did nothing to soothe Dan's vicious mood.

"Frankly, I don't think there'll be any more attacks." He continued his strategizing without responding to Garrett. "I think this was how they planned to get to Medio Sawyer. They know if he thinks Chloe and her closest friends are in danger, he might agree to sell. This is classic Wretchkinsides. He loves for his victims to be in constant fear, never knowing what he's going to do next. But I don't think they have any intention of actually harming the players. They want the team to continue to be highly profitable."

"They've been pretty cruel with Chloe," Garrett reminded him.

Dan gave him a sorrowful nod. "They know if they can force Medio Sawyer out, the team is theirs. I really am sorry about everything that's happened to her." Cold cruelty was the way of the Interfeci. They just had to figure out a way to put an end to it all.

Dan's cell rang, and he jerked it off the table. "What'd you find out?"

"We only got one print and it was a partial," Officer Indite explained. "It belongs to an International Iodex officer. The print's sealed. You'd have to put the order in to unseal it, Dan," she explained.

"Did you find anything else?" He had no intention of explaining that he already knew which International Iodex officer's prints were on Fionna's gas hook-ups.

"I couldn't swear to you that it didn't just crack next to the valve. That's a pretty old house. If it was cut by someone, it wasn't spilling into her home. It wouldn't have hurt her unless she went outside to smoke or something. It would've hissed loudly. She would've noticed it. Basically it's vandalism at best. It'll cost her some money having the feeder replaced and a day or two with no heat and no hot water, but that's about it."

"Yeah, I figured. Have you gotten anything back on the car?"

"My team's just getting back in. We won't have the fingerprints for a little while, but I can let you talk to Testarino. Hang on."

"Heya, Dan," Testarino barked in his heavy Boston accent.

"Were they cut?"

"Maybe, couldn't say absolutely though."

"What do you mean?"

"Coulda been the weather. They were pretty dry. It coulda been yanked apart. Didn't look like a knife. They musta been left by a thread. She weren't meant to go far enough to get herself in trouble. If somebody did this to her car, they never intended for her to leave the driveway, you know."

"Yeah, that's what I figured. Let me know if you get any prints."

"No problem. We took a load, but I'm guessing they're the owners."

"All right, thanks for your hard work."

"Anythings for yous, you know that."

Dan couldn't help but grin. Testarino's accent got him every time.

Everyone waited to hear what Dan had been told. "No prints other than yours," he huffed to Fitzroy.

"Figured that."

"They don't want to do anything that might shut down the board meeting Friday night. They just wanted to scare the leaders on the team and to terrify Sawyer into selling. I really don't think they'll make any more moves on the team, but that's not a chance I'm willing to take. So, I suppose you two are getting a pretty sweet assignment." He gestured to Garrett and Rainer.

"I assume you're just going to go ahead and include yourself in that with us." Garrett finally achieved a genuine chuckle from Dan.

"Yeah, I guess I am. Just remember that part of keeping Fionna safe means that you can't be seen out with Chloe too often, and that Chloe is the one they seem willing to physically hurt. Don't leave her side."

Garrett nodded his agreement.

"As for the rest of you, you'll each be given a player. You'll have to stay at their houses. It's only two nights. Tell your wives to call me if they feel the need to screech at someone." Dan was certain he'd be receiving numerous phone calls.

"I'm just gonna go ahead and beg you to give me Sasha since her husband is a pharmacist at the hospital where my wife works. She knows and trusts him, so that would make my life a hell of a lot easier," Logan begged.

"Done," Dan instantly agreed.

"Connor and Katie are still fairly friendly. Even though they're not dating anymore, Mom and Dad wouldn't mind her staying at the farm. No one will bother her there," Garrett offered. Dan agreed, as he was quickly running out of officers.

He turned the office over to Portwood and assigned Angels to Ericcson, Ramier, and Tuttle. He filled in the rest with Non-Elite officers and then sighed. "I'm short one man."

"Hey, let me help," Fitz jumped in. "I can guard one of the Angels, or I can switch with one of the guys guarding the owners' families."

"Are you sure?" Dan felt bad that Fitz would be working nights, when he was really only here to help with the sheer amount of evidence they'd taken in. The smirk Fitz shared with Dan let him know *why* he might not mind not being in the house with Fionna and Dan.

"I don't fly out until Saturday. We can celebrate after we get the job done Friday night." Fitz, who was much better at team morale than Dan had ever been, united the men in their mission. "When the ladies aren't here practicing, we'll be with them."

Garrett was glancing back and forth between Fitzroy and Dan. He'd caught Fitz's earlier smirk. Part of what made Garrett Haydenshire such an excellent officer was his ability to notice every single detail. It was also what made him so popular with women, in Dan's opinion. As Garrett started laughing, Dan wished he hadn't figured out what Fitz was insinuating.

"All right." Dan drew everyone's attention back to him and away from Garrett's laughter. "Our main concern for the rest of the week is obviously keeping everyone safe, but also to make absolutely certain that by three o'clock Friday afternoon, every one of Wretchkinsides's bank accounts that we're aware of has been seized and shut down.

"I need every piece of information in that briefcase gone over with a fine-toothed comb. If there are other accounts, I sure as hell need to know about them. I plan to force whoever shows up to purchase the available stock to show their hand. When they try to access the accounts, there better not be any available money."

Rainer was visibly impressed with the plan and seemed to have forgiven Dan for his reprimand after being told that he was being assigned to be in Emily's presence constantly for the next sixty hours.

"You know if it's Pendergrath, he'll show up with a briefcase full of cash hoping to catch Kent's eye," Fitzroy pointed out.

"I know," Dan sighed. "But he'll do that in hopes of actually getting the stock at a lower price. Kent's not stupid. Neither is Magnus. Not to mention that in their shortsighted plan, if they are the ones threatening Magnus's family, even if he sells, he'd rather sell to me than to Pendergrath.

"They're counting on Sawyer not wanting the press to find out that a large percentage of stock is going up for sale. Sawyer doesn't like having too many owners to deal with. They don't think there will be any other buyers available that night. I'm monitoring the accounts closely and so is Buffett's team. I'm not shutting them down until a large withdrawal is made. Then we'll know what we're dealing with. I want to know what they're going to go in with as their opening bid."

This time the entire table looked impressed. Dan smiled. He'd earned his title even if he was rather young when he received the job.

"The Angels are working out in the gym until lunch, so I want you to continue going through the documents we were going over yesterday. I'm heading back to the office to hand out the other assignments and then I'll be back."

CHAPTER 50
THE HEART OF FIONNA STYLER

By that evening, Dan had worked the Elite team hard, and they were all complaining as they showered and redressed.

"Can it. Your significant others will thank me. I plan on pointing out that they like that you don't look like a bunch of sloths when they call me up and demand to know if I really assigned you to stay with one of the Arlington Angels."

Thus far, Tuttle had been the only person excited to be assigned two nights with one of the Angels. Mostly out of spite, Dan had switched Tuttle to the person who would be keeping tabs on Bridgette for the rest of the week. She was still spying on Wretchkinsides's guys, and she still wanted the paycheck from the Senate. Though Dan never wanted to see her again and was ashamed that he'd agreed to date her only to gain himself access to the information she had, he did feel responsible for keeping her safe.

As soon as practice was over, Dan helped Fionna pack to go to his house. He heat-casted all of the pipes to keep them from freezing until the repairman could come. Dan had phoned an old friend of his father's who he trusted, and Mr. Wheaton was meeting Dan at the house at ten the next day to repair the lines. As Wheaton was Non-Gifted, he had no idea who Fionna Styler was or what Dan did for a living.

"I just really want to spend Christmas here," Fionna fussed as she packed.

"Of course, baby. I just want you at my house until Friday." He paused and then corrected. "Actually, that isn't true. I want you at my house all the time."

"You sound a little desperate there."

"For you, always. I told you that." He wasn't backing down. He'd prove it to himself, and he'd prove it to her. He just had to keep her safe.

She turned thoughtful again as she continued to pack clothing. She'd packed enough to stay for several weeks, but Dan didn't see this as a good sign. He was well aware that women almost always over-packed and always wanted options.

"You said the gas lines would be fixed tomorrow. Why should we stay there until Friday?"

Dan tried not to be offended that she very obviously did not want to stay at his house. He reminded himself that since he'd worked her from a one-night stand, to his girlfriend, to what he hoped would someday become his wife in just a very short time, she'd been through quite a bit.

"Wretchkinsides did this, sweetheart. He had men here, and I'm holding it together pretty well, but that scares the shit out of me. I'd just feel better if you were somewhere he didn't know about."

She nodded and tried to hide her fear inside a smile. "Your house isn't all that hidden away. It's in a nice neighborhood. Is it unlisted or something?"

"As unlisted as they get, and it's a completely Non-Gifted neighborhood. I don't own a landline telephone. I bought the house in cash, so there's no paper trail of the purchase. The deed is registered to an alias that I have used only for the purpose of buying the house. All of my utility and credit card bills are sent to a Senate PO box that is also not registered to my name. I use a different address for my bank accounts and my checks but also a PO Box."

"Wow." She looked simultaneously impressed and concerned.

"Do you need anything else? We could grab some movies." Dan hoped to change the subject and for her to have things that would make her more comfortable in his home. She blushed and gave him a sheepish grin. He was instantly intrigued.

"Can I bring my pillow?"

"Of course." Dan grabbed her pillow off the bed. "Just this one?" He was perfectly willing to pack her entire bedding ensemble if that's what she wanted.

"Do you think that's weird?"

"No. If that's what makes you comfortable, then that's what I want you to have."

She looked relieved as she glanced around her room wistfully.

There was more she wanted. Dan studied her but couldn't put his finger on any one thing. She shivered, and he set down the bags and pillow and moved to her. He formed a heat cast around her as he pulled her to him.

"Why don't we go get you warm?"

She nodded but still didn't seem to want to leave. "Dan," she choked on the verge of tears.

"What's wrong, baby? It's just two nights. I'll bring you back Friday." Defeat settled harshly in his gut. It clawed at his shield. She wasn't going to ever move in with him if she hated his house that much. He didn't understand it.

He had a very nice home, safer than any in DC. It had a great deal of potential. He'd just never cared enough to do much with it, but she was so good at seeing the possibilities in everything around her, especially in him. Why didn't she want to see the possibilities in his house, unless she didn't really want to spend that much time with him? His shield tensed. When he was with her, it was perfection, but she just seemed to keep pulling away.

She looked embarrassed by her own emotional display. "I do want to stay with you." She'd read his heartbreak in his rhythms.

"I may not be much with emotional energy, but even I know when you're lying."

Tears tracked down her face as her chin trembled. His eyes closed in regret. She buried her face in his chest. Her entire body braced for rejection.

"Honey, what is it?" He had no idea how to make this better. Even if she wanted him to leave and never to see her again, he had to keep her safe until he made certain she wasn't being targeted because Wretchkinsides wanted the Angels.

If she ordered him away, he would still make the purchase. He would keep her safe whether she wanted him or not. *If she walks away, Vindico, you might as well go ahead and dig your own grave. Life isn't worth it without her. You tried it that way, remember?*

"Dan, I do love you. Please, please don't feel this way. I just…I just want to bring my teapot."

"Okay." Of all the things she could have said, that wasn't one he'd counted on. Giving up on ever figuring out women, Dan managed a nod. He wondered why on earth she wanted to bring her teapot. He had numerous ways to heat water, one of them being his own hands. Most Gifted people didn't even own a teapot. Not to mention the fact that her teapot was rather worn and in need of replacement. Dan had planned on purchasing her a newer, fancier one for Christmas.

"I know that's weird, and I'm being such a big baby."

"It's fine, sweetheart. Will you tell me why?" He kept her tucked against him. He rubbed her back and kissed the top of her head. Her tears began to permeate his shirt.

"It was my mom's."

Realization flooded through him. "Oh, baby, I'm so sorry. I didn't understand. The house…"

She nodded and tried to swallow down another round of emotion. "I made my house feel like the house I grew up in on Kauai. It reminds me of my Tutu's. Whenever I miss my mom really badly, like at Christmas, or when I've had a rough day or week, I make the Hawaiian tea my Tutu makes me. My Papa grows the tea leaves, and Tutu dries them and has her own line of tea just for Receivers. I just miss Kauai so much, and I miss my mom every day. But that doesn't mean that I don't love you or don't want to stay with you. I just…" She shrugged, unable to explain what he already understood.

"Look at me." She turned her tear-filled eyes up to gaze into his. "I want you to bring anything at all that makes you feel safe and content and helps you be the absolutely amazing woman that you are. I'm sorry we can't stay here, but if you want me to box up your entire

420

room, or your entire kitchen, or hell, the entire house and get a truck, and move it just for the week, I will. I will do anything to make you happy. I'm sorry I pressured you to move in with me. If you never want to leave here, I'll understand."

"It's just moving is really hard for me." Another shiver quaked in her rhythms. "Until I bought this house, I never felt like I got a say in where we lived. Daddy forced me to leave my farm and my island right after Mama died. He dragged us to Texas for two years then moved us up here. He kept saying he was doing it for me, but all I wanted was to go back to my island, and that was the one place he'd never go again. He hated when I went to visit my grandmother. He'd say awful, mean things to me every time I went. He still says mean things about it. I just tried so hard to make this house mine. This is my little Kauai."

Dan swayed her back and forth and recalled the conversation they'd had sitting in the hotel room in Sydney. "Do you remember telling me that it was okay for me to miss Amelia?"

Her brow furrowed, and she gave him a hesitant nod.

"It is okay for you to miss your mom, sweetheart. It's okay not to want to move, and you absolutely should have made your home a place that makes you comfortable. It's also okay not to want to share all of that with me. I understand. I want to help you. I want to help you heal and feel more like you. Maybe, when you're ready, I could go to Kauai with you. I'd love to meet your grandparents and see their farm, but for now, I'm going to stop pressuring you to do anything at all. We'll stay here until you say you want to leave, if you'll just stay with me this week."

"I would love to take you to Kauai some time. That would mean the whole world to me. I think it's all just been a little fast, and everything seems to be going wrong. Eric kept calling the arena today. I told the admin assistant that I wasn't speaking to him, but he called over and over constantly. I didn't want to tell you because you're already so busy. I don't know what to do."

Dan bit back the urge to scold her for not immediately telling him that she was being harassed. He'd been right there in the arena with her, and she'd said nothing. He drew a deep breath. He needed to work in order. She was cold in the house with no heat and he could fix that now.

"We'll talk about Eric and everything else later, okay? I'll get all of this." He indicated the bags and pillows on her floor. "Why don't you go get the teapot and anything you need to make you, *you*. We'll go get settled at my house and then we can talk." It took every ounce of chiseled determination that radiated through his musculature to remain calm and to reassure her.

From what he'd learned about Fionna Styler thus far, he'd say her father was a selfish asshole. Eric Kent wasn't going to go away quietly. Wretchkinsides wasn't going to give up the Angels without a fight. Being with him could still get her killed, and their life wasn't going to get any easier any time soon.

On their way out, Dan grabbed the quilt off Fionna's couch that he knew was her favorite, a few vintage Hawaiian cookbooks from the shelf in the kitchen, and the thick romance novel complete with a duke and a woman in a ballgown from the coffee table. She'd been reading it whenever she'd gotten a chance to sit down. Fionna beamed as he placed them in the Expedition.

"Best boyfriend ever." She leaned over and kissed his cheek as he cranked the car.

CHAPTER 51

LOCK, STOCK, AND BARREL

Dan, Rainer, Fitzroy, and Garrett all stood reticent in the financial-planning offices of the Senate at two o'clock Friday afternoon. The rest of Iodex was either with the team owners or at the arena watching the Angels practice.

Magnus had alluded to the fact that he was going to sell, and word had gotten back to Wretchkinsides. If he purchased Magnus's and Kent's shares, he would hold thirty-eight percent of the team—certainly enough to do a great deal of damage.

The Angels had brought the Summation Cup home to Arlington three years ago. It was then that several other teams decided it wasn't equitable that Chloe Sawyer's father owned a large percentage of the team she captained.

Formal complaints were filed against Sawyer and the Angels. The Senate gave a new ruling. No one person who was related either by blood or marriage to a player could own more than twenty percent of the Summation team that the player challenged for. To the dissenters' irritation, Sawyer had been allowed to keep his stock in the Angels. He was grandfathered in.

Dan hadn't explained the problem to anyone, but it ate at him. Rainer Lawson, who was now the owner and sole proprietor of the Lawson family fortune, could buy the thirty-eight shares without even emptying one of his many, many bank accounts. Dan could not. He could split the available shares with Rainer as long as the stock remained at its current value.

If Pendergrath made a low-ball offer, Rainer and Dan might be able to get the stock for less. Rainer, who would be marrying Emily Haydenshire in a few months' time, couldn't own more than twenty percent of the team, and Dan would have to liquidate most of his assets to acquire the other eighteen.

Buffett had invested Dan's money well, and Dan had secured an excellent salary as the Chief of Iodex, but things could get dicey if Pendergrath managed to come up with more money. *This has to work.* Dan prayed that he had knowledge of all of the accounts that Pendergrath had access to without having to contact Wretchkinsides.

"Here we go," Will Haydenshire, who'd been named one of the VPs of the Senate bank a few months before his father had taken office, called to Dan as he constantly refreshed a computer screen. "He's requested $780,000 in hundreds." Will's brow furrowed.

Dan rolled his eyes at the antics. "That's how much will go in a standard Halliburton." After receiving several impressed glances, Dan continued to watch the screen as numerous cashier's checks in varying amounts were handed across the marble counter to Pendergrath.

"That was a draw from three different accounts, one not on the record you gave us, Dan."

"Add it to the list and shut it down," Dan ordered.

"Total in checks was $17.6 million."

Dan and Rainer edged behind Will.

"The stock dropped after the last loss." Rainer stated what Dan was already well aware of.

Dan nodded. "He's shooting low, just like I said he would. He's hoping that if he brings in wads of cash, Kent and Magnus will start drooling, take it, and run."

"He's leaving. Street-cam outside the Gifted Bank on Wall Street." Garrett held up the security feed on his tablet. They all huddled around Garrett.

Pendergrath's driver opened the trunk. Dan's heart sank. Four

Halliburton briefcases were already in the trunk. He had no idea if they contained cash or the amount they held. If he drove the stock up any more than its current value, Dan would have to mortgage his home and sell his bike to make the buy. Magnus and Kent weren't going to wait for that. The Angels, Fionna, all of them would be run by Dominic Wretchkinsides. Dan shook himself.

"Shut them down, and drain them now," he commanded the entire financial team that had been assigned to the case.

With a nod, Dan watched as twenty-eight of Wretchkinsides's bank accounts containing millions upon millions of dollars became seized property of the American Gifted Realm. Fitz offered him his hand. To date, this was their biggest triumph over the Interfeci.

If Dan hadn't been so terrified over Fionna's safety and their relationship, and so concerned that he was going to be left with nothing but a meager savings account, he would have bought the entire Senate a beer.

No one knew about Dan and Fionna. Other than limited funds, there was no reason he couldn't own more than twenty percent of the team.

Knowing that they had to discuss what they'd both been avoiding, Rainer had humbly walked in his office the afternoon before. He'd offered to loan Dan money to secure the purchase should Pendergrath show up with more.

Despite Rainer's plea that Dan never have to pay him back, just to keep Emily's team out of Wretchkinsides's clutches, Dan couldn't accept the loan.

If he made the purchase with Rainer's money, he would then promptly be fired for knowingly breaking the law set by the Senate regarding Summation owners. It wouldn't take much of a lawyer to make the Senteon believe that Dan had accepted a bribe so that Rainer could own more of the team, and Wretchkinsides's lawyers were the most lethal in the business.

"If I wasn't a completely freaked-out mess, I would be all over you right now." Fionna stood in Dan's bathroom with him, as he tied his tie and she reapplied mascara. Dan shook his head at her hyperbole. "I'm serious. You, in an expensive suit and tie—yum. I could be persuaded to do many, many dirty things with you dressed like that." She shot him a devious grin that made his muscles tighten in need.

While laughing at her outright, Dan moved behind her and wrapped his arms around her waist. He cuddled her closely. That sexy little ass of hers nuzzled at his zipper line, and made him wonder if he had time before the meeting to help her out of the jeans she was wearing. "I will definitely have to remember that," he growled in her ear as she swayed her backside over what she now felt begging for her attention.

"Are you about ready?" He paddled that luscious ass with a few quick slaps before he willed away his sudden distraction by remembering everything that had to happen that evening before any celebrating could be done.

He shoved his wallet in his back pocket and picked his suit coat up off the bed. He stowed his cell phone in the jacket pocket and then moved to one of the bedside tables.

He laughed as he noted that the only things in the drawer were his favorite pistol, the Colt .45, and a piece of paper with a heart drawn on it with his initials and Fionna's drawn in a crossed pattern. All of the condoms were gone.

She was grinning sheepishly while trying very hard not to meet his gaze. Dan shook his head as he moved to one of the closets in the room. He pulled out the holster he typically wore under his suit coats and slung his arms through it as he slid the Colt under his arm.

Fionna's eyes goggled, and Dan tried not to let her see his grimace. "Why are you wearing a gun?" Panic set in her face.

"Baby,"—Dan moved back to her but didn't touch her as he was currently strapped—"Pendergrath is an extremely dangerous man. He'll bring some of his thugs with him, and I'm hoping that I'm about to thoroughly irritate him. I don't believe he'll do anything violent, but I can't be certain of that." He tried to sound calm and soothing. "I'm an officer of the Realm. Actually, I'm the lead officer of the entire American Realm. I not only have to keep the Angels' stock safe tonight, but I have to make certain that everyone at that meeting is safe as well."

Terror broadcast from her entire being. "What if you get hurt? I…I can't…." She choked. Her chin trembled.

Dan flung the holster off, laid it on the counter, and wrapped her up in his arms. His shield radiated around her. She liked to keep him guessing, that was for damn sure.

Every reaction to every situation they encountered taught him something new about her. She really seemed to love him as much as he loved her, even if he couldn't get the words to form on his lips just yet. "I'll be fine, sweetheart. This is what I do, and in just a little while, I'll be back to the farm to pick you up, and then we'll all go out and celebrate."

Fionna, Emily, Chloe, and most of the Angels were all staying at the Haydenshires' farmhouse, with Garrett and Logan and the Elite team, while Rainer and Dan went to the board meeting.

Fionna nodded as she pulled away from him. "I don't want to get makeup on your shirt." She made her excuse as she backed away.

"Fi," Dan soothed, "I'll be fine. I promise. I know what I'm doing. You sure you're okay with Lawson and me dividing the shares?" he asked for the tenth time that day, hoping to get her mind off the danger the evening held.

She nodded and then gave him a hesitant smile. "Yeah, of course."

"I don't want it to be odd for you. Believe me, I'll be a silent partner." He didn't feel like he knew enough about Summation or the Angels to offer the team more than money.

"It's fine. I can't believe you're doing this for me. It's more than I could ever have asked for. Maybe the twins will get my mind off everything."

"Governor Haydenshire really appreciates all of you helping decorate the farmhouse tonight. They're trying to get ready for Prince Nguyen's arrival, and the pregnancy isn't getting any easier."

Fionna nodded her agreement. "Poor thing has been on bed rest for so long, but when I'm around her I can feel that the baby is going to be really special. If I told her that, she'd think I was crazy."

"Emily's a Receiver, and Mrs. Haydenshire is a Double-Predilect with Receiver energy, even if it isn't nearly as strong as her Occamy Gifts. She wouldn't think you were crazy."

This brought a genuine smile to Fionna's face. She trailed out of the bathroom, grabbed her purse, and began drawing measured breaths as Dan pulled the holster back on and covered it with his jacket.

"I'll call you as soon as we're finished, and if you get scared,"—bile rose in his throat as he forced himself to say—"Garrett will be there."

"Garrett isn't you."

His heart gave a quickening beat. He laced his fingers through hers as he led her to the car. "No, he's not, and I will not let Wretchkinsides, or Eric, or anything hurt my girl."

CHAPTER 52
THE CASTLING MOVE

"Wanna drive?" Rainer held up the keys to his new Porsche. He was still trying to apologize for his slight disrespect earlier in the week and the uncomfortable conversation about loaning Dan money.

"Sure, Lawson. Thanks." Although it was a very nice car, Dan had far too much on his mind to care how he got to the meeting. He knew Rainer wanted to both impress Dan and try to make up for the quip about keeping the Angels safe, so Dan feigned excitement.

A chill came over him as he guided the Porsche into the Angels parking deck. Tension and revenge mixed readily with the gas fumes that permeated the crisp air outside the arena.

Rainer's mouth hung open as he stared longingly at the black Aston Martin Vanquish parked near the door.

"Do not look impressed. He's driving that to be intimidating and impressive to the investors. He is the lowest form of scum on this earth, and I intend to bury him and his car under the rock he crawled out from under at the earliest possible opportunity."

Rainer seemed uncertain as to how to respond to Dan's palpable fury. He casted his Porsche, and they entered the arena. Turning north, they headed toward the opulent boardroom.

Dan's veins filled with chilling hatred as he took in Candor

Pendergrath, seated between Shane Ganzmore, one of Wretchkinsides's lesser accountants, and Adrian Malicai, a smarmy half teen, half grown man that Nic was personally training. He'd been released from prison a week before.

Pendergrath scowled as Dan entered with Vivian Scardoza, and Rainer followed Will into the room. In the Realm financial office, only Buffett was higher paid or higher skilled. Pendergrath was surprised by Dan's arrival but tried to hide it.

"Why, Chief Vindico, what a pleasant surprise. Didn't get to speak with you the last time we met. It was difficult to catch up with you while you were fleeing the country," Pendergrath drawled spitefully.

Dan refused to speak, although several choice phrases pulsed acridly in his mind.

"Careful now, Adrian. You know when children don't get their way they tend to pitch fits," Pendergrath sneered at Malicai, who gave the required chuckle.

Medio Sawyer looked extremely concerned as he sat at the head of the long marble table.

"Vindico, tell me," Pendergrath continued since no one could stop him, "do you and Amelia have children yet? Oh, right, I forgot," Pendergrath tsked, "that didn't work out." He feigned sorrow, and Dan's hands clenched into tight fists as Rainer and Will gave him a sympathetic glances.

Just before the meeting was called to order, Crown Governor Haydenshire made an entrance with none other than Buffett behind him. He took a seat at the table and gave Pendergrath the signature Haydenshire smirk. The one all of his sons had in duplication.

"Why, Governor Haydenshire, how nice of you to come. I haven't gotten the chance to congratulate you on your victory. I suppose good taste and refinement just don't hold water in this Realm," Pendergrath sneered.

"That's Crown Governor, Candor. Don't ever forget that."

Dan, Will, and Rainer all held back their grins and tried to remain professional as immense pride swelled through them.

Thomas Kent entered and looked highly irritated as he fell into his seat. Pendergrath slithered excitedly in his chair. Laptops from all of the financial counselors were heaved onto the table and set up. Pendergrath pulled out the sleek Halliburton briefcase he'd gotten from the bank, and Dan gave him a cocky smile that left him visibly wondering, much to Dan's delight.

After the reading of the minutes from the last meeting, Medio Sawyer opened the floor up to new business. Kent stood, and Dan's stomach turned. Eric and his father ranked just above Pendergrath and Wretchkinsides, in his book.

"Medio Sawyer, board members," he greeted, "I have decided to liquidate my stake in the team. I'll be focusing on my son's campaign."

Magnus stood. "I think I'll be selling as well." He glanced nervously at Pendergrath, who looked like the cat who swallowed the canary.

Sawyer sighed as he nodded. "And I assume you gentlemen are all here to try to purchase the available shares."

Dan, Rainer, and Pendergrath all nodded. Sawyer glanced toward the Crown Governor, but seemed to think better of asking why he was at the board meeting.

Pendergrath stood. "I'm fully prepared to purchase both of these men's shares." He dramatically popped the clasps on the briefcase revealing the $780,000.

Pendergrath picked up a bound stack of hundreds and placed it in Kent's hand. "You'll find, gentlemen, that cash spends quite nicely. If, say, you didn't want to reinvest it and deal with pesky things like taxes and such."

Governor Haydenshire narrowed his eyes. "I'd be careful with talk like that, Candor. The Crown Governor and the Chief of Iodex are sitting right here, and you're suggesting these men commit tax fraud."

"How much is that?" Magnus pointed to the briefcase. As most men had never seen that much cash, Dan wasn't surprised he looked intrigued. "Not that I won't be paying taxes, Governor."

"That, sir, is only the beginning." Pendergrath's sly half smile formed on his greasy face.

Magnus scoffed, "My shares alone are worth several million."

"Yes, they are," Dan stated confidently. The current value of the Arlington Angels stood at just over $64 million dollars, not including the current season's ticket sales or the value on the arena.

Kent's and Magnus's shares combined were worth just over $24 million. Dan and Rainer each had $12 million in cashier's checks in their pockets. Rainer had quite a bit more in his wallet but was trying to keep the price low. Dan could not afford to spend over $13 million on this investment.

With a nod to Rainer, who smiled and stood, Dan let Lawson have his day.

"Chief Vindico and I would like to split the available shares for the current value of the stock. We're prepared to give you $24 million right now."

Suddenly the briefcase full of cash didn't look so appealing, in light of the fact that the Crown Governor was watching the exchange.

Pendergrath looked mutinous as he glared at Dan, who gave him a sneering grin.

"Fine, I'll give you $40 million." Pendergrath pulled a few checks from his jacket pocket.

"Put your money where your mouth is, Soap." Dan laughed outright at Pendergrath's self-assigned thug nickname. "I don't think you have forty mil with you. Let's see the funding." Dan gestured his head to Ganzmore.

Pendergrath scoffed as Dan went on, "This man is a criminal. He's been imprisoned on numerous occasions, all for financial crimes. If I were you, I'd want to make absolutely certain you're going to get paid. He's very, very slippery."

"Let's see the funding," Magnus agreed.

"Daniel, you amuse me. Show them," Pendergrath huffed.

As Ganzmore began typing passcodes and PINs into his laptop, Pendergrath turned to Kent. "You know, if we work something out here this evening, I could ensure a victory for your son. Elections happen to be my specialty."

Kent was instantly intrigued. Governor Haydenshire looked sick as he pulled his cell phone from his pocket. He casted the phone and laid it out on the table.

"Lachland, this is Stephan. I'm so sorry to bother you and Yvette this evening. I just needed a quick favor." Certainly no one was going to interrupt or stop the Crown Governor, so everyone waited and listened intently. "I do hope you're doing okay."

"We take it a day at a time," Peterson spoke quietly. "What did you need, Stephen?" Dan noted that he didn't sound put out by the request. He sounded as if his life had left him with nothing more than bone-weary exhaustion.

The Petersons had buried their only daughter just a few weeks before. She'd been killed when Peterson had taken the offer made to him by Wretchkinsides, promising him that he'd be the next Crown Governor. Samantha had been a pawn in the sick game, and when Peterson had lost to Governor Haydenshire, she'd been the punishment as well.

"I'm currently sitting in a room with Adrian Malicai and Candor Pendergrath. They've just offered to help Thomas Kent get his son, Eric, elected to your old seat on the board. I just wondered if you might give Mr. Kent some advice before he accepts their help." Governor Haydenshire stared Pendergrath down.

"Put him on the phone," Peterson demanded.

Dan shot Pendergrath a smirk. Governor Haydenshire gestured to his cell phone on the table as Kent nodded confusedly and picked it up. Governor Haydenshire immediately dropped the cast.

"This is Thomas Kent," he stated warily. Whatever Peterson decided to share, he leapt immediately and the table watched as Kent's eyes goggled. He gasped audibly a minute into the conversation, and Dan narrowed his eyes at Pendergrath. His face was glowing red in his fury, and utter hatred etched his facade.

"You'll find that consequences have very little pity, Mr. Pendergrath," Governor Haydenshire huffed.

"Yes, uh, well, thank you for your advice, and I'm terribly sorry for your loss." Mr. Kent ended the call and handed the phone back to the governor.

Kent turned to Magnus. "I really think we should accept Chief Vindico and Officer Lawson's offer. It's more than the stock is worth after the last loss."

"Yes, but his offer is almost double the price." Magnus gestured to Pendergrath.

Ice-cold sweat dripped down Dan's neck. He didn't have $20 million. He couldn't match Pendergrath's offer, and he still didn't know how much money was in the Halliburtons in the back of that ridiculous Vanquish in the parking deck.

Rainer's hand brushed over the checkbook in his pants pocket, almost without conscious thought. He was desperate to buy the stock and ignore the new law.

Dan braced. Pendergrath, even more than Wretchkinsides, did not like to lose

"Sir, I can't seem to access any available funds from your accounts." Ganzmore looked reluctant to explain the problem to Pendergrath. "I've checked all four of your personal accounts and each of the business accounts as well."

Pendergrath was mutinous. "What do you mean, you blubbering imbecile? Where is the money?" He turned back to Magnus and tried to plaster on confidence. "He's an idiot, and he will pay for this. I have $30 million with me tonight, gentlemen. That is a very fair price for what you're offering." The panic in his voice did nothing to soothe either Magnus or Kent.

Dan willed his heart to beat in rhythm. He couldn't match $15 million, either. He was going to lose, and he was going to do the very thing he'd sworn to Fionna he'd never do. He was going to let her down.

Suddenly, he was wounded by his own stupidity. Every promise he'd made her, every vow he'd made to himself that he could keep her safe and make her all his own was massacred in his defeat.

How could he have been so incredibly foolish? He could never have anything good. He didn't deserve her. He never would. He was nothing more than a forced sacrifice in this deadly game that he'd stupidly made her a part of.

CHAPTER 53

CHECK MATE

"I'm not certain what your financial woes might be, Candor, but I'd like to make another offer." Governor Haydenshire's soothing intonation brought a shock of air to Dan's lungs. Everyone turned their attention to the Crown.

"I'd like to split the available stock three ways. It seems to me the more you divide the shares the less possibility there is of someone getting their hands on it who might not have the team's best interest at heart." He glared at Pendergrath. "I think it would be wise for my son-in-law and his boss to give you both $8 million. I will write you a check this evening, gentlemen, for $16 million dollars. I assume that might be something we can all agree on."

"Yes," Kent and Magnus both agreed readily.

"Draw up the paperwork," Magnus commanded the lawyer for the Angels.

Unable to wade through the harrowing emotions and the terror, it took Dan a moment to locate the checks in his pocket. Rainer's eyes closed in supreme relief.

Dan kept his eyes locked on Ganzmore and Pendergrath. They were both staring at the laptop screen with outraged acrimony.

"You're an idiot! You've entered something wrong!" Pendergrath shouted.

"I didn't. I swear," Ganzmore begged for his life. "That's one of the business accounts. The balance is zero." He pointed to the screen.

Pendergrath turned to glare at Dan. He slid his folded arm forward on the table just enough to let the 357 Magnum show under his jacket.

Dan gave a complacent chuckle. He edged his left elbow out to lean against the chair beside him. The grip of his Colt .45 gleamed under the fluorescent lighting. He'd never show Pendergrath that he'd lost just a little of his ego or that he was consumed with anguish.

At that moment, nothing would've suited Dan more than to bury several slugs inside Candor Pendergrath.

Before he could allow that fantasy to consume him, new contracts were drawn up, signed, and notarized, while the governor, Rainer, and Dan smugly handed over checks.

Pendergrath scowled as Dan and Rainer stood to shake Sawyer's hand. He stood, dramatically flipped the briefcase full of cash closed, and stalked toward the door, with Malicai and Ganzmore hot on his trail.

"By the way, Vindico," he drawled repugnantly as he narrowed his eyes and turned back to Dan, "Nic says to tell you thanks for finally moving on."

Dan's blood turned to ice as his heart stuttered and seized. It seemed unable to pump the solid mass through his veins.

"Oh my God," he panicked as soon as Pendergrath was gone. His chair shot backwards as he raced from the room, grabbed his cell phone from his pocket, and sprinted into a supply closet on the upper level of the stadium.

"Answer the damn phone," he spat on the third ring. He paced frantically in the suffocating space.

"Hey, good-lookin'. Is it over?" He heard the sweetest voice in the world, and his heart thundered back to life and began to fly.

"Fionna, baby, are you okay?" His voice shook. Hot tears of failure pierced his eyes.

"Dan, what's wrong? I'm fine. What happened?"

Air managed its way back into his lungs.

"Dan, what's wrong?" He suddenly heard Garrett's low tenor demand.

"I think he knows," was all Dan could manage.

"You think he knows what?"

"About Fi. Pendergrath just thanked me for moving on." His entire body cringed in terror. His head throbbed, and he ached with the pain he'd tried so hard to bury in that grave a decade ago. It haunted his weary soul.

"All right, man, just calm down," Garrett soothed. "He doesn't know anything. He's trying to get to you because I'm guessing you just pissed him the hell off. She's standing right here beside me. I've got my arm around her. I'm holding her. She's safe. We'll keep her safe. I will not let anything happen to her."

It took Dan a few seconds to wonder why her being tucked up in Garrett's arms didn't piss him off, but the only emotion available to him at that moment was thankfulness that she was alive and safe.

"She was playing blocks with the boys. They adore her, and the farm is perfectly safe. Don't freak. I'd never let anyone hurt her. And he doesn't know anything. How would he? You haven't so much as cast a shadow her direction."

"Get her away from the windows. I'm on my way." Dan exited the room and sprinted toward the parking deck until he remembered that he didn't have a vehicle.

"Dan, get it together. You're scaring her," Garrett commanded.

"Dammit, Garrett, just do what I said."

"Daniel," Governor Haydenshire called as Dan rushed down the corridor. "Get it together, son. You make incredibly poor decisions when you let your emotions rule you."

Dan bit back the words that were forming on his lips. "I need to go."

"We're going, and you're riding with me. Fionna is perfectly safe. She is with Garrett and a gaggle of other people at my home. Pendergrath knows nothing other than the fact that he is angry, and he was beaten badly. So this time, why don't you let his temper play him for a fool instead of you playing that part for him?

"Get in." Governor Haydenshire pointed to his minivan, and Dan tried not to grimace as he sank into the passenger seat. "I'm aware it isn't my future son-in-law's Porsche, but thus far he hasn't let me drive it."

"I'm sure he would," Dan forced his lips to move. The governor's remark was barely audible to him. His mind was still in a wind tunnel of horrifying fear as he tried to locate calm.

"I think of Rainer as one of my own. I always have. He would do anything in the world for Emily. So, he's not only a son I'm very proud of but also a son-in-law I couldn't be more thankful for. He's also a whole lot like his old man, and a hell of a guy in general. But right now let's talk about you."

"How did you know I couldn't afford the stock?" Finally giving up on making any sense of his own thoughts, Dan rubbed his temples and settled into his own defeat.

The governor smiled. "Let's call it a lucky guess, but that's not what I want to discuss. I certainly won't pretend that I know at what stage you and Ms. Styler are in this whirlwind relationship you seem to have stumbled upon." The governor gave Dan a sideways glance as he continued, "But I will tell you this, you are a better man when you are with her, a better officer, a better person, and she loves you, in spite of everything you've been through."

"I know that."

"Do you? I'm not so sure you do. You're either lying to me or you're lying to yourself. Because I still don't think you believe anyone could love you. But hear me say this, she, just like your parents, Lillian and I, the entire Senate, Will, Garrett, all of your friends, all of your officers, all of your family, and even Amelia's parents, do not blame you for Amelia's death."

"Well, you should." Dan was unable to keep the words from escaping.

"No, we shouldn't, because you didn't fire the pistol that horrible night. You were a victim just like she was. But you can't stand to let yourself believe that. You can't stand to see it that way, and that's why you can't seem to forgive yourself." He shook his head. "I came unglued one day at the office during the election. I was convinced something else was going to happen to Lillian or one of my kids at the hands of Peterson and Wretchkinsides. I took Lillian's Suburban out to see Sam. I wanted it inspected by someone I trusted. I had to make certain it was safe. He gave me some excellent advice. He always does. If the Realm really wanted the best man for Crown, they should have elected Sam."

Dan tried to listen. He did want to hear the advice over the roar of impending doom occupying his brain.

"He told me that nothing can kill love like fear and vice versa. Truer words were never spoken. You've got to let go of the fear. For me, try to love her and to let her love you."

With a steadying breath, Dan decided to really listen, instead of trying to come up with excuses to combat what the governor was saying.

"You need to have a little faith, because let me tell you something, if you leave her and force her away because you're trying to protect her, that will be the stupidest thing you've ever done. And that includes telling the Russian Crown to suck your cock." Governor Haydenshire's tone turned vicious. "No one has the power to hurt her like the man who holds her heart in his hands."

"That was a pretty specific threat." Dan couldn't allow himself to believe what he was hearing.

"The likelihood that you would've gone on for ten years without ever really being involved with anyone else was very slim. It didn't seem like much of a leap to me. You've been dating a few weeks. One of them was in Sydney. You haven't been photographed at all. The press tends to shy away from you. I don't see how he could possibly have known anything. He gambled on the fact that you would be seeing someone, as you are a thirty-two-year-old, warm-blooded, male. Trust me, it isn't just the good guys who know you blame yourself for Amelia's murder. Rainer said Candor plunged that knife in as soon as you arrived, so he decided to twist it before he left, nothing more."

Dan wanted so desperately to believe the governor. He just couldn't quiet the terror in his soul. He needed Fionna. She was the only one who could ever turn the tides of his self-hatred and pull him from their piercing, drowning depths.

"Go get her." The governor gestured to Fionna. She was sitting on the swing on the side porch of the Haydenshires' farmhouse. Garrett was standing near her. His arms were crossed over his chest as he kept constant scan on the horizon. He was keeping her safe.

CHAPTER 54
UNITED IN TIME

Dan's heart began to beat in rhythm as he watched her sip a mug of something warm enough to form steamy swirls in the cold night air.

"This isn't exactly away from the windows," Dan lamented as he ran up the stairs.

Garrett laughed. "Sorry, I kind of assumed by now you know her better than I do, but if you think for one second that Fionna Styler will stay anywhere she doesn't want to be, maybe I was wrong."

Fionna gave him his smile as Dan took the seat beside her. "Go away, Haydenshire."

Garrett slapped Dan on the back as he followed the governor into the kitchen.

"I'm sorry I came unglued," Dan began as Fionna nestled her head on his shoulder. Dan let the peace of just being in contact with her wash through him.

"I assume that I am now sleeping with one of the owners of the Arlington Angels."

Dan nodded his agreement. It was the first moment he'd even given thought to the fact that he was now an owner.

"Yeah, since I'm an owner now, I think I might renege on my offer to be a silent partner and demand that those contracts are rewritten to include sick days without penalty for all of you."

"Do you want to tell me what happened or do you want to listen to what I have to say first?" Fionna's tone was soft and soothing, but there was a steady strength Dan hadn't expected.

"Governor Haydenshire, Lawson, and I split the available stock. We basically barred Wretchkinsides from ever hoping to get a foothold again. I couldn't have done it if the governor hadn't stepped in."

Fionna leaned up and brushed a tender kiss on his cheek. "There are a lot of people who love and care about you and about us."

"Fionna, I have never been so terrified in my entire life as when Pendergrath thanked me for moving on." He just couldn't keep the terror at bay. Even in her presence, it began to permeate his soul again.

Fionna nodded and then took his hand. She forced her intoxicating love and soothing peace through the depths of his terror.

"I can't let anything happen to you," Dan choked as he shoved his thumb and fingers in his own eyes in an effort to dam the emotion pooling there.

"Listen to me. I don't think you really heard what I was saying when we talked in Sydney, so I'm asking you to really listen this time. You can't keep trying to do this alone, and I can't let you continue to try. I love you too much for that. I am safe. No one who shouldn't know about us knows that I am completely in love with you. I wish, just for a moment, you could feel things the way I feel them. Don't you see? You've forever changed me, and that's what was supposed to happen. But now our timelines have to form together. They've united. I can feel when something bad is going to happen to me. If one of them found out, I would know. I could feel that. I knew I would be safe tonight. I knew you would be safe, even if I got a little scared because I love you so much. But…you're not the only one who's resisted our path."

She was so confident, but how could she always know? How could he really believe that their need and desire for one another wasn't influencing her reads?

"It's not." She stared through him. In the depths of his eyes, she accessed his soul. Without ever dropping his frenzied gaze, she'd just proven her awe-inspiring powers. "I want to move in with you."

"No." He shook his head adamantly. "I don't want you to do anything just because that's what I want. I told you I'm a selfish asshole."

Fionna gave him another one of his smiles, and Dan swore the effect could cure the most heinous of diseases.

"And I told you that you're not. You're scared, and that's okay. It's a perfectly normal emotion. But we aren't made to be apart anymore. Tutu says our path has formed as one." Her face suddenly glowed in embarrassment.

"You talked to your grandmother about us?" She cast her sheepish gaze downward. Dan felt the absence as she pulled away.

"What else did she say?" He just needed her to keep talking. Her voice carried his life's blood.

"That it wasn't going to be easy," she sighed. Dan wondered what that meant exactly and just how much Tutu really knew. "We've intertwined our lives, and that means I have to change too. I can't hold on to my house, or my island, or my past because I'm willing to give all of that away to have a future with you." She stumbled over her plea. Her eyes desperately sought agreement from his.

Dan smiled at her adoringly as he snuggled her closer. "Tutu sounds almost as smart as you, sweetheart, and I would love to give up my past and trade it for a future with you. We both have to change because we have to change together, right? I just need you to give me a little time. My past will keep hunting me down. It won't let me go. I have to end it."

A broad grin of relief formed on those luscious lips. She nodded. Unable to help himself, Dan leaned in and kissed her hesitantly. He traced her bottom lip with his tongue. He needed to taste her. She pulled him closer, and he added to the intensity. He groaned from the heavenly taste of her as she filled his mouth.

Feeling like he was sixteen again, they made out on the side porch of the Haydenshires' farmhouse. They both kept their hands in places the governor would approve of, even though Dan pulled a quilt off the swing and covered her in it.

They stayed lip-locked for a solid half hour before going back in the kitchen.

"'Bout damn time," Garrett laughed. "No one could leave."

Fionna giggled. "You could have left. We wouldn't have stopped, but you could still have left."

Rainer held up his cell phone. "Fitzroy's called three times. He wants to know where we all are."

"We're all going to Frye's to celebrate," Garrett reminded all of the Angels and most of Iodex, who'd all taken refuge in the kitchen. No one wanted to interrupt Dan and Fionna's talking or their kissing.

Anxiety consumed Dan. Fionna was still holding his hand. She shook her head at him.

"Since all of Iodex and all of the Angels are going, wouldn't it be more weird if I wasn't there?"

"We'll all be there. Just don't hang all over her, and this will be fine. Come out into the world, Danny. You will survive, and so will she," Garrett continued to chastise.

Dan immediately formulated rules for their evening. He'd stay away from her, as hard as that would be. She wanted to go have fun, and he just wanted to keep her safe.

"Let's take the Expedition. I'll even drive," Garrett offered. "You coming, Dad?"

The governor shook his head. Mrs. Haydenshire bid everyone good night and told them to have a good time. She cupped Dan's face in her hands, tearing up slightly, and patted his cheek. "I'm just so happy for you."

Fionna cracked up as Dan tried to think of a response.

"I think I'll stay home with your mother and celebrate." The governor took his wife's hands and guided her away from Dan.

"Ugh, Dad, please." Logan pretended to gag as everyone headed outside.

"Your mom looks much better," Rainer commented to Emily as they moved into the barn where all of the cars were parked.

"Yeah," Emily giggled, "they took her off bed rest yesterday, because Adeline started to notice that the baby does better when Mom's actually using more of her own energy." Dan and Fionna listened intently to the good news. "Adeline monitored her, and today they took her off '*pelvic rest.*'" She used finger quotes and gave a slight shudder. Rainer and Dan both cracked up.

"I thought the governor was a little eager to get home." Dan had no idea how he was able to joke, but Fionna laughed and pulled his arm around her shoulders. She was right. They were forever changed.

He couldn't go on without her. He just had to keep her safe.

CHAPTER 55

INFORMATIVE NIGHT OFF

Dan and Fitz enjoyed a glass of Scotch while Chloe, Emily, and Fionna and all of the Angels began downing glasses of wine. Dan had relaxed some when he discovered that Frye's was virtually empty that late at night. As it was the restaurant where Iodex, the Senteon, Senate officials, and the governors ate most often, it wasn't a likely hangout for Wretchkinsides and the Interfeci.

Adeline sipped wine as well, though not with nearly the same vigor the Angels were downing drinks. Fitzroy shook his head at Fionna. "I'm not gonna get any sleep tonight either."

Dan laughed and shook his head. If she wanted to blow off a little steam with her friends and a few bottles of wine, she definitely deserved that. "Are you kidding me? If she keeps going like that, in about a half hour, I'll be carrying her to bed sound asleep."

Fitz chuckled. "Ah, a sleepy drunk. Well, that sucks for you, my friend, but I gotta tell you, she's amazing. Don't scare yourself out of this. You need to hold on to her tight."

"You're the second guy who's told me that today." Dan tried not to let his gaze linger too long on Fionna. She was laughing with Emily. Her cheeks held a rosy glow. Her hair hung loosely down her back, and the low-cut shirt she was wearing showed just enough of her cleavage to make him long to see more. He couldn't seem to keep his eyes off her curves.

"I really don't think he knows, Dan." Fitz's comment dragged him away from his visual safari over Fionna's lush hips. "I think the governor's right. He was just trying to get to you. He always is."

"I hope so. I still think I'll watch her like a hawk though."

"If you do that too much, you might just watch her walk right out of your life. Give her space when she wants it. She seems pretty happy when she's with you, so just keep making her happy."

"That is definitely my plan." Dan nursed another sip of Scotch. Laughter from the Angels' tables permeated the air.

"I happen to have information that you want desperately," Garrett announced as he took a chair at Fitz and Dan's table, spun it around, slung his right leg over the seat, and looped his arms over the back.

"Oh, yeah, what's that?"

Garrett grinned and leaned in. "I happen to know what Fi is really wanting for Christmas."

"I'm listening." Dan had already ordered several things he thought she'd like, but they were relatively small, and he desperately wanted to spoil her. He'd become accustomed to the irksome jealousy that always came with Garrett's knowledge of Fionna, but it still stung.

"You're either gonna need my mom or her mom to help you."

"We're having dinner at her parents' tomorrow night." Dan sincerely hoped he could win her parents over, but her dad seemed like a real piece of work.

"By the way, man," Garrett interjected suddenly, "do you think you could get her to stop telling me how good you are in bed? I do not want to know that." Garrett shuddered as Dan and Fitzroy laughed.

"Nah." Dan shook his head as his ego restored itself. "If she feels the need to share that, who am I to stop her?"

Garrett rolled his eyes. "Yeah, yeah, I got it, but if I hear 'he's the best ever, better than I ever dreamed of' again, I will puke." Garrett did a horrible impersonation of Fionna.

"At least you didn't have to *actually* hear it," Fitz joined in as Dan narrowed his eyes. This time Garrett cracked up as Dan took another sip of his Scotch.

"Christmas?" he reminded.

"Right, okay." Garrett tipped his beer bottle up, drew a long sip, and then set it on the table. He leaned forward again.

"This is women for you. She really wants a new sewing machine, but she doesn't want to get rid of the one she has which is ancient and hasn't worked right in years. I've casted it. She's casted it. I think it's just given up the will to live."

Dan furrowed his brow. He would definitely either need Mrs. Styler or Mrs. Haydenshire's help.

"Em might be able to help you, but she doesn't sew near as well as Fi. Mom would be a better choice. Anyway, the one she has is one her mom gave her or something. Not sure why that means she can't get rid of it if it's not working though."

A peace and a certainty that Dan hadn't been able to access until that moment fortified him. He understood vastly more than Garrett for once.

"So, she wants one that works, and I guess to just keep the other one to look at. I don't know. You know chicks are crazy."

"I got it. And thank you for everything. Seriously."

"No problem. Like I said, I want this to work for both of you. I've never seen either of you so happy."

They chatted about the board meeting, and Dan retold the story of the governor's heroics.

"Yeah, Dad's kind of a badass, just don't ever tell him I said that."

"Hey, just out of curiosity,"—Dan glanced at Fionna, still making certain she was all right—"has Fi ever dated any guy worth his salt, or have they all been douchebags of the highest caliber?"

Garrett continued to sip the one beer he'd allowed himself since he was driving.

"She has had one or two guys I thought were decent. There was one guy, Jared, for a while. I couldn't stand him, but I figured she was into him."

Dan suddenly wished he hadn't asked.

"I thought they were really going somewhere. Dude would squeeze a penny 'til Lincoln puked, but," Garrett shrugged as he recalled, "I guess he treated her right. He had a good family and all that. Fi broke it off with him, broke his heart, and swore she never wanted to see him again. She told him she hated him. She was vicious, and Fi is never vicious. I still can't figure out what brought that on.

"He called me up the next day and told me she'd dumped him. He thought she had a thing for me, so he asked me to take care of her. She said he just didn't get her and that he wanted to change her." Garrett shook his head and shrugged. "I have no idea why anyone would want to change her, but you already know that."

Dan had several ideas of what it was that Jared might not have gotten, and he was immensely thankful for each and every one of them.

Things got risky several minutes later when Fionna sauntered over to Dan's table. There were about a dozen people who had gathered at the bar seating in the restaurant as the night had worn on. His eyes goggled as she almost half seated and half fell on his lap.

Garrett quickly caught her hand and spun her into his own lap. With his fists clenching under the table and fury bubbling in his gut, Dan tried to remember how thankful he was for all that Garrett was doing.

"Hey, baby. You ready to go home?" Garrett was laughing quietly at both Fionna and Dan.

She stared confusedly at Dan. She didn't seem to understand how she'd ended up in Garrett's lap, but she tucked herself into his embrace and laid her head on his shoulder. "I'm not that tipsy," she explained to Dan.

"Uh-huh, I know," Garrett answered her.

"I'm not." She blinked several times in an effort to focus.

"Maybe you should have some coffee before you go." Dan waved to the waitress.

"Maybe just a little and some water, a little."

Dan finally chuckled and nodded his head.

"She is a very happy drunk. Everything's hilarious until she falls asleep in a matter of minutes," Garrett informed Dan in a whisper, as Fionna became distracted by Emily. "Any idiot who thought they might get her tipsy and then get her in bed has been sorely disappointed. She falls asleep in the car every single time." Garrett laughed at the stories he was clearly recalling.

"She deserves a night off." Dan let Garrett order her a strong coffee and a large glass of water.

Fionna fell asleep in Dan's lap on the way home.

"I don't think we'll be up too early." Dan scooped up Fionna and carried her up the steps to his front door. Fitz unlocked it as he chuckled his good night.

Even though he was well aware that Fionna normally slept completely naked, Dan would have felt like a jerk to strip her when she was barely awake. He couldn't do it. He pulled one of his T-shirts from a drawer and swathed her in it as she curled up on her pillow and was out.

Gazing at her for a long minute, Dan let the governor's words and Fitzroy's warning echo in his mind. He pulled the light from the lamp and shed his clothes as he climbed into bed with the only thing in his world that really truly mattered.

ABOUT THE AUTHOR

J.E. Neal (aka Jillian) vastly prefers coffee to tea, guac to salsa, the beach over anywhere else, and the world inside her head over the one outside her front door. She also loves not having to choose.

Driven by the question 'what if,' J.E. Neal's world began to manifest. What if there were people with powers the rest of us couldn't see? What if the energy of our world could be summoned and used at their will? Characters with these amazing abilities took shape in her mind. She created—and continues to create—an endless number of stories full of delicious escape from our reality where emotions are visible, desire is palpable, and danger is universal.

Learn more about J.E. Neal at JillianNeal.com

facebook.com/jilliannealauthor
twitter.com/JillianNeal_
instagram.com/jilliannealauthor

ALSO BY J.E. NEAL

ENERGY OF MAGIC

Shield and Shattered Cages (Book 1)

Shield and Faltered Steps (Book 2)

Shield and Splintered Oaths (Book 3)

Shield and Humbled Crown (Book 4)

Shield and Vile Serpents (Book 5)

Shield and Coveted Splendor (Book 6)

Shield and Guarded Shadow (Book 7)

Shield and Worthy Sinner (Book 8)

Shield and Sacrificial Heirs (Book 9)